When Twilight Comes

also by

Roger Derham

Novels

The Simurgh and the Nightingale (2001)

And as

Alex Skalding
The Colour of Rain (2002)

When Twilight Comes

Roger Derham

To Tim
with very best wishes
Roger

Wynkin
deWorde

2003

Published in 2003
by

Wynkin
deWorde

Wynkin deWorde Ltd.,

PO Box 257, Tuam Road, Galway, Ireland.
e-mail: info@deworde.com

A CIP catalogue record for this book is available from the British Library

ISBN: 0-9542607-3-2

Typeset by Patricia Hope, Skerries, Co. Dublin, Ireland
Cover illustration by Roger Derham.
Jacket Design by Design Direct, Galway, Ireland
Printed by Betaprint, Dublin, Ireland

Acknowledgements

My deep and sincere thanks to the citizens
of Granada, Corsica and Armenia,
each in its own way, places of wonderment.
And to Valerie Shortland for her
editorial belief in this book.

Lines 1-6, 25-28 and 40-46 of *Solomon and the Witch;*
Lines 184-188 of *The Gift of Harun Al-Rashid;*
Lines 43-47 of *Lapis Lazuli* and Lines 1-4 of the *Magi* are
from *W.B. Yeats'* Collected Poems, Wordsworth Poetry Library,
1994 Edition and are used with the kind permission of the
publishers.

Dedication

This could only be for Brenda
and also for my father
Joseph
and always for David, Heather and Nicole

and of course, for all the strangers and friends
met on the journey to understanding

Saeculum

Now as at all times I can see in the mind's eye,
In their stiff, painted clothes, the pale unsatisfied ones
Appear and disappear in the blue depth of the sky
With all their ancient faces like rain-beaten stones

From W B Yeats, The Magi

The Edge of the Sky

Not all dreams are like this, I thought, as I warped in and out of the flickering reality. The images that enveloped me had such frightening clarity, such attendance, they dazzled all perception of that reality.

I am a nine year-old boy again; standing naked, shivering and dripping wet, on the cold blue-black-granite slate slabs of the kitchen yard to the rear of my childhood house. My father is talking to me, back over his shoulder, as he slowly tilts the rim of a tinker's beaten bathtub. I cannot make out what he is saying over the noise of the cascading water and so, settle for watching the warm dirt-laden liquid as it waltzes and swirls down through the rusted grill cover of the outside drain; the released thermals of moist air are spiralling up into the cold January night air and, high above the two of us, the bright stars of Orion shimmer as they continue their bear-hunt across the winter sky.

My father stops what he is saying, stands up suddenly and, with hands on hips, arches his back to look up at the constellation. He smiles wistfully, as if wishing Orion well, looks back down at me and soon realises, from my vacant purple-faced expression, that I have not taken in a word of what he has been saying.

'In the beginning, Michael,' he repeats, while drying me off with a coarse-woven towel. 'In the centre of our universe was a huge whirlpool. It led down into the deepest darkness and, like a swollen river trapping a drowning child in its current, it did everything in its power to suck in the light of the stars. But near the edges of that swirl, near the edge of the sky, where the pull of the black current was least, just enough pulses of light escaped from the funnel to warm our world and favour our lives. Remember Michael, there is always a beginning and an end, and there is always darkness and light. Life is lived between the twilights, in the transit time between risings and settings.'

He spoke earnestly, as he always did, to an adoring son.

These were the images and sounds that disturbed me as I became conscious. My father, who had been compelled by the financial and personal obligations of my unplanned but imminent birth to abort his doctoral thesis and become a school teacher instead, always had a habit of talking down to me and filling the distance, and void, between us, with words and ideas. Much later I learnt that those ideas were generally borrowed and sometimes stolen and the sharing had involved me in the conspiracy.

It had been a long time since I had dreamt about him and now, as my mind cleared, I wondered momentarily why that particular memory had surfaced. It was all too obvious. That evening in the kitchen yard was the last time we were alone together. He committed suicide less than a week later, a day before my tenth birthday. A morbid fear of cancer and suffering, my family had said. My mother remained silent, as always. Her's was a fear of happiness, I'd always thought.

The fugitive colours and sounds of the dream faded further as a far more tangible, harsh, mechanical noise kept intruding. As I struggled to determine where it was coming from I realised I had no clear perception of foreground or background. I was in a vacuum with no centre and no horizon.

Sheshh-shup . . . Sheshh-shup . . . Sheshh-shup . . .

Was it the sound that had that woken me, I wondered. How long had I been asleep? Where was I? Unanswered questions posed in the confused twilight of waking moments.

Caught between nonsense and sense, between entrapment and escape, I felt groggy and un-refreshed but became increasingly alert to other noises in my vacuum. Like soft rhythmic clapping, the sounds were sometimes fast and sometimes slow. What could they be? I wondered. *Footsteps . . .Yes, footsteps!* Echoes of rubber-heeled shoes beat out their passage across a hard-surfaced floor. Where were they coming from? Again, I could not be sure.

Sheshh-shup . . . Sheshh-shup . . . Sheshh-shup . . .

I tried to reach out and switch off the monotony of the repeating sound, but couldn't. The clapping sounds changed their pitch. Their rhythm slowed, then stopped.

'What's his name?' a throaty whispering voice, suddenly asked.

I needed to see the speaker but couldn't. I wasn't even certain as to whether or not my eyelids were open. I had very little perception of light, just a dense haze, like walking in a freezing fog on a pitch-black winter's night and yet, there were moments when darker undefined shadows moved in and out of the cloud. I wanted to touch my eyes. *Rubbing them would surely help.* I tried to touch my eyes but nothing happened, no light came in!

What's happening to me? How long have I been like this? Where am I? I panicked in deafening silence.

I felt no pain; in fact I had little feeling of any kind save an intermittent stretching sensation, somewhere in my chest, I think it was my chest but again, it was proving difficult to orientate myself. In the surround, and I now realized completely synchronous with the stretching sensation, the repeating mechanical noise continued.

'According to his passport his name is Michael Mara.' A tired sounding woman, with a Caribbean accent spoke.

'Irish?' another woman asked, younger with a Scottish brogue.

'No. Well . . . don't know for sure. Had an American passport.'

'What happened to him? How long has he been here?'

My questions exactly! The voices and moving shadows were really close to me.

'We're not sure as to what exactly happened. He was brought in three days ago and he's remained in a coma since then,' the nearest shadow answered, with West Indian fatalism.

Three days ago! Jesus! I screamed out into the vacuum.

'Brought in from where?'

'Heathrow. He apparently collapsed in the arrivals area.'

Heathrow! Collapsed! What happened to me?

I forced myself to try and remember.

Crepesculum

EVENING TWIGHLIGHT

Granada, Spain.
1 September 2001

The blistering, late-afternoon, Andalusian sunlight of that September Saturday was still oppressive enough to force many of my fellow tourists, and even some of the locals, to stop their promenading on the Paseo de Los Tristes and seek the welcome shade of the plaza umbrellas. In the midst of the bustle I was relieved to find an unoccupied table near the wall that separated the Rio Darro from the Paseo. The Paseo itself was once an elegant avenue of elms that the Moors called *al-Gharsa*, but most of the trees were long gone and in their stead was a canopy of coloured nylon fabric.

At the base of the wall, the parched riverbed was a testament to the long summer and upstream bleeding by irrigation schemes. From its far bank the Monte de la Assabica rose majestically to a plateau where Granada's red acropolis, the Alhambra, glowed crimson on the skyline. I pulled out a chair and positioned it in such a way that my back would be to the mountains and I would have an unimpeded view of the turrets of Yusuf's palace. I remembered the words from the wall of the Garden of the Adarves, '*There is nothing more cruel in life than to be blind in Granada.*' and muttered them aloud as I looked around me.

Sitting at an adjacent table was a large family party, loud in their banter and laughter. The group appeared to include grandparents, parents and children and from the scattered coffee cups and empty liquor glasses they were obviously coming to the lazy but loquacious end of a prolonged midday meal. As I continued to watch them, I was struck by the uncannily close physical resemblance between the different generations of men and how this resemblance seemed compounded by the near-identical mouth and hand gesticulations that accompanied their manic conversation. In contrast, the women at the table were as dissimilar as the men were similar. They appeared peripheral both to the banter and to each other.

At that moment there was the metallic screech of a chair being pushed back and the young woman with her back closest to me suddenly stood up. Agitated initially, she quickly calmed to walk gracefully and unhurriedly towards a small child who with loud wailing lay crestfallen nearby. Her long legs and taut bottom were framed by a tightly tailored white linen suit and when she bent to lift the crying child a quick flick of her red-black hair away from her shoulder revealed a finely chiselled beauty.

From the left edge of my field of vision I could also see that mine were not the only eyes that were focused on the scene. I noticed that the other younger – and altogether much frumpier – woman at the family table was also intently following the linen-clad beauty, albeit with less admiring eyes than mine. Suddenly looking across she caught my glance and, just as quickly, as if somehow discovered in an act of treason, tried to hide her discomfort by reaching for a cigarette packet in front of her and turning with exaggerated attention to the stony-faced elderly matron on her right. I followed her movements giving her a small wry smile, wanting to convey to her that I also understood the difficulties of trying to match up to the beautiful of this world, particularly within the suffocating boundaries of a family group.

There and then, I had decided to dislike the linen-clad lady for no reason other than the sadness I saw in what I surmised was her sister-in-law's eyes. My resolve was disarmed somewhat when, as the beauty returned to the table with the by now happy child perched contentedly on her hip, she stooped down effortlessly to retrieve a handkerchief that had fallen silently to the ground from my pocket and flashed me a beautiful smile as she handed it back. Nodding foolishly I tried to avoid, unsuccessfully, the knowing smirk from the furiously smoking frumpish woman, and stood up to pull out the linen-clad lady's chair. Once again I was rewarded with yet another resolve-shattering smile before finally slinking back, guiltily, into my own chair.

Reaching down into my knapsack I retrieved my cigarettes and two guidebooks, which I placed on the table in front of me. While searching for a lighter in another pocket I could not resist drawing the prodigal handkerchief slowly past my scenting nostrils to blot away some real but very convenient sweat droplets from my forehead. 'Chanel,' I whispered, scenting her perfume as I inhaled the first long drag of a newly lit cigarette. This was my one real holiday indulgence as the pervasive leprous attitude towards smokers in the politically correct and sanitized part of California where I worked meant I did not smoke there at all, at least not in public spaces. Exhaling with relish, I carefully folded the handkerchief and packed it away, deep in a knapsack pocket.

'Buenos tardes, Señor.'

I watched as the waiter quickly wiped clean the surface of the table and reluctantly paused to allow me to lift my books from the path of his napkin. He then stood there without making any eye contact in a way that reminded me of a desert meerkat, surveying nervously with quick head movements and darting eyes the other tables of his kingdom for any potentially difficult orders.

'Una Limonada y un café con leche, por favor,' I ventured.

'*Si, Señor.*' He had already turned and was walking quickly away.

'*Camarero!*' I growled after him in a loud voice.

Reluctantly, with slouching evasive shoulders, he again stopped in his tracks and glared back.

'*Un helado de frambuesa tambien, por favor*,' I added.

The waiter nodded his head and scurried away to his restaurant burrow on the far side of the street returning, impressively, soon afterwards with my order.

After gulping down the lemonade I began to spoon small lumps of the delicious ice cream onto the tip of my tongue where the raspberry taste instantly, as it always did, brought back the ripple days of my childhood and mollycoddled memories. Reaching for the slightly tattered version of my two guidebooks I lifted the fraying ribbon bookmark and levered it open to find the chosen yellowed page. Near the bottom of the page was a general description of Granada and how it was situated at the base of two mountain spurs that ascended gradually from west to east. I searched for the information about the part of the city where I now sat.

'The northernmost of these long-stretched hills is the Albaicín, from the Arabic *Rabad el-bayyazin*, 'quarter of the falconers', the oldest part of Granada and once the favourite seat of the Moorish aristocracy.' I was reading quietly aloud when a voice interrupted.

'*Perdone, Señor.* Is that chair taken?'

Startled somewhat and thinking of falcons, I looked up to find a tall girl, her head haloed by the sun, hovering over me with one hand on the chair opposite. She was wearing a large pair of very dark sunglasses and it was impossible to see her eyes. I got the impression that I was somewhat in her peripheral vision, enough perhaps to detect any reluctance on my part, as she searched for an alternative seat.

'Yes . . . Sorry, I mean no. It's not taken.' I mumbled while standing up awkwardly and unwinding slowly so that I might gauge my own height against hers. Thankfully, I was a little taller and I smiled when pointing to the vacant chair. 'Please sit down,' I said.

She ignored my invitation as she called to the waiter.

'*Hola, Sancho. Un Café solo, por favor*.'

Sancho immediately stopped taking an order from an elderly

Japanese couple. They watched him scurrying across the street to the restaurant with the open-mouthed astonishment of half-delivered orders. The Japanese man recovered first and began to scan the menu card and a guidebook as if trying to determine whether this behaviour was a recognized quirkiness of this particular restaurant. His wife waited in vain for an explanation.

'*Gracias, Señor.*'

The girl accepted my invitation and was smiling as she turned back to look at me. She settled into the chair and immediately raised her face towards the sun. The rim of the chair must have been sun-baked hot as she had to arch one shoulder forward and then another until the contact was comfortable. She has a nice neck, I thought as I watched it sway from side to side. Stubbing out my cigarette I looked behind me, as I sat down again, to find the waiter. I need not have worried as the frenzied Sancho nearly fell over my chair in his rush to bring the girl her coffee. I pulled it forward quickly. He glared down at me before panting to a stop in front of her.

'*Muchas gracias, Sancho.*'

'*No hay de que, Isabella.*'

Just my luck, I thought, the love struck meerkat Sancho will be hovering over us from now on. I watched as she brought the cup to soft full lips and gingerly tested its heat. Letting the cup down she ran the tip of her tongue quickly along her lightly tinted upper lip and looked directly at me.

'Are you English?'

She spoke in a peculiar, precise and officious way. It was not the accent she had used when she first came to the table and my developing fantasy of the chance to chat-up a local princess evaporated quickly. The way she spoke reminded me somewhat of a painfully thin French piano teacher I had when I was ten and I smiled at the memory.

'*Francais? Deutsche?*'

I was still smiling stupidly to myself as the memory of Mademoiselle Porridge – as children, we called her that, although Fourage was her real name – floated by. 'I'm sorry,' I responded, trying to excuse my hesitation. 'I'm Irish or to be more accurate, Irish-American.'

She nodded once, pursing her lips slightly, before reaching for her cup again.

'And you?' I asked.

She seemed anxious to ignore the question as she took a long sip of her coffee. 'You smiled earlier when I asked if you were English. Is that an Irish or . . . how did you describe yourself, an Irish-American sensitivity?'

Forgetting the expected and often amusing arguments with minor and major uniformed bureaucracy, and the occasional early morning pool-side German, there had been very few times in my adult travels where the opening salvos of a conversation with a complete stranger were so obviously confrontational.

For me and many other travellers, there is usually an accepted etiquette of enquiry. This would define your nationality, your reason for travelling, your enjoyment of the visit, your opinion of the weather and where you were off to next. The protocol was also suitably softened by a genuine apology on your behalf for the difficulties you had with the language and a compliment to the stranger on their command of English. This was not to be one of those conversations.

'*No!*' My reply was a little terse. The woman had been very direct and I decided to be likewise.

'Was it something else?'

Also very perceptive, I thought. 'What? Oh No! I was just thinking of . . .' I started to tell her about the anorexic piano teacher of my youth and then stopped. ' No it's . . . it's nothing.' A silence threatened the space between us until she spoke again.

'It is very hot, this afternoon. We have had a long summer.' The girl's accent softened as she arched her neck and pushed up the large sunglasses to the crown of her head. Her hair was earth-brown and had an Afro quality. Keeping her eyes closed she fanned her face with a menu card.

'Yes, very. I was glad to get some shade.' I relaxed, thankful that normal protocol was being restored.

She leaned towards me and touched the battered guidebook that I'd been reading. She looked up and it was the first time that I'd seen her eyes. The irises had the most amazing turquoise-green speckled pattern and I wondered at first whether she had those fashionable tinted contact lenses but could not see any evidence of this. An intense blue cylinder-shaped pendant she wore, attached to a simple gold chain around her neck, complimented the opal flecks of the irises. I could only see the top of the pendant, where the chain passed through, as she was wearing a high necked silk blouse.

'May I?' She asked as she lifted the book.

'Of course,' I said and watched as she ensured that the red and black bookmarks were carefully in place before closing the book to look at the cover.

'Hmmm! An old *Baedeker* guide to Spain and Portugal! How quaint. You do not see many of these being actually used by tourists.'

I was surprised by her knowledgeable interest and how good her English really was.

'No. You are right, not many people use them. Mind you, that is a second edition, 1901. I have a first edition at home. Do you know much about *Baedekers*?'

She smiled. 'A little. Do you collect them?'

'Yes. I have about seven first editions. Always on the look out for more.'

'I know a bookseller who might be able to help. His name is Alonzo Aldahrze. He lives quite nearby in fact, in the street behind San Juan de los Reyes.' She continued to turn the pages slowly. 'They are beautiful in their own way. The bibles of a lost age when travelling was the preserve of the idle rich and knowing what steamers and railways to take was considered essential knowledge.'

I laughed. 'Yes and with loads of really helpful advice on why a traveller should be prepared to alter his habits somewhat but not to the extent of adopting some of the less moral habits of the natives. Poor Baedeker was obviously worried that his North

European and English pilgrim travellers would be seduced by the charms of the South of Spain.'

The girl smiled for the first time. 'It has happened anyway . . . to our cost.' She handed the book back.

Taking a pen and small notebook from my breast pocket I began writing. 'Alonzo . . . eh . . . Allarze, you said? The name of the bookseller?'

'Al*da*hrze.' She smiled indulgently. 'May I trouble you for a cigarette?'

'Of course. I'm sorry, I should have offered.'

'No need to apologize, I rarely smoke.' Taking the cigarette she leant forward to cup her hands, unnecessarily given that there was very little wind, around my proffered lighter. The touch of her skin against mine was light, cool and fleeting.

'Are you from Granada? I must say that your English is excellent.'

'I am from Seville originally but my mother is from Gibraltar. I read for my master's degree in Oxford, hence the accent.'

'In what?'

'Pharmacology.'

'Interesting.'

She laughed this time, a curt easy laugh. 'You managed to say that without sounding bored. Yes it was and is.'

I blushed. 'I'm sorry! I did not mean it like that, I . . .'

She touched my hand again. 'You really must stop apologizing. I was only teasing you. I am a doctoral student in the University here.'

'What are you doing your thesis on?'

'Basically I am investigating new ways of delivering drugs to specific parts of the body.'

It was my turn to smile. A slightly smug smile of satisfaction, which I barely concealed, creased my face. 'Using trans-membrane proteins as the piggy-back carrier?'

She was caught off guard. 'Yes! How did you know? Are you a scientist?'

I held my hand out to her. It was the first time I'd felt

comfortable. 'I know your name or at least your first name. Isabella is it not? Mine is Michael Mara and I'm pleased to meet you.'

The girl accepted the handshake, her grip was firm but somewhat distracted and she continued to look at me with a puzzled expression.

'How do you know so much about me?'

'Oh that. Well with your name I had some help.' I pointed to the hovering Sancho, who took it as a signal to immediately approach.

She smiled as he arrived.

'Would you like another espresso, Isabella?' I asked with as much familiarity as I could dare, without the scowling Sancho killing me there and then.

She nodded without looking at me. 'Yes, thank you. A black coffee please.'

'Otro café con leche y un café solo, por favor.'

'Si, Señor.'

This time the meerkat glared at me before sulking his way across to the restaurant.

'I have a distinct feeling that I've crossed into his territory . . . his attention to you, I mean.'

'Don't mind him. His mother is my landlady and they have sort of adopted me. Sancho considers himself to be the big brother I never had and feels he needs to protect me.'

'Or cage you!'

'Yes, perhaps that also. He is harmless though.' She laughed lightly before looking at me with an inquisitor's gaze. 'You still have not answered my question. How did you know about my work?'

'Oh that! An educated guess really.'

'Explain.'

'I'm in Granada for the pharmacology conference at the Centro de Congreso and I happened to listen in on a presentation about trans-membrane carrier proteins. It was given by Alvorro Martinez, the Professor of Pharmacology in the University here in the city. I just guessed that is what you might be working on.'

'You are right as it happens. Professor Martinez is my supervisor and most of the work he presented was mine.'

'Do I detect a tone of resentment?'

'No, not really. That is often the fate of a student's doctoral thesis work. He is the professor and my work is only the next stage of his life-long academic commitment to developing new drug-delivery systems. We agreed that he should present, although it was a joint paper.'

I reached down and retrieved the conference programme from my knapsack. Flicking quickly through the pages I came to the section that detailed the session I had attended.

'Ah I see! Alvorro Martinez and Isabella Sanjil, Department of Pharmacology, University of Granada. Your surname is Sanjil?'

'Yes. And you? Were you presenting a paper at the conference?'

'No. Not a research paper. I was invited to give the keynote lecture on the first day.'

'Who invited you?'

'Your professor as it happens, Alvorro Martinez. He is chairman of the organising committee. But then you know that!'

'Of course. Do you know Professor Martinez well?' She looked puzzled again and I thought the question had a slightly concerned edge to its tone.

'No. Don't worry, Señorita Sanjil. I will not tell him about his student's rightful but muted annoyance. The invitation to speak, in fact, was a very unexpected honour.'

'Why? Are you not also a pharmacologist?'

'No, as it happens. I am, or was at least, a molecular biologist but now, increasingly, a reluctant businessman.'

'What do you mean by that?'

'I'm a biotechnology entrepreneur developing gene products for commercial exploitation.'

'You do not sound very happy about it, Michael. I thought that this was the dream of all scientists to have control and reward from their years of work. Is it not very lucrative?'

'Very . . . well, at least on paper. The industry at present is at a volatile stage. Reward comes with the ability to patent and protect your developments and neither the consumer legislation nor the ethical debate can keep pace with the rate of new gene products being developed. That is what I gave the talk about to the conference.'

'What is your company?'

Retrieving my wallet I opened it and pulled out one of my cards. I handed it to her and she examined it carefully.

'Doctor Michael Mara. Both an MD and PhD I see. Very impressive!' She looked at me with raised eyebrows as she read the card, running her fingers over the gold-embossed lettering. 'President, Hoxygene Inc. San Clemente, California. May I keep this?'

'Sure.'

'Are you in Granada for long?'

'Unfortunately not. I leave tomorrow.'

She continued to examine the card before looking up at me. 'How are you *exploiting* hoxygenes?'

I ignored the unnecessary emphasis. 'Basically, as you are aware, they are site-specific short-chain DNA genes that initiate and direct cellular repair. There are about seven known, but ours, which targets cardiac muscle, is at the most advanced stage of commercial development. It will be licensed for human use by the FDA early next year.'

'Very lucrative indeed!' She lifted one eyebrow while tilting her head slightly. 'The "plant of immortality, the plant of the heartbeat".'

I had heard those words before and tried hard to recall from where. Suddenly, I did remember and like a teacher's pet began to blurt it out. 'Gilga –'

Sancho had returned with the two coffees causing Isabella to look at her watch and interrupt.

'My apologies, Michael. I must go. I start work in ten minutes.'

'*Work!* On a Saturday evening? Very dedicated.'

Isabella smiled. 'Not the lab. I work as a part-time masseuse in the old Moorish Baths, down the street, to earn some extra money.'

'That's an amazing coincidence. I've been cooped up so much in airplanes and meetings that I was thinking of having a relieving massage. What do you suggest?' I hammed this last question out like a bad afternoon-soap actor while, in Marx brother fashion, rubbing my lower back furiously. Isabella laughed out loud as she stood up.

'That was the most pathetic cameo of locker-room humour I have ever seen and it is reflective of a repressed American hang-up of what a therapeutic massage actually offers. If you are genuinely interested, why not call to the bathhouse and make an appointment. I am working until nine and there might be a vacant time-slot.' She hesitated for a moment. 'I am usually booked out though.'

'I'm not surprised,' I offered and immediately regretted. Isabella Sanjil was already walking away, waving to Sancho as she left. She stopped for a moment and looked back over her shoulder towards me.

'Mention that you are a friend of mine to the receptionist and she will try and fit you in. You were right by the way. The quote was from the epic of Gilgamesh. *Adios*.'

I watched her go, standing up to get a better view, hoping she might turn around again.

'Si, Señor.'

It was 'big brother' Sancho. Where had he come from? 'Oh . . . *La cuenta, por favor.*'

'Si, Señor.'

'Graçias.'

Sancho began to walk away but then stopped and turned. '*La señorita, tambien?*'

'What? Oh . . . *si* . . . yes, yes of course! *Graçias.*'

It was the first time that he had smiled at me.

Michael had walked up and down the narrow street a number of times before he started to mutter to himself. He was increasingly concerned at the conspicuous way he was inspecting all the doorways and peering into the darkness through the few un-shuttered windows. The street itself was deserted apart from a small ginger cat perched nervously on a sill where he was catching the final rays of the day's sunshine.

Finally he stopped, and while shaking his head in exasperation had one more look at the map he carried before deciding to give up on the quest. Barely concealing his disappointment, he began to walk towards the steep road that would bring him back down the hill to the city centre. At that very moment he heard one of the doors creaking open behind him and turning, saw an elderly man, dressed in a finely tailored white-cotton suit, step out into the street. He hesitated for a moment, to watch while the man locked the door behind him before approaching.

'*Perdone, Señor. Habla ingles?* Could you possibly help me? I'm looking for a bookshop on this street,' Michael said loudly, in a tourist's habit of deafening communication.

The elderly man looked at Michael with an amused expression before answering in a quiet voice.

'A bookshop! Here! No I am sorry.' His English accent was very precise. 'This is a residential street. You will have better fortune finding such a shop in the area closer to the central markets.'

The old man pulled out a fob watch and flipped opens the lid. The casing was tethered to his waistcoat by a chain of rose-coloured gold. He shook his head. 'In any event the bookshops will be closed by now.'

Michael blushed. 'I know. I mean to return tomorrow but as I was walking nearby I thought I would check if there was a bookshop here. I'm sorry to have disturbed you.'

'It is not a disturbance. Perhaps you will have better luck tomorrow.'

'Perhaps. It's . . . it's strange though.'

'What is so strange my friend?'

' I was told by somebody I met earlier today that there was a bookseller on this street.'

'I see. What is the name of this bookseller that you seek?'

Michael pulled out a notebook and opened it. 'Alonzo Aldahrze. Do you know of him?'

The old man was taken aback somewhat and immediately began tapping the ivory-handled and metal-tipped wooden cane that he carried, on the cobblestones of the street. Small sparks flew up and caused the lounging cat to jump from the nearby sill and dash between the two of them with an irritated shriek. Quickly looking up and down the street the old man then stared, without speaking at Michael. The silence was awkward between them.

'I am sorry, Señor. Did I pronounce the name wrong? Have I said something to offend you?' Michael ventured.

'It depends. Who gave you this name?'

'A lady called Isabella Sanjil.'

'That is very interesting! Very interesting indeed!' The old man visibly relaxed. 'Come, my lost young friend. I was about to take my evening stroll and you can accompany me. Let me lean on your arm.' He leaned forward and with his free arm linked that of Michael. 'What do those English gentlemen call it . . . a constitutional? Are you English?' he asked as he began leading them both off at a brisk pace along the street.

'No! American. I don't understand,' Michael blurted out, feeling slightly awkward with the unfamiliar physical familiarity.

'Of course you do not, my dear boy. I am Alonzo Aldahrze, the man you are looking for, although a collector rather than seller of books. I certainly do not have a shop.' He paused for a moment to size up Michael again. 'Isabella sent you? That is indeed most interesting. She would know well that I do not have a bookshop. How is the dear princess? I have not seen her since she came back from America.'

Michael stopped. 'America? She never mentioned that. I'm sorry Señor Aldahrze, I only met her for a brief time today. I was reading an old *Baedeker* guide and she told me that you might be able to help me source some more. Perhaps I misheard her when she said bookseller, she might have said collector.'

'It is of no concern. What is your name?'

'Michael Mara.' Michael unlinked his arm and removing his wallet opened it and handed the older man a card. Alonzo looked at it carefully before pocketing it.

'She is an attractive young woman, our Isabella. No?'

'Very.'

They walked in silence until reaching the Plaza Nueva. The older man stopped suddenly and examined the card again.

'Well Doctor Michael Mara I will try and help you with your *Baedekers*, but you will have to give me something in return.'

'Sure. Of course . . . What would you like?' Michael appeared on guard, wondering what the older man would demand of him. Alonzo smiled at his hesitation.

'Do not worry Doctor Mara. I would just ask for the pleasure of your company for a while. I am an old man and I like to talk as well as listen. I have few people to converse with, particularly in English, and if you can spare the time, join me tomorrow evening for my walk. I will meet you here at the same time.'

Michael blushed. 'I was due to leave tomorrow but I have decided to change my plans.'

Alonzo smiled again and like an indulgent uncle, squeezed Michael's arm gently. 'Good, that's settled then. I am sure you will find that the effort will be worth it. Until tomorrow then Doctor Mara.'

The cell phone suddenly vibrated into life against my chest wall. While reaching into my pocket to retrieve it I realised I must have forgotten to switch it back to ringing mode after the conference had ended that morning. Sitting down on the bed I flipped the lid open and saw from the number display that it was Rod Mallory calling. Only he, Willard Adams, my personal secretary and my wife, Caroline, had the number. I pressed the receive button.

'Hello, Rod.' According to my watch it was midday in San Clemente.

'G'day cobber. How's it going mate?'

Rod Mallory's strong Australian accent bounced off the

satellite and hurtled to earth; neither warped by space nor distorted by the many years he had spent away from his native Kangaroo Island in South Australia.

Rod had been a champion surfer and martial arts expert in his youth but it was his intellect, often cunningly shrouded, that had brought him, first to the University of Hawaii and then to the Massachusetts Institute of Technology. That same intellect was to propel him to a quick and substantial fortune as an offshore investment banker. At a time when I was seeking both finance capital and business acumen to help develop and market my genetic products he had come on board and helped establish the company. Rod Mallory was currently the chief financial officer of Hoxygene.

'Good Rod, thanks. The conference was reasonably informative and Granada is a beautiful city.'

'Washington Irvine the second eh, cobber? Are you staying in the Alhambra as well?'

Little of Rod's prodigious memory ever let him down but it was very, very unusual though, for him to interrupt his sacrosanct Saturdays to make a business call: even to me. I looked at my watch. Normally at this time of the day he was to be found lording it on the tennis courts of the country club where we were both members. I did not play tennis much, a reflection more of my skill than inclination, preferring the solitude and challenge of hill walking that took me well away from the atmosphere of crass greed and vanity in the club. There, a better facelift, a larger yacht, a bigger house or a killing on the stock exchange defined your present worth, and prompted envy even amongst people already hideously wealthy, and that was just the men. The mountains were a necessary escape to sanity.

I remained a member of its enclaved pomposity for the sake of my wife Caroline, whose characteristic cool and dignified restraint rapidly evaporated when preparing to serve. She and Rod Mallory had formed a mixed doubles combination that had dominated the local veteran's circuit for the past three years and on the few occasions that I had had a chance to watch them play

I found that the intensity of their game was often jealously unnerving.

'No, not really, Rod. I'm slumming it on the lower slopes. Still a good view though.' There was silence on the line. 'Rod are you still there? Rod!'

There was a banging sound in the background and a pause before he came back on the line.

'Sorry mate, I just had to shut the door.'

There was still some persistent background noise, which sounded like running water. For some reason I suddenly wished, at that point, I had access to one of those Taiwanese electronic surveillance facilities that I'd seen written about in a recent copy of the *International Herald Tribune*. You dialled a special number and it would play back all the background peripheral sounds, with the voice screened out of the person you were in contact with. According to the report, Taiwanese women wanted to know what their husbands were up to, and where and the replayed sounds helped localise them, particularly if they emanated from houses of pleasure.

'Are you at the tennis club? It sounds like it's raining.'

'What? Oh yes. I'm in the pro's office. The sprinkler system just came on and I needed to shut the door. It's splattering against the windows. *Michael?*'

'Yes, Rod.'

'Are you sitting down, cobber?'

'Yes,' I lied. This type of enquiry nearly always automatically caused me to start pacing. I got up and moved to the window, pulling back the curtains, to look out at the city. It was twilight and the streetlights were beginning to flicker on. 'What is it, Rod?'

'Charles Alexander rang me with an offer. It's incredible.'

Charles Alexander was the President and Chief Executive Officer of Alpanna BioPharm, one of the biggest biotechnology conglomerates in the world. They held patents for a diverse range of gene products: an eye pigment regulator, a complete activating sequence from the HIV virus which was now being used for vaccine production, a lung cancer associated protein, and a gene controlling disease resistance in soybean and rice. The present big money spinner for Alpanna, because of its implications for the paper industry, was a gene controlling the amount of structural proteins in the Eucalyptus tree.

Hoxygene had been negotiating with Alpanna BioPharm for development funding in return for the commercial production rights.

'What do you mean, Rod? Will they give us the funding?'

'More than that, Michael!'

'Get to the point, Rod!'

'They want to buy a majority stake in Hoxygene.'

'*What!* No way, Rod! We agreed that we were not open to offers.'

'Easy cobber. You've not even heard the –'

'I don't care what the offer is. *Hoxygene is not for sale.*' By this time I was pacing furiously, my free hand clenching and opening in frustration. '*Do you hear me, Rod?*'

There was silence apart from the running water sounds I heard earlier.

'*Rod.*'

'When you've calmed down, you arrogant shit, I'll speak to you. This is a business call and not some playground battle over who has the most marbles.' The tone of his voice was loaded with venom.

I could feel myself breaking out in a sweat, caused by a mixture of anger and fear. I fought hard to compose myself. 'No . . . You are right, Rod, I'm sorry for shouting. Stay on the line.'

'That's better, mate. I hate playing silly games to haul ivory-tower scientists down into the real world.'

I tried to recover some of the lost ground. 'Have you spoken to Bill?'

Willard 'Bill' Adams was the 65 year-old chairman of an old, family-run Wall Street investment bank. A few years previously, he had immediately recognized the potential of the prospectus that Rod and I had put together and rather than farming it out to other investors had committed the family money to the start-up costs for Hoxygene. This had amounted to about $9,000,000 and gave the bank a fifteen per cent stake in the company. While I controlled 45 per cent of the issued shares, Rod had 24 and in addition, there was about ten per cent placed with large institutional investors. The remainder of the shareholding was tied up in a family trust controlled by Caroline, and her brother Max.

Caroline was English. We had met by chance, about ten years ago, while skiing in the same group in Copper Mountain, Colorado and married two years later. Encouraged by Caroline and Max, their then living father Jack, a wealthy London industrialist, invested in Hoxygene. I never liked the grumpy bastard much, as he was often too patronizing to his 'American Paddy' son-in-law but I did appreciate his commercial vote of confidence. After Jack's death his shares were put into a family trust for the benefit of Caroline and Max.

'Yes. Bill was with me yesterday when we met with Alpanna BioPharm.'

'*Yesterday!*' I shouted down the phone. 'That meeting was scheduled for next week . . . *After I return*.'

There was silence again on the line apart from the sound of another slamming door.

'Michael, I'll not be shouted at. I'm way past the time when I need to tolerate such behaviour, *from anyone*. Alpanna asked for the meeting to be brought forward and I obliged. If you can possibly extract your head from your arse for one moment, I want you to listen up to what is on offer. Either, use that cold, detached analytical ability that you are wont to wallow in, or piss off.'

The venom stung. Although Rod and I had developed a close working association over the years, I still knew very little about his personal life away from Hoxygene. Apart from the contact necessitated by his tennis arrangement with Caroline, we rarely socialised together. We were not die-hard mates, as he would say, but that was my fault as I was jealous of his easy and warm relationship with Caroline and tended to steer clear. This reservation meant that I had little opportunity to probe him on his inner thoughts and he never volunteered.

I regretted this reticence of mine because it had been Rod who had originally approached me at a conference and announced, in his blunt way, that he had money to invest and that his researches had indicated I was the man to back. He had made the money, he said, in offshore banking in Belize and the Caribbean and bored with it decided that genetic biotechnology was the way to go. Encouraged by his enthusiasm and apparent unlimited access to investment funds, we had founded Hoxygene together.

I had always admired his ability to diffuse the patronizing formality of American business negotiation with judiciously used 'out-back' charm. In all our time together we had never had an argument where I had heard him resort to such unfettered venom with me as the object of that venom.

'Rod.' My voice was calm.

'Yes.' His was still sharp.

'I am beginning to feel like some African or South American dictator who heads to Switzerland for a prostate operation only to wake up and find that a well-planned coup has removed his need for a toilet at home.' I was not in any mood to apologize any further. There was a silence for a moment and then loud laughter filtered down the line.

'Idi Mara. The name suits you, Michael, just do not catch the dick-rot.'

'Rod, what is the offer?'

'Listen Michael, I can sense how unhappy you are about what's happened but it was Alexander who rang me requesting an urgent meeting. He also indicated that if I did not agree to do so straightaway then all negotiations for funding were off. What was I to do? Given the stance of the arrogant dickhead I brought Bill along for support. At the meeting the original agenda, that you and I had agreed, was immediately discarded by Alexander, and we were handed a summary proposal on a 'take it or leave it' basis.'

Doors were opening and closing in the background and there was still the constant sound of running water.

'Go on, Rod.'

'$190,000,000 for yours, mine and Bill's shares. You are to become a board member of Alpanna.'

'And you?'

'Hey! I'm out of here mate. I plan to spend the money. I'll buy bloody Queensland, or a third world country! Whatever.'

'And Bill?'

'Home to New England I'd imagine. Happy in the knowledge that the Adam's family mansion is safe for another generation of puritan coin-collectors.'

'Rod, I'll think about this and will talk to you on Friday.'

'Friday! I thought that you were due back tomorrow evening.'

'I've changed my plans somewhat. I'm staying on in Granada for a few more days and will fly back via London on Thursday night.'

'Alpanna BioPharm want an answer by next weekend.'

'They'll have to wait until I return.'

'Michael.'

'Yes, Rod.'

'You sound about as happy as a bastard on father's day. What's up? The women of Granada are meant to be some of the most beautiful in the world. How can you fail to be enchanted?'

'I'm not like you, Rod.'

'And you would know mate, with your head stuck under an extraction hood all the time.'

'I thought that it was you antipodeans that kept your heads down.'

'Wow, very quick. Perchance sharp Irish wit to blunt my jesting barb. For your information I like having my legs in the air.' Rod really did have a way of calming my impatience. 'But seriously, Michael, you do sound pissed off. Why?'

'I don't know, Rod.' I was not entirely sure that I really wanted to get into an explanation of something I could not understand myself.

'That's a cop-out, Michael. Enlighten me a little.' He wasn't letting go.

'Despite the success of Hoxygene I am feeling a little unfulfilled. It's as if I'm seeking a new direction to my work but do not know where to turn. I need to re-energise but cannot find either the time or the stimulus. It feels a bit like hitting the marathon runners 'wall'. Do you understand what I'm trying to say, Rod?'

I wasn't really sure whether I wanted him to understand or commiserate with me. There was a prolonged silence from Rod's end of the connection and when he eventually spoke again, his voice was serious.

'Does this impasse extend into other areas of your life as well, Michael?'

'You mean with Caroline. God no! Why should it?'

'I just wondered.'

'Well stop wondering, Rod. It's not related. I'm more than capable of separating my work from home.'

'Of course you are, cobber, but sometimes even the most capable of us are unable to prevent an overlap of frustration.'

'Listen, Rod, I appreciate the psychotherapy but it is something I will work out. I just need some time to myself.'

'Sure.' He did not sound that convinced.

'Thanks, Rod. I'll talk to you during the week.'

'Michael.'

'Yes.'

'Do not pass on the Alpanna proposal. It . . . it might be outside of your control.'

'What do you mean, Rod?'

'Oh . . . Nothing, mate. Think about the offer and I will see you Friday. Enjoy the extra few days. Alexander and Alpanna have asked us for a joint meeting to take place with them and their financial advisors on the eleventh.'

'Where?'

'Manhattan. The WTC, south tower; 9.30 am.'

'I'll have to think really hard about this, Rod.'

'I'll arrange a time for you, Bill, Caroline, Max and me to meet on Monday in New York before briefing the legal and financial whiz kids. Bye.'

'What's Caroline –' The phone went dead.

As I looked out the window a few fireworks were exploding over the southern edge of the city. Isolated and unchoreographed, their impact soon fizzled out against the vast expanse of the cloudless, moonless, but not yet star-filled sky. I tried ringing Rod back on his cell phone but there was no reply.

The only occupant of the room was a middle-aged man with short-cropped, silver-grey hair who sat in a high-backed swivel chair, which was turned away from the desk. He was rocking back and forward with a slow rhythm as he looked out through the panoramic window that dominated the room. At this elevation, on the Utliberg Heights, it afforded him an uninterrupted view of the Zurichsee Lake as it stretched away to the southeast. In the far distance he could just make out the Glarnisch crest and he thought of his ski lodge in the valley of Flims beyond it. His line of sight was following the horizon southwards and just as it reached the Todi peak the intercom on the walnut desk activated. He swung back, away from the window and pressed a button on the console panel.

'Yes, Fraulein Schmitt.'

'Your call to Granada sir!'

'Thank you, Fraulein Schmitt. I will take it on my personal line. You may go home now.'

'Yes, sir. Thank you, sir. I'm transferring the call through now.'

The silver-haired man removed the dark tinted glasses that he wore and laid them on the table. He allowed the telephone to ring a couple of times before picking it up.

'Hello. One moment please caller.' The man loosened his tie before standing up and walking across the room. He opened the door that connected to his secretary and looked into the outer office. Satisfied he returned to his desk and settled into the swivel chair. He picked up the phone. 'Go ahead, caller.'

'Am I speaking to a friend?'

'The beginning of love is search –'

'But the end is rest.'

The silver-haired man smiled as he heard the familiar code words. *'Masa 'l-khair, Solis sitti!'*

'Masa 'n-nur, Sahib al-Zuhur baik.'

'Have you any progress to report?'

'Yes, but I am not sure that this line is fully secure.'

'There is no evidence of that at my end, Solis but be discreet and I will understand.'

'As you wish, Sahib al-Zuhur. I arrived back yesterday morning but was unable to contact you before now. I met with our horticulturist, as we had arranged, and that meeting was successful and very helpful. His information is that the effect of the new fertilizer on the crop growth has exceeded all expectations. He is prepared to provide us with samples but has indicated that the cost of harvesting has increased significantly however.'

'The horticulturist is getting greedy. Is there any danger of cross contamination in the seeds? '

'Not so far. If I do suspect that, then, I will cancel the order, permanently. '

'That is good. How did the other meeting go? Did the wholesaler arrive?'

'Yes. Your information was accurate. He was there as anticipated. How did you manage to arrange it?'

'Alvorro . . .' A look of irritation creased the man's face. He brought his hand up and ran it through the silver-grey hair. 'I was owed a few favours. How did the meeting go?'

'The fruit is ripe for picking.'

'Very good. Proceed with caution Solis, as the market is a bit saturated at present and I do not want to alert any competitors. I have made an offer to the other partners of our friend for their distribution rights and demanded a quick answer. Let them apply the pressure on the wholesaler. Do you agree?'

'Yes. I will be able to monitor the wholesaler's response at my end.'

'And Zoë?'

'She has watched my back.'

'I have to be in Corsica by next Friday and would like to meet you both there, either on Friday or Saturday.'

'Why Corsica?'

'I will explain when I see you. I'll leave a message on your answering service on Thursday as to the time and place. We need to discuss a strategy as I have arranged for a further meeting with the distributors for the eleventh.'

'Where?'

'New York.'

'That's fine by me. By the way, will I arrange for the horticulturist to come to Corsica as well?'

'Yes. That's a good idea.'

'Fine. I will see you then.'

'Solis.'

'Yes.'

'Bring your dowry. It is time for the joining.'

'Perhaps! *Mesik bil-khair*.'

'*Messaki Allah bil-khair.*'

Vesper

EVENING DUSK

Granada, Spain.
2 September 2001

As I climbed the short flight of steps, which led up from the pavement of the modern Carrera de Darro to the older street level of the fifteenth-century avenue, I looked ahead of me, searching for the doorway of the small Moorish bathhouse or *bañuelo*. It had been quite an overcast morning and it was only now, early in the afternoon, that the sun was making a brief appearance. The doorway was framed by deep shadows and I paused for a moment before entering to let an exiting customer leave. He looked pleased with himself and flashed me a giddy smile.

The carved, wooden outer door was not that thick, yet once closed behind me the street noise instantly, and near completely, faded. I made for the small reception area where I had made the booking the evening before. There was nobody about and while I waited for somebody to appear, wandered into a small narrow courtyard where a stone fountain and seat and an unkempt orange tree stood. There was a decorative, iron, external balcony-walkway overlooking the courtyard and I thought I saw some movement at one of the doors that opened out onto it.

'Hello. *Hello!* Is there anybody here?' I called up. There was no immediate answer from above only the clatter of footsteps down the narrow staircase, which I had seen just inside the entrance. A bronzed, blonde and blue-eyed girl with pierced nostrils and eyebrows appeared.

'*Perdone, Señor*. I did not hear you coming in. Are you waiting long?' Her tongue was also pierced and I had trouble keeping my eyes off the silver orb as it danced to the strong Scandinavian accent. She also had a small defect in the lobe of her left ear.

'No. Not really. I have an appointment for a massage at 1.00pm

She checked the ledger in front of her and then looked at her watch. 'Oh yes. Doctor . . . eh. . .Vara is it not?'

'Mara, yes.'

'Well it is good, you are on time.' She reached down behind her and retrieved two thick bath-towels, which she then handed to me. 'If you go into the changing room there,' she said as she pointed to a small wooden door, 'and remove your clothing, you then go to the baths. When Isabella is free she will come to you for the massage.'

'Do I pay you now?'

'Sure. It is normal.'

Having handed over the agreed sum and deposited my wallet and passport in a safety deposit box I gathered up the towels and walked to the changing-room door. Crouching a little to enter I stepped down into a mould-smelling and poorly lit room. To my left was the open archway entrance to the baths with its faded decoration of blue-and-white Moorish tiles and directly ahead there was a set of pegs for hanging clothes. On one of the pegs hung what looked like a woman's tracksuit and shirt. I wondered whether they belonged to Isabella.

Turning right, I entered a small cubicle at the end of the room and began undressing. Opening my knapsack to retrieve my swimming shorts I found that I had left them at the hotel. This oversight annoyed me a little and while muttering to myself, I half-wrapped a towel about me and pushed open the cubicle door. I stopped just as suddenly at the sight of a young woman, who had her back to me, reaching fully naked to retrieve her clothes from the peg.

'Oh! *Perdone, Señorita,*' I spluttered as I hastily tied in my towel and made to go back into the cubicle.

She turned and smiled at my obvious discomfort. 'It's OK! There is no need for you to be embarrassed. I will not be long.'

The accent was of mixed origin but I thought it had the cadence of deep-south USA. She was in her early 20s, with the toned body of an athlete and spiky red hair. I noticed that there was a wet swimming suit on the floor and pointed to them. 'I forgot my trunks. I wonder if they supply them here.'

The girl carried on dressing, and turning towards me, oblivious to her nudity and my awkwardness, began pulling a simple black T-shirt over her head. The collar must have been tight and as her arms lifted to ease it on I could not help admire the way her small firm breasts rose up as well. Her pubic area was completely shaved, the hair replaced by a small tattoo of a poppy.

'I don't know,' she mumbled from beneath the cotton shirt. 'Why not ask at the desk?'

'I'll do that. Thank you,' I said as I brushed past her to re-enter the courtyard and make my way to the desk.

The pierced Scandinavian looked up, a patronising smile creasing her face.

'I forgot –' I began to explain before the blonde held up her hand dismissively.

'It is not a problem, I think. It is a Sunday and we close soon, yes. You are the last client and so there is no one to frighten. Isabella will not mind. Go ahead into the baths, Doctor Vara. I promise not to stare.' She giggled sarcastically.

I gave the mocking Scandinavian a sharp look but without replying turned back for the door that led into the changing room. The athlete was just leaving; she smiled at me.

'Enjoy the baths. Is this your first time?'

'Thank you. Yes it is my first time here. Where are you from?' I wanted her to stay and talk.

'Granada.'

'But the accent?' She wore no jewellery but I now noticed that there was small triangular area missing from the lobe of her left ear, which was uncannily like the defect that the receptionist had. She caught my stare and pretended to brush her hair back.

'I'm on an athletic scholarship to Georgia Tech. Hurdles.' She continued on to the desk and retrieved her belongings. After a few words with the blonde receptionist she left, giving me a small wave as she went. I watched the outer door close behind her.

'Oh, Doctor Vara.' The silver pinioned Nordic tongue called out. I looked at the bobbing bits of metal coming towards me.

'It's Mara,' I said with too sharp, and probably unnecessary, emphasis.

'Ah, I see! The archdemon!' She laughed as she said this and I over reacted.

'What did you say? I thought that all you Scandinavians were a polite people.'

'We are. Do not be so serious, man. Relax!'

'What did you mean by archdemon?' I asked.

'Oh that! I'm a Buddhist and in my religion Mara is the tempter who along with his daughters, Desire, Pleasure and Restlessness, inhibits us from achieving Nirvana and Enlightenment. I had always hoped he might pay the bathhouse a visit at some time. Your name is such a coincidence.'

'It's an Irish name.'

'Whatever! I go now, so here is your deposit key. Ask Isabella to make sure the door is locked when you are finished. Good afternoon Doctor . . . Mara.'

I took the key and entered back into the changing room, lonely now without the redhead. Turning left I walked along the tiled passageway towards the cool resting area at its end. Along one wall were open cubicles with unusual double-seated small shower baths that you stepped into. Steam was coming from a narrow passageway that opened into the cool-room and following the drafting mist I entered into a large vaulted room, which had the shape of a cross. Along the nave was a rectangular pool from which the steam rose and in two side chapels there were beds for massage.

There was no electric lighting and the natural light that was available outside filtered grudgingly through small stained-glass panels cut into the domed ceiling. The tinkling sounds of running water coursing through a series of tiled channels on the floor, echoed off the walls. After a while these noises became part of the atmosphere and in the otherwise hollow quietness of the murky tropical dimness I began to feel somewhat unnerved. I thought that somebody was watching me so I removed the towel quickly and slid into the shallow bath. Suddenly a voice came from the direction of the passageway.

'Relax in the warm water for twenty minutes or so. I will be with you then.'

Was that Isabella's voice? I could not be sure. It sounded different. The time passed slowly, the room becoming darker and darker. I wished there was music.

'OK, I am ready for you now, Michael.'

I could just make out a ghostly figure carrying what appeared to be two wicker-lit oil-lamps into the upper apse. These were placed on wall mounts and after a little adjustment a cedar-scented yellow glow soon lit up the shadows. I edged out of the pool and pulled the towel around me. Walking towards the shadow figure I saw that it was indeed Isabella. She appeared to be dressed in a finely woven muslin shirt that reached down to her ankles. When she moved towards me across the beam of the wall-mounted light the impression I got was that she was naked underneath. Indeed where the material was damp it clung, almost transparently, to sallow glistening skin.

'You may remove the towel and lie face downwards, on the bed. Are there any areas of your body in particular that are stiff or sore.'

'No.' I lied as I dropped the towel and lay on the bed as instructed.

'I am first going to rub you down with a kese cloth. This gets rid of all the dead skin.'

Isabella worked my arms and legs and then my back until the skin tingled. Turning me over she covered my midriff and did the same on chest. There was very little eye contact. When she had finished she lifted a bucket of soapy water and poured it over me. I held onto the towel for safety.

'Turn please.'

I did what I was told. The towel fell to the floor. I watched the stream of suds disappear into a drain. There was the sensation of silk air bubbles cascading over my skin. It was like nothing I had ever felt before. What was she doing?

'Turn over again please, Michael.'

She had her back turned to me and was dipping the lower part of her long shirt into a bucket of hot soaped water. Turning she gathered up the hem and pinching the material into a balloon shape blew into the neck until it expanded like a bladder. This she then patted from my neck to my knees in one descending movement until the air was gone and the fabric deflated. The sensation of air hitting my skin through the fine weave of the muslin was like that of champagne bubbles moving mercurially everywhere. The whole cleansing procedure had taken about five minutes.

'You may face downwards again please.'

I noticed, as I turned that one of her nipples, protruded erect and proud against a damp area of her gown.

'That was a truly unique experience, Isabella. Fantastic.'

'Thank you, Michael. Now I am just going to cover you with some warm towels, while I dry off and change my shirt.'

She disappeared through a side door I had not noticed and about five minutes later returned this time in the standard white trouser and short-sleeved jacket uniform. Her hair was tied back.

'It's an interesting place this, Isabella. A little bit eerie though. Who was that girl I met in the changing room?'

'Which girl?' She sounded irritated.

'The red-headed athlete.'

'Oh that girl. That was Zoë, my previous client. She is also, in fact, my cousin. Nice body. Did you notice?'

Did I what. 'Yes. Are all your family so gifted?'

'Only the women!' She laughed at her own wit and at my expense.

I squirmed a little, my naked self, feeling exposed and cold all of a sudden. Almost on cue Isabella placed a warm towel over my buttocks and legs and began working on my back

'I thought you were meant to be going home today.' She began massaging my neck with firm but agile fingers.

'I changed my mind. I wanted to stay in Granada a little longer, to see a bit more of al-Andalous.'

'Your Arabic pronunciation is not bad.'

'Do you speak Arabic, Isabella?'

'Yes.' Her tone was matter of fact and as she continued to my lower back a silence descended. I was enjoying her skill and as the time passed felt more and more relaxed. As she began massaging my upper buttocks the movement caused them to rock from side to side. I could feel myself becoming erect. Jesus do not turn me now, I pleaded silently.

'Michael.'

'Yes.' Panic in my voice.

'I am going to work on the back of your legs now. I will just put another warm towel on your back.'

'Sure. Thanks.' There was a woody sweet scent from the oil she applied. 'What's the oil you're using?'

'Frankincense. The resin of relaxation.'

'It's beautiful,' I sighed in pleasure as Isabella's hands began to massage the inner part of my upper thighs. Her fingers occasionally touched the skin of my flattened scrotum causing the nerve ends to ripple. Unable to resist the sensation, I gambled and tried closing the gap between my legs hoping to grasp her hands, if only for a moment. She ignored my clumsy movement and continued to knead until finally embarrassed, I relaxed and she moved lower without comment. The massage on my calves was deep and definitely more painful. My earlier excitement waned fast.

'Turn over, Michael. I want to do your chest and head.'

Isabella moved to the top of the table and began moving her

hands from my neck to my stomach in slow deep movements. As she leant forward I could see her eyes and feel the touch of her breasts against my head.

'You should not lie so badly, Michael.' Her large eyes bore down into mine.

'What do you mean, Isabella?' I was startled at the directness of the comment although it was said in a soft gentle voice. More an admonishment than accusation.

'You stayed in Granada to see me again. Did you not?'

She began massaging my scalp with fine circular movements of her fingers.

'Yes,' I admitted.

'That's better. There is no necessity to hide one's true intentions. It is a waste of effort and willpower.'

'I –'

The fingers stopped moving. Her voice sweetened and cut across my useless defence. Isabella whispered close to my ear:

> ' "*Were she to lose her love, because she had lost*
> *Her confidence in mine, or even lose*
> *Its first simplicity, love, voice and all,*
> *All my fine feathers would be plucked away*
> *And I left shivering*".'

'Very apt.' I theatrically shook my shoulders as I spoke, trying to ignore the astuteness and directness of the observation. 'Yeats.'

'So, *you are* an Irishman after all! It's from *The Gift of Harun Al-Rashid*. Appropriate to the setting and the atmosphere. Don't you think?'

'Yes it is.'

'*Na'iman!* We are finished. Turn over again and rest here for a few minutes. After that you can go and change. Do not shower. Let the oils work.'

'What does "*na'iman*" mean?' I looked up at her as I revolved.

'Michael, you really do have some gaping omissions in your

education. Have you never read Burton's Thousand Nights and a Night?'

The beautiful eyes watched me with a feigned pity as I guiltily shook my head.

'No.'

'You should, for many reasons. *Na'iman* is the polite greeting after being in the bathhouse, as we are. The modern reply is *Allah ykhallik*, God preserve you.'

'*Allah yuhanniki.*' A sensuous but unfulfilled night of long ago in Marrakech came flooding back to my rescue.

Isabella smiled and flick-slapped me on the bottom with the wet corner-point of a damp towel before turning to leave. She stopped at the arched doorway and looked back.

'*Allah yuhanniki* . . . God pleasure you . . . Very good, Michael. You have the makings of an oriental yet even if you have avoided Burton.'

I looked at her for a moment before speaking:

> ' "*And thus declared that Arab lady:*
> *Last night, where under the wild moon*
> *On grassy mattress I had laid me,*
> *Within my arms great Solomon,*
> *I suddenly cried out in a strange tongue*
> *Not his, not mine.*" '

I had dredged my memory for the words and then failed miserably in trying to hide my accompanying smirk of satisfaction.

'*Touché, Michael!* Yeats' Solomon and the Witch. I am not sure whether to feel complimented or insulted. I will see you in a little while.'

'Isabella, wait! I need . . . I want to talk to you. *Please.*'

'Of course you do, Michael. Sure. No problem. I will wait for you at the reception desk. Perhaps we could go for something to eat. I am hungry and I know a very good restaurant near by. Would that suit you?'

'Yes. Yes, of course. I'd like that.'

The two men were walking slowly, in the near-dark evening shade of Wellington's elms in the valley below the Alhambra. The air was warm and with most of the visitors gone the predominant sounds were those of running water and the far-off chimes of the cathedral bells. Alonzo was dressed in a baggy, linen safari-suit and walked with the aid of his carved ivory-topped cane-stick. They had been walking and talking for the best part of two hours and Alonzo was beginning to hobble a little bit more as the strain on his leg began to hurt. Finding an empty park bench he brushed away some fallen leaves and sat down. He motioned for his younger companion to take a seat beside him.

'Michael, I must rest for a bit. My leg is complaining loudly.'

Michael looked concerned. 'What happened to your leg Alonzo? Were you injured?'

'No. My doctor says it is part and parcel of my age. I disagree of course.' Alonzo smiled. 'Too much time spent chasing the beautiful women of my youth and turning abruptly on the knee when my attention was caught by yet another heavenly body passing in the other direction.'

'Would you not consider a knee replacement?'

'The pain is tolerable and somehow it brings pleasure in the memories of its origin. If I ever become truly incapacitated I will consider it. Do you believe in fate, Michael?'

'Yes and no,' he replied.

'Explain,' Alonzo persisted.

Michael looked up at the trees, the upper branches of which were waving in the evening breeze and appearing to swipe at the returning rooks. 'In my work, I sometimes feel so empowered by the clarity of the best of my ideas that I have no doubt about their successful proof. The intensity of those moments is so palpable that I often feel that I am destined to achieve greatness and, to a large extent, I have. The strong force driving that success is sometimes so powerful I'm unable to explain it. Some might call that fate.'

He paused, as if exhausted by the uncertainty.

'Go on, Michael,' Alonzo said gently.

'Unfortunately, the same clarity doesn't often extend to other areas of my life so I'm beginning to question what fate has in store for me. I'm a little confused as to what direction I want to go in.' He looked at the older man. 'I'm probably not making sense.'

Alonzo patted him on the leg and began drawing interconnecting circles on the ground with the tip of his cane. He did not look up as he spoke. 'On the contrary, Michael, it makes perfect sense. Fate is just a meeting point where, at different moments in time, all the forces that play out their tunes on the strings of our lives condense in a single note of harmonious illumination. Perhaps what you are really saying is that your life lacks that harmony?'

Michael stared down at the circles. 'Yes . . . yes, perhaps I am. I've not tried to vocalize it before. Somebody else recently questioned me along the same lines but I drew back from an explanation. I'm . . . I'm afraid of the consequences of analysing it too much.'

'What about God, Michael. Do you believe in God?'

'Yes, but He is distant. Uninvolved. Disinterest on both our parts.'

'That was Saint Augustine's fault.' Alonzo rested his cane in the centre of one of the circles and rolled it between his palms as if trying to start a fire.

'I don't understand.'

'The early Christian church had difficulty in resolving the obvious and prevalent presence of evil in the world and in order to remove the heretic notion of God being somehow responsible distanced Him from it, and subsequently from the faithful, by making mankind fully responsible for that evil.'

'I do not have too much of a problem with that concept. Evil, as far as I am concerned, *is* a human failing. The difficulty of a hidden God, unapproachable as it were, is the fear of having to confront that evil, on your own.'

'Do not be afraid, Michael. Evil is of this world and, dare I say it, necessary. Knowledge will help you overcome your fear of it.'

'How?'

Alonzo turned his head slightly to look at Michael then leant his hands on the carved handle of his stick and rested his chin on these. It was a few moments before he replied.

'Michael, I have greatly enjoyed your company and I truly believe that fate has brought us together at this time. The work that you are engaged in sounds fascinating but it strikes me that you are being isolated by its physical and intellectual demands. You are too reliant on your own capabilities and the perceived value of your work. You have a great need to be understood as a person but you also need to understand the onus that this places on other people. It appears to me that this balance is absent in your life.'

Michael lit a cigarette and watched as the older man straightened his arthritic knee. He felt suddenly vulnerable and spoke quietly. 'I do not follow, Alonzo.'

'I think you do Michael, but it does not matter. I sense that you are ready to try and find that complete harmony but you lack the knowledge of the path you must take in order to achieve it. All of us need guidance and fate has determined that I should be your guide. That is my responsibility.'

Michael brusquely stood up, shaking his head, as if suddenly threatened by the older man whom he had only known for such a brief time. He paced along the path for a few minutes before returning to face Alonzo. He began rubbing out the circles on the ground with his shoe.

'This is all very strange, Alonzo. Do not get me wrong. I do not want to appear impolite or ungrateful, but I hardly know you. Even if I am searching in some way for the harmony that you describe, why would you, a complete stranger, be offering to be my *guide*? What responsibility do you owe me? What right have you to assume that responsibility?'

'Do I seem like a stranger, Michael?' Alonzo lifted his chin off its resting place and looked up at the younger man. His gaze was unwavering, almost accusatory. Michael bristled but then just as suddenly sat down again.

'No.'

'Good. I understand your reservation, Michael. Believe me when I say that this situation is also difficult for me. I have known for a long time that I had one more unfinished task to complete, before my own destiny was fulfilled and its terminus reached. My offer of guidance is freely given and does not demand either reliance or dependence. Each of us has to find our own way to the elusive harmony that we all seek. My responsibility is to show you the doors; you must cross their thresholds.'

'What unfinished task, Alonzo?'

'Michael, may I tell you a story?'

'Of course, Alonzo.'

'It might take some time. Do you need to be somewhere else?'

'No.' Michael's answer was emphatic.

'Good.'

Alonzo's gentle face and earnest eyes reminded Michael of another old man he had known as a child. He was the father of Mary, the girl who came to their family's house to look after the children and lived in a small village about ten miles away. She had an old Vespa scooter and as the children grew up would often take them, in turns, on the spluttering machine to her home. There, her father, or Pa as children called him, would sit Michael down and tell him the most wonderful stories, while his wife fed them with currant soda-bread, layered with wild blackberry jam.

Michael had never known his own grandfathers well. To a small child they had both seemed austere, distant and in any event had died, like his father, when he was very young. Pa was all the grandfathers that he could have wished for.

Michael's memories were cast aside as Alonzo began to speak:

'This story has its beginnings about 6,000 years ago in the small valley of Diwanah Baba which is nestled in the Hindu Kush mountains of the Nuristan region of modern-day north-eastern Afghanistan.

Try to imagine that it is the time of the vernal or spring equinox. The morning air, at that altitude, still feels bitterly cold. Half way up the side of a high, southwest-facing valley wall there is a small level area of ground hidden within a grove of sturdy holly oak and pink flowered deodar. Surrounding the grove is a cordon of imperious cedar and junipers, which shuts out the morning sun as it rises over the mountain ridge behind. On the flattened piece of ground there is a carpet of yellow asphodels. On –'

'The Greek flower of death and the underworld,' Michael interrupted with a schoolboy's smile of satisfaction creasing his face.

'Yes. You are right. A credit to your education.' Alonzo touched Michael lightly on the arm before continuing:

'On the valley floor below, one can just make out where goats graze close to the tightly bunched wooden dwellings that lie near the river's edge. At intervals, along the banks of the ice-green torrent, are scattered knots of willow and mulberry and where the waters disappear into a narrow gorge its entrance is framed by a blaze of purple orchids and lilac primulas. If one could see well enough this is where the hoopoe and bee-eaters play. At the northern end of the valley the dust raised by the salt carriers announces their safe arrival through the pass.

In the grove all is quiet apart from the sound of cascading water. A little to the side of where the first of the holly oak trees are rooted, a spouting waterfall exits from a narrow crevice in the white cliffs that rise majestically to the sky behind. It sprays the ground with rainbow colours, converging again to form a small stream that skirts the grove before meandering down the valley wall to join the river below.

Despite the late spring-heat, warming the meadows below, at that elevation there is still deep snow on the ground and the footprints of ibex and snow leopard can be seen on the tongues of white snow that probe the spaces between the mighty cedar trunks. The thin air is scented with pine, wild rose, tamarisk and . . .'

Alonzo appeared to lose his own thoughts as he involuntarily looked around the small glade where they were sitting and began sniffing the air. He looked at Michael who leaned forward like an excited child, eagerly encouraging him to continue the story:

'Imagine the stillness rippled by the sounds of a small party of people edging themselves carefully around a large rock outcrop on the narrow track that leads from the valley. They are pulling a reluctant, small, stocky horse behind them, that, despite being un-laden, is having difficulty with its footing on the brittle surface of thawing shale. On occasions it stumbles and drags its handler back.

The party all look greatly relieved when they finally reach the level ground of the holly-oak grove. Panting to catch their breath they first kneel to touch the ground before moving to the stream to quench their thirst.

Once recovered one of the group leads the horse to the far end of the grove where a circle of upright stones about the height of a small child stand. The horse is tethered to a fallen tree by means of a loose bridle of coarse-wound fibre and it snorts loudly while nuzzling a hollow in the snow to chew on emerging vegetation. Its handler, a beardless youth, remains close to the stone circle where he begins to gather kindling and fallen pinecones to lay down a fire.

The remainder of the party, which consists of six men and one woman, move to the centre of the grove and position themselves to sit cross-legged on the ground, facing each other in a rough circle. Because of the bitter cold they all keep on their coarsely tailored sheepskin coats.

One of group is sitting with his back to the valley and looking up at the sky. He has a hand outstretched to reduce the glare of the midday sun and is much older than the others, with many missing teeth. He has his head covered by a bearskin cap with upturned edges and from beneath its rim long, black-grey hair lies matted and sweat-soaked against his neck. He is stroking a large, bushy beard with his other hand while his attention is suddenly focused on an adult lammergeyer gliding on the updrafts of the valley walls.

"See there!" The old man points upwards to the large bird of prey. "The bearded messenger-bird of the Sky God awaits his reward."

"It is a good omen," one of the others replies as he looks upwards at the large vulture. The older man nods before turning his attention back to the group.'

Michael smiled as he listened to Alonzo begin to characterize each of the voices. The performance was achieved with the just the slightest change of accent and flicker of the mouth and eyes. It was as effortless as it was appropriate and was the magical art of a natural storyteller. Michael remembered that Pa used do it too:

' *"Once again we have made"*,' Alonzo continued in the voice of the old man of the mountains, ' *"on this the day of equal light and dark, the difficult journey to this the sacred grove. In celebrating the festival of Hekamaad we give thanks to the gods for bringing a new season of rebirth. It is good that the omens are with us as we have much to do."*

The older man is looking intently at the weather-beaten faces of his friends. They remain silent, waiting for him to continue. Scented-cedar wood smoke from the by now roaring fire drifts across the grove.

"You and I, my friends, are the seven ka-anuman, *the guides, the guardians of all our people's wisdom. In the thousand winters we have lived in these valleys, those of the* ka-anuman *who have gone before us interceded with the gods, were the judges of disputes, interpreters of dreams, pathfinders of destinies and tellers of the story of the people.*

Each of you, your own destiny determined by being the first of twins of the same soul, was chosen at birth by the great Sky God to inherit the guide's birch-pole of the ka-anuman. *The navel cord of your brother or sister soul is wrapped around that pole and binds you to their home amongst the stars. Today is the day that another is brought amongst us. I can count my remaining teeth quickly and will not see another winter and thus I have brought my inheritor Nadaksin to the mountain. He is not yet one of the seven but I have had a vision which I must share with you and him."*

The group murmur amongst themselves and look in concert at the youngest, beardless, newcomer Nadaksin who had been busy clearing a shallow pit in the centre of the stone circle. The only woman in the group speaks first.

"Ebabu, this is not possible. You have many seasons left. What visions do you speak of? You must be eating too much of the fruit of the mushroom tree."

The older man smiles. 'Thank you, my sister, for your concerns. No, this vision came only with fasting.'

"I also am hungry to understand," one of the others adds.

Ebabu, the old man, smiles again. "In the time before the thousand winters, before we came to these mountains, our people lived in the land between the sea of the one thousand islands and the sea where they hunted the long-nosed fish of many eggs."

The listeners all shake their heads in agreement as Ebabu continues.

"In the beginning, there was Manuru, the Sky God, the god of the light, the father of all the gods. One day he saw his reflection in the warm waters of Eana, his daughter, the goddess of the waters, and desiring that men be created in his image planned to sow his seed. The coiled serpent God of Darkness heard of this plan and during the time of the first day-night, caused by the Moon God copulating with the Sun God, the serpent sowed his seed in the waters of the Goddess Eana and thus created men. The Goddess Eana, seeing that the God of Darkness had deceived her, decided to create, from pure water uncontaminated by the serpent's seed, the first seven ka-anuman, *so that they could guide all the other children of the serpent.*

It was she who told the first seven to lead the people away from their land and to follow the white path of the great Sky God, Manuru. It was she who showed the seven the river of beech that led to these mountains.

At one time, all the people spoke with the same tongue and had a common memory of our gods and there was no conflict between the peoples. That has all changed and now there are many tongues and differing memories. Each year brings new oxcarts and conflicts from the plains to the high valleys.

I have been shown in a vision *by our mother Goddess Eana, that the great people who live between the two rivers of the night house of the Sun God, Ansham and who trade with us for the sacred blue stone of these mountains will soon suffer a great flood. All will be lost, all memories.*

I have seen in my vision the Goddess Eana directing the seven ka-anuman *to depart this land and once again to lift our birch-poles and like the winter geese follow the sky-path down from the mountains. The* ka-anuman *are to take our knowledge and wisdom to plan the rebirth of the drowned nation so that they might thank our gods."*

The group are somewhat puzzled by the revelation and look at each other with questions in their hearts.

"Ebabu, our father. If we are to leave our mountains how will the people in the drowned lands know what we know? What if we forget or are lost on the journey?" It is the woman who speaks again.

The old man, Ebabu, points over to where the young man Nadaksin has lit the fire.

"Look over there," he says. All of them turn towards the pit. "When you see a fire, you see smoke and you know that wood is burning. But in your hearts you also know that a fire is warmth, is danger, is a signal, is useful in our metal work, is useful in splitting the white rocks of the blue stone and a protection from wild animals. A fire is more than a fire."

"I do not yet understand Ebabu," one of the other men says quietly.

'I will tell more of my vision. I have seen the Goddess Eana asking her father, the great Sky God Manuru, how is it in the lands of different tongues that her people's story and the story of the gods be told. The great Sky God tells the Goddess Eana that

the ka-anuman *already know the houses of his children, the stars, in their learning. He asks that we look at the houses and by carving marks on clay and stone, as we do with mountains and rivers on our water pots, then the houses will never be destroyed. Each house will have a name and will announce a story of our people. Each house will have a sound and will remember the tongue of our people. Each house will have a door to announce the wisdom of our people."*

"But there are only seven of us!"

"Remember the fire. Each house will remind us of more than just one memory. In my vision the great Sky God Manuru tells his daughter, the mother Goddess Eana, that our people the Weiminstan, are the people of the star path. We have to show other people the way of our gods by means of these marks. Then if our voices be silenced our marks will remain on the earth of the God Enanll."

"But how will we achieve this?"

"Our mother the Goddess Eana has told me in my vision, the path we must take. We must, like the geese follow the sky-path of the winter. Our people will travel for another thousand winters through the lands of Indadra to reach Daraum the island of the blessed and the land of Enlladam. In my vision it is in the land of Weikushanni where we will stop wandering."

Ebabu stops suddenly, as if exhausted by the effort of telling the story. He starts to sway from side to side and a number of the group rush forward to steady him. After a moment he is composed again.

"Ebabu, how are we to achieve this?" the group speak nearly as one.

Ebabu reaches into the shoulder bag he had carried with him and takes out seven gemstones. These have been roughly cut into the shape of short, flat cylinders the size of which would just fit in the palm of a closed hand. He places them, one at a time, in front of each member of the group with the exception of his own, which he holds up in front of him. As the sunlight catches it the stone appears to radiate an intense blue colour with occasional glints of gold.

Each of the stones has a small raised central knob through which a fine hole has been bored and which allowed the passing of a chord that it could then be tied around the neck.

"Look at the smooth side," Ebabu speaks without taking his eyes off the stone.

Each of the group lifts their respective gem and examines it carefully. Into each a figure of a seated man holding a river in one hand and a snake in the other has been precisely carved. Above the figures are the sign of the Sun God and the upturned crescent of the Moon God. Surrounding the figures are a number of carved symbols and on each stone these are different.

Ebabu continues. He is getting tired.

"Each of you must wear the stone around your neck and learn the marks of the others. Press these into the potter's clay and the story will be told. The stones will be the tongues of our people; tell the people of our great Sky God Manuru and of his children the Sun and Moon who move from one hand to another; tell the peoples of our womb-mother of the waters, the Goddess Eanu, who gave us life and of her deceiving consort, the serpent God of Darkness, with whom she created our people and who waits to bring them to their final home; tell the peoples of the great Sky God Manuru and his struggles in keeping the twin strands of our destiny apart.

We, my friends, are the voices of Manuru. We must explain to the people the reasons for the twin judgments that determine their paths. We must show that wisdom and folly, knowledge and ignorance, life and death, peace and conflict, beauty and ugliness, food and famine, good and evil is necessary and will be with us always. That is the inheritance of the ka-anuman, *that is the story of our people."*

The members of the group began comparing the marks on the stones. The woman amongst them spoke again.

"Ebabu, most pure elder, how is it we will know when we have reached the new home of our people, this Weikushanni?"

The old man once more reaches into his bag but this time withdraws a ball of still-soft potter's clay. He places it on the ground and flattens it into a disc. Leaning forward he takes back each of the gemstones from the others and begins pressing them at intervals into the clay. When he finally has placed his own he speaks quietly.

"This is the final secret. There are seven of us and we are also the children of the messenger of the sky, Araum, the God of the Time that governs us all. In his house the first seven ka-anuman of our people found their immortal home. It is from his crotch that we are reborn. In the night he is always carrying on his shoulders the twin Sky Gods, as you must in your judgments. I have placed the seven stones to show his house at the middle time of the longest night. Remember the house and when we see it again in the same position at the same time then our people's travels are over. That is my vision. That is our vision."

He pulls out the stones from the clay and after handing them back to the others turns the clay tablet so they can all see the pattern they have made. Nothing is said as each studies it carefully. Ebabu shivers. It is getting colder on the mountain.

"Come my friends. The day has nearly passed and the Sun God is restless for sleep. We will talk of this again. It is time to take the mead and then offer the sacrifice of the horse to the gods."

Later when the light is almost gone and most of the group are huddled around the fire for warmth, Ebabu draws apart to the dark end of the grove to look out over the valley. Behind him the cold night air is filled with the inebriated sounds of the goose-bone music. He is intent on the horizon and does not turn when Nadaksin joins him.

"You did well today, Nada, I am proud."

"Thank you, master."

"Do you see over there on the horizon." The old man points to the west, "that mountain of faint light reaching to the sky from the night home of the Sky God?"

The sky was almost pitch dark but Nadaksin could just see rising up from the horizon a pyramid-shape of faint light. They watch for a while until it disappears.

"That is a sign from the Sun God. When we leave these mountains we must raise ourselves up again in their shape to be closer to him. This we must tell the drowned peoples to do."

"Yes, master." '

Alonzo stopped abruptly. The story was over. He leant back in the chair and took a long draught of water from the bottle they had bought at the kiosk earlier.

'An interesting story, Alonzo.' Michael spoke with genuine warmth. 'I presume it is a traditional myth of our pre-diluvian creation and origins. Where does it come from and what by the way is the *Hekamaad*?'

Alonzo watched Michael carefully for a while, tracing and erasing a geometric design on the ground with his cane.

'The story is as it is. It has not been written down but has been transmitted as an oral tradition in a secret language from one generation to the next. The language is very precise and thus does not allow much in the way of change. The difficulty is translating it into English.'

'What's the secret language?'

Alonzo ignored the question. 'You asked me about the *Hekamaad*. This word literally means "horse-drunk". There is increasing archaeological and linguistic evidence to suggest that most of the Neolithic ancestors of the Indo-European races, the so-called Proto-Indo-Europeans, were to be found in a five-hundred-kilometre-wide band that linked the Black and Azov seas in the west to the Caspian and Aral Seas in the east. From there they spread out in all directions bringing their proto-language and traditions to dominate the original inhabitants.

To these people the horse was their most valuable possession and sacrifice as the numerous pit-grave excavations show. The word for horse in most European, Indian and Iranian languages has the proto-Indo-European *ekwos* as their root; the word *meydho* for mead is more obvious. The ritual of Hekamaad or *ekwo-meydho* is a spring festival involving both the horse and drunkenness.

The people of the secret language have a tradition that stretches back 8,000 years and which implies that their ancestors first migrated from near the Aral to the valleys of the Hindu Kush. About 6,000 years ago, because of pressure from the Aryans, they then moved down to the Indus Valley. From here they migrated by coast and sea to Elam and finally as a people established the Mittani empire.

Along the way *they* were the first to develop the rudiments of writing and astronomy and that was their power. They were the original Magi of history and brought that wisdom to the early Sumerians and Egyptians. Their language was of the group we call Indo-Elamo-Dravidian, the first language of north-west India, Pakistan and Afghanistan.'

Michael cursed silently, annoyed at his ignorance of the origins of language, and tried a different tack. 'It's a fascinating story. I would like to understand it more. What of the blue stones? It sounds like they are still a significant legacy for the people you talk of.'

Immediately Alonzo's face lit up. 'That is it. I *knew* you would realize the most important thing. I told them so.'

'Told who?' Michael asked with a puzzled expression.

Alonzo hesitated. 'The blue stone is *lapis lazuli* which in its purest form is only mined in one valley on the Daryz-ye Konkce River in north-eastern Afghanistan. For thousands of years, before even Alexander or Christ, it had been traded from there to Sumer, Harappa and Egypt. Its azure hue, the original ultramarine, decorated the idols and effigies of all the greatest civilizations. Its relative softness allowed easy carving and it was used to make seals of identification. They –'

Michael smiled as he interrupted the older man:

' "*Every discolouration of the stone,*
Every accidental crack or dent,
Seems a watercourse or an avalanche,
Or lofty slope where it still snows." '

Alonzo looked puzzled. 'What are those lines and why the mirth?'

'I'm sorry, Alonzo. They are from a poem called Lapis Lazuli by Yeats, the Irish poet. Your fable of the stone seals from the mountains and valleys of Nuristan reminded me of the lines. Somebody teased me earlier this afternoon about my ignorance of

Yeats . . .' Michael hesitated, as if he were about to expand but then decided against it. 'Forgive my rudeness, Alonzo. Please go on with your story. What of the people, the *Weiminstan,* I think you called them?'

'Well remembered, Michael! The people of the secret language have always controlled the trade of lapis lazuli and their most sacred totems were the seven seals carved of that stone and given to the *ka-unuman.* '

'Do they *still* exist?' Michael asked incredulously.

'What? The people or the seals?' Alonzo was testing him.

'Both.'

'Is it not obvious?' The older man sounded disappointed. He leant his chin on the knob of the cane-stick, the inlaid eyes of the carved-ivory dragon-head held Michael in their fixed stare. It was a few minutes before Alonzo spoke again.

'I am of the people. Despite the efforts in the past of the Aryans, Persians and Greeks, and in more recent centuries those of the British and Russians; the people have survived. Even the so-called Tailiban patriots of the Darul Uloom Haqqania madrash have failed to eradicate the true inheritance.'

'And the secret language that you spoke of?'

'Although Brahui is the remnant Dravidian language of Afghanistan, the secret language of *our* tradition is called in Kabul, Zargari, the language of the Afghan goldsmiths and traders in precious stones. It has been considered, by the few linguists who have been allowed to study the language, to be closest to the peculiar dialect of ancient Persian, known as Gurani. Deep in the past the people must have adopted the language of their commerce in lapis and spinel balases.'

'What about the seals?'

Alonso smiled. 'I would like to tell you the full story of the seals, Michael, but, in doing so, it means that you too become part of the story. It also means that you willingly accept my offer of guidance. Given your reservations earlier . . . are you prepared for that?' Alonso was studying Michael's reactions with an intensity that undermined any attempt at levity.

'Yes . . . I think I am. Yes. It feels right somehow,' Michael blurted out with false bravado.

I was pacing forward and back, like a caged animal at feeding time, across the heavily stained carpet of the hotel-room floor while waiting impatiently for my call to be answered.

'*Come on* Caroline. Answer the goddam phone. Where are you?' I barked into the receiver. Suddenly, the connection was made.

'Hello. The Mara residence.' My wife had never lost her clipped Oxford accent to the lazy drawl of the West Coast.

'*Where were you, Caroline*? This is the third time I have tried in the last two hours. I couldn't reach you yesterday either?'

'Hello to you too, Michael. I'm fine but let me put my life on hold while sitting by the phone waiting for my master to ring.'

'Very funny,' I said quietly.

Penetrating sarcasm was Caroline's deadliest weapon and I had learnt to be very wary of its unleashed power. I stopped pacing the room and sat on the edge of the bed. 'You're right Caroline. Sorry . . . but where were you?'

'I was next-door with Marcia, raking over the embers of yet another failed relationship.'

'That woman goes through men with the zeal of a meat factory renderer. No wonder it always ends in tears.'

Marcia was the, relatively young and extremely wealthy, widow of an auto parts manufacturer. His wake had been consummated by a succession of carnal interviews for the vacant position.

'She has a higher expectation of men than is reasonable or justified. Now let's talk about you, Michael.'

'Ouch.'

'You walked into it!' There was a small pause and when Caroline spoke again it was more conciliatory. 'How did the conference go?'

'Good,' I said truthfully.

'You must be in London now. What time is your flight?'

'That's what I want to talk to you about.'

'That will be a welcome change.'

'Caroline, what's up with you?'

'Michael, dear. You are about to tell me that you have decided to stay on in Spain for a few extra days and that not to expect you until next weekend.'

I looked at the clock on the bedside locker. It was nearly midnight. Its red glow pulsed in the darkened room. I lay back on the bed exasperated at the need for the games between us. 'How did you know? *Oh I see!* Rod told you, I suppose.'

'Yes.'

'He was very quick off the mark. You must be in constant communication.' My sarcasm was childish.

'At least he does communicate.'

'What do you mean by that Caroline?' There was another pause. Her breathing sounded heavy, almost tearful.

'Michael, your whole life has been dictated to by a need to identify problems and provide, brilliantly at times, solutions. Increasingly, in recent times, conversations between us have lapsed into a strict formula of identification of mutual responsibilities where reason and rationalization will provide solutions. In order to minimize conflict you have made a convenient virtue of apologizing for your shortcomings before they are even tested. That is an arrogance which I accept might work in the business but leaves me isolated.'

'But Caroline –'

'Listen, Michael. I am not a problem to be solved. I want you to ask me 'How are you feeling?, What are your needs?' and to be there for the answer. I do not expect you nor, if I really think about it, particularly want you, to come up with an instant solution so that you can relax feeling that "the Caroline problem" has been dealt with. I want only that you understand that we should explore our feelings and needs more and to be receptive to that.'

There was a background sound of muffled voices.

'And I suppose Rod does. Is he there with you now?'

'What do you mean?'

'I thought I heard voices.'

Caroline's laughter reverberated down the telephone link. It was a genuine, light-hearted and slightly amused laugh this time.

'You see, Michael, you are even getting paranoid. No. I was just telling Mrs Sanchez that you would not be home and there was no need to prepare a meal.'

Caroline and I had never had children. "Unexplained infertility" the experts had said. Both of us had balked at the suggested intrusion of in-vitro fertilization and declined its temptation. I don't think either of us ever regretted that decision. Caroline declined to consider adoption as well and for the most part not having a family had never been an issue between us.

It was at times like this however, when we argued, when we questioned each other's motivation, that the idea of our being possibly unfulfilled in our lives occasionally crossed my mind. It somehow only served to confirm her accusation of me being a solution driven partner. I knew she was right, I had let our economic security become the guardian of our dreams.

'You are right. I have let *us* slip.'

'*We,* have let us slip. ' Her voice sounded tired rather than despondent.

'Listen, Caroline. I'll change my plans again and return tomorrow. We will take the same time together instead or could . . . would you join me here?'

'No, Michael. I cannot. I'm flying down to La Paz in Baja tonight. I will be there for about three days.'

'Why? You never mentioned it.' I felt as if I had been found out somewhat as the 'you get on with your life and I'll get on with mine' scenario had not entered my calculations. My tone was defensive.

'An urgent situation has arisen and the Columbian Financial Intelligence Unit have requested a meeting with us and the Mexicans.'

Caroline was an honours graduate of the Royal College of Art and Design and had obtained a doctorate in Paris with cutting edge experimental work on the application of new metallic inks in printing. From there her career had evolved into Caroline becoming one of the world's leading experts on security features incorporated into the printing of banknotes to prevent forgery. She was currently contracted as a consultant to the United States Bureau of Engraving and Printing.

In recent years her expertise and appetite for change had taken her away from the sterile atmosphere of design, manufacturing and bank offices and into the shady and dangerous world of 'field' operational counterfeit detection and interception measures. To my mounting concern this work increasingly seemed to involve her operating in an undercover capacity. Caroline on the other hand was enraptured by her work. It appeared she had a natural aptitude for subterfuge and the US Treasury saw her as their brightest star, if only she would relinquish her stubborn hold on Her Majesty's passport.

'Who are you travelling with?' I asked.

'Randy Coors from FCEN, the Financial Crimes Enforcement Network; John Cortes from the Secret Service and some young hotshots from the State Department.'

'Are you in the field.'

'No! Not this time. I shall be cosseted in the plush environs of a posh hotel. It's planned only as a short-stay briefing session.'

'Why La Paz?'

'Who knows? Whales perhaps.'

'What?'

'Lighten up, Michael! Remember that trip we made to follow the whales along the coast of Baja. Sand, sun, sea combined with environmentally friendly and frequent sex. It was a good time if I remember properly.'

Caroline's words were accompanied by a brief wistful nasal giggle which quickly evaporated as she switched into reality tone. 'I suspect La Paz was chosen both for secrecy and convenience for all parties. I will ring you with the hotel number when I get there.'

'I could join you in La Paz, Caroline. We'll take a few days together and relive some of the memories.'

'No, Michael. There is no need. Do not change your plans again. Take the extra time in Spain to chill out on your own and think. I have to, in any event, be back for the charity tennis tournament on Thursday and we can talk when you get back.' There was more light laughter. 'You are on your own, aren't you?'

'Hold on, I'll just check.' I was glad of the opportunity that Caroline had deliberately, in her cunning way, provided to check my edginess. It was a natural, and disarming, accomplishment of her people management skills. 'Imagine that! *She* has gone and not a word of thanks. Like with all the other women in my life I obviously didn't make a huge impression.' I laughed.

'That's better, Michael . . . Did Rod tell you about the offer?'

I sat bolt upright on the bed and suddenly, feeling very nervous, very paranoid, hesitated with my reply. My head was beginning to throb. I thought I could hear a creaking noise in the background of the connection. It sounded like a door opening and a voice whispering. It was probably Mrs Sanchez going about her work.

'Yes but why . . . why was he so keen to involve you Caroline?' I was being very cautious.

'As a matter of course, Michael. You know that. Max and I control six percent of Hoxygene. He would have to discuss the offer with us.'

'But we, you and I, Caroline, had always agreed that you and your brother's shareholding would be allied to mine.'

'Yes, I know, but Max is now anxious to divest and Rod has made a convincing argument for the deal.'

'But, Caroline, I would lose the company and everything I . . . we have worked for.'

'Perhaps you might lose control, Michael, but you could gain so much more. A chance to regain the freedom we appear to have lost along the way. It really sounds like a good deal.'

'A bloody betrayal more likes. You, Max and Rod can go fuck yourselves. I'm not selling out.' My frustration and anger welled up and spilt out in an icy blast.

'Group therapy! Not a pleasant thought.' Caroline's voice was sharp again.

'Well, you and Rod so. You appear to be so much in tune with each other.' I instantly regretted the bitchiness of the comment. It brought into the open, in circumstances where I'd little control of where it would lead, secret jealousies and fears that I had suppressed about the true nature of Caroline and Rod's relationship.

'Given your current attitude, Michael the prospect is particularly tempting, although, I doubt I would satisfy his criteria.'

'What do you mean?' I was puzzled.

'I should have said this to you before now, and you are not to let on who told you, Rod is the country club queen of hearts. He's gay. '

'I don't believe you!'

'Nevertheless, it's true.'

'Jesus! How long have you known that?'

'About a year.'

'And you never told me!'

'Listen, Michael. Nearly every second man we know is gay. It's not that important an issue and in any event Rod made me promise that I wouldn't.'

'Why?'

'He thought Irish-Americans to be the most homo-phobic people on the planet. He was anxious that it would interfere with your working together.'

'Jesus! I don't believe it. He always has beautiful women hanging from his arm.'

There was the sound of a door opening and then closing on the line.

'He talks to them, he doesn't shag them.' Caroline rarely let her reserve down to curse and so the impact was even more pronounced. 'He's also very discreet.'

'Why did you tell me now?'

'Because your paranoia is obscuring your vision. This is far more important than Rod's sexuality. It's . . . It is important for us, you and me.'

'I'm not paranoid. I don't give a fuck whether Rod is queer or not, although you should have told me. I care about Hoxygene.'

'Michael.'

'Yes, Caroline.' I was dismissively cool.

'Look! This is not a done deal. Rod has not even approached the institutional shareholders yet. Max and I want you to think about the benefits for all of us, and we will discuss it when you return. Nothing more will be done in the meantime.'

'Thank you for that, Caroline. Perhaps Max and I can arrange to travel on the same flight from London. We could meet you in New York and jump off the Empire State together.'

'Yes. That's a really good idea, Michael. Very inclusive! You won't mind if I don't jump. I'd rather push.'

I let out a long sigh. 'Caroline, I'm sorry about the way I'm reacting. It's just that Hoxygene means so much.' The bedside clock alarm began to sound. I cancelled it quickly.

'I understand Michael.'

'Listen. My head is pounding and I can't think straight. I'm going to take a shower and then turn in. I'll ring you tomorrow. Give Marcia a hug for me. Ok!'

Caroline laughed again but this time it was sarcastic. 'Sure. Am I dismissed?'

'I did not mean it to sound like that, Caroline. Honestly. I am tired and this offer has upset me. I'll sleep on it and will talk to you tomorrow. Have a good trip to La Paz and ring me with the hotel number when you get there. Goodnight sweetheart.' My mind was already drifting to the problem and the solutions.

'Goodnight . . . Oh . . . *Michael. Are you still there?*'

'Yes.'

'A General Arnold telephoned about two hours ago. He was looking for you urgently and asked that you should contact him. He was very insistent and wanted your cell phone number. Who is he?'

I needed to shower badly. The oils had missed their mark. I was exhausted but not relaxed. 'He is with the army. I have being doing some work with their viral labs. I will contact him tomorrow. Thanks, Caroline.'

'Goodnight, Michael.'

'Oh, Caroline.'

'Yes.'

'About . . . about what you said earlier. I've been doing some thinking while in Mexico.'

'Good.' There was a silence as I tried to figure out what I was going to say. I really was very tired. 'And?' Caroline prompted me tetchily.

'I have met some very interesting people here and they have opened my eyes to a different view of things by challenging some of my precepts. You should come and meet them. You would like Alonzo in particular.'

'Who?'

'A guy called Alonzo Aldahrze. A book collector and an extremely fascinating man.'

'I cannot, Michael. I must go to Mexico.'

'But . . .'

'It's just not possible, Michael. I'm glad that you have found such stimulating company and you can tell me all about them when you come back. If this Alonzo character has managed to widen your perspective, even a little, then we will *both* be in his debt. I look forward to meeting him sometime.'

'I would like to talk to you about it . . . about him.'

'Michael, I have to go to the office before heading to the airport and I'm way behind. I'll ring you tomorrow and we will talk then. All right?'

'Sure . . . Sure, that's fine. I'll talk to you tomorrow.'

'Michael, promise me you will think carefully about the Alpanna offer. It's too good an opportunity to miss.'

'I promise.'

'Good night. Sleep well.'

'Good night, Caroline. Have a safe –'

The phone-line went dead and I remember staring at it for an age before wearily undressing and heading for the shower.

The telephone rang twice before it was answered. The sound seemed to echo throughout the deserted building.

'I am the servant of the powerful.'

'For you there will always be light!'

'Is this connection secure, Sahib al-Zuhur?'

'It is secure, Sahib al-Sa'igh.'

'Did you follow up on Solis's intelligence? Is the information about the effectiveness accurate?'

'It looks very promising. We will have to be very careful though. The South American *magicos* must not get wind of it. If the Israeli is willing to sell to us he may also be willing to trade with them. I do not trust his motivation completely yet it is such a great opportunity, we must not let it slip. How is the price holding up?'

'Hovering about $70 per kilo for raw material. Between the drought and the activities of those sanctimonious sons of the Pakistan brothels, prices are rising.'

'I thought they were only paying lip service to Europeans and American drug agencies.'

'Sucking on each other more like. They enjoy abusing the revenue and are only destroying hectares in areas they do not control. The Taliban has recently gone as far as defending the right of Afghans to produce the crop saying it is the responsibility of the West to control the consumption amongst their people.'

'They are playing right into our hands.'

'Yes indeed, but we need to take more control. The Nigerian vagina-packers are getting about $3,000 per kilo for getting the refined shit onto the streets in London and Paris. Our take is only a third.'

'The ketamine and ecstasy labs in Belgium are up and running and the routes to the States being established. We will soon be able to dispense with the services of the Nigerian motherfuckers and control the full trade and the profits.'

'Yes, the timing is critical. My costs are escalating and I need access to hard currency.'

'You and your people will be provided for. Have I not been generous?'

'Yes, but it is to your great advantage.'

'It is to all our advantage, al-Sa'igh. Your needs and mine are mutual and in satisfying them the great design will be fully achieved. The Israeli is coming to Corsica and once we have the samples he will be disposed of. Solis will see to that.'

'Overlord. There may be one other problem, on that particular score.'

'What is it?'

'I have had a contact from Zoë. She feels that Solis has made an error of judgment and wonders what should be done.'

'What do you mean?'

'The Pir-i-Roshan may have been compromised. Solis has introduced him to the American who the Israeli is working with. There is no telling what damage to our cause might result.'

'I trust Solis implicitly. If she has compromised the Pir she must have had her reasons.'

'Be that as it may, it is still a concern. What would you like me to do?'

'Eliminate the Pir.'

'*Eliminate!* Are you sure Sahib al-Zuhur?'

'Yes. Now is the right time, for many reasons. The symbol has to be destroyed to permit us access to the pure Idea. Get it done.'

'I will tell Zoë –'

'No! Do not involve Zoë for this task. Ask our mutual friends, the *Khannakiya*.'

'It will be done as you stipulate, Overlord al-Zuhur.'

'And, Sahib al-Sa'igh . . .'

'Yes, Overlord.'

'Bring back the glass of the desert grains.'

Rod Mallory uncoiled himself slowly from the deep white leather-clad chair.

'*He talks to them, he doesn't shag them,*' He imitated her voice with eerie accuracy as he sauntered across the room to a small refrigerator. 'Very profound, Caroline. Did you have to tell

Michael about my preferences?' Opening the door he pulled out a bottle of beer and held it up. 'Do you want one?'

Caroline shook her head. She sat on a high barstool chair, staring at the telephone she held in her hand. She didn't look up at the tall, tanned Australian as he leant on the counter-top facing her.

'I hate lying to Michael, even if he is being stupid about all this.'

'What do you mean?'

'You only came in half way through the conversation. He suspected that you might be with me and that we were plotting against him. I needed to distract him from that, so I had to tell him about your . . . your sexual preferences.'

'Well it's all true, even if put a little crudely. You weren't lying. I'm here with you and we are in a sense plotting against him. I'm worried though that he might look at me differently. '

'Why do men assume that we women have nothing better to do than worry about their sensitivities? I was talking about me, Rod, about my reservations and my concerns. Can you possibly understand that?'

'Ouch, Caroline. That hurt me.' Mallory's voice hardened. 'Though, from the conversation with Michael you strike me as being pretty good at word-hurt.'

'Asshole.'

'Not as much as I would like recently.' Rod Mallory squealed in a high-camp voice. He flashed a ponce's smile at Caroline as he prised the telephone from her hand and replaced it in the charger. She couldn't help but laugh.

'Disarming bastard.'

'The true skill of a 'fag-hag' as you post-modernist feminists would categorize me. But sadly, enough of me . . . What was Michael's reaction?'

'Obvious and immediate. He does not want to part with Hoxygene. He seems . . .' Caroline hesitated.

'He seems what?' Mallory persisted as he started peeling off the moistened label of the beer-bottle.

'He seems distracted, distant. I don't know, Rod. Lately we are not communicating. It's as if we . . .' Caroline's eyes stared into empty space as her voice trailed off.

'What, sweetheart. You know you can confide in me.'

'Thanks, Rod. It's just that we used to be able to anticipate each other's moods, what our needs were. That's not there at the moment. Michael is in his own world and I am no longer made to feel a part of it. To tell you the truth I am pissed off and frustrated by it. I am not sure what to do.'

'It happens pet. Hoxygene is at a very exciting stage in its development. It is bound to absorb much of his energy.'

'If it was just Hoxygene, I would understand or at least be a little more tolerant. No, it's him. He is defensive and distracted and somewhere else in his head.'

'Did he sound depressed? Is Spain such a bore?'

'On the contrary he is loving it there. He said he has met some interesting people in Granada and wanted me to join him there.'

'Oh, oh. I sense danger.'

Caroline nodded her head and took her time in answering. 'I know.'

'Will you go?'

'No . . . I can't. I must go to Mexico.'

'Whereabouts?'

'La –' Caroline stopped herself short. Even her friendship with the Australian did not override the need for maintaining secrecy about her work. She regretted mentioning Mexico but was glad that Rod had only joined her half way through her conversation with Michael and thus did not hear the details about the trip to La Paz. 'I'm not sure exactly.'

'Fair enough super-sleuth. *If you were to tell me then you would have to kill me*,' Mallory slurred in an uncannily good Sean Connery imitation.

'Exactly.' Caroline gave a little laugh as she tried to hide the edginess in her voice. Rod missed very little, she thought, and she would need to be more circumspect. A silence descended between them broken by the Australian slurping back the last of his beer.

He finished pulling off the label and reaching forward stuck it onto Caroline's forehead. He gave a mock salute.

'Here's to America's saviour, the Budweiser medal of honour. Bloody rice water,' He gargled. 'Give me the nectared effluent from the Swan or Torrens any day.'

Caroline peeled off the sticky paper, its glue smudging her makeup.

'I must go, Rod. I need to get ready. You, Max, Michael and I can talk next weekend.'

'Are you backing off the deal, Caroline?' Mallory stared at her. His eyes were suddenly cold and calculating. One mask replaced by another.

'No. It's a good deal but . . . I don't know if I could go against Michael's wishes. It means too much to him. If I do it will cause irreparable damage to our relationship. That is my gut feeling.'

'The faithful and dutiful wife, eh?' Mallory's tone was savagely sarcastic.

Caroline's eyes flared as she glared at him. 'Thank you for that, Rod. I hope that observation was a slip of the tongue and not a idiotic commentary on the secrets . . . my secrets, that I have been foolish enough to share with you.'

'I am sorry, Caroline. I didn't mean –'

'Fuck off, Rod.'

'Caroline. I didn't mean it as it sounded.' Mallory looked suddenly agitated and unsure. Reaching across the counter he tried to take her hands in his. Caroline pulled away and getting off the barstool walked to the door and held it open for him.

'I need some space, Rod. Please go.'

'Caroline.'

'Go. *Now!* I'll talk to you next weekend.'

Conticinium

DARKNESS – SILENCE

La Paz, Baja California, Mexico
3 September 2001

They had convened in the smaller of the two conference rooms on the second floor of the hotel and huddled in small groups beside the panoramic windows which looked out over the turquoise-blue waters of the Gulf of California, where morning squalls were whipping at the waves and driving the multi-coloured emblazoned sails of the windsurfers across their crests. The room itself had little in the way of decoration apart from a woven Mexican rug on one wall and its space was dominated by a large oval table with matching high-backed chairs, made from imported madroña burr, above which hovered a projection system, tethered by its umbilical arm to the ceiling.

As Caroline entered the room she was struck by the orange glow that the table reflected in the morning light. Nobody was wearing identification badges and there was an awkward silence between the three huddled groups that had gathered at different points of the table until a loud voice, at the end of the room, called them to order.

'*Señores e señora*, please take your seats. At the instigation of our Columbian friends the US-Mexican High-Level Contact

Group on Drug Control has asked that this working group meet. I will first make the introductions and then we can get down to work.'

Vincente Ayala was a jovial man in his late 50s from San Cristobal de las Casas in the Jovel Valley. Caroline had met him on a number of previous occasions and admired his affable yet focused way of dealing with people. He never tired of reminding her of his brief but 'beautiful' time in England playing professional soccer for Chelsea and how he loved, and was loved by, the English women. A shattered ankle had put paid to that career. Returning to Mexico, he had entered Government service and after rising up through the ranks to head the money laundering investigation unit, he had become one of the most senior figures in the new Secretariat for Public Security and Justice.

There was a shuffle of chairs as people sorted themselves out. Caroline made a beeline for the far side where she could continue to watch the unit.

'On my left is Randy Coors of the Financial Crimes Enforcement Network; John Cortes of the US Treasury's Secret Service; Jack Jago from the US State Department's Bureau of International Narcotics and Law Enforcement and last, but not least, the beautiful Caroline Mara of the Bureau of Engraving and Printing.'

Caroline gave Ayala a stern frown but he just smiled mischievously back at her, before continuing.

'At the far end of the table, beyond the beautiful Caroline, are Miguel Montana from the Columbian Financial Intelligence Unit, Fabio Calamar of the *Direccion Nacional Estupefacientes* and Escobar de Alarcon of the Columbian Prosecutor General's Office.'

There was a great deal of nodding acknowledgement and as Caroline was nearest she took the opportunity to lean forward over the table to shake their hands. Ayala watched her movements admiringly and waited for her to sit down again before giving a quick wink and hurrying to finish.

'Finally, *playing* for Mexico as it were, are Commander Diego

Rios of the Federal Preventive Police's Maritime Interdiction Force, Juan Hidalgo de Morales of the Mexican Attorney General's office and myself, of course.'

Caroline smiled at the two Mexicans. The Attorney General's man was pale and slightly precious looking. He returned her greeting with a nervous grimace.

'I hope your *players* do not give us Columbians the elbow again.' It was Miguel Montana who spoke, with a sarcastic laugh.

Rios, the federal policeman, shot out of his chair and storming around the end of the table pulled out Montana's chair and glared at him.

'What do you mean by that?' he said angrily.

Rios was about 40, Caroline thought, and in contrast to nearly everyone else in the room had the wavy, unbleached, blonde hair of a Californian surfer. Although his features were hard they had a rugged handsome appeal. She found herself looking at his hands. He had long fingers with precisely manicured nails and they hovered as if ready to throttle Montana.

'Nothing. It was just a joke. Do not take it so seriously, Commander.'

'Diego! Please retake your seat. We are all friends here.' Vincente Ayala looked flustered and watched with mounting horror as Rios swung the palm of his right hand towards Montana's face. 'Stop, Diego!' he cried out.

Rios laughed as just at the point of contact he held the blow and let his fingers lightly brush the skin of Montana's cheek. 'I am only joking, Vincente. Of course we are all friends.'

'What the hell's going on here?' Randy Coors asked out loud as he watched Rios walk back towards his seat.

'I suspect there is some bad-blood over the recent Copa Americana. Boys will be boys!' Caroline smiled sweetly as she gave Vincente a slight nod.

'I don't understand, Caroline.' It was Jago's turn to look puzzled.

'Columbia beat Mexico in the recent final of the Copa Americana. It's the biggest soccer tournament after the World

Cup. Near the end of the match one of the Mexican defenders elbowed a Columbian in the face and all hell broke loose. The referee lost control and the match ended in sour circumstances. I do not think Commander Rios appreciated the reference.' Caroline spoke as she looked at Montana and then Rios in turn. The Mexican moved first.

'I'm most impressed, Señora. You know your football.' He brushed his hand through his hair.

'I watched a great deal of it on television, Commander. It was a great tournament, full of skill and passion. I can well understand the frustrations it aroused. I gather that Mexico have finished third or second on the last three occasions.' Caroline could see Vincente Ayala nodding furiously.

'That is true but . . . it is no excuse. I apologise to Miguel for my behaviour.' Rios walked back to Montana and held out his hand. The Columbian looked relieved and shook it vigorously.

'I also, for my bad taste in jokes.' Montana smiled at Caroline. Everybody at the table had begun to relax a little when Rios, before retaking his seat, suddenly leant across the table and held out his hand for Caroline to shake.

'I am Diego Rios, Señora. I am delighted to make your acquaintance.'

Caroline obliged but was quite surprised at the cold laxity of his grip.

'Good. Now that's all settled . . .' Vincente Ayala pressed a button on the console in front of him and watched as the curtains began closing 'Perhaps we can get down to business. Jack Jago will first give us an overview and then discuss specifics.'

The room was nearly in darkness as Jago walked to a small lectern set out at an angle from the wall in the top corner of the room. Ayala pressed another button to activate the dimmer lighting and then moved his chair to offer an unimpeded view to the others of the projection screen behind him. The overhead projection unit flickered into action as Jago removed a disc from his pocket and inserted it into the lectern's slim-line laptop computer. While waiting for it to boot up he checked a small laser pointer by flashing it against the farthest wall. One of the Columbians had started smoking and the laser beam darted between his clouds. Randy Coors let out an irritated cough, to little effect as Ayala lit up his own cigarette. Caroline leant towards him and whispered in his ear.

'Don't make an issue of the smoking, Randy. You're in Mexico, remember.' She threw a look in Jago's direction. 'I haven't seen Jack lecture before. I hope he's not a squiggler with the laser pointer. I hate squigglers.'

Coors gave a small snort and even in the dimness Catherine saw both Ayala and Rios look in their direction. She flushed slightly in a schoolgirl way before leaning back in her seat to listen to Jago. The screen suddenly flashed up an image of the great seal of the United States of America and its all-seeing masonic eye.

'Good morning, everybody. My presentation will take about twenty minutes after which I will hand over to John Cortes.'

A map of the Eastern Pacific Coast stretching from Guayaquil in Ecuador to San Diego in the USA replaced the first image. There was a large red arrow originating from Columbia and ending near the tip of Baja California. A small graph descended from the upper margin to superimpose on the centre of the arrow. The laser pointer began darting about the graph in a manic dance.

'Shit. He's a squiggler,' Caroline leaned across and murmured into John Cortes ear.

'In the past two years it is estimated that the Coca crop in Columbia has increased from about 122,000 hectares to about 136,000. Averaging a yield of, just under, half a kilogram of paste per acre this represents about 54,500kg per crop harvest. With an average of seven harvests a year this amounts to a total production of 370,000kg or 370 tons from Columbia alone of which nearly 60 per cent ends up in the US. With the price of coca paste at source of about $500 per kilo and $4,000 per kilo on hand over to a US dealer it is obviously a significant part of the Columbian economy.

The good news is that we think that the hectarage has peaked. With the full implementation of all the strands of Plan Columbia, starting this summer, we are expecting to start seeing a sustained and significant reduction both in crop production and final product supply. Can everybody hear me?'

Jago scanned the room like a junior schoolteacher for any obvious dissent or distraction.

'Good,' he continued, satisfied with his authority. 'I will now turn to Mexico. Although cannabis hectarage has increased both opium and cocaine production has been markedly reduced. If we are half as successful in our Columbian efforts as the Mexican government has been in decimating their illegal crops over the last year then we will be doing great. We can –'

'Crop field-surveys have indicated that Mexican cannabis plants have become more robust with a greater flowering area, higher levels of THC . . . eh . . . tetrahydrocannabinol, and a greater resistance to herbicides.' The pale Mexican Attorney General's man interjected.

Caroline was secretly pleased that he had the gumption to interrupt Jago. She tried giving him a smile and a slight nod of encouragement.

'Thanks for that. . . eh . . . Juan.' Jago looked annoyed at the interruption. 'To continue. The first bit of bad news, particularly for our group, is, as I have already touched on, that 60 per cent of the cocaine and heroin entering the United States, is of Columbian and to a lesser extent Mexican origin. This trade is primarily routed through Mexican traffickers and, as yet, shows no signs of tailing off despite increased interception of land, air and maritime routes. In addition the Mexican traffickers in particular have begun anticipating the probable change in their main source of income and are branching out into other lucrative areas such as counterfeit. Let me hand over to John at this point.'

'Thanks, Jack.' John Cortes squeezed Caroline's arm as he stood up and whispered so only she would hear, 'What is it worth to you if I don't use the pointer?' As he hobbled slightly towards the lectern, his ankle sore from where Caroline had kicked him,

Cortes pulled out his own disc and inserted it into the drive mechanism of the laptop.

'Counterfeit production has been a relative sideline in Columbia until recently but with the availability of increasingly sophisticated copiers the Treasury have had their work cut out keeping ahead of the forgers. Caroline will address those issues in a little while but I want to deal with the current status of the Mexican situation in particular.'

A picture of two young men flashed on the screen with the word WANTED theatrically stamped in red across the lower section.

'These are the Arellano Felix brothers who are well known to our Mexican colleagues. Through a system of intimidation enforced by the so-called "juniors", they have controlled the major portion of the sea and land transport of cocaine from Mexico and Columbia into the US for about ten years.

As Jack Jago has already mentioned briefly, the Mexican Government has been very successful in attempting to break up the power of the Arellano Felix Organisation. The AFO group's activities and direct Felix family control of those activities has declined significantly. It is our information, however, that one of the 'juniors' of the family, an associate of the captured financial controller of the AFO, Jesus "Chuy" Labra Aviles, has stepped into the vacuum and is slowly establishing himself. It appears that his expertise was counterfeit currency and money laundering and he has expanded the operation here in Mexico to fund his push for total control.'

Cortes paused for a minute to allow this information to be digested. He then continued in a less optimistic tone.

'The bad news, from our point of view, is that up to now we have had no idea who this new player was. We had no obvious target. But, with help from our Columbian friends, and that is the reason for this meeting, we have been able to add a few clues to the puzzle.'

Cortes nodded across the room to the smoke-enveloped Columbians. Their faces all remained impassive as if trying to deny who was responsible for passing on the information.

'The man in question was also a close associate of the recently arrested Carlos Guzman, who served as the go-between for the Columbia-Mexico shipments to the AFO. He is rumoured to be originally from the town of Siquiros, in Sinaloa State, and is codenamed, Diablo. The counterfeit operation is thought to be centred in Mazatlan and is producing good quality forgeries of the Series 1997 $50 notes. The money laundering is conducted through the unregulated "*casas de cambio*" here in Mexico and off-shore banking facilities in Belize.'

The screen flashed and a picture of a $50 bill appeared which then split to give a close up view of Ulysses Grant and the metallic strip to the right of the portrait.

'At this point I will hand over to Caroline Mara.'

Caroline stood up and smiling at Ayala walked slowly to the lectern. She was wearing tight-fitting blue denim jeans and a white T-shirt and in the smoke-laden gloom of the room the eyes of every man followed her long-legged movements.

'Thank you, John. Gentlemen . . .' She pressed a button on the console and the screen split to also show a picture of a boat surrounded by smiling policemen. 'This bill was recovered in a maritime seizure of a "go-fast" catamaran speed boat, last November, in an exercise co-ordinated by the Maritime Interdiction Working Group and directed by Commander Rios.' Caroline thought she caught an appreciative display of pearly white teeth on the other side of the table. 'There were 3.2 metric tons of cocaine and $2,000,000 of these forged bills on board. The quality is excellent . . . Of the currency, I mean. '

Caroline could hear John Cortes burst out laughing. Others around the table followed suit and she waited for them to settle before continuing. Her face was flushed.

'The watermark, green-black colour shift and fine line concentric background printing are all top-notch. Even the UV yellow glow of the metallic strip and micro printing in the collar of Grant's shirt has been achieved.'

The slides changed as Caroline highlighted the details.

'A few major errors such as the omission of the micro printing on the flag in the metallic strip and the numeral height being 13.8 instead of 14mm makes them easy for experts to spot however the overall improvement in the quality is quite extraordinary. There is truly a craft combination of engraving and printing.' Caroline pressed a key on the laptop and the projection image shut down. 'I'm finished with the projector, Vincente. You might pull back the curtains and we can open up for questions.'

As the curtains whirred back the mid-morning sunlight flooded into the room. Caroline was blinded momentarily and struggled to suppress a sneeze. She walked to the other end of the room and opening the fridge pulled out a bottle of chilled water. She was still pouring it when the first question came.

'I am not sure why our Columbian friends are here. This counterfeiting seems to be a Mexican issue.' Diego Rios spoke through a cloud of smoke.

Vincente Ayala at the head of the table frowned and when Caroline caught his eye he threw a quick glance upwards towards the ceiling. John Cortes leant forward.

'I'll take this if I may. The cocaine that you recovered, Commander Rios, as you know, was Columbian and destined for a dealer whose contact with the Medelin cartels was through Guzman. It was also the first maritime seizure where counterfeit money was also found in great quantities and this stroke of luck has provided us with the first possible lead to the mysterious Diablo and his direct links with the Columbians.'

Rios said nothing but examined his nails in a distracted fashion.

'In addition the paper for the forgeries was Columbian although the metallic printing ink has a Mexican spectroscopic fingerprint of origin.' All eyes turned to looked at Caroline as she commented in a matter-of-fact tone while removing her disc from the laptop.

'How do you know, Señora Caroline? *We* do not have that information.' It was Fabio Calamar.

'Analysis of the paper shows a linen-cotton mix which deviates marginally but significantly from the Crane and Company Standard of US notes. I only received the paper analysis and database comparisons yesterday and it gives a 98 per cent probability match with a type that is only produced by a single mill in Bogotá. I am sure that this will be a fruitful area for joint surveillance and I will include the information in your briefing pack at the end of our meeting. I needed to clear that first with the Bureau of Engraving and Printing.'

'See. They . . . the Americans do not trust us.' It was Diego Rios who spat out the words. The pearly teeth were enveloped in a sarcastic sneer.

Caroline could feel that both Randy and John were about to pounce on him so she decided to strike first. She toppled the glass she had been drinking from and a small amount of water spilt across the table towards the blonde Mexican commander.

'Oh dear. How clumsy of me.'

'No problem. No damage done,' Vincente Ayala placated as he leant forward and mopped the water up with a flamboyantly produced pocket-handkerchief. Caroline returned the glass to an upright position. She smiled apologetically to Rios firstly and then to the Columbian officials on her left.

'With regard to the results of the paper analysis and the information on the paper mill in Bogotá it is my fault that it is not available for you at this session. I was delayed on my way to the airport and in my hurry I left the briefing documents behind in the office. I've contacted the Bureau and they are being flown down this evening on the commercial flight from LA. You will have them tomorrow. My apologies again.'

Nobody said anything but Caroline saw that Randy and John had relaxed back in their seats.

'I think that is enough for this morning. We will break for lunch and meet again at 2.00.' Ayala was already standing and as there was no objection the participants began filing out.

'Caroline, could I have a word.' Ayala looked up at her as he watched the others leave the room.

'Sure, Vincente.'

'Thank you for earlier. You saved a very difficult situation with your knowledge of soccer. Most impressive.'

'My husband Michael coaches a high-school soccer team in Los Angeles. We watched the match together. We wanted Mexico to win but don't say that out loud.'

'I won't. Thank you again.'

'I'll see you later, Vincente.' Caroline was just at the door when Diego Rios, who had obviously waited for her, approached. She saw that John Cortes and Jack Jago were also waiting and waving at them indicated for her colleagues to go on ahead without her.

'Doctor Mara.'

'Yes, Commander Rios. Please call me Caroline, by the way. We are all friends here, right? Trying to tip the scales of good and evil to the side of the just.'

'That's what I wanted to talk to you about. I apologize for my rudeness inside. It has been a difficult week.'

'I understand Commander –'

'Diego.'

'I understand, Diego. I took no offence. As you might have gathered I am English and as a nation we also have a well established, and even occasionally well founded, mistrust of our neighbours, the French. Sometimes minor domestic upheavals or misunderstandings, such as a soccer match, can become international incidents. My work in comparison to yours is almost cocooned in its safety. Direct operational confrontation with the cartels must be very stressful, for both you and you family.' Caroline watched for a reaction, but there was little. 'Anyway, a little warning shot across the bows of Uncle Sam's good old boys, every now and then, does them no harm at all. No harm at all.'

Diego laughed aloud. 'I am glad that you understand.'

'I will see you after lunch, Diego. I have a few calls to make.' Caroline giggled conspiratorially as she shook his hand and headed for the elevator, where Randy Coors waited for her

'You handled that well, Caroline. Luckily Vincente had warned us that Rios was a bit of a hothead,' he whispered as he pressed the floor button.

The blonde hair and flashing teeth are confusing me. 'What do we know about him? He's not a typical Mexican,' she said.

Randy pursed his lips and tilted his chin to one side. 'Very little as it happens. Used to work in the Office of the Special Prosecutor for Drug Crimes; or the FEADS as it's known, but was promoted and switched to the PFP when Commander Cesar Jimenez of FEADS fled after been suspected of involvement in Arellano-Felix-linked murders. He has top level security clearance though, but I'm not sure about his herpes status!'

Caroline punched him hard in the midriff. 'Rude bastard. That's not what I meant.'

Randy had to take a large intake of breath before answering. 'Ouch. That's some forehand you've got. How is Michael by the way?'

Caroline could see her reflection in the mirrored panel of the elevator. She looked downwards and pretended to shuffle her notes.

'Fine, Randy, a little confused but fine. He's in Spain at the moment but will be home at the weekend.' The elevator stopped on Caroline's floor and she stepped off it. 'See you later.'

'Ok.' Randy watched her walk down the corridor. The doors closed. 'Boy. That is one gorgeous woman,' he spoke to his own reflection as he brushed back his thinning hair with his hand and inspected his teeth.

Isabella was fashionably late and I was trying hard to avoid looking like somebody who was about to be stood up when her voice announced her arrival.

'Hello, Michael.'

I put the book that I'd been reading down and stood up to greet her. She was standing at the other side of the table and was wearing what I think was probably the skimpiest black cocktail dress I'd ever seen, obscuring the distinction between lingerie and daywear to the limits of designer perception. I often thought, when looking at the pictures of strutting catwalk models, that in order to carry the fashions off you either had to be young, brave or foolish. The dress terminated in a hemline just below an acceptable level for decorum in a public space.

It was hardly surprising then, that every male eye in the restaurant had been following her movements and continued to watch as there was an immediate territorial stand off between the maître d'hôtel and myself in our efforts to pull out Isabella's chair. I lost, and, to the smug satisfaction of the other males waited in a half crouched position for her to sit down. I'd wanted to greet her in the continental way, to feel her skin against my cheek, but instead had to settle, awkwardly, for a handshake.

My hotel concierge had recommended the restaurant, which was in a dark alleyway that led onto the Zacitín, and it was obviously popular. The room, that lunchtime, was filled with elegantly tailored and bejewelled diners who after the interruption, and in the case of female accompanied men, the prompting of their glaring partners, soon returned to their eating and loud banter.

'You look stunning, Isabella.'

'Thank you my kind *gentil homme*.' She had noticed my efforts! 'I am sorry that I had to rush away yesterday afternoon without us having had the chance to talk. Some urgent family business needed attending to. It was very good of you to arrange for another opportunity.'

'The curse of modern communication. You are always instantly available. I was very happy, however, that you were able to make it today. Is everything ok with your family?'

'Oh that. Sure. A minor crisis averted.' Isabella smiled at me before looking around the room for people that she might know. This was done expertly with only the slightest movement of the head but with eyes that scanned in a complete arc. I watched as she used the excuse of hanging her shoulder bag over the back of the chair to complete the reconnaissance of the diners sitting behind us. Turning back, to look at me again, she gave a small smile of satisfaction.

'What would you like to drink, Isabella?'

'I like the local *vin seco*, if that is acceptable to you?'

'Sure.' I called the waiter over and asked for the wine list. He soon returned and handed me a particularly thick leather-backed volume?'

'Would you like water Señor? Señorita?'

We both nodded. Isabella asked for non-sparkling and while waiting for the water I chose one of the scarce but better Granada vintages. The wine waiter nodded approvingly, more for the benefit of Isabella than me, but I appreciated the professional courtesy and smiled at him warmly. Isabella leant over and looked at the book I had been reading.

'*The Dumas Club*. I also like Perez-Reverte. Have you read any of his others?'

I picked up the book and placed it out of sight on the ground beneath my chair. 'Yes, most. I liked *The Fencing Master* and *The Flanders's Panel* equally well. Less obviously cerebral but better focused and paced than Eco.'

'True.' Isabella was studying the menu and did not look up as she spoke.

I did likewise and, having made our choices, we passed the next hour or so enjoying the food and the nut-brown wine. That brief interlude for me was the only time that I remember with Isabella where a detente of non-confrontation or truce pervaded, allowing a polite civilized probing of each other's work and lives.

It was only when the desert plates had been removed and coffee served and Isabella reached back into her bag for cigarettes that I noticed she was not wearing the blue pendant I had seen at our first encounter. A plain gold chain around her neck sank into the groove of unsupported breasts. She noticed my interest and inhaled deeply as she transfixed me with a quizzical and slightly conspiratorial smile.

'Does your wife suspect that you are having dinner tonight with a young, impressionable Spanish maiden?'

The noise and activity in the rest of room seemed to suddenly evaporate in its irrelevancy. The detente was over. I brought my hands up and linked them under my chin as a rest and looked at Isabella for a long time before answering. Her use of English had always been precise, measured.

The chasm of difference between suspicion and knowing was, to the scientist, acolyte or cheating husband, the obstacle that they had to rationalize, to overcome. For many it is a beginning, for others a termination. Isabella's question was a test, an initiation and a departure. I gave her a rueful smile and her dilating pupils and slightly arched eyebrows showed that she knew I had understood.

'I doubt that you were ever easily impressionable Isabella, but in answer to your question, no she does not either know or suspect. Would it matter?' I needed confirmation that this arrangement was mutual. It came but not in the way I had anticipated.

'Not to me, Michael, because I am here with you by choice. As you are with me, for that matter! Your wife . . . eh . . . Caroline is her name, no? She has had no choice in our arrangement. Does that mean you lead separate lives?'

'No. . .' I hesitated. 'Not really.'

'But surely not discussing your lives, away from each other, would undermine trust between you?' Isabella's question was neutral in tone, inquisitive without accusation or pre-judgment.

'Perhaps, but it would be difficult to explain my desire to explore other relationships away from the accepted conformity of a married partnership. It would arouse jealousy and conflict.'

'Only because the reasoning for your actions would give cause for jealousy and conflict.'

'I do not understand what you mean.'

'Of course you do only you do not want to face it.'

'Explain.' I flushed with irritation but Isabella blithely ignored it.

'To me, and remember I am a virtual stranger, your very obvious inclinations are to try involve yourself physically within those relationships where *you* deem that the effort is worthwhile. I suspect, from our contact so far, that you obtain a great deal of pleasure and delight in ensuring the satisfaction of others but that is a patronising approach. As such, and although perhaps intense and exciting for all involved, it carries no weight of moral conviction and is doomed in the end to failure.'

'I would see that ensuring happiness is a duty, and as such does carry a moral worth.'

'I agree. If your inclinations are followed through from duty as distinct from beneficence then they do carry a moral strength. Your actions demonstrate a continual desire to move beyond the parameters established by your primary relationship with your wife. These parameters of course are different for different couples, and some even encourage this avenue of exploration. For you apparently, this type of freedom is not an option and the betrayal of trust, as I see it, means ignoring, for your own satisfaction, the established boundaries. Your inclination for happiness is offset by an inclination to ignore other obligations. You must recognize that.'

'You . . . you are right, Isabella.' She was indeed. My voice was cracking, and I could feel my heart pounding from the danger of the insight. 'I do have the inclination to find happiness in new and unexpected shared experiences and have rationalised my desire to explore those needs.'

'Needs? You say that as if it is enough of a justification of your actions. Are you a serial philanderer so? Am I a number to be notched up?'

'No! Of course not! It's just that . . . I'm captivated by you.'

Isabella gave me a dismissive look. 'But that is purely sexual, spreading your seed as it were. If you are that desperate let's go into the toilet or if you prefer, your hotel, and have sex right now. Remove it as an objective. Every other man in this room would jump at the offer. Is that what you want, Michael?'

'No of course not! You make it sound trite, dirty even. I explained myself badly. I don't just want sex but want to explore the potential for a shared happiness. Yes, I've had other relationships but cannot remember feeling the intensity that I do right now.'

'A temporary phenomenon.' She laughed loudly as she said this.

I was defensive. '*No*. Not true. You and I were destined to meet, Isabella. That is my conviction and the justification for my actions. I really want to know and understand you.'

'I doubt that, Michael. The feminist writers would consider that reasoning a *phallusy*, I think the right term is.' Isabella blew smoke in my direction. I waited for it to clear surprised by the uncharacteristic mispronunciation.

'What do you mean by fallacy?'

My question was sharp in its tone, reflecting some of the discomfort I suddenly felt. Isabella leant forward and held my hand. The hairs on the back prickled erect in an electric response.

'I said *phallusy*, Michael, not fallacy. Faulty reasoning engendered by a penile assessment of me as an object! Do not misunderstand me. I am sure you are a very beneficent lover. Patient, attentive, adventurous and even sympathetic. I am also sure that few of your secret women friends would have faulted you on that score but it does not equate to knowing or understanding them. I suspect that you have never completely given of yourself and they instinctively would, as I have, recognize that, and be prepared for ultimate disappointment. You compartmentalize, you separate, you move on. Your inclination is to secure happiness but you are afraid of the duty involved.'

'What is it about people that makes them all want to be bloody psychoanalysts?' I was irritated.

'What do you mean, Michael?'

'Ah . . . Nothing. It is just that recently everybody, both here and in the States, has said much the same thing to me. I must be a sad case.'

'Perhaps, but not terminal. There is a cure.'

'What's that?'

'Get off the intersection, Michael. You are straddling the compartments you have conveniently contrived for yourself. Go one way and you can tell the world and your obligation to duty to 'get fucked'. You can play the games but at least be honest and admit that it is for your satisfaction and yours only.

Go the other and you will open your mind and life to experiencing, without pretence, real relationships with the world, women and even other men for that matter. The choice is stark but necessary.'

'Thank you for that advice.' I was fumbling with my napkin, sweat-battered by the frontal assault. 'And you Isabella, what do you want in a man? What do men think of you?'

She smiled sweetly and squeezed my hand before withdrawing hers. 'Do you mean sexually or as a friend?'

'Both.'

'I love men with a firm tight bottom and nice eyes,' Isabella taunted and then watched as I shifted uncomfortably in the chair.

It was at that very moment however, when I think about it now, that I first felt the waves of release washing over me. A tidal cleansing of my soul, as it were. Relieved, ecstatic almost, I began to laugh loudly, ignoring the initial amusement and then annoyance of the other diners. It was almost manic in its intensity. Composing myself slowly I crossed my eyes and stared back at Isabella across the table.

'And there was I wishing for a bigger penis.' She nodded her head and blew me a kiss. 'Thank you, Isabella.' I really meant it.

'It is my pleasure, Michael. In answer to your question, although I see it is no longer an issue, as a friend I give my trust to few people and as a sexual being I am celibate.'

'I find that hard to believe. You must be one of the most sensual women I have ever met. Why?'

'Are you asking about sex or trust?'

'Sex.'

Isabella laughed. 'I see we are getting back down to basics.' She stubbed out the cigarette and immediately lit another. 'I am celibate as a matter of choice, of discipline as it were. It is hard to explain.'

'You mean, like a priest or nun?'

'No, not really. I am not Catholic but I suppose in its original intention it is not that different. There was a famous Sufi mystic and writer called Ibn 'Arabi from Andalusia who in the twelfth century said that it can only be in woman that man may truly contemplate God.'

'The Shaykh al-Akbar. Born in Murcia I think. I read his book of poetry dedicated to the Lady Nizam during a romantic summer long ago.'

'I am impressed, Michael. It means you possibly understand.'

'In what way?'

'In remaining celibate I have purified my soul. I have reached a spiritual stability which the Sufi's call *tamkin*. In recompense there is insight, knowledge and wisdom. Ibn 'Arabi suggests that a celibate woman is the ultimate *jamal* or beauty describing the relationship of mankind with God.'

'Have you always . . . eh?'

'What? Been celibate?'

I nodded and Isabella's unfettered laughter, once more, made us the focal point of the room.

'You are persistent! No, Michael, I am not a virgin. I have had to travel through a number of degrees of ascent to achieve this state of inner peace. You were observant earlier about my sensuality and, believe me when I say this, the transition has often been difficult. Duty for me has meant sacrificing some very strong inclinations. Can you understand?'

'Yes, although it is hard to rationalize the sacrifice.'

Isabella squeezed my hands again. 'Cheer up, Michael. There is some hope. I reserve the option to review that choice at any time. I consider that the pursuit of pleasure, material or sensual, is a wilful choice and not the result of original sin or inherent evil. For me however my duty to secure happiness is served best by the opposite course. There is an additional value in the energy saved by needless games and this allows me to develop trusting relationships with my Creator, others and myself. You should consider it.'

'I thought that the Sufi's felt that in making love to a woman man reaches the state of *annihilation* and that the couple's sins were absolved.'

'Yes, but that annihilation is only in the context of absorbing the light of God. In its intention it is a stage on the path to understanding. Salvation requires that we release ourselves from the constraints of matter, lust, and belonging to reach a higher awareness. This I must do alone.'

'Have you never met the right man?'

'Person you mean. It does not automatically mean a male is necessary.'

'You are right, but then I am looking at you from a male perspective.'

'You should stop looking *at* me, Michael and look *into* me instead.'

'I would like that.'

'I wonder whether you are up to the challenge though? Are you really ready to contemplate *annihilation* as you put it?' Her eyes were probing.

'Try me.'

'Even if we never consummated our relationship?' Isabella's question was not posed with a tone of finality and it left an avenue that was generous in its possibilities.

'You were right earlier, Isabella. As a lover and friend I have serious shortcomings, if you can excuse the pun, and I would hate to disappoint you, in either category.'

'But you hardly know me, Michael. Why would what I thought matter?'

'I do not really know, Isabella but, all of a sudden, it *is* really important to me. Perhaps I have been searching for this . . . for someone like you. Who knows?'

Once again she took my hands and lifting them to her lips kissed them gently.

'What are you doing later, Michael? Would you like to meet?'

'Yes, I would . . . but . . . I'm meeting Alonzo at 8.00. Perhaps we can arrange to see each other after that.'

'Alonzo who?'

'Alonzo Aldahrze of course. Remember! You told me about him.'

'Did I?' Isabella looked strangely perturbed and hesitated for a moment. 'Of course I did. The *Baedekers*. I had forgotten. You managed to find him. That's . . . good. How is Alonzo? I have not seen him for a while.'

'Yes, he said that you had been in America.'

'Did he? Yes, I was . . . I was at a conference presenting my work.'

'Where was that? I'm sorry I missed it.'

Isabella was still holding my hands and squeezed them again. 'Thank you, Michael. You are sweet. It was in . . . Chicago and it was boring. This is much more enjoyable. Come closer.'

I complied and Isabella, keeping her eyes locked on mine, leant forward and gently kissed my lips. I could feel her tongue run quickly and lightly along their join. She pulled away before I had the chance to respond.

' What did I do to deserve that? I must remember.'

'You are a nice man, Michael. Listen! Meeting tonight might not be possible. How about tomorrow? It will have to be late as I am working. Would you come to my apartment?'

I tried controlling, unsuccessfully, my nodding head. 'Sure. What time? Where do you live?'

Isabella's voice lightened as she let my hands go and reached back to get her purse. 'I will give you my personal card. Let's meet at say . . . 11pm.' She pushed the card towards me with a long fingernail pointing to the address.

'That will be fine. I am sorry about this evening.'

I looked at the card before putting it in my wallet. This movement brought the attentive waiter to the table with the bill. I extracted my AmEx credit card and handed it to him, after signing for a more than generous tip. He returned with the card and a smile that was, for the first time during the meal, directed at both, Isabella and me, equally. She smiled back at him before turning to me.

'Michael, shall we venture out together into the light?'

The late afternoon sunshine was barely penetrating the shaded room.

'Yes, but don't let me forget the hurricane lamp.'

Isabella laughed as we stood up, and linking my arm

possessively paraded me out of the restaurant and on towards the Zacitín.

The two men stepped off the dimly lit street and passed through the heavy wooden outer doorway of Alonzo's house. Inside there was a small atrium in which a *maastaba* seat rested against the facing wall. Turning left the older man, limping a good deal more after their walk, led them down a narrow corridor that led from the atrium and terminated in a Mozarab archway. It also had a heavy wooden door but this time was more elaborately carved in Arabic script. Alonzo paused and touched one of its panels, tracing the script with his finger. He turned to Michael.

'A prayer to Allah giving thanks for the safe return of the traveller.'

The archway door led into a rectangular shaped courtyard along whose perimeter ran a vaulted open corridor. In the centre of the courtyard was a pencil-like pool with three fountains that were carved in the shape of water lilies. Fine jets spouted upwards from these only to fall again in geometrically split cascades. It was very similar in style to the beautiful Patio of the Acequia, where they had walked earlier. Alonzo flicked a switch and the pool's waters were immediately bathed in a soft yellow light. There were orange and mulberry trees and from the upper floors purple Brazilian bougainvillea cascaded to the ground.

'This way, Michael.' He opened a door and Michael followed him into what appeared to be a study.

The floor was covered with smooth ochre-coloured marble tiles and in the middle of the room set away from the wall that faced the door was an elaborate desk with fine Italian marquetry panels. Michael saw that the design effect on the uncluttered surface was that of a cosmological map of the heavens. On the legs were representations of various astrophysical instruments. To one side of the desk was a smaller table on which sat a computer and telephone console. The desk faced the inner wall, in which two windows looked out on the courtyard pool.

He noted that there was only one other item of decoration and this was a large map hanging on the wall at the far end of the room. It was set off-centre because of another arched doorway to one side. He was immediately drawn to its jumble of flags and figures and a large, gold-leaf embossed windrose that dominated one side. Moving closer he could make out it was a map of the Mediterranean and North African coastline but that the lettering of the multiple place names was all in Arabic. Instinctively, Michael put out his hand to touch the map but was immediately embarrassed as the almost imperceptible clear glass plate that protected it repulsed his fingers. He turned to Alonzo.

'This is magnificent. A portolan I guess. Fifteenth-century. Catalan?'

'Very accurate, my young friend.'

'The Arabic script is unusual though.' Michael turned his head sideways to try and read the writing on a red flag that dominated the edge of the map. Below the flag in heavy ink and almost certainly a later edition was a single word written in what seemed like Old Spanish or Portuguese. 'I have never seen one like that.'

'You will not again.'

'Where is it from?'

'It was produced in 1486 at the workshop of Jehuda ben Zara, a mapmaker in Alexandria, as a commission for one Hamid al-Zagri. It was never much used by its owner hence its condition.'

Michael pointed to the Spanish graffiti that he had noted on the map. 'What does that mean?'

'*Acanaveados*.' Alonzo pronounced the word slowly. 'Acanaveados was the name given to Christian converts to Islam who when captured fighting for the Moors of Granada were used as live targets for spear throwing contests by the forces of Fernando. I suspect that Hamid al-Zagri met his fate in this way, and thus the graffiti of the victorious scribe.'

'Who was al-Zagri?'

'The Arabic writing on the red flag reads 'There is no conqueror, save God' and it was the motto of the Nasrid dynasty Amirs who ruled Granada for three centuries until its fall. Hamid al-Zagri was the military governor of Malaga who held out against the Christian forces until the 20 August 1487. As part of his responsibilities for the main port of the kingdom he had commissioned the map, two years earlier, in order to be fully conversant with the most up to date information on the Mediterranean. Most navigation maps, of that time, were drawn in heavily censored workshops and the agents of Christian kingdoms zealously guarded the information included. Hamid al-Zagri had to have his pirated copy reproduced in the relative safety of Alexandria.

After Malaga fell, al-Zagri was captured and, it was supposed, sent into slavery. However the graffiti implies that he met his death like a Christian convert. This would have been done as a final and deliberate insult.'

'How did you come by it?'

Alonzo smiled. 'God willing, that is a story for another day. Come, I want to show you something else.' Taking a disproportionably large key, it seemed to Michael, Alonzo opened the small door beside where the map was hung and then stood aside to let Michael enter.

'Wow!' Michael found himself in a large library. Three of the walls were completely occupied by neatly arranged bookshelves to the height of the second-floor ceiling. A narrow, wooden balcony divided the walls into two levels. There was an octagonal reading lectern in the centre of the room and against the far wall a low glass display cabinet. The natural light that entered the room was muted and came through a stained-glass dome in the ceiling. On the one bare wall were two prints. He moved towards the centre of the room and circling the lectern continued to stare at the rows and rows of books. 'This is fantastic.'

'Thank you. This is my paradise on earth. Please look around. I want to organize some coffee.'

Alonzo disappeared from the room and Michael walked slowly past the rows, occasionally touching a binding or lifting a book out to inspect the title page. He felt like an intruder at times and avoided lingering too long with any one book. Most were very old but in good condition. He was looking at the wall above the display cabinet when Alonzo returned.

'Are they *original* Durer's?' Michael's face had a disbelieving look.

'Yes. They are metal engravings rather than woodcut though. Most likely copper, although there is some debate. That on the left is the *Knight, Death and Nemesis* from 1513. It is an early impression on ribbed paper with the Pitcher watermark. That on the right is *Adam and Eve* from 1504 on paper with the Bull's Head watermark. This is particularly rare as it is a very early impression with no inscription on the tablet hanging from the tree. Do you see?'

Michael nodded. He felt out of his depth. 'I wish I knew more about the artist and his work.'

Alonzo smiled in a paternal way. 'We call him a Master, but do not let that irritate you. I am an old man and have little else but time to distract me whereas you, on the other hand, carry the cares of the world on your shoulders. Come, let us go and have coffee.'

Michael turned to follow him but stopped. 'Alonzo, what are the books in the display case? Are they the most precious in your collection?'

Alonzo stopped and watched Michael for a moment. 'Yes and no. I change the display to compliment the guests I bring here.'

'Did you do that for me?'

'Yes.'

'I am flattered but also very embarrassed because I do not know what they are.'

'The book on the left is a fine copy of the *Muquaddima of Ibn Khaldun*. This was the introduction to his universal history but near the end is an account of the development of natural sciences and a lamentation that the advances were now coming from the west instead of the east. You and your science are the continuation of that trend.

The middle of the three, with writing that looks Asian in character, is a beautiful vellum manuscript of the *Haran Gawaita*, written in Syriac about 300CE, and is an account of the history of the Mandaeans and the traditions of the Magi.

The final book, on the right, is written on papyrus paper and is a copy of the *Hypostasis of the Archons* or otherwise called the *Book of Norea*. It is a Gnostic book written in Sahidic Copt and dates from about the same time.'

Michael stared at the books, trying to figure out their relevance to him. He turned to inquire only to find that Alonzo was already leaving. Despite his lame leg the older man continued at a fast pace out of the study and further along the courtyard corridor until he entered a modern-furnished sitting room.

'How do you like your coffee, Michael? It is Arabica.'

'No milk and one sugar, please.' Michael watched as the older man poured the coffee. Adding a sugar cube he stirred the dark brew quietly. 'Alonzo, what–'

'Have you had the chance to meet with Isabella again, Michael?' The older man sat down on a seat opposite his guest and balancing his cup on the armrest began to fill a pipe from a pouch that lay on the table. He smiled at Michael whose face had reddened a little. 'Smoke if you wish.'

'Thank you. Yes, I have met Isabella again, today in fact. I had a late lunch with her before coming to meet you.'

'A very attractive woman, Isabella.' Alonzo's facial expression was inquisitive. 'It must have been difficult to pull yourself away from her company.'

Michael squirmed a little in his seat. 'Very! Intelligent and sharp witted. I find her company . . . stimulating.'

'Better than that of an old man, no doubt.'

'It is a different type of stimulation, Alonzo . . .' Michael paused, unsure of how to proceed. 'It is as if she and I are playing a game of chess. Each makes a move and the other counteracts. Perceptions on my part are challenged by anticipation on hers; insight is clouded by confusion, partial knowledge by complete ignorance. Whatever chemistry brought us together she controls the formula. I am intrigued and daunted by her. Can you understand?'

'In Isabella's case, yes. Is the relationship sexual?'

Michael let out a nervous laugh. 'Steady on, Alonzo. I

suddenly feel that a prospective father-in-law is interrogating me. You're not, are you?'

The older man laughed as well. 'No. I am sorry to pry Michael, but it is important.'

'Why? I am afraid you have me at a loss.'

'To explain I need to tell you more of the story of the people and the seals. Can you be patient?'

'Sure.' Michael lit a cigarette and as his exhaled smoke mingled with Alonzo's he settled back into the comfort of the chair. Alonzo refilled their coffee cups while Michael looked around the room. There was a domed skylight in its ceiling as well, although a little smaller than the one he had noted earlier in the library. By now the study was quite dark and he could see stars appearing in the night-sky above. They appeared to shimmer in the blue-tinted glass.

'You asked yesterday, Michael, if the seals still existed.' He spoke in a quiet voice, as he watched the younger man stare up through the skylight. ' They do!'

Michael stopped looking upwards and concentrated on what Alonzo was saying. He tried to keep the look of amazement of his face. 'Are you *serious*? That's fantastic. Where are they kept?'

'The seals have had different collective names over the millennia. Some generations have called them the seven *Khnumu* or architects, others the *Hydria*, but in the language of our people they are best known as the Seven *Voices*.'

'Has that something to do with what you were explaining to me yesterday, Alonzo, about the development of language? Are they called *Voices* because they and their hieroglyphs are a key to understanding the origins of the Proto-Indo-European language you talked about?' Michael was very keen to show that he had being paying attention.

'No, not quite.' Alonzo leaned forward to rest his elbows on his knees. Ash and loose tobacco fell, ignored, to the floor from the tilting pipe. 'What *do* you understand by language and its development, Michael?'

'Necessity, words and their meanings, stories, parables, communication, understanding, commerce, history, ideas.'

'Not ideas, Michael, not ideas!'

'What do you mean?'

'Most academics have given up the quest for a universal proto-language, accepting that onomatopoeic imitation of the noises of nature and the accidental sounds of human contact, rather than divine imprinting, were responsible for the development of language. Sounds were joined, as metaphors, and understood. The differences in the development of the identified major language groups probably related more to the anatomical structure of the larynx and the resonance of their stage of development at that particular locality.

Ideas on the other hand are different. They, perhaps, *are* the divinely imprinted wanderings of the conscious and sub-conscious, the pathways to gnosis. Ideas, like time, fill the void and only materialize when briefly constrained by the metaphors of language.'

'I do not understand the link to the *Voices*, Alonzo.'

'The hieroglyphs or symbols carved into the face of the seals, Michael, are not the keys to an ancient language. They are the marks of the covenant, the pictograms of the ideas of our race and the bargain with the Creator. Can you understand?'

'Ideas and time captured in the matter of stone seals and their never-ending journeys.'

'Exactly! If, at any point in that time mankind loses its way, degenerates as it were, then with reasoning as a starting point and the ideas acting as an intermediary, the way can be regained, regenerated.'

Michael nodded vigorously. 'I understand. It's a beautiful inheritance.'

Alonzo smiled weakly. 'Yes, but it also brings trouble. The collective acquisition of the *Voices* however, from earliest antiquity, has always been a magnet for men and sometimes women acquainted with their history, or suspicious of their power. There is an ancient tradition within the lore of our people which suggests that when the seven are gathered together once again, time will stand still and that the ideas, the gestures of our existence, will lose their ability to regenerate forever. *Eschatos!*

With the loss of the *Voices*, the Lords of the Void, the truth can never be attained and all the powers of heaven and earth will reside in the gatherer.'

'Has that ever happened?'

'No, but it might be a reality soon.'

'How come. Where are they?'

'Patience, Michael. Let me tell you their stories first, or at least as much as I know, and then I will answer your questions.'

At that moment both men could hear the telephone ringing. It came from the direction of Alonzo's study. Alonzo himself looked irritated as he stood up looking at his watch.

'Excuse me for a moment, Michael. It is unusual for someone to telephone me at this time. It must be important. I will not be long.'

It was about ten minutes later when the older man returned. He looked very tired all of a sudden.

Michael got up from his chair. 'Is everything all right, Alonzo?'

'Michael, I must apologize. I have to go out. Perhaps we can meet again tomorrow. Would you care to join me for supper?'

'That will be fine, Alonzo. About 5.00.'

Alonzo was distracted and appeared not to hear. Michael looked at him waiting for an answer.

'Oh yes. 5.00 would be fine, Michael. Let me show you out.'

The dial tone indicated a free line and as I waited for my call to be answered there was a gentle knock on the bedroom door. I had a quick look through the security fish-eye before disengaging the lock and opening the door to the night porter. He was carrying the club sandwich and tea I had ordered on my way through the lobby earlier.

'Your sandwich, Señor.'

'Thank you.' Pedro was a pleasant, overweight man who had helped me out in recommending the restaurant that I had met Isabella in earlier. 'Please put it down –'

'Hello,' a voice interrupted. 'US Army Advanced Biological Research Center, Manassas. General Arnold's office.' The voice was polite with a soft southern accent.

I was having difficulty in holding the phone against my ear as I signed the chit. Searching for a tip I pushed a bundle of coins from my pocket into his hand before directing him to the door. His face showed a distinct lack of amusement at their meagre weight and I tried giving him an apologetic smile, pointing to the phone with one hand, while placing my thumb over the microphone portal. 'I will catch up with you later, Pedro,' I whispered as I shut the door behind him.

'*Hello!* General Arnold's office.' The receptionist on the other end of the connection was not amused with the delay.

'I'm sorry. I was just closing a door to get some privacy. General Arnold, please.' I resisted the urge to immediately bite into the sandwich.

'Who is that calling?'

'Doctor Michael Mara.'

'Oh yes, Doctor Mara. General Arnold is in a conference right now but instructed me to disturb him if you called. Will you hold for a few moments?'

The line switched to a recording of the Bourrée from Handel's Firework music. It was only when it had just begun its third repeat that the southern voice broke in again.

'Sorry for the delay, Doctor Mara. Ah am putting you through to the General, raaght now.'

The connection was seamless. 'Bob Arnold here. Is that you, Michael?'

'Yes, Bob.'

'I'm sorry about the delay but had to transfer your call to a secure line in my office. I've been trying to track you down since yesterday.'

'I know. Caroline told me.'

'Then, why didn't you contact me?'

'Many reasons, but most of them are none of your business,' I said in a good-humoured voice. 'I'm on holiday as of yesterday and I wanted to enjoy the first day at least. It always spells trouble when you start looking for me, Bob.'

'Where are you, Michael?'

'Spain.' I was not prepared to be more specific than that.

'That's good. We can speak safely.' He sounded very serious.

'What do you mean, Bob?'

'Our SatIntel and intercept monitoring is at 'A status' in Spain. Any attempt or suspicion of interference will automatically lock-out your call.'

The military loved their games. 'Is all this cloak and dagger necessary, Bob?'

'Yes, Michael, it is. There is a 'Priority 1' level only, clearance on this conversation. It will be taped.'

'Say what?'

'The Director of the CIA, Marshall, the Secretary of State, Freeborn, and Burns of the Advanced Research Projects Agency will be made aware of all that is said between us, but it is off limits to everyone else. Is that understood, Michael?'

I looked at my sandwich regretting I'd not eaten it before making the call. I poured some tea. 'Sure. It must be important. Go on, Bob.'

'The parallel piggyback vector-study trial results have started coming in from Beltsville and our Israeli friends in Bet Dagon, a bit earlier than expected. They . . .' Arnold paused, as if hesitating before giving some bad news.

'And?' I asked, wary. The results had not been due for another month. There was another prolonged silence. Oh Jesus, I thought, just get it over with.

'They have exceeded all expectations,' he said in a deadpan monotone.

'Bastard! You had me worried there.'

'Couldn't resist it, Mikey boy. Great news . . . yeah?'

'Give me some specifics, Bob.'

'As you predicted in the gene sequence design, enzyme activity has been reduced to about one percentage of normal. Almost undetectable! The Anx-P works a dream.'

'That's encouraging, Bob.' I tried to suppress my own excitement.

'*Encouraging!* It's more than fucking encouraging, Michael. We have the bastards licked, boy.'

I had worked, before starting up Hoxygene, on a project to isolate and identify the gene sequence for the enzyme that controlled the cocaine production in the leaves of *Erythroxylum coca*. Funding for the experiments had been provided by a Federal grant from the Advanced Research Projects Agency. The patent for the isolated sequence had been secretly filed and approved in 1994, but field trials of a follow-up technique, using the sequence information to design an inhibiting probe to suppress the action of the enzyme, had only begun in 1998. We had called the blocker sequence that we developed 'an anti-expression probe' or 'Anx-P'.

'Not really, Bob. We still have the problem of being able to deliver the Anx-P to the plant with predictive effect and accuracy.'

'It's no longer an issue, Michael. You're not listening to me.'

'What do you mean?'

'Don't you understand? Your solution has worked a dream. Nobel prize stuff!'

I reminded myself that Bob Arnold was an army general and, at times, given to hyperbole to justify his expenditure. My solution was elegant but hardly the stuff of a Nobel prize. In order to be able to deliver a new gene sequence carrying the blocking instruction to the cocaine producing plants it would either, have to be done at the time of the plant's fertilization in a lab, or alternatively by using the vector of a natural plant virus to carry the sequence along with it, when it infected the plant. I'd concentrated on the second solution.

The US Department of Agriculture had isolated a leaf-mosaic virus that affected the *Erythroxylum coca* plant in 1989. The initial hopes for the virus by the Department were dampened however by early studies which showed that it had a very low virulence and penetration and thus in the wild caused little damage to the cocaine-producing leaves.

By this time I had established Hoxygene and the Department of Agriculture approached me to see if there was some way of enhancing the virus activity. With the help of an Israeli colleague, Moshe Hertzog, I found a way of splicing into the leaf-mosaic virus, with the help of a short unique insertion code, a gene sequence from another plant species pathogen, the *Tobamovirus*.

This gene sequence from the *Tobamovirus* had a very specific function. It directed the production of, what plant virologists called a "movement-protein". These movement-proteins allow viruses like *Tobamovirus* to accelerate their own rapid transfer between cells and thus increase their infectivity.

By incorporating the *Tobamovirus* gene sequence into the cocoa leaf-mosaic virus, it then gained an ability to direct a movement protein and we were able to increase the penetration of the mosaic virus by about 300 per cent.

The necessary luck, that sometimes accompanies hard scientific work and which occasionally allows unexpected discoveries, was with us. We found that the addition of the *Tobamovirus* movement-protein sequence into the middle of the leaf-mosaic virus structure had also altered one of its terminal sequences. This unexpected alteration provided us with the opportunity to then chemically attach, or piggyback, the Anx-P onto this sequence.

This new "modified" coca leaf-mosaic virus had therefore, a movement-protein, borrowed from the *Tobamovirus*, to increase its penetration and the attached Anx-P blocking-enzyme sequence, which would then activate to inhibit cocaine enzyme activity without any obvious reduction in the enhanced infectivity of the new virus.

The Anx-P sequence itself was one of the first patents granted to Hoxygene and to a large extent the future of the company depended on its successful application. The field trials that Bob Arnold referred to were the first completed studies on the infectivity and cocaine-inhibiting effect of the altered virus.

'Go on, Bob.'

'If anything, infectivity is further enhanced. All plants

analysed, so far, show a 100 per cent penetration and expression of the virus. In addition both *E.coca* and *E.novogranatense* are equally affected.'

'And?'

'That's the beauty of it, Mikey. The plant structure is not altered. The leaf-mosaic virus appears to modify its previous characteristics to concentrate fully on the role of piggyback delivery. In addition, in the second and third generation studies that have just come through, the altered plants, although no longer producing cocaine, appear to have a preferential growth over native uninfected stock. We could not have hoped for a better result. We have codenamed it MSV – *Mara's Stealth Virus*.'

'That's excellent new – *ssslurrp*'

'What did you say, Michael?'

'Sorry, Bob, I was just taking a bite of a sandwich. It just arrived as I phoned you and I'm ravenous.' I wiped the dripping mayonnaise from my mouth and waited for the bolus of food to swallow. 'I said that is excellent news. We should however wait for at least ten generations to analyse any down sides.'

'*That's* the first problem, Michael. We may not be able to wait that long.'

'What do you mean, Bob? We agreed on this in the protocols.'

'I know, but the President, with the advice of the State Department and their scientific advisors, has authorized full scale MSV production with the intention of beginning high altitude airborne dispersion in the Putamyo-Caqueta region of southern Columbia next January. Peru and Bolivia will follow soon after.'

'But that is preposterous, Bob! It is far too soon. We must fully evaluate any other human and environmental impacts. Remember the problems you are encountering and have encountered with both the glycophosphate herbicides and the EN-4 fungus. Without full evaluation you will also contravene the 1975 Convention on Biological Weapons. Neither I, nor Hoxygene will be associated with that plan. Please set up a meeting with the President and his advisors for me. I will be back on Sunday.'

'It's too late, buddy. The President signed an executive order yesterday.'

'I'll withhold the virus patent.'

'It's too late for that as well, Michael.'

'What do you mean, Bob?'

'In the interests of National Security a second executive order rescinded your patent and transferred it to the army.'

'I do not believe you. That's illegal.'

'The United States has one of the most powerful dictatorships in existence. An executive order in the interests of National Security supersedes many legal rights. By way of compensation you are to be paid $11,000,000, raised by the CIA venture capital firm, In-Q-Tel.'

'That's bloody piracy, Bob! It's worth twenty times that to the company, but at this juncture the money is not the issue. I have got to be fully sure of the altered virus's impact. We must act responsibly.'

'Give the money to me if you like, Michael, I know the price of my soul. In any event, we are being responsible and for a very good reason.'

'Who's in charge, Bob?'

'Jack Mitchell, Assistant Secretary of State; with responsibility for the Bureau of International Narcotics and Law Enforcement. A good man. Used to be an ambassador in Peru. He reports directly to Sec State and the President. West Hemi is out of the inner loop.'

'Why?'

'You did not hear me say this. He's weird.'

'I've never met him.'

'Oh Jesus! He gave a press briefing in March and lectured the hacks on herbicide use in the alpha quadrant of our planetary system and on how the US of A wakes up every morning wanting to save the world. We were all diving for cover.'

'This is definitely a new administration, Bob. Alienate the Europeans with CO and the Chinese and Russians with treaty-busting reactivation of "Star Wars" missile testing. In fact, alienate everybody by dispensing with all international treaties!' I tried taunting him but he ignored it.

'The present administration are however, to their credit, going all out on implementing "Plan Columbia" of the Clinton administration. In addition to the $750,000,000 the Columbian army counter-narcotic battalions for helicopters and other equipment the President has even directed that the ARPS-funded "High Altitude Endurance Unmanned Aerial Vehicle Program" be moved to the Patrick Air Force Base in Melbourne, Florida and seconded to the new INL task force under Mitchell. A total budget of one billion dollars has been approved. MSV has entered the secret stratospheric world of emergency supplemental budgets.'

'Jesus!' I tapped out a cigarette from the packet lying on the bedside table and lit it with a shaking hand. I needed time to think.

'Michael, are you still there?'

'Yes, Bob.'

'There is one other problem.'

'Only one, Bob?'

'I'm being very serious here, Michael. In fact, I'm being deadly serious! We suspect that the news about MSV has already leaked out.'

'*To who*?' I almost shouted.

'INL suspect that a secret organization with links to the Asian opium trade have got wind of the experiments and want to take it into their control.'

'Who? Is it the warlord, Khun Sa? *How* did he get that type of information so quickly?' The smoke from my cigarette was filling the room.

'The INL boys do not think the Burmese are involved. The intelligence was obtained from a source in Afghanistan, but it points to a European-based organisation. There may have been a leak about the field trials at the Israeli end and the information passed to an intermediary.'

'Who?'

'We think that somebody working for the pharmaceutical firm, Alpanna BioPharm, paid for the information and passed it on to the Afghans. An investigation is underway as we speak.'

'*Alpanna*. Charles Alexander. The bastard! I should have guessed his company might be involved.' I could feel sweat forming droplets on my forehead. I needed to be careful about what I divulged to Bob.

'Do you know him, Michael?'

'Alpanna BioPharm has just made a hostile bid for Hoxygene. This is industrial espionage. If the news breaks about the virus, it will not only make us a target for every pissed-off cocaine producer but also when it is known that the American government has appropriated it, the company's shareholders will want to bale out. No virus, no profits.'

'Listen, Michael. We're not sure if Alexander is involved in getting the information or what his relationship, if any, with the opium boys might be. The CIA has placed him under surveillance as of yesterday.'

'This is very disturbing, Bob.'

There was a long pause at the other end of the line. I could hear another phone ringing and being answered in the background.

'Michael, be very careful. Ring me tomorrow.' Bob was rushing his words.

Suddenly another voice came on the line. It was curt, electronic in character. 'This connection is terminated.'

The line went dead.

The satellite videophone connection took some time to establish and even then the picture was of very poor quality.

'*Ali baik salaam*' A man wearing a balaclava spoke from through the haze.

'*Akzabti*.'

'Who wishes to use our shade?'

'I have been instructed by the Overlord to ask a favour of the Khannakiya.'

'And that is?'

'For the Pir-i-Roshan to find the truth.'

'But he is the *Sahib al-zaman*, the Lord of Time. Is this truly necessary?'

'There is a passage, my friend from the Persian poet Sa'di's Gulistan which says that 'a lie, which does a good work, is better than truth, which breeds confusion'. Just accept that it is deemed necessary by the Overlord.'

'*So be it!*'

'One other thing.'

'Yes.'

'Recover the hourglass of his guardianship.'

'It will be done.'

The late-evening sunset sky was a spectacular display of orange and crimson colours as the two perspiring players finally walked off the tennis court and made their way to the poolside bar. Both of their faces, streaked with the clay-soiled sweat of the game, showed the strain of intense exercise. Little was said between them as they quickly ordered and swallowed a glass each of iced lemonade while standing at the bar.

'Would you like to sit down out here for a while to cool off, Caroline?'

'Sure.'

'What would you like to drink?'

'A gin and tonic please, Diego. Lime not lemon.'

While he ordered their drinks Caroline moved to a table that overlooked the seafront. Directly ahead of her at the water's edge, two small children, finally free from the day's heat, danced with excited shouts in and out of the small waves that lapped against the sand. Their mother, heavily pregnant, watched over them anxiously, and called out whenever they waded out too far. Further along the beach a few barefoot couples were taking a day's-end walk on the warm golden sands of the shore. As Diego returned with their drinks she watched one couple turn towards each other and kiss tenderly.

'I needed that lemonade . . .' Caroline spoke softly as she accepted the drink and sat down at the table. 'It's still very hot.'

'When Vincente told me that you played tennis, he didn't say how good you were.' Diego was wiping the sweat off his forehead with a towel.

'You're no mean hand yourself, Diego.'

'I thought so but it's a long time since I have had such a hard match. I do not like to be beaten.'

'By a woman you mean?'

'By anybody!' He laughed.

'Where is gallantry gone?' Caroline looked directly at him. The blonde hair was matted down against his temples. He looked a good deal older after the exertion.

'Its funny you should say that, Caroline, as I had fully intended to let you win. As part of a well-executed charm offensive I was going to play hard but not too hard. However, it was soon apparent that I was in a more than equal contest and my 'macho' survival instincts took over. All that preparatory effort in brushing my hair and teeth swept aside by that forehand of yours.'

'I like a man who is not a complete hostage to his vanity.' Caroline laughed as she called the waiter; her first gin and tonic had quickly followed the way of the lemonade. She turned back to look at Diego, an inquisitive smile on her face. 'Is the charm offensive over, then?'

'Does it offend you?' He was a little taken aback by her directness.

'What woman or person, for that matter, could be offended by charm?'

'If it was, perhaps, seen as false, a tactic as it were, to take advantage of a beautiful woman on her own in a foreign country.' He flashed a tooth-filled smile.

'Thank you for the compliment, but you should give women more credit than that, Diego. Most of us can see through men, charming or otherwise, before they even get a so-called offensive off the ground. If a woman allows herself to be taken advantage of, as you put it, then it is a matter of choice not inevitability.'

'That is not my experience, at least not here in Mexico at any rate. Women here *are* taken advantage of.'

Caroline's attention was diverted for a moment by the young couple she had seen kissing on the beach passing by close to their table. She smiled up at the girl who grinned back at her. She continued to watch as the couple walked towards the hotel, their hips pulled close together by fondling hands deep in each other's back pockets. Diego moved his chair in an agitated fashion.

'I'm sorry, Diego. I was distracted by young love. I heard what you said but . . . whose fault is that? There is a difference between victims and equals. In choosing victims as a target for your charms you become an oppressor not a liberator of passion,' she said as she wiped her forehead with the back of her hand.

Diego Rios stood up suddenly and went back to the bar where he filled his towel with ice-cubes. Returning to the table he offered it to Caroline who removed one, to press against her neck. He watched as the melted water flowed in a steady stream downwards into the cleavage of her breasts. He smiled contentedly as he noticed that her nipples, still partially engorged from the exercise, become fully erect beneath her thin cotton shirt, in response to the ice-cold water.

'Are you a woman of passion, Caroline?' He wrapped the ice-filled towel around his neck as he spoke.

'Yes, I can be. Depends on the stimulus though.'

'What? The man you are with?'

Caroline laughed as she wiped off the last drops of ice water from her neck and upper chest with her towel.

'Why confine it to the sometimes limited stimulus of a man? My passions can be ignited by friendship, loyalty, disloyalty, work, a miscarriage of justice, even the desire to win a tennis match.' It was all very true, she thought.

'So I noticed. Are you married, Caroline?'

'Why do you ask?'

'I was just wondering how any one man could sustain the energy to quench all those fires of your passions.'

'I'm married, yes. Are you?' Caroline suddenly felt a little defensive.

Yesterday's conversation with Michael had left her with an uneasy feeling in the pit of her stomach. Sure, she had expected his reaction to the Alpanna offer but there was something else, something that she couldn't quite put her finger on. Something was changing between them. Not in her, she thought, but in Michael. She knew that her own changing had begun some time previously, around the same time that she took up the offer for undercover work with the Bureau. Perhaps Michael was just catching up and given time they could sort it out.

Looking at Rios, as he sipped his chilled martini, she did not think there had been any undue malice or condemnation in his observation but she was not yet prepared to open up to him, a stranger.

'No.' He looked at his watch. 'Well not for . . . let's see, the last fourteen days.'

'What happened?'

'Her lawyer, who incidentally was English-trained, summed it up as disinterest, disloyalty, distrust, disillusion, dismay, disgust, disdain and divorce. In that sequence.'

'Was it true?'

'Yes and no. I am no saint but . . . You know how these things are? Half-truths and half-lies. At the end it is a trade off.'

'And how do you feel about it now, Diego? The divorce?'

Caroline thought that there was a genuine sense of hurt in his voice and she found herself responding to its hint of injustice. She was not sure however whether this was because he had lost his wife or that he had lost the battle. His forehead became a map of lines as he pushed up his eyebrows with the tips of his fingers.

'I could add two more words. Disaster and disembowelment! I have been cut off from my children. Do you have children, Caroline?'

'No. What ages are yours?'

'My son, Tomas, is nine and little Maria is four.'

Caroline saw that his eyes reddened a little as he quickly brought his towel up to wipe his forehead again. She waited for him to finish.

'It must be very difficult when children are involved?'

'You are very lucky, Caroline. The desire to protect them impairs rational judgements.' Diego put his hand up and clicked his fingers to get the waiter's attention. 'Would you like another drink?'

'I don't think so. I'm already feeling a little woozy.'

'Woozy! What is that?'

'Mildly drunk. Not fully in control of myself.'

'Hey! So what! This is Mexico. You can sleep it off later. I've never had such a good-looking, or understanding, padre confessor before and I don't want you to go.' He laughed out loud.

Caroline blushed. 'Well! When you put it so charmingly, how could I refuse? One more drink and then, I must go. I have to telephone my husband and prepare my notes for tomorrow.'

'Where is your husband?'

'In Spain. At a conference.'

'What's his name?'

'Michael.'

The drinks arrived and Diego signed the chit while the waiter cleared the used glasses. Caroline offered to pay but he would have none of it.

'That's a strange coincidence.'

'What's strange, Diego?'

'My wife's . . . my ex-wife's name is Michaela.'

Neither of them said anything as they turned to watch the sun finally set below the horizon of western hills. The sky became dark quite quickly, the twilight a very brief interlude to the coming night. Caroline shivered slightly and he, noticing that her skin prickled, stood up and placed the jacket of his tennis tracksuit around her shoulders. His hands lingered on her shoulders a little longer than Caroline thought absolutely necessary but she did not object. The fingers were no longer cold or lax in the pressure they exerted. She turned her head slightly to look up at him.

'Diego, I really must go. It's getting cold and I need a shower.'

'Sure, me too. That red clay gets everywhere!' He lifted his hands off her shoulders and walked back to his side of the table. Lifting the martini glass he swallowed the contents in one quick movement before looking directly at her and speaking in a soft voice. 'Caroline?'

'Yes.'

'Would you have dinner with me tonight?'

She stood up, and a little unsteadily picked up her racquet from the ground. She handed him back his tracksuit top.

'I don't know. Some of the others are heading into La Paz to eat. They want me to go and have a night on the town with them. I said I would think about it but I'm not sure that I want to. I think I might just have a sandwich in my room.'

'Listen, Caroline. Have your shower and get some rest. I will ring you at . . . say 9.00. If you are still here and you feel hungry, have dinner with me. If not, I will see you tomorrow afternoon.'

She looked at him. 'I won't be here tomorrow afternoon Diego. I have to be back in LA by then. I am doing the morning session and catching a flight at midday.'

'So soon. That's a great shame. I am unable to come to the morning session and therefore it is even more of a reason why we should have dinner tonight. Think about it, Caroline. Please!'

'I will, but no promises. Thanks for the tennis game. I really enjoyed it.'

'My pleasure. Until 9.00 then.'

She walked into the hotel, already regretting the three quick drinks taken on an empty stomach and it was only when she was handing her racquet back to the receptionist that she realized she had left her room-key on the table by the bar. Returning to the poolside she saw that Diego was still sitting there. His back was to her and he was talking animatedly into a cell-phone. She touched him gently on the shoulder as she reached the table.

He twisted sharply to glare at her while she leant forward to retrieve the key. He looked very angry at the unexpected intrusion, not unlike the earlier incident at the meeting when he had flared up at Miguel Montana. His eyes flashed coldly for a moment, until he realized who it was and hastily softened.

Caroline suddenly felt like an intruder and annoyed by his reaction, held up the key and dangled it in front of him.

'Did another bloody football match go against you then, Commander? I just happened to forget my key. I'm so sorry to have disturbed you,' she said sarcastically before turning on her heel and walking away from the table.

Diego Rios abruptly terminated his conversation and closed the flap of the cell phone. He got up and rushed to get around in front of her. With waving arms, he tried forcing an exaggerated and apologetic smile as he shuffled backwards ahead of her.

'I am so very sorry, Caroline. Please forgive me. You caught me off guard.' He pointed to the phone. 'Idiot subordinates. Incompetent fools, all of them. I cannot be gone for one day and they botch things up.'

'It's not enough of a justification to take your anger out on me,' she said sharply.

'I know. I am so sorry. Please stop for a moment and let me try and make it up to you.' He was pleading.

'Be quick.' She stopped.

'A problem has arisen and my second in command now needs me to sort it out. It was his incompetence that was the cause of the problem in the first place and I'm so sorry that my hot-tempered reaction has ruined a wonderful afternoon and the friendship between us.' He brought his hands together as if in prayer, moving them up and down to emphasise his atonement.

'Do you have to go somewhere?' she asked. Her own irritation had eased.

'*No*,' he almost shouted while opening his hands to press hers between them. 'Well, not until tomorrow at any rate, thankfully. I would not pass up on the possibility of having dinner with you Caroline, even if the US suddenly invaded Mexico. It is still a possibility, I hope, dinner that is?'

Caroline smiled. 'Perhaps. Depends on how the war goes. Ring me at 9.00 and I'll see how I feel.'

'Thank you, Caroline. I am so happy.' He stood back to let

her pass and she was nearly at the door of the hotel when she turned around to look back at him.

'Oh, Commander Rios,' she was aware of the hotel porter watching her.

'Yes.' He almost ran towards her.

'If, and it's a big if, we do have dinner we are not going to discuss football. Ok!'

'I promise.' He was still laughing as she crossed the foyer to the elevator bank.

Isabella opened the door of the apartment and turning left walked into the living room. There was the sound of running water from the far end of the corridor.

'Is that you Isabella?' A muffled and slightly distorted voice called out.

'Yes. I'm in the living room Zoë,' she answered while quickly checking through the envelopes she had recovered from the lobby mailbox. 'Don't leave the bathroom in a mess. I know what you Georgia Tech hurdlers are like.'

'Very funny.' Zoë's voice was suddenly more distinct.

Isabella looked up to see the slim blonde girl walking completely naked into the room. Her head and face were partially covered with a bath-towel as she busied herself drying off the last wetness of a recent shower. Isabella smiled as she admired the movements of the lithe and supple body and the almost innocent and carefree way the naked girl found, and perched on, the soft armrest of a chair. Isabella immediately moved closer and letting her hands linger on the moist shoulders, massaged them gently. The younger girl arched her neck back in response and purred out a pleased sound, like a stroked cat. After a few minutes, Isabella slowly lifted the towel and looked into the cool eyes before gently kissing her cousin's lips.

'I can see why our scientist friend found the sight of you so exciting. You flaunt that body with total abandon.'

'They are so uptight, those Americans.'

'Irish-American, apparently.'

'Even worse! How did you get on, Isabella? Was the scientist equally enraptured by your own displayed, but withheld charms?'

'You have never complained.'

'No! You are right but then, I'm not very fussy.'

Isabella laughed and pulled at the naked girl's ear.

'As it so happens, everything is going to plan.'

'What do you mean?' Zoë stood up and began to wrap the towel around her. As a mother would, Isabella finished the movement by taking the final corner and tucking it within the fold that lay across the younger woman's chest.

'As we anticipated, his attraction to me is the typical male response. It is rooted in the principals of action and not of reception. With careful handling I can ensure that the attraction will remain seated in his will and not his senses. In that way it can be easily manipulated.'

'And fully erect!' Zoë laughed.

'For as long as is necessary for our purposes.' Isabella joined in the laughter and the two women hugged, tenderly.

After a few moments Zoë withdrew. She walked across the room and pulled back the lace curtains a fraction to look down on the street below. She turned her head slightly in Isabella's direction.

'And what if it becomes more than that? Don't forget how well I know your failings, Isabella!' she said, concerned.

'You mean the possibility of love?'

'Yes.'

'Any potential for a greater involvement, particularly in this instance, must be avoided at all costs and any inclinations towards it to be instantly undermined.' She paused for a second to join the younger woman at the window. 'I do find him attractive . . .'

'I could sense that.' Zoë spoke sternly.

'But I also recognise my weakness for love. As an affliction it cannot be commanded or controlled and it would negate *our* efforts.'

'I'm glad you realise it.' The girl pulled away as Isabella leant forward to kiss her.

'Don't be harsh on me, Zoë. Isn't it for that reason that I have you, my sweet shadow? If you sense me drifting, you can haul me back.'

'It is a dangerous game, Isabella or should I call you, Solis.'

'Yes, but exciting . . . and necessary.'

Intempestiuum

MIDNIGHT

Granada, Spain.
4 September 2001

Michael arrived at Alonzo's house a little before the agreed time. After a long wait an elderly housekeeper with sad eyes opened the door. She led him along the outer courtyard corridor and through a small archway to an inner courtyard where orange blossom and jasmine scented the air. A small table with two chairs had been set in the shade of a small wooden pavilion, whose roof arched up to a narrow point and whose sides were a series of exquisitely and intricately carved lattice panels which appeared to expand and contract in response to the light or shadow that fell on them.

The housekeeper was pointing to a chair for Michael to sit on when Alonzo appeared. The distressed features of the previous evening were gone as he grasped Michael's shoulders and kissed him on both cheeks.

'You are most welcome my friend. Please take a seat. Would you like a glass of wine?'

'Thank you. White please.'

It was only then that Michael noticed the inner ceiling of the pavilion. It appeared to descend to meet him in a series of green-

and-gold-coloured tiled stalactites like cascading verdant comets from a glittering sky. His mouth automatically opened at the wonder of its design and execution. Alonzo stood beside him, stretching up his hand as if to catch the stars.

'This is the pavilion of my pleasure, the house of my heart, the true centre of the garden of my happiness. It once belonged to a Sufi mystic *shayk* who once lived in Cordoba. He had called it the *Khalwat el-rumman*. Wonderful, is it not?'

'Incredible. What is *Khalwat el-rumman*?'

'*Khalwats* were the spiritual retreats where Sufi's could 'remember' God and *el-rumman* is the pomegranate fruit. In Sufi mysticism the pomegranate was the fruit of the Garden of Essence, the final stage in their journey of exploration and the symbol of the Unity of Being.'

While Michael continued to stare upwards Alonzo turned away to speak to the housekeeper in Spanish. She ambled off towards what Michael supposed was the kitchen. Alonzo was laughing as he sat down.

'Señora Hernandez and I have been together for nearly twenty years. I have no idea what age she is only that she is much older than me and I am 72. She is going to bring us the food and wine and then go home. Her cooking is never predictable but always substantial. I am glad there is someone else to share it with.'

'Last night. Was everything all right?'

'What? Oh! The need for me to go out? Yes. There was no real urgency after all. I am sorry that it interrupted our evening.'

Señora Hernandez soon shuffled back with the food and wine, flashing a big toothless grin at Michael as she placed an overflowing plate of cold meats and cheeses in front of him. She then said her good-byes and Michael could hear a nearby back door locking behind her as she left. The two men ate in relative silence until satisfied they had both done justice to her efforts.

'You were about to tell me the story of the seals, Alonzo. I would still like to hear it.'

Alonzo pulled out his pipe and making sure that it was well filled took obvious pleasure in lighting the tobacco. After a ritual series of puffing and packing manoeuvres he finally appeared satisfied and watched Michael for a while through a fog of billowing smoke.

'Are you a mystical person, Michael? Do you believe in fate or do you still find the circumstances and discourses of our meetings a bit strange or offbeat?'

Michael pondered the question for a moment before standing up to touch the roof of the pavilion and to walk the full circle of its inner perimeter. He was behind the older man when he replied.

'That is a difficult question, Alonzo. I have generally determined my own destiny but I enjoy chance encounters. Perhaps it is more a natural inquisitiveness but I am happy to allow the encounters follow their course. If that is fate then I welcome it. Meeting you seems right somehow, comfortable, and I have not questioned it. Should I?'

'A little perhaps but it is not important at the moment. What about the mystical aspect?' Alonzo did not turn to look at his visitor.

'Like many people I have at times come across the writings of both modern and medieval esotericists in their promotion of an ancient, and continuing, wisdom. Similarly I have read some of the recent scholarly works on the concept of secret organisations and their possible impact on society, be it benign or malign. To be honest with you, I have often enjoyed and responded to their sometimes well-argued hypotheses but shied away from their strident advocacy. Nothing I have read or encountered became a revelation or offered a life-changing philosophy but . . .' Michael returned to take his seat. He searched Alonzo's features for a response, but the older man's face remained impassive. 'When I look around me here and listen to you there is a real sense of timelessness and inheritance. In answer to your question I always accepted that mystery, and mysticism, existed but it was not an exploratory path I wanted, or was prepared to undertake. My life and work has been . . . is dedicated to the solution of questions posed by the physical world surrounding us and not the soul.'

'You corrected yourself, Michael. Any reason?' Alonzo was smiling.

Michael nodded, realising that that the answer was already obvious to the older man. He also realised that, where Alonzo was concerned, it was necessary for him to vocalize that answer and he pondered silently on his response for a few minutes, before replying.

'My life is sterile, responsible yes, but devoid of real emotion, real understanding. I'm selfish, self-contained, compartmentalised in my relationships and sometimes cold. I have no misconceptions about my own mortality but before that happens I now feel that I want to lay myself open, fully exposed to the wind and rain of other experiences.' Michael paused. A frown creased his forehead skin.

'Go on, Michael. Spit it out, as you Americans say.' Alonzo reached out to touch Michael's knee.

'I wonder, however, if this is just a further indulgence because I'm in the financial and intellectual position to make that choice. Am I running away or towards something? I don't know, Alonzo. I'm confused, yet in the last few days there have been momentary glimpses of the possibilities of such inner peace that I want to reach out and hold on to them. Am I making sense?'

'Yes, Michael, but only because I have travelled the same road. . .' Alonzo paused for a few seconds. 'I do not know why it was determined that my life and the legacy of the *Voices* should be so interlinked. I resisted the demands of such a legacy, for many years.' The older man placed his hand on Michael's and squeezed it gently. 'In pursuing the possibility you, my young friend, are opening far more doors than are being closed behind you. But are you willing to continue?'

Michael felt a strange sense of euphoria. The frown disappeared to become the excited face of a nine-year-old boy again. He did not hesitate. 'Yes . . . *Yes,* I am!'

Alonzo settled back in his chair, flicking fallen ash from his pipe off his shirt.

'Good. So be it! Would you like more wine?'

'No thanks, Alonzo. Please go on.'

'All of the lazuli seal stones have ancient names which are

passwords to their history. The first, called *Syrbeth* has never before left its homeland in the high valleys of Nuristan, the land of the Divine Light, in Afghanistan. Its guardians, both good and evil, have always been the people of those mountains.

About 800 years ago *Syrbeth* became part of the traditional initiation ceremony of the leader, or malik, of the goldsmiths of Kabul. In a final act of submission to their cause the new malik kisses the seal. Few, if any, of the guild leaders have known the true origin of their seal of office, yet were and are prepared to guard it with their lives.

At present it is in the possession of Hasan al-Sa'igh, the current malik of the guild of goldsmiths in Kabul, but he plays a very dangerous game.'

'In what way?'

'Hasan al Sa'igh is a friend of the Arabs of the al-Qae'da terrorist group who are helping the Taliban impose their regime in Afghanistan, yet he is also the leader of a secret Karmatian organization, known as the Badhriya, which is loosely associated to the Northern Alliance and dedicated to the overthrow of the Taliban in Afghanistan. Al-Sa'igh is the warlord who controls most of the output of the poppy crop of the region.'

'I don't quite understand the connection.' Michael spoke with a puzzled frown.

'In past centuries opium was a sideline business for the goldsmiths, who always had controlled the trading contacts, but now is their main source of income. Hasan is greedy and it has brought him into open conflict with the Taliban who are determined to control the opium industry from Afghanistan as a statement of their intention to restore the rule of *shair'a* law in the country.'

'I read something about the tonnage they have destroyed so far.' Michael spoke quietly.

'I suspect, sometimes, that it is an empty gesture. There are too many of the old mujahadeen within the Taliban hierarchy.' Alonzo shook his head from side to side, a pained look on his face. 'The danger for *Syrbeth* is that, in Hasan's attempts to fund his conflict with the Taliban, outside parties have learnt of the seal and are attempting to acquire it. In addition, within Afghanistan, a carved stone like *Syrbeth* is seen by the Taliban as an idolatrous object to be destroyed.'

'Like the Buddhist statues of Baiman?'

Alonzo took the pipe from his mouth and accompanied by a slight nod of his head pointed it at Michael in acknowledgement. There was a silence again as Alonzo refilled their glasses.

'The second seal, *Abrape*, having descended from the high valleys, remained for most of its existence on Indian soil and did not leave that sub-continent until the late seventeenth century.'

Alonzo lit his pipe again. Michael watched the smoke drift to the sky. He had not noticed it earlier but was now sure that he detected the distinct smell of hashish. He said nothing as the older man continued.

'The seal and its successive guardians had journeyed, with the other *Voices* that had left the Hindu Kush, across the mountain passes and down the Indus Valley to the sea. About 2500BCE, 1,000 years after the other seals had departed, *Abrape* was to be found in Mohenjo-Daro but with the invasion of the Aryans it moved south-eastwards to the Banas culture at Adar. Its history after that is a little confused but its guardians appeared to become the Brahmins of the early Hindu faith.

Abrape made, what you might call 'its public reappearance' in the twelfth century of our time.

It was in the keeping of Jasodhar, a Brahmin of Pali, and a town very close to the ancient Adar. It was given as a tribute to Siha, the first of the Rathor Rajputs. He had it incorporated into a jewelled *khilat* ceremonial dagger and later it was part of the dowry of Harkha, the daughter of the Rajput Bhar Mals, when she married the Mughal emperor, Akbar, in 1562.

About 200 years later it was given to the Shah Shuja-ud-Daula of Oudh, for his support of the disintegrating Mughal Empire and when Warren Hastings, the Governor General of the East India Company, confiscated the treasure of the Oudh begums it came into his possession and was transported to England. After

Hastings's death the *khilat* passed through the hands of a series of private collectors and *Abrape* now rests in a bank vault in Switzerland.

It has for company one of the other *Voices* and there are rumours that two or three of the others will join them soon.'

'You mean there are possibly five in the possession of one individual.' Alonzo gave a grave nod of his head. 'Who is the gatherer?' Michael spoke excitedly. Alonzo held up his hand.

'I will tell you later, but let me finish the stories of the *Voices*. It is important. They have nearly all been together before.'

Michael sat back. 'Sure. Sorry.'

'The next three seals, *Nergimmel, Ayatau* and *Saclaresh*, have a similar early history. Arriving in Uruk about 3700BCE the guardians kept our people in lower Mesopotamia through Sumerian, Elamite and Akkadian upheavals until founding the Mittani homeland, centred at Washukanni about 1600BCE.

If you remember the story I told you, it was predicted that the people would find their new homeland when they saw the constellation of Orion at the same latitude as the grove in the mountains.'

'Yes.' Michael nodded.

'Well, Washukanni is at that latitude and it was there that these three *Voices* separated for the first time. *Nergimmel* went with the sea tribes, that part of our people driven from the western areas of Mittani land by the Hittites, to re-establish their culture in the coastal Phoenician cities. The guardian of this *Voice* subsequently made his home around 1000BCE at Lefkandi, on the island of Euboia off mainland Greece. Euboia used to be called Peran, the country beyond the sea, by our people.

Nergimmel remained there until travelling with Magasthenes in 730BCE to found first, the Euboian colony of Cumae on the Italian mainland and then Zankle, modern day Messina, in Sicily. After that it moved to Syracuse with Gelon and through Greek, Roman, Vandal, Gothic, Byzantine and Arab times it remained there until Roger II, the first Norman King of Sicily, became its guardian.

Ayatau and *Saclaresh* went east. First to the Assyrian capital Nineveh, and then to Ekbactana, or modern day Hamadan, of the Median Empire about 612BCE. *Ayatau* remained in Mesopotamia through all the empires until it was brought to Palermo in Sicily, by its then guardian Abu Abdullah Mohammed al-Edrisi, in 1039CE. Roger II was then able to gather it as well.'

Alonzo stopped for a moment and looked at Michael as if to ensure he was paying attention.

'*Saclaresh* has a much more mystical history. It is known also as the Voice of the Magi. From Hamadan it moved further east until Zoraster became its guardian. It then remained under the care of the Magi priests until Darius killed the usurper Magian king, Gaumata, at the fortress of Sikayahuvati in 521BCE.

After the defeat of Darius III and sack of Persepolis in 330BCE, Alexander became its next guardian. *Saclaresh* remained in Babylon after Alexander's death and in the third century of our time it became the possession of Mani and later of the Manichean Perfects, the priests of that religion. In 1038CE George Maniakes, the Byzantine General, conqueror of Syria and a Perfect, led his Varangian Norsemen and Bulgar irregulars to Sicily. *Saclaresh* was deposited in the church of Santa Maria di Maniace in Maletto until stumbled upon by Adelaide, the mother of Roger II, King of Sicily. She gave it to Roger at his coronation.'

Michael shifted in his seat. He was having some difficulty in following the history and was glad that Alonzo was skipping over many of the details. 'Alonzo?'

'Yes, Michael.'

'The names of the *Voices*. Do they not all end in Hebrew letters? Why is that?'

'About 900CE the head of the Afghan gold merchants, and guardian of the first seal, *Syrbeth*, was a Jew called Alut Tagar Hiwi. Somehow he came to be aware of the significance of the seal and the story of the others. He decided it was necessary to be able to identify the *Voices* by a secret code and attached a Hebrew letter to each of their names. It has remained so to this day.'

'I see.' Michael was stiff. 'Alonzo, do you mind if we take a walk in the courtyard while you continue?'

'No, of course not. Let us go.' Michael and his host stood up and linked arms as they walked the courtyard perimeter.

'The other two *Voices,* Alonzo. What of them?'

'The next is *Nefradaleth,* sometimes called the Woman's Voice. After leaving the Indus valley the people settled first in Dilmun, or what is now called Bahrain. This, for our people, was the Isle of the Blessed. From here when three of the *Voices* went northwards to Susa, *Nefradaleth* travelled onwards to Sheba by sea. The land of Sheba would comprise most of modern day Yemen. About 3500BCE our people in Sheba crossed the Red Sea, first into Punt and then northwards into Egypt. Keeping to the coast they found the Nile by travelling inland along the Wadi Hammamaat and followed it to the Delta. The guardians became the *Khnumu* priests of the ram-headed God Khnum and our people advised and assisted both Djoser and Khufu in their monumental building works.

The *Voice*, *Nefradaleth*, always stayed with a woman Pharaoh Queen such as Sobeknefru or Hatshepsut and finally was with Cleopatra VII of the Ptolemy's in 51BCE. After the Roman occupation of Egypt, *Nefradaleth* became the responsibility of the chief Archon priestess, Sophia of the Gnostic settlement in Chenoboskion, on the east bank of the Nile near Qena.

The rise of Islam saw it journey, first to Alexandria, then to Cyrene, and then to Tunisia from where it moved to Palermo. In 1111CE the *Voice* was given by Rebecca ben-Gerbi to Queen Adelaide when she moved the capital of Norman Italy to that city. *Nefradaleth* had been altered somewhat in its travels and in addition to the marks of our people, its total surface had also been covered in a series of hieroglyphic, Gnostic, Arabic and Hebraic symbols.

Because of these strange marks, and their meaning, Adelaide directed that the *Voice* be deposited in the Antoine ascetic convent of Monte Vergine near Avellino in Campania. When Roger II built the church of S.Giovanni degli Eremiti in Palermo,

Nefradaleth returned with the monks and nuns of Monte Vergine to administer the church. Roger II of Sicily now had control of four of the *Voices*.'

A breeze from the mountains was making the night air chilly and both men were happy to return to Alonzo's study. Soon the sweet smell of hashish once again wafted through the room.

'Roger II commissioned al-Edrisi to create a map of the known world, which he did on both paper and in a silver planisphere. The four seals were incorporated to represent the four cardinal winds and the huge planisphere was stored in the palace in Palermo. Palermo was the true centre of the multi-national, multi-religious and tolerant society that was Roger's Kingdom of Sicily.

On 9 March 1161, however, there was a palace revolt against William I, Roger's son and King of Sicily since 1154. In a four-hour orgy of looting, the palace treasury was ransacked and the planisphere disappeared. The strange thing was that the revolt was put down only *two* days later, yet there was no trace of the planisphere. It had already been broken up for its silver and the *Voices* were already dispersed.'

'*Nefradaleth* became the responsibility of Clementina, Countess of Catanzaro and lover of Mathew Bonnellus, chief of the revolt against the King of Sicily. It was suggested that it was she who planned the coup, as she wanted to get all the *Voices* but had to settle for just one. William came after it to her fortress at Taverna but *Nefradaleth* was gone. Clementina also disappears from the pages of history.

It next surfaces within the Cathar community at Montesegur in the Languedoc. On the night of 16 March 1243, the last night before the citadel commander Mirepoix and the remaining occupants resigned themselves to their fate, a female Perfect called Esclarmonde de Foix, along with three others, secretly escaped from the fortress and recovered the Cathar treasure that had been hidden two months earlier in the cave of Sabaoth. It became the responsibility of successive female Perfects of the Spanish Cathars who went into hiding, first amongst the Mara

Gatos people of Astorga and then in 1259 to the newly established Kingdom of Majorca. The tradition continues to this day in the guardian-ship of the highest female initiates of the Alumbados.'

'What happened to the other three?' Michael interrupted.

'*Nergimmel* was quickly recovered and incorporated into a jewelled chalice that became the property of Richard the Lion Heart of England, when he was given it as a present by Tancred, King of Sicily at Catania on 3 March 1191 in exchange for the supposed Excalibur sword of King Arthur.

Later the following year Richard, on his way back from Acre, was shipwrecked on the small isle of Lokrum near the city of Ragusa, or what today we call Dubrovnik. He was only able to salvage a few personal possessions, one of which was the chalice. He gave it to the priests of the new cathedral that was being built in Ragusa, in thanksgiving for his survival.

Ragusa was destroyed by an earthquake in 1667 and in the widespread looting of the city that followed, *Nergimmel* disappeared. Much later, Napoleon was thought to have acquired it when he created his Illyrian States but it soon disappeared again, only to turn up recently in the vaults of a Swiss bank. I hope I am not going too fast for you, Michael.'

'No, but I wish I had a tape recorder.'

Clouds were forming over the distant Glarnisch as the phone call was put through. On the waters of the Zurich See, far below, the silver-haired man could see the wind whipping up the crests of small waves. The line crackled as he spoke.

'*Sabah el-khair, Shaikh al-Shurat.*'

'*Sabah en-nur, mein der Freund.*' The speaker switched from Arabic to lightly accented German with ease.

'You would prefer to speak in German?'

'Yes.'

'I was surprised at your message for me to make urgent contact. Is this line of communication secure.'

'Yes!'

'What is the problem?'

'I have heard some disturbing rumours and I want assurances from you.' The voice on the phone line was harsh and abrupt.

The silver-haired man swivelled in his chair to lean heavily on his desk. A concerned frown crossed his face as he answered cautiously. 'Have I not always been honest with you my friend? Have not you, and the al-Qae'da always been assured of my support?'

'Your generosity is not questioned my friend, without your support it would have been difficult to continue the jihad.'

'Well then. What is the problem?'

'The rumours, I have heard suggest that you might have become involved with some of the elements of the *Badhriya* opposition group in Afghanistan. Is this true?'

'Ramzi –'

'No names friend!'

'You know that I believe, as you do, that the route to paradise must be littered with the bodies of the Jews and Crusaders. I fully supported the fatwa of 1998 and will continue to help you in any way I am able.'

'What is your connection with the *Badhriya* friend? I do not have much time. Be truthful!'

'I have long believed, and you know this because we have discussed it, that the control of the supply and distribution of narcotic drugs into any country is by far the most effective way to destroy its fabric. In addition, the financial benefits allow me to support those movements fighting for a new world order, such as yours. At present, the American government is putting a huge effort into eradicating the Mexican and Columbian narcotic trade into the United States and the opportunity is there to supply the market from somewhere else. It is true that I had made contact with some of those involved in the opium trade from Afghanistan but I understood they were only a marginal part of the Badhriya and the opposition to the Taliban.'

'They are vermin!'

'But useful vermin my friend. They are the carriers of the plague and may be used for our purposes. I am just walking on a different road to the same great khan as you. Trust me!'

'I trust very few people my friend. If your opium traders are in any way connected to Ahmed Shah Massoud they will very soon find that the ground beneath their feet opens up to swallow them. I would advise you to finish your business with them quickly. Give me their names so I can keep them under surveillance.'

'I will.'

'When?'

'Next week when my use for them has diminished.'

'What is happening?'

'I will soon have access to a technology that will allow me control the world's cocaine production. That power will be mine . . . ours to dispense. After that, the opium traders in Kabul will be of negligible importance. Both our ends will then be served by me giving you the names.'

'Very well. One week!'

'I thank you, *Shaikh al-Shurat*.' The silver-haired man's face jerked with anger as he spoke. He did not like being pushed into a corner.

'One more thing, my friend.'

'Yes.'

'Stay away from America next week.'

'Why? What are you planning?'

'Just stay away. This is my advice. The *ashab al-kahf* are awake. *Allah ykhallik, maah es-salameh*.'

The connection terminated with a loud click. The silver-haired man got up and paced around the table. Stopping, he suddenly banged his fist in fury on the surface causing the papers he had been working on to jump into the air. He leant forward and touched the console button.

'Fraulein Schmitt,' he growled.

'Yes, Sir.'

'Telephone a Mr Rod Mallory, in California. I need to speak to him.'

'Yes, Sir. Is there anything else?'

'No . . . yes! Yes there is! Cancel my travel arrangements to New York for next week and the appointments that we had made in the city. Also, I want you to ask Ziffel, my broker, to come here straight away.'

'Will I endeavour to rearrange the New York appointments?'

'No. Not for the moment. Thank you.' He slumped back into his chair, rocking back and forth in it silently, before turning again to look out at the mountains.

The afternoon shadows were lengthening as the two men blew smoke into the air. Alonzo Aldarhze was the first to break the silence.

'You said you wished you had a tape recorder.'

'Yes.'

'There is no need. The history of the *Voices* is only a brief overview. Their travels are not your primary responsibility, Michael. Your destiny lies elsewhere.'

'What do you mean, Alonzo?'

'Let me continue and you will soon understand better. Is that okay?'

'Sure.' Michael's face flushed.

The older man smiled at him in a fatherly fashion. 'I had not completed the story of *Saclaresh*. After the planisphere of Roger of Sicily disappeared, and was presumably broken up, the mystical Voice of the Magi somehow surfaced in Damascus. The next guardians, of note were the early Sufi masters Al-Suhrawardi, Ibn Arabi and Mahmud Shabistari. It then moved further east with Shah Ni'matullah Wali before returning to Shiraz.

In the early 1500's, when Isma'il I of the militant Safavid Sufi's took power in Persia, his Pir or spiritual guide was a man called Sahkulu Baba Tekeli, nicknamed Seytankulu or 'slave of the devil'. Under this man's influence Shi'ia became the state religion and Sunni's were persecuted, a situation which continues to this day.

Sahkulu was thought to have cemented his position in the Safavid court by magically producing a miraculous Qur'an. It was considered particularly so as it was written in the new *nasta'liq* script developed by the famous Persian calligrapher, Mir 'Imad al-Hasani. Sahkulu is said to have hidden *Saclaresh* within this Qur'an's elaborate binding.'

Michael slapped at a mosquito that hovered near his neck. He reached forward to retrieve a cigarette. 'I'm afraid I don't understand the significance of the script, Alonzo.'

'Let me explain it a little bit better, Michael.' Alonzo seemed in a hurry to continue. 'Most copies of the Qur'an were written in one of the six accepted variants of *kufic* script. The Ottomans, who were traditional Sunni, favoured the *nesih* variant and would not use the newer *nasta'liq* style of the Shi'ite Persians for copying the Qur'an because it smacked of heretical innovation and tampering with the Prophet's words.

The few Qur'ans that did exist in the *nasta'liq* script were probably produced by the Safavid Shahs to be presented by their ambassadors in their dealings with the Ottoman court. This was a deliberate attempt, of course, to confront the Sultan and trick him into accepting a Shiite Qur'an, and its truth, as protocol dictated that they could not refuse a gift. To prevent such an embarrassment the Sultan would have a copy of his own Qur'an nearby and when the gift of the Shi'ite *nasta'liq* version was announced he would solemnly lift up his own and kiss it, thereby affirming its sanctity.'

Michael was amused. 'The pen is mightier than the sword. Eh!'

'Indeed.' Alonzo was anxious to continue his story. 'The "Devil's Qur'an", as it was soon called after Sahkulu's nickname Seytankulu, with *Saclaresh* still secreted within its binding, was in Isma'il's possession until his death. Recovered at that point by Sahkulu's family, it remained in their guardianship until 1638 when the Ottoman Sultan, Murad IV sacked Baghdad. From there it travelled, with its Sahkulu guardian, a famous musician, to Istanbul.

In 1705 the "Devil's Qur'an" was put on the market and acquired in Istanbul by a Prince Demetrius Cantemir of Moldavia who brought it with him to Russia. In 1785 his son Antiochus, the Ambassador of Czarina Catherine to George III of England, brought the Qur'an to England. It was once again put on the market and in 1792 was acquired by a man called Sir Gilbert Elliot who was soon to become Viceroy of the very temporary Anglo-Corsican Kingdom. In the confusion of Gilbert's departure from Corsica, in 1796, the Qur'an was somehow left behind in Ajaccio and was later given to Napoleon when he stayed there in 1799.

Napoleon gave the Qur'an as a present to Gaspard Monge, his confident and after Monge's death in 1818, the copy was sold to the Parisian branch of the Armenian Balian family.

One of the most famous members of this family was Karabet Belian who was to become the architect of the famous Dolmabahce Palace in Istanbul. It was he who discovered that part of the leather binding of the Qur'an appeared to have been stiffened by an old piece of parchment with faded cuneiform writing on it. Belian was very anxious to have this translated and arranged to have the Qur'an sent to a Reverend Edward Hincks, the rector of a small parish in Ireland, and one of the most brilliant cuneiform experts of that time. It was Hincks who, when having to carefully strip the leather cover to release the parchment, found *Saclaresh* hidden within the damaged binding. Coincidently perhaps, it was also at this point that Hincks began to publish his own major discoveries.'

'What do you mean, Alonzo? What discoveries?' Michael had never heard of Hincks.

'The Reverend Hincks, like you Michael from what you have told me of your life, was born in Cork, in the south of Ireland. He entered Trinity College, Dublin at the age of fifteen and received his Doctorate of Divinity from there in 1829. In 1826 he was appointed by the College to the small parish of Killyleagh in County Down in Ireland where he remained until his death in 1866.

By force of sheer intellect alone, as he did not travel to Egypt or Mesopotamia and was a little removed from the academic world, he was the scholar who confirmed the significance of Egyptian name "cartouches", who determined the Egyptian system of chronology and who applied the final polish to a full understanding of hieroglyphic grammar.

If this was not enough he also, with even greater success, turned his attentions to Mesopotamia. It was Hincks who first determined the syllabic nature of Assyrian cuneiform and by 1852 had provided the basic decipherment of Akkadian. This is why the Balian family sent him the Qur'an. Quite an extraordinary man really and almost forgotten! He should be spoken of in the same awe as Champollion!'

Michael startled at the sudden intensity of Alonzo's impassioned words. The older man, noticing the effect, calmed himself quickly.

'I am sorry Michael to get so excited. The decipherment of ancient languages is a hobby of mine and I have always felt that Hincks did not get the recognition he deserved. Let me continue with *Saclaresh*'s story.

After Hincks's death in 1866 his possessions dispersed and there was no mention of the "Devil's Qur'an" or of the seal. The book itself eventually reappeared in 1916, when it was bought at an auction at Christies in London. It is now in the Chester Beatty Library in Dublin. They, of course, do not know or catalogue it by this name nor are they fully aware of its true provenance. Indeed the original binding has gone completely to be replaced by a new binding, which must have been done in London by somebody not used to dealing with Qur'ans.'

'Why?'

'The new binding, a close copy of the original perhaps, has been attached upside down in the wrong fashion. *Saclaresh* had disappeared again.'

Alonzo stood up and tapped out the burnt remnants from his pipe into an earthenware pot containing a small mulberry bush.

'Why so much detail about *Saclaresh*, Alonzo?'

Alonzo immediately began to fill and pack his pipe again and it was a few minutes before he seemed ready to continue.

'Because its fate intimately concerns you, Michael!'

'In what way?'

'I'll return to it but let me finish the stories of the other *Voices* first.'

'Sure. Sorry Alonzo.' Michael looked puzzled but the older man ignored this as he retook his seat.

'Finally there was *Ayatau*. After the break up of al-Edrisi's planisphere, *Ayatau* went west from Sicily to Majorca in the guardianship of the Jewish Charazes family of mapmakers who had helped el-Edrisi make Roger II's planisphere in the first place. It and its surrounding silver mounting from the map were fashioned into an hourglass about 1500 and it has remained in the care of the Timekeepers since. I am the latest in that line.'

'*You mean you have one?*' Michael sputtered out.

'Yes.' Alonzo was watching Michael's face intently.

'May I see it?'

'Of course. Let us go back to the library.' Alonzo led Michael out of the study and back along the courtyard corridor to the first room they had entered. Saying nothing the two men entered the library and Alonzo went to the reading lectern that stood in the centre of the room. Depressing, what Michael assumed was, a hidden lever the octagonal top of the lectern opened and a plinth, with an elaborately carved, silver hourglass set on it slowly rose up. Alonzo waited for the movement to stop and reaching forward lifted the hourglass off the plinth and handed it to Michael.

'Look at the top.'

Michael's grip was nervous and he was suddenly afraid that the fragile looking glass might break. Both the top and bottom had a lid of about four inches of solid silver, which were linked in delicate latticed arches to the neck of the glass. The heaviness of the hourglass surprised him and yet, he was certain he could still sense the gentle vibration of the shifting grains of sand as they moved through the narrow channel when he turned the glass in his hands.

In the centre of the top lid, set almost flush with the silver surface, was an azure-blue stone with a primitive but delicate carving of a horned man holding either two snakes or two rivers. There was a pair of hieroglyphs to either side of the figure, who sat cross-legged beneath a carving of the crescent moon and oval sun.

'This *is* fantastic. What did you say you were called Alonzo? A Timekeeper.'

'Yes. A *sahib al-zaman*. Look at the bottom lid Michael.'

Michael inverted the hourglass, slowly, to look at the bottom side. Set with balas rubies he recognized that it was a representation of the constellation of Orion.

'Orion?' Michael thought of his father.

'Yes, or in the language of the people, *Araum*, the God of Time. It is appropriate, as the *Voices* are really the archons of time. Astronomy, language, history, science, philosophy are really tools to help us understand and define the concept of time but it is an impossible task. Saint Augustine once astutely remarked, when asked about time, that he knew 'exactly what it was but couldn't explain it'. Time past, time present and time future are without matter. When all else is destroyed, time will remain.

It is the mastery of time that will allow us to penetrate new dimensions both within and without ourselves. The *Voices* are the seven gates between birth and death. Only in harnessing the power of all seven, when the Archons of Time are gathered, do our people believe that time can be controlled. The responsibility of the Timekeeper is to ensure that does not happen.'

Michael had upturned the hourglass again and, as he watched the cascading sand, was tracing the stone carvings with his finger. His brow was furrowed with deep lines of concentration. 'I swear that I have seen something like this before. It was recently but I can not remember where exactly.'

Alonzo smiled. 'With Isabella?'

Michael looked startled. 'Yes. *Of course!* She was wearing something similar on a neck chain the first time we met. Does she have one of the *Voices*?'

'Isabella is the guardian of *Nefradaleth*.'

There was a long silence as Michael tried to digest everything he had been told. He began thinking out loud as he replaced the hourglass on the lectern plinth.

'Why . . .'

Alonzo touched the lever and the plinth sank down again. 'What is it, Michael? Ask anything you want.'

'Why have you told me all of this, Alonzo? What is my role in the story?'

'You are to be the next guardian of *Saclaresh*.'

'But you said it had disappeared.'

'Think of it not being lost but more like waiting to be found. By the person whose fate it is to do so, of course.'

'Where do I start?'

'Etschmiadzin perhaps. I also suspect it will probably find you.'

'Etschmiadzin? Where is that?'

'Near Yerevan in Armenia. It is the monastery complex that is the seat of the Supreme Patriarch and Katholicos of the Armenian Church. I am now fairly certain that *Saclaresh* was returned by Hincks to the Belian family and that they gave it into the safekeeping of the Katholicos.'

Michael had barely touched his coffee and now that he reached for it, found it to be cold. The aroma had left with its heat.

Alonzo got up. 'I will get some more. Are you sure you would not like some more food Michael? Perhaps some fruit?'

'No thank you, Alonzo. Coffee is fine.' Michael watched him shuffle out and went back to look at the books in the display case once more before leaving the library and taking a seat in the outer study. He could hear the rattle of the cups and saucers as the older man returned.

'Who is the gatherer, Alonzo?'

'A man called Charles Alexander.' The older man was blunt with his answer.

'*Charles Alexander!* Not again! I don't believe it.' Michael nearly knocked the tray from Alonzo's hand as he brought his hands to his forehead in exasperation.

'The same. Do you know him, Michael?'

'This is the second time recently that I have had to answer that question, Alonzo. The man is beginning to irritate the hell out of me.'

'Do you know him?'

'His company has just made an offer for mine. I have never met him personally although I did hear him speak once.'

'He is an extremely wealthy and powerful individual and wants to gather all the *Voices*.' Alonzo sighed as he put the tray down on a small side table and began pouring Michael his coffee.

'Thank you. Why?'

Michael was more than disturbed at the coincidence of hearing Alexander's name in connection with the *Voices*. Up to then it had been a story, not real, not grounded in reality surely, it was just a story. Alonzo stopped pouring.

'Why does any powerful man seek more power than he has the ability to control? Sugar, Michael?'

'Thank you.' He stirred in the cubes as he watched Alonzo pour his own coffee and then sit down.

'Power is the ultimate prostitute. It is the mistress of enchantment which fills the void or vacuum in men's lives. In gaining it, a price is extracted, an arrangement made, a Faustian deal with the devil accepted. Vacuums are spaces in men's hearts devoid of everything except time. In order to be fully empowered it is also necessary to expel time from that void. He, Alexander, if he is the gatherer, the green man, wants to control time.'

The older man wearily closed his eyes and arched his head back as he finished. Michael sensed that this weariness was almost a recognition that Alonzo's responsibilities as the Timekeeper, had exhausted his energies. Alexander might win out.

'What is Isabella's role in all of this, Alonzo? You said that two or three more of the seals might soon join the *Voices* that Alexander already has. Does that include *Nefradaleth*?'

'Perhaps.' Alonzo spoke hesitantly. 'I will talk to you about it another night. I am now quite tired. Would you mind if we stopped for this evening Michael.'

'No. Of course not.'

'Thank you Michael. Excuse me for one moment.' Alonzo

went back into the library and after a few minutes returned with a package. 'I want to give you something but I want you to promise me not to open it until you have left Granada.'

'Why, Alonzo?'

'I like to give my foreign guests presents but I never want to embarrass them into returning the compliment. It is human nature to assess a present and then to judge what would be an appropriate response and the tendency is to rush out and acquire something in the city. By waiting until you leave Granada then if you wish to do so, it will be something from your heart and not expediency. That is my pleasure and my request.'

Michael took the package and placed it on his lap. 'Thank you, Alonzo. I will wait.'

'Good, now let me show you to the door. We might meet for a walk tomorrow, perhaps?'

'Yes, Alonzo, I would like that. Same time?'

'Yes, Michael, same time. God willing.'

The two men walked slowly to the door. There was a light evening rain falling and Michael could feel the chill of the cold wind. One of the street lamps was flickering, struggling to fully light up. Michael turned back to say good night to Alonzo and was struck by how aged the intermittent weak orange light made the older man look. The eye sockets were deep in the shadows of his face as Alonzo looked up and down the street.

'Alonzo, what about the seventh *Voice*. You did not tell its story. Why?'

'The seventh *Voice* is called *Ammonkaph*, the Silent One, the last gate. Its history has always been shrouded and only revealed to its guardian. These guardians have been reputed to include Hermes Trimegistus, Pythagoras, and Plato and perhaps even Francis Bacon. I suspect, that for most of its journey it was to be found, like *Nefradaleth,* in Egypt, but cannot be absolutely sure.'

'That's a pity, particularly when you know so much about the others,' Michael said sadly. He could sense Alonzo's disappointment. The older man nodded his head.

'Ammon in Egyptian means the 'hidden one' and it was also

the Hebrew name for Alexandria. An Arab writer suggests that the *Voice* was known as the Caliph's Seal, which was supposed to have been in a secret lodge called the Abode of Learning, in Cairo about 800CE. That is the only reference I have found.'

'Perhaps it's fated to remain hidden.'

'I'm not so sure. *Ammonkaph* is rooted in the matter of this world and waits just below the horizon of our lives to greet the rising and setting of the light,' Alonzo added bleakly.

The hairs on the back of Michael's neck stiffened and he shivered as they were suddenly doused by a heavier shower funnelling up the narrow street. Quickly stuffing Alonzo's present under his jacket he took the older man's hand and shook it warmly.

'Good night, Alonzo.'

'I know it must be difficult for you Michael to be suddenly enveloped by such a metaphysical and, perhaps your intellect is screaming, seemingly fantastical sequence of events. All that I ask is that you open your heart to the gestures of our existence.

All that I have told you normally takes many years and stages of full understanding, but there is not enough time for that. You do not fully realise it yet but your destiny is one of enormous responsibility and importance. Goodbye, Michael.'

'Alon–' Michael shivered again, as his words were cut off by the closing thump of the heavy door as the older man quickly retreated back into the house and closed the door behind him. He thought about ringing the bell, but stopped himself short. Pulling up his collar Michael turned to face into the, by now, driving rain of the electrical storm that had descended on the city.

Once again my call to Bob Arnold's office was accompanied by a series of security checks. He sounded agitated.

'Hi buddy, where are you?'

'Spain still.'

'Michael, I need you to be more specific than that.'

'For what reason Bob?' I was looking at my watch. It was

nearly 10.00pm local time, and I'd arranged to see Isabella at 11.00. Even Bob Arnold was not going to stop that.

'A very good reason. Your *life* Michael!'

'Come on Bob, don't be melodramatic.'

'Michael. We've had some further information come in to confirm some of the concerns you expressed yesterday.'

'Which concerns, Bob? There were many,' I said sharply.

'We think that there is some sort of contract out on you and that there might be a kidnap attempt. I need to know exactly where you are. Don't mess me around on this!'

'OK, Bob. Take it easy!'

As I gave him the address of the hotel in Granada I walked into the bathroom of the large suite that I occupied. Its narrow-arched Moorish window with frosted-glass overlooked the plaza of the hotel entrance. I released the catch and slowly pushed out the window a fraction to look down at the activity below. All appeared quiet apart from the arrival of a taxicab but then if somebody were waiting for me they would hardly make themselves known.

'*Michael!* Are you still there?'

'Yes, Bob.'

'I need your cell phone number. Please leave the unit on from here on out.'

'Why, Bob?'

'Until a team gets to you we need it.'

'What team? What do you mean?'

'Langley is dispatching two teams from Lisbon and Madrid, ASAP, to protect you.'

'Is this really necessary, Bob?'

'Yes, buddy. Leave your phone on . . . just in case.'

'Just in case of what?'

'In case something happens to you. We can use it for triangulation and thus track your location. When this call is over dial in *42** 783 and set the cell phone for repeat call. This will then make it work like a transmitter. Do you follow, Michael?'

'Yes, Bob, I mean General, Sir.' I deepened my voice in an attempt at a little levity.

'Michael, this is serious man, *you are in grave danger*. Secure the room and wait for the teams. The first should be there in about three hours. I will –'

'This line is being terminated.' The metallic voice broke in and the line went dead.

Unsettled, both by the conversation and the sudden cessation of the telephone call to Arnold, I waited for a few minutes before trying the number again only to become even more frustrated when encountering a continuously engaged signal. I kicked out at the bedside table causing the innocent alarm clock that had squatted on its surface to bounce in the air and then tumble towards the floor where it wedged itself under the base of the bed. Retrieving it, I saw that the clock face protested the disturbance with a blurred red-flashing 10.45, which did not move on. Time was standing still.

I then tried Isabella's number again, without luck. After what Alonzo had told me, I needed to talk to her. More than that I needed to see her. Perhaps she would come to the hotel instead? I looked at my watch and after waiting again for a few minutes, dialled her number again. No answer.

The excitement I felt was a mixture of fear and desperation, an alchemical elixir that I had seldom experienced since I was a teenager. Bob Arnold's warning was flashing into my consciousness but served only to prompt a memory of me, as a lad of fifteen, sneaking out for love from the seaside house, a corrugated-tin-roofed shack that my mother used to rent for the summer. At that age, in my first truly physical relationship, Mary Delahunty was much older than I was and also happened to be dating somebody else. I recognized no fears save those of rejection and her boyfriend.

Late night secret summer rendezvous, mounting excitement spurred on by my stepfather's warnings of dire consequences if I were to cause my mother any trouble in his frequent absences. Truth be told, I sometimes felt she too would have welcomed the chance to sneak out, sneak away. She was less lucky in love.

I stared at the phone. Presented with the rare opportunity of recreating some of those remembered feelings, I decided I had to go. If I hurried, I reckoned, I could get to Isabella's apartment and return before Langley's goons would arrive. Turning off the lights, first in the bathroom and then in the bedroom, I threw one more quick glance down through the narrow opening in the toilet window to the now empty plaza below before tiptoeing across the carpeted floor of the suite to the balcony doors.

Drawing them open slowly I inched forward to the alabaster-capped railing and for a few minutes scouted the shadows of the hillside that sloped down from the hotel. The night horizon was a phosphorous sea of stars and glimmering city lights. Satisfied, I returned to the room, put on my shoes and, after opening the main door as silently as I could, furtively prodded my head out and gave a thief's look up and down the corridor. There was no sign of friend, or foe for that matter, and with pounding heart I stepped out before closing the door quietly behind me.

I made for the emergency stairs and nearly stumbled down the top steps as a sudden crashing noise, from a new batch of cubes being churned out by the ice-maker on the stairwell landing, caused my legs, and heart, to lose their rhythm. Composing myself, I took one of the ice-cubes to moisten my dry mouth and ran down the steps at speed to the basement garage level. There I pushed at the release mechanism of the fire exit door and found myself in the narrow laneway and cool night air at the back of the hotel. As the heavy metallic door closed behind me I thought I could hear the sound of a muted alarm bell and voices in the stairwell.

Alarmed, I ran blindly along the pitch-black laneway kicking the empty boxes of that day's deliveries out of my way. The laneway passed around the side of the hotel and opened onto the steep hill that ran down towards the Campo del Principe. Stepping into the shadows when any car or taxi came from the direction of the hotel I finally flagged an empty cab about to ascend the hill. Grunting, the protesting driver executed a labour-intensive turnaround and fifteen minutes later deposited me outside the address that Isabella had given earlier. I kept a watch throughout the journey for signs of somebody following us but there did not appear to be any evidence of danger.

The cab sped off and in the darkened doorway I eventually found an intercom button with the name Sanjil written above it. The identity label looked new. I pressed it and the reply was immediate.

'Hello.'

'Isabella, it's Michael. I'm sorry I'm so late.' It was nearly 11.30.

'I am glad you could finally make it Michael. Come on up. Third floor.'

The buzzer went and I pushed through the unlocked door into a marble-floored atrium. There was an old staircase to one side and an even older-looking grilled elevator set deep in a recess in the opposite wall. I took the stairs and soon reached the third-floor landing. Here there was a tattered carpet covering, in places, darkly stained and slightly warped wooden planks, which creaked both in isolation and symphony as I made for the one door I could see at the end of a short corridor. I was just about to knock when I heard the elevator mechanism engaging. I quickly retreated back to the stairwell and waited in its shadow to see if it stopped on that same floor.

To my mounting panic, it did. After a protesting metallic opening back of the grill doors I could hear creaking footsteps and, cautiously looking around the corner, saw a young woman approach the door at the end of the corridor. She was wearing a baseball cap and, though her back was towards me, her movements seemed somewhat familiar. There was also a small defect in her left ear lobe. It was the red-headed nude hurdler.

I coughed as I stepped out and the girl turned around to look back. She did not appear surprised by my sudden appearance and smiled warmly.

'Ah! The man from the bathhouse. Are you breathless from the stairs?'

'Zoë, is it not? Athlete, Georgia Tech. Isabella's cousin.'

'Well remembered, I'm impressed.' She did not look like she was. 'And you are?'

'Michael Mara.' I held out my hand and she took it in a firm grip. 'It's nice to meet you again.'

'Are you here to see Isabella? She did not mention you were coming. I hope I don't intrude . . .' She winked as she released my hand and turned to the door. 'A "wallflower" or "gooseberry" I think you say.'

I blushed. 'No . . . of course not.' I was relieved that she did not appear to notice as she knocked.

The door opened and the welcoming Isabella kissed her cousin on both cheeks while throwing me an apologetic glance over the girl's shoulders. Zoë moved on in and Isabella waited for a moment before stepping forward and kissing me lightly on the lips.

'I am sorry, Michael. I'm never sure when Zoë might call. You know what family are like? She will not stay long. I promise.'

'She said that you weren't expect . . . It doesn't matter. I'm just glad you're here,' I mumbled. 'I tried telephoning earlier with no success.'

Isabella smiled as she took my hand and led me into the apartment. 'Come in. You are most welcome. I've only just arrived myself. I was worried when you were late that you were not going to make it or that I had missed you.'

'Wild horses would not drag me away, I –'

'Zoë, make yourself useful!' Isabella interrupted to shout at her cousin. 'There is some champagne in the fridge. Will that suit you, Michael?'

The living room was long and narrow with scattered Persian carpets and silk-covered divan type couches placed against the wall. The windows were shuttered with latticed doors and what little light there was in the room was generated by two very tall flickering wax-candles set on ornate stands in the far corner. There was little other decoration save a large antique smoking water pipe on a small cabinet in the corner nearest the entrance. The air was scented with jasmine and rose.

It was a private room, feminine, I thought as I looked around.

'That would be fine. Thank you, Isabella.'

'Excuse me for a moment, Michael. I want to shower and change my clothes. As I said, I was not here that long before you.'

'Sure!'

As Isabella left and walked towards the bedroom somewhere down at the other end of the apartment Zoë returned with the uncorked bottle and three glasses. She plans on staying, I thought to myself. She smiled as she expertly poured the frothing wine and passed the glass to me.

'Do not worry, Michael. When Isabella returns I will disappear into her room. I have some work to do on her computer.'

I blushed and smiled guiltily back. 'When do you return to America for your studies?'

'Next week, and you Michael, when do you go home?'

'Home! Too soon unfortunately. I will miss Granada.'

'It has that effect on some people. Once caught in its snare you never want to leave. Are you married?'

'Yes.'

'Is your wife here?'

'No.'

'Has she ever been to Granada?'

'I don't think so.'

'You should bring her next time. She should see the city that has charmed you.'

'Yes.' I gulped down the wine and accepted a refill. 'Next time perhaps.'

At that moment Isabella reappeared. She was wearing a full-length cotton kaftan with silk borders. Her hair, still wet, was wrapped in a turbaned towel. Around her neck was the gold chain and hanging from it . . . *Nefradaleth*. I couldn't take my eyes off it.

Zoë noticed my interest as she handed Isabella the bottle. She smiled back at me before winking at Isabella. 'I will leave you two in peace. Michael and I were just talking about being seduced.'

'What!' I protested.

'By the city and its charms, of course.' Zoë gave another wink and after stretching out a hand to touch Isabella gently on her cheek disappeared from the room.

'She is always teasing. Do not mind her, Michael.'

I moved up on the divan and Isabella sat down. I could feel her body heat and the seal appeared to glow. I could not help but put out my hand and touch it, almost like the strange need of people to touch the swelling abdomen of pregnant friends and strangers. It was a primeval, unlearnt, instinctive reaction to something that was so basic to our existence. I wanted to draw from that energy. Isabella seemed to understand and did not pull away.

'She is right though about the seduction of the city.'

'Is that what you want, Michael? To be seduced?'

'I would be lying if I denied it.' I pulled back a fraction to watch her eyes but as I did so she took my hand from the seal and placed it over her left breast. I could feel the nipple rise erect beneath the cloth. She placed hers over mine and pressed it inwards gently.

'Do you feel my heartbeat? Flesh and blood Michael. I am not some mystical creature. I am neither an ideal nor a phenomenon.'

'I know but . . . you are different. The seal for example . . . *Nefradaleth*.'

Isabella startled and jumping up from the chair to hover over me, left my hand grasping thin air. '*You know its name!*'

'I know the names of all seven *Voices*. Alonzo told me.'

'Even I do not know that, Michael. You must be marked out in some way for Alonzo to divulge the secret of the *Voices*. Somebody special.'

'I don't know about that. He is a fascinating man and I have learnt so much from him, even in such a short time. We are meeting tomorrow again.'

I could hear cackle-like noises coming from the corridor and tried looking in their direction. Isabella refilled our glasses before sitting down beside me again.

'That's Zoë. She is on an Internet voice and visual link to her American coach. The speakers are of poor quality. What else did Alonzo say about *Nefradaleth*?'

'He is concerned that it might fall into the wrong hands. Something about a Swiss collector.'

'This is very unexpected.' Isabella began to pace the room.

'What is?' I asked.

'You knowing the story of the *Voices* and having a conversation about them with me, as if they were a normal subject for discussion. It is very strange.'

'It was you who put me in touch with Alonzo. You must have known this would happen.'

'Believe me, Michael when I say that I did not anticipate such a development.'

'Alonzo is very concerned, Isabella. I think he hopes I might help prevent the gathering of *Nefradaleth*.'

'That will never happen Michael. I am its guardian until I die. *Nefradaleth* not only brings with it the responsibility of care but also great peace and fulfilment. Can you understand that?'

'I understand responsibility, but despite all my academic and commercial success I have seldom been able to contemplate, or experience, true peace and fulfilment. Until now that is.'

Isabella walked to the small cabinet where the antique water pipe stood. She opened a drawer.

'Will you smoke a joint with me, Michael. It is pure Afghan gold'

'Sure.'

She brought the two rolled and tapered cigarettes and after lighting one off the wax candle handed it to me. She then lit her own and sat down cross-legged on the floor in front of me. Both of us took two large inhalations, sucking in air like a back draft to aid the rush. The sweet-smelling smoke tingled in my nostrils.

'Tell me about your responsibilities, Isabella. Alonzo mentioned something about an organization called the Alumbrados.'

'The guardianship of *Nefradaleth* is a sacred duty. It demands an acknowledgement, and acceptance, of the principals of light and dark. The *Voice* is one of the Portals of Matter through which we can experience the true essence of God. The ancients held that God and matter were of equal importance and interdependent and that the limitations of matter such as evil, both moral and physical, were a positive force rather than a defect. Matter in its purest form, man's soul, can only contemplate God by total absorption in the essence of his beneficence.'

'But what is your role?'

'I am a Perfect and must be "quiet" by example. This allows me approach a level of gnosis of God that few are able to penetrate. I am continually in His presence and the light courses through my veins. I can deny my needs, my wants, my desires, knowing that they have already been truly fulfilled. Yet also, I may indulge those needs without staining the soul. I can accept outside authority without distortion of my inner self. I am passive to God's will and intuitive to God's design. *Nefradaleth* is the key to that intuition.'

Isabella's eyes glazed over a little as she spoke, before focusing back on me, and waiting for my reaction.

'Why was Alonzo so concerned about the possibility of *Nefradaleth* ending up in the wrong hands?'

'Alonzo has less faith than I in the intuition of men's souls and their relationship with God. His real responsibility is not concerned with resolving the philosophical conflicts of monism or dualism but only with his guardianship of the journey of that discovery and its universal ferryman.'

'I don't understand.' I was wishing I had paid more attention to my Plato and Aristotle. 'What do you mean by the ferryman?'

'Time Michael, *time*! Alonzo is the Timekeeper. He is convinced that once all the *Voices* are gathered together then time will lose its ability to govern the journey of men's souls. Both the attraction and separation of God and matter, light and dark, will be lost. Chaos will reign. Again!'

'Is that possible?'

'You tell me, Michael. You are an intelligent man and a rational scientist pushing at the boundaries of knowledge. Have you enough faith in your ability to fully understand all of the ramifications and responsibilities of your work? By asking the question, if what I and more importantly, what Alonzo have already told you is possible then you have already accepted that it might be so. I do not concern myself unduly about the questions but accept whatever consequences will accrue.'

'Does that not worry you, Isabella?'

'No. Why should it? I have annihilated myself before God's will. If it is to be, it will be.'

I could feel the combination of hashish and champagne stripping away all of my reservations. Once again the sensation of utter relief was washing over me, only this time it threatened to drown me. Isabella was somebody I could talk to. I was desperate to open my soul, to be free, as she was. She must have sensed my longing and held out her hand. I took it. Tears were welling up in my eyes.

'I would so like to have found what you have, Isabella. In fact . . . Jesus, I hope I'm making some sense here. . .' I squeezed her hand tightly. 'I would like to be with you, body and soul, lust and love, passion and peace. *All of you!* I too would like to be annihilated, as you put it, by what you have: by what you are.'

'I think you are drunk, Michael.'

'*No, I'm not!* Well, perhaps a little. It's great pot.' Releasing her hand I leant forward to touch *Nefradaleth* again. 'All of a sudden I feel a tremendous clarity of purpose. Nothing else matters.'

'Nothing?'

Isabella asked as she stood up. Unravelling the towel she let her hair fall free before standing between my knees. She rested her hands on my shoulders and slowly leaning forward let her wet-ended hair drape over me. In one movement, she lifted *Nefradaleth's* chain over her head and let it slide down her hair to place it around my neck.

'The truth, Michael!'

'*Nothing!* I really mean it, Isabella. This is so important.' Isabella withdrew and stood watching me as I touched the stone that rested on my chest. It felt almost warm.

'What about your wife, your work?'

'I love Caroline. Don't get me wrong. We . . . We've a good

relationship. She's very strong and the best judge of people I know. I have leant on her far more than she ever has on me.'

'And yet you are here with me. Have you told her about me?'

'No.'

'Why not? Remember what we spoke about yesterday. Surely if this being here with me is important to you, she would understand. Nothing has happened between us.'

'I don't agree. I feel that something great has happened between us. I had hoped you felt the same.' It was difficult to keep the hurt from my voice. Isabella placed her finger on my lips.

'As it happens I do feel the same, Michael but I also want no part of a deceit. Be true to your heart. It will cause less pain in the end.'

'I was hoping to talk to Caroline this evening, before coming here, but she is in Mexico and I've had difficulty contacting her.'

'Why is she in Mexico?'

'Doing some work for the American Government.'

'Secret work?'

'Yes in a way. She's a counterfeit expert . . . Anyway I was waiting for a phone call from her but it never came. I had intended to tell her about you, Isabella and how important my feelings for you and Alonzo had become. I think, in fact I now know, that I have spent far too long compartmentalizing my responses, my emotions and have never allowed myself to be completely open about anything, particularly my needs. I always assumed it would cause conflict with Caroline so I held back. Afraid! Maybe, as you have pointed out, Caroline would understand. I don't really know. I have never asked. I have never wanted to put our . . . my concept of love to the real test.'

'Are you prepared to lose everything for your want of this freedom, for your want of me?'

'Yes . . . I think I am and it's not a fantasy. After talking with Alonzo and now with you, I have suddenly realized how infinitesimal my time, our time is, and that it is better to grasp the moment than pretend I can delay its mortal thread. I *am* now . . . and to embrace you is to embrace more than an ideal. It is a duty and a way of fulfilling that duty.'

'You are getting very profound, Michael. Is this your passage beyond the Pillars of Hercules?'

'I don't know, Isabella. Perhaps. The moral certainties and the reasoning I held dear are being very readily undermined.'

'I am not an idealist, Michael. The concept of a rigid unity of being or purpose has no attraction. There is good and there is evil, there is darkness and there is light, there is wisdom and there is ignorance, there is substance and there is chaos. What we make of these forces is for God to orchestrate both within and without us. I will not judge your desire to change only support its necessity. I will not have you covet me but will open your mind to the concept of a greater belonging. A greater love.'

At that point I was floating, in love and at peace with the world and myself. It was this clarity of determination that thrilled my every sense.

'I am ready.'

Isabella smiled as she began stroking my cheek with the rim of her champagne glass. She laughed an easy laugh, a compassionate laugh.

'You must need sex very badly to give it all away so easily.'

'It's not about sex, Isabella. Honestly. If . . . If that ever happens between us it will be a bonus. I just want the freedom of knowing you, truly knowing you.' My speech was slurring, my brain less clear.

'We will see.'

'What do you mean?'

Isabella stood up and in one whirling movement lifted the kaftan over her head. She was fully naked underneath with a slim body, small firm breasts and sculptured hips. There was little in the way of pubic hair. 'Take off your clothes, Michael and lie back.'

I did not feel strange in doing this and soon, naked and erect, I lay back on the couch. Completely exposed and yet completely safe.

Isabella came forward and lifted *Nefradaleth* from around my neck. I watched as she tilted the champagne glass and the bubbling liquid coursed down my chest and hastily indrawn stomach to circle the base of my pulsating penis.

'I want you to do something for me, Michael.'

'Anything, Isabella.'

'I am going to stand here and I want you to never take your eyes off me, no matter what happens or what you feel. Do you promise?'

I readily obeyed and locked my eyes on her as she began to move from side to side in a gentle rocking motion. At the same instant I thought I could feel a gentle breeze on my leg as if somebody was blowing on it. Isabella continued to move, her hands were circling up and down her body. Hair flowing, back arching, fingers delving. My head was spinning. I could feel a warm body slide beside me on the couch, holding my penis, mounting me, tight rocking movements, moist and warm, forward and back, forward and back.

'*Do not look away, Michael!* Watch me?

Isabella drew closer and closer, holding herself and my eyes. My heart was pounding, suffused. My ears ringing, confused. I was coming, too soon! Quicker movements, groaning noise, telephone ringing, impending explosion, implosion. Night closing in. The dancer disappeared.

'Isabella, *Isabellllla.*' I screamed and remembered little else.

When Caroline reached her room, she showered for a very long time. Eventually, after stepping out of the cubicle, she draped herself in a huge bathrobe and moving into the bedroom picked up the bedside phone and tried to get a connection to Spain, with no success. Annoyed, she lay down for a while on the bed and suddenly very tired, closed her eyes and was quickly asleep.

It was nearly 45 minutes later when she woke and, refreshingly alert, looked at her watch.

'Shit. It must be nearly 5.00 in the morning in Spain.'

She decided to telephone Michael anyway as she needed to talk to him. Their last conversation had left a pall of confusion hovering over her feelings. What did he mean by saying he had been doing some thinking?

'Thinking about what?' she said aloud as her hand probed around the floor for her electronic organizer. 'Where the hell is it?' she grunted before finally finding it under the bed. She wondered for a moment at what point it had fallen from her hand while she slept.

After locating Michael's number she lifted the receiver and dialled. This time there was a ringing tone, but no immediate answer. Caroline looked at her watch again. A sleepy voice came on the line.

'Halo. Hotel Palacio.'

'I am looking for Doctor Mara.' Caroline spoke in Spanish.

'Hold on.' There was a repeating dial sound that rang unanswered for two minutes. 'I am sorry Señora. There is no answer from his room.'

'Would you please check again? It is important,' she pleaded. 'I'm telephoning from Mexico.'

'Señora, it is nearly five in the morning here. He must be in a deep sleep.'

'Please try again. I'm his wife and I need to talk to him. I will wait.'

It was nearly ten minutes later when the receiver was picked up again. 'I am very sorry, Señora. Doctor Mara is not there.'

'Are you sure?'

'Of course. I went to his room. The bed has not been slept in. Perhaps he has friends in Granada or is travelling in the mountains. He told me yesterday that he likes mountains. We have beautiful mountains here,' the hotel voice said with awkward confidence.

Mountains my backside, Caroline thought as she struggled to restrain her annoyance. 'Maybe. I don't know. Thank you for your help. I'm sorry to have disturbed you.'

'It's not a problem. Will I leave a message that you telephoned?'

'Don't bother . . . No, please do. Thank you. Write in the message that I called and will be at home. 4.00 pm, Los Angeles time.'

'4.00 pm Los Angeles time. That's done.'

'Thank you again. Good night.'

'Good night, Señora Mara.'

The connection terminated.

'Fuck you, Michael!' She shouted at the phone as she next tried calling Rod Mallory's number in Los Angelus. It was answered by a male voice with a strong South American accent.

'Hello.'

'I'm looking for Rod. Is he there?'

'And who is looking, may I enquire?'

'It's Caroline Mara. Who are you? I want to speak to Rod.' Caroline shouted angrily down the line.

'Oh, Señora Mara. Rod said you might ring. My name is Roberto. I am a friend of Rod's from Belize.'

'Where is Rod?' she asked impatiently.

'He said to tell you that he has gone to Europe for a few days. Something to do with a Swiss deal. He said to say he was sorry to miss the tennis tournament but that you would understand. He will be back on Sunday.'

'That's a pity. Thanks Roberto. I'll probably get a chance to meet you in LA with Rod sometime and I'm sorry that I shouted down the phone.'

'It's no problem, Señora Mara. I will look forward to meeting you. Rod has told me a lot about you. You're like a sister to him, he said.'

'Good night, Roberto.'

'Good night, Señora Mara.'

The bedside radio-clock showed her that it was nearly 8.45.

'What shall I do? *What shall I doooo?*' Caroline muttered as she got off the bed and paced across the room. She moved to the wardrobe and pulled the slide-door a little way along its track. Hesitating, she peered into the darkness for a moment, before shaking her head and fully sliding back the door. The automatic wardrobe light flickered on. Her hand moved to one of the hangers, and she gently rocked it back and forth. Suddenly the rail attachment mechanism accidentally released itself and the black cocktail dress, it had supported, fell in a heap on the floor.

As Caroline stooped to pick up the crumpled dress she caught her reflection in the full-length corridor mirror. She looked at her half-crouched image for a long time, then rose to her full height. She unravelled the dress from the hanger and held it against her chest.

'Come on old girl. Snap out of it. Go for it! If Michael can be sneaking about so can you. Where the hell is he, anyway?'

She spoke to her reflection before crossing the room and laying the dress out on the bed. Clapping her hands and rubbing them together for further encouragement she let the towelling-robe, she had been wearing, fall to the ground. Now naked, she danced on tiptoes across to the bathroom and, humming to herself, entered the shower cubicle again. Her shower was quickly taken, this time, and after drying herself off she brushed on a light make-up foundation and some pale eye shadow before pursing her lips to apply a very light pink lipstick.

Satisfied, Caroline began to brush her hair turning this way and that to admire her shape in the full-length but slightly misted bathroom mirror. As a final manoeuvre she held her hands under her firm breasts and after a brief and reassuring elevation let the breasts fall back to their natural position. A quick squeeze of one nipple was met by an instant response.

'Way to go sweetheart! We're in good shape!' she said happily.

Returning to the bedroom she chose and pulled on a new pair of silk panties and in one movement slipped the simple cocktail dress over her head. It was a tight but near perfect fit and with just a minor adjustment required to the position of her unsupported breasts she was pleased with how it looked. Her satisfied smile changed somewhat after stepping into her shoes.

'Blast it. They're not quite right. I should have brought a different pair.' Caroline was still talking to her feet when the phone rang. 'Oh shit! Too late, girl, to do anything about it now though.' she shouted aloud as she looked at the clock on the bedside table. It was exactly 9.00. She sat down on the bed, still talking to her self. 'Take it easy, don't appear too anxious.' Or too easy, she thought. She lifted the receiver.

'Hello.'

'Caroline.'

'Yes, Diego.'

'Are you still available for dinner?'

'I'm really not sure, Diego. I'm very tired and I might not be very good company.' Caroline smiled at herself in the mirror as she stood up and half-turned to ensure that the fall of her dress across her bottom was smooth.

'Please, Caroline. You would do me a great honour.'

'Well if you put it like that Diego, how could I refuse? I am hungry.'

'Magnifico! That's great! I will meet you at the restaurant bar in say, ten minutes. Would that be okay? I know how you ladies like to take time getting prepared.'

'Do you now? I'm so glad to be in the hands of such an expert. I will be down in five. I'm not planning to go to much trouble.'

Caroline put the phone down. Returning to the bathroom she put on a simple pair of black pearl pendant-earrings and complimented this with three simple gold bands on her right wrist. Removing her watch and rings she placed them in her slim shoulder strap Chanel bag and as a final flourish liberally dabbed perfume to her neck and wrists and to the cleavage of her breasts.

She was just about to lock the door of the room when she stopped and rushed back to the bedside telephone. Picking it up, she dialled Michael's hotel number again. The connection to Spain was quick.

'Halo. Hotel Palacio.' It was the same voice. Awake this time.

'It's Señora Mara again. Has my husband returned yet?'

'No. I am sorry, Señora Mara.'

'Fine. Please tell him I called. Good night.'

Caroline looked at the phone for a long time before slowly replacing the receiver. Locking the door behind her she initially waited for the elevator to come but then decided to walk down instead.

Commander Diego Rios was waiting at the bar. He was wearing a white linen suit with the merest hint of silver silk thread within its weave. With a small cigar dangling from his lips and a glint in the steel-blue eyes he reminded her of Robert

Redford in Butch Cassidy and the Sundance Kid. Seeing her approach he shot out of his stool and rushed to meet her.

'You look sensational, Caroline. I will be the envy of every man here.'

That worried her somewhat. Most of that evening's diners had already deserted the bar and she tried glancing over his shoulder into the dining room. There was no obvious sign of any of the others and she assumed that they must have headed for town as planned. She was relieved.

'Thank you, Diego.'

'I hope you don't mind, but the maître d'hôtel is a good friend and he has kindly arranged a table for us in one of the private balcony dining rooms. It has a spectacular view and the music filters up without intrusion. Would that be acceptable?'

'Yes. Perfect.'

Caroline was relieved at the privacy afforded by the arrangement as she followed Diego and the headwaiter along a side passage to a small door near the end. Climbing a short set of marble stairs they stepped onto a balcony that had been decorated with overflowing vases of different coloured roses. Petals were scattered across the floor as if they had been windblown. The dining table looked out over the bay and she could hear the waves crashing onto the rocks nearby.

Diego moved towards the table and after removing a already opened magnum of champagne from a nearby ice bucket, began to fill the crystal flutes he held in his left hand.

'Dom Perignon Brut Rose. 1982. I hope you like it.' He smiled as he proffered the half-filled flute.

Caroline accepted the glass and moving to the balcony looked out over the sea. The fragrant nose of the champagne wafted upwards. She sipped the pale crimson liquid and let it bubble across her tongue. The Mexican was watching her closely.

'They must pay the commanders of the Federal Police very well to afford all this, Diego.' She smiled.

'I'm owed many favours, and have a very creative accountant. This . . .' He waved his hand across the room like a frontier farmer. 'This I will hide deep in my expense account, although no man in his right mind would want to hide you, Caroline.'

She blushed. In the background, music of blended Arabic voice and Spanish guitar was haunting the night air. Accepting the chair that the waiter held out for her, she sat looking at the rising moon.

'The music is lovely. What is it?'

'Listen to the words, Caroline.' He looked directly at her as he repeated and simultaneously translated the song:

'Vivire para besarte. . . I live to kiss you
vivire para besarte . . . I live to kiss you
acariciar tu cuerpo . . . to caress your body
para poder amarte . . . so that I can love you
tu eres primito . . . you are the fountain
la fuente donde yo bebo . . . I drink from . . .'

His voice faded and Caroline found herself blushing even more. Rios had noticed.

'It is from the combined talents of Rocio Alcala and Juan Martin on his album *El Alquimista*. I could not trust the hotel trio to replicate it and, as I wanted to express my sentiments, I arranged for the CD to be played.'

'Are you an alchemist then, Diego?'

'The only mystery about me, Caroline is a complete inability to dance. I say that in case you are wondering why I am not sweeping you off into a rumba. Nothing like trodden toes to ruin a perfectly good evening.' He laughed, disarmingly.

She laughed as well, and remembering her earlier annoyance at the lack of choice in shoe selection, she now decided to slip them off to savour the coolness of the marble flooring against her feet.

'I'm famished. What will we have to eat, Diego?'

'If you do not mind taking the risk, will you allow me choose for both of us?'

'In for a penny, in for a pound!'

'What did you say, Caroline?'

'Oh . . . nothing. It's just an expression. Please go ahead and choose for both of us. I am now in your capable hands.'

While he studied the menu her attention was momentarily distracted by the crashing noise of a large wave pounding against the rocks below the balcony. As she leant forward to look down over the railing towards the water she did not notice the slight twitch at the angle of Diego's thin-lipped smile.

'The fish served here is some of the best in the country but, and I know it is not very Mexican, the head chef makes the greatest southern fried chicken with mashed red-skinned potatoes that you are ever likely to taste. I would recommend it. There is also a surprise dessert you must try.'

'That will be fine. I like dessert, so no first course for me. I have my figure to consider.' she said with the right amount of self-depreciation.

'What nonsense? You will never have to worry about the way you look, Caroline! If you will forgive my bluntness I think you are beautiful and I love the perfume you are wearing. The perfect scent for a beautiful night.'

So much for subtlety, she thought. 'Enough of the compliments, you charmer!' Caroline could not help blushing again at his directness. 'The atmosphere in here is already heady enough and I might get carried away on its promise. Tell me more about your work, Diego.'

'Talking about work is boring. I would rather talk about you.' He put down the menu.

'Do you mean, that your type of work couldn't possibly be of interest to a mere woman?' She teased him with a taunting smirk. 'Do you have a problem with my involvement in the meeting, Diego? Am I threat to a cosy male cartel?'

'No. *Of course not!* I did not mean to imply that at all.' It was his turn to be somewhat uncomfortable. 'It is just that, talking about our work is too much like business, and tomorrow morning we will have to return to it. Tonight, I thought that we, you and I, could forget the ugly underworld we are involved in and instead enjoy the beautiful opportunities of the other aspects of our lives. These are some of the rare moments in paradise that two people can share, in blissful ignorance of the world beneath.'

'You really *are* a serpentine charmer, Diego. I will need to be very careful in this Garden of Eden.' She smiled at him. 'I think I'll have an apple for dessert.'

'What? Why?'

'I'm just joking.'

'Oh, I see.'

Caroline knew that he hadn't, at least not fully, but for many reasons it did not seem to matter any more. She relaxed and decided to let the atmosphere between them determine its own course and with that decision, she could feel the champagne and the potent red wine that Diego had chosen, washing away many of her remaining inhibitions and caution. As the dinner plates were being cleared she found herself looking out over the balcony again. The moon was much higher in the sky and much brighter.

If Michael is prepared to throw caution to the wind then there was no damn reason why she couldn't. 'No damn reason at all! Sauce for the goose, sauce for the gander,' she murmured as her foot suddenly touched Diego's. Caroline felt a shiver of excitement in the pit of her stomach before she quickly moved her leg from beneath the table and pretended to rub away an imaginary itch. She waited and then watched as he shuffled his chair closer and bent down to gently lift her leg.

'You have beautiful ankles, Caroline,' he whispered as he pulled a rose petal out from the space between two of her toes and showed it to her. He used this to gently brush the dust from the sole and, while looking at her closely, rested her foot on his chair between his legs.

She did not withdraw her foot and instead, arched the toes forward to move slowly and rhythmically against his crotch. She could feel his penis bulging beneath the linen cloth of his suit and she used her toes to delve below the underside of its hardness.

Diego was about to say something when the young waiter

suddenly entered and immediately interrupted the mood and the opportunity.

Caroline quickly withdrew her leg from its nest between his legs and gave a slight cough as the waiter began to hoover the crumbs off the tablecloth. Rios's face flared at the unwelcome disturbance and in a torrent of abusive language began to berate the cowering boy.

'Wow!' Caroline spoke in a louder than necessary fashion to stop him. 'That wine was very powerful, Diego. My head is spinning. What was it?'

'A 1991 Caymus Cabernet. I'll order some more,' he said, expansively.

'Oh no! I have had more than enough.'

His anger dissipated as quickly as it had risen and he waved away the relieved waiter with an instruction to bring their desserts. 'Once again I must apologise for my behaviour. It is my Latin temperament! I get too passionate at times. I just wanted everything to be perfect tonight.'

'I would not see that as a fault. You are quite a connoisseur?' Caroline touched his hand.

'You mean the champagne and the wine?'

'Yes.'

'I have a small confession to make.' He held his hands up and a boyish grin softened his features.

'What is it?'

'I hope you won't think me ignorant, but I did cheat a little. I love wine but can never remember one vineyard or vintage from another. I either like it or I don't and I asked my friend, the maître d'hôtel, to choose.'

'Does that apply to women as well?'

'No! Never! With women I remember everything. Their clothes, their scent, their private noises, and the way they move and like to be moved. Everything!' He pushed out his chair and half-crouched, pulled it around the table closer to hers.

'It sounds like there have been many.'

'None as special as you, Caroline.'

The young waiter returned with the desserts.

Diego ignored him and let his hand slowly drift downwards beneath the table. He watched for her reaction as he found and then began to stroke the inner side of her thigh. For a moment she returned his look but then closed her eyes. Her breathing quickened and she began to inhale in rapid short bursts.

The waiter couldn't hide his embarrassment and Caroline opened her eyes as he fumbled, when placing the plate in front of her. She smiled up at him and he nodded nervously before turning quickly and rushing to leave the room. Looking down, the deserts seemed more like a cocktail than a dessert. In each crystal bowl, a small scoop of crème-fresh ice cream floated on a generous pool of blue Curacao liqueur.

Content with their proximity, Diego's fingers began to glide around her thigh and move higher and higher towards the moist warmth of her groin.

She pressed her pelvis forward to allow him enter, her thigh pushed out against his. She felt his fingers slipping beneath the loose folds of the silk pants she had chosen to wear.

She dipped a finger in the pool of liqueur and tasted it.

'Wow! More alcohol, Diego?'

'These are very special desserts, Caroline. The liqueur will wash away any lingering taste of cayenne and allow the tongue to enjoy all other sensations again.'

She hardly heard his words as she felt his fingers suddenly delve deep to finally find and tease their target. Her whole body felt as if it was about to melt. She could feel the spasms beginning and was fighting for air.

With a sudden and loud exhalation Caroline pulled her legs together and pushed back her chair. 'Phew! It's very hot, Diego. Excuse me for a moment please. I need to use the powder room.'

'I understand.' He smiled, as he smelled the tips of his released fingers. Pushing his chair back, he stood up and coming around behind Caroline, held out hers.

Shakily getting to her feet, she managed to compose herself a little before walking barefoot towards the narrow passageway, where the waiter had earlier indicated that the restrooms were situated.

As she reached the top of a small flight of steps, she felt the power drain from her legs and, out of Diego's line of view, had to lean heavily against the passageway wall to prevent tumbling down. She rested there for a moment, breathing deeply, then descended the steps and found the restroom doorway. She pushed heavily against it and as it swung open, was relieved to find that the toilet cubicle was directly ahead. She entered quickly and locking the door behind her, sat down.

'What are you doing, girl?' she asked the vague reflection in the green gloss paint of the door.

What I want to! she thought. This type of opportunity for abandoned excitement had presented itself before and she had declined. Why had she bothered? she wondered. She was sick and tired of patiently waiting for Michael to change his priorities and of the fall off in physical affection he showed her. She wanted to feel that excitement again, even if it was only for a short time. She wanted to feel herself desired, ravished. What harm would it do? She rationalised. There was a red-blooded Mexican waiting to take her and she wanted to be taken. She'd make sure he took precautions.

Her hands rested between her legs as she leant back against the cistern, breathing slowly. She could suddenly feel the warmth. Her toes arched against the cold tiled-floor. The spasms began again and this time she didn't stop them, couldn't stop them.

'Oh God! *Oh Goddddddd!*' she cried, as their intensity doubled her forward. She collapsed across her knees.

It was some time before she could safely stand up. She left the cubicle and moved to the washbasin. After freshening herself up, she checked and rechecked her appearance in the mirror, applied a liberal sprinkling of perfume and returned to join Diego at their table.

He looked concerned as he stood up and came forward to meet her. 'Are you ok, Caroline? You were a long time and I was worried. You look flushed!' He held out his hand.

'I'm fine, Diego. Much better now, in fact.' She took his hand and allowed him to guide her back to her chair. He waited until she sat down before returning to his own chair, which during her absence she noticed, he had moved back to its original position. The ice cream desert had all but melted yet the taste was still superb and with renewed relish, she finished it all.

'How do you feel, Caroline?'

'I *feeeeel* great, Diego. What a wo . . . wonderful night.' Caroline felt pleasantly drunk again and slurred some of the words.

'Tell me about your husband, Caroline?' he asked.

'Must we talk about him? Michael is probably out sha . . . shagging a frustrated Spanish lab-rat with big tits, as we speak. Bunsen burners instead of candlelight! No, that's unfair of me. He . . . he has probably talked himself out of the opportunity. Poor man!'

'You don't sound happy?'

'No, that's not true. We are happy, in a way. I love Michael but he doesn't do it for me anymore. Sexually I mean. Isn't . . . isn't that really sad?'

'I cannot understand why, Caroline. You really are so beautiful.'

'Thank you, Diego, you . . .you're a real man.' She suddenly pushed back her chair and stood up to lean across the table and kiss the Mexican on the lips. Immediately her tongue slipped into his mouth and began to explore. He responded and she could feel his hands on her breasts before, to his very obvious surprise, she withdrew and flopped back into her seat.

'God. I feel so dizzy . . . randy but dizzy.'

'Come, Caroline. I think you have had enough to drink. I'll bring you back to your room.' He stood up.

Caroline waited for Diego to walk around. As she stood up, she leant heavily on his arm. Turning towards him she placed her free hand on his still bulging trousers and whispered into his ear.

'No, my Mexican lover. Take me to yours,' she slurred.

'Are you sure?'

'Very.'

By the time they had stepped into the elevator Caroline could feel the warmth in her pelvis rising again. Once the doors closed she watched his reflection in the polished mirrors and followed his eyes as his hand moved between her buttocks. Separating her legs slightly to allow him, she smiled mischievously as she watched his face change when he suddenly realised that she had discarded her silk pants.

The spasms came quickly as the requested floor arrived and the doors opened. Reluctantly she moved forward onto the corridor while he kept his hand where it was, toying with her. Reaching the door of his room, Caroline struggled to insert the key card he had handed to her. On the third try, she succeeded and once inside the room, turned and began to fumble at the buckle of his trousers belt. She couldn't understand how uncoordinated her movements were. Her head was spinning.

Diego Rios suddenly grabbed at her hands and holding the wrists pushed her away from him. 'Not so fast, Caroline. I want to savour these moments for a while. Stand over there against the bed with your back to me.' He closed the door behind them.

She glared at him in mock defiance, turned and staggered towards the bed. She leant forward slightly to lean on the end board and looked back over one shoulder to watch him watching her.

'Like this, lover?'

'Yeah. Now take off your clothes for me. *Slowly,*' he demanded.

With a shaking hand she pulled the thin straps of her dress over her shoulders until she could lift out her arms. Swaying from side to side she then used one hand to tug at the hem of the dress until it just began to slide over her skin. Her breasts were suddenly free. She kept her back to him and placed her hands on her head. She enjoyed performing for him. With alternating rising and dropping movements of her hips she was able to make the dress slither down her body and legs until it finally lay in a discarded heap on the ground. Kicking the dress away, her hands then came to rest on her buttocks, gently prising them apart so that he could see all of her.

'Did you like that, Diego?' She smiled back at him.

'Very professional.'

'You have only seen a glimpse of my skills.'

'Show me more.'

She turned slowly and walked towards him. Stopping about a hair's breadth away she leant forward and began tracing the line of his mouth with her tongue. He pushed forward sucking at her lips, biting at her tongue. Her hands had dropped and were moving slowly up the inside of his thighs. She could feel his erection trying to burst itself free.

His hands were now struggling with his belt.

She grabbed his wrists and suddenly jerked them away. 'I'll do that lover. It's my turn!'

She undid the belt and slowly pulled down the zip of his trousers. Releasing the top clasp, she inserted her hands between the skin and the material of his shorts and clumsily began tugging at them. His erection sprang free as she quickly pulled the shorts over it and downwards towards the ground. His trousers followed suit to fall about his ankles. Looking up at him from her crouched position her tongue darted out to lick the underside of his penis. She straightened up, pausing to squeeze his testicles as his throbbing cock pushed against her skin.

Diego Rios was in a desperate hurry to pull his shirt off. Buttons popped and flew like bullets across the room. He pulled at her hair forcing her head back down to take him in her mouth.

Caroline obliged and watched him with upturned eyes as she teased and licked the pink exposed tip before opening her mouth to draw in the shaft. Her hands massaged the lifted testicles, running back and forth to the rim of his anus. His back arched, his breath came in short bursts. She kept it going until he seemed about to ejaculate.

'Sancta Maria!' he cried.

She pulled away and standing up turned back towards the bed. 'Hardly.' She smiled as she took his hand. 'Did you like that, Diego?'

'If you fuck as good as you suck woman, then I am a lucky man,' he said coarsely.

She glanced back at him. The coarseness excited her even more. She increased the rhythm of the movements of her hips so that her firm buttocks began to rise and fall in time with her breathing.

He moved in closer. His hands began at her neck and tightened and squeezed in a downward descent. He found her again and began to tease the skin apart.

Her legs separated as she felt the building orgasm. It came quickly, wet, and then built again. He was pulling at her folds. Her knees began to buckle.

'Quick, Diego. Quick. Take me! Fuck me now!' she pleaded.

'Good things come to those who wait, *bitch!*'

He stepped back as he spoke and bending down retrieved the thick leather belt from his trousers on the floor. He hung it around his neck as he slowly stood up, running his hands along the inside of her thighs. He watched her quiver to his touch. Suddenly his hands moved to her breasts, crushing the soft tissue back against her ribs. He plunged violently into her from behind, his weight grinding her down against the bed. Caroline could feel the spasms cascading over her in one wave after another. She put her hand back and pulled at his hair.

'Deeper. Go deeper!'

'Like this, you gringo slut?' He pulled away her hand.

'Yes! Oh God, Diego. *Yesssssssssss!*' she cried.

'You like it like that, don't you, whore! Bark for me like the bitch in heat you are.' He suddenly withdrew and pulled the belt from around his neck. Swinging it in a wide arc he slashed her hard with the buckle end across the skin of her bottom. The mark of the metal was instantly imprinted with a bleeding weal.

Caroline felt all sensations of pleasure suddenly evaporate. She was left with just the pain. She cried out as she turned to look at him. 'Jesus, Diego, that hurt. What the *fuck* did you do that for.'

'Shut up, whore!' he shouted as he pushed into her again.

His movements became more and more brutal. Her breasts were hurting with the vice hold he had across her chest with his left hand. He was hurting her. She felt another searing pain scorch across her back. She managed to pull his hand off her breasts but suddenly found her head snapping back. With his now free hand he was tugging at her hair. One of her earrings tore through the skin of her ear lobe as she shook her head trying to free herself. He bit into her neck. Caroline screamed.

'*Diego! Stop it!* You're hurt –'

'Shut up, you slut. Take your fucking like the *bruja* you are.'

His hand now came around to suddenly cover her mouth and nose. She was very frightened. She could not breathe and tried to pull away from him. He was still in her, driving her down, not letting her free. She felt him come. He went deeper and deeper. Her skin was tearing. She tried hitting back with her elbow. She bit at his hand. There was suddenly a noose around her neck. It tightened. She needed to breathe. Her head was spinning. She wanted to vomit. She could feel her urine running out as the darkness came.

The video-telephone link was of poor quality. The man pulled the jeep over to the side of the road. Trucks heading for the border roared past.

'*Ali baik salaam*' The voice link cackled.

'*Akzabti.*'

'Who wishes to use our shade?'

'Is it done?'

'Not yet. It is set up for tomorrow night.'

'And the hourglass.'

'Will be on its way by courier to Corsica the day after.'

'Good. We are very pleased.'

'It is our duty to the inheritor of Kaya Rudbari.'

'You will find great reward in heaven.'

'Allah will not begrudge an earthly reward as well.'

'Of course. It is already lodged.'

'Shukran, Sahib al-Sa'igh.'

'Ahlan wa sahlan, Sahib al-Sirr.'

Caroline was not sure whether what she was feeling was part of a dream or reality. There was movement, pain and noise. Somebody was violently shaking her awake and shouting in her ear.

'*Wake up, you bitch*,' the voice screamed.

She flickered-open her eyes to find that the light hurt her. She couldn't focus. Who was talking to her? What had happened? She didn't remember anything.

'*Wake up, you bitch*,' the voice screamed again.

She was lying face down on a bed. What place was this? There was a taste of vomit in her mouth and soiled sheets about her head. She couldn't move her hands.

'Where am I? Where are my clothes? Is that you Diego?' Caroline had to spit out a plug of blood-stained food before she could shout the words.

'Yes, whore.'

'Why are you speaking like that, Diego? Why am I tied up? Why am I so confused?'

'Rohypnol in the dessert, bitch. Your brain and ass were roched, as it were. Ha Ha.'

'Why? Why are you doing this?' she shouted.

'*Shut the fuck up, whore.*' He rolled her over on the bed so that she was looking up at him. 'Tell me about your husband's work with the American army.'

'What?' She wanted to move her hands to cover her breasts and pubic area but couldn't. Her wrists were tied behind her. She struggled but the chords or wires holding her just cut deeper into her skin. She started crying. 'I don't know anything about work he has done for the army.'

'You're lying!'

'I'm not. I swear. Oh God I don't know anything. Please stop hurt –'

Her pleading was interrupted when Rios leant down, grabbed her hair with his left hand and jerked her head backwards. His face was a sweating mask of hatred. She could feel the retching begin again. He had a half-smoked cigarette in the other hand and was bringing its crimson tip closer and closer to her eyes.

'Tell me.'

'I don't –' She screamed as he suddenly pulled the cigarette away from her eyelid and buried it into the flesh of her cheek. She could smell the burning flesh. She wanted him to stop. He must stop hurting her. 'I . . . Please stop hurting me, Diego. . . I only heard of one name. A General Arnold. I swear.'

'I don't believe you, bitch. Make it easier for yourself and tell me about the Mara Stealth Virus.'

'The what? I don't know anything, Diego. Please. Pleassssse!'

She screamed again as he held the cigarette close over the skin of her right breast. She could feel the heat getting more intense as he circled it towards her. All of a sudden he stopped and looked down at her for a moment, as if thinking about what to do next. The hard facial features softened and the voice grew kinder. He pulled back the cigarette and with his other hand began pinching her nipple gently, until it was engorged.

'Do you know, Caroline, that when the Spanish arrived in this part of the world they thought they would find the fabled race of Amazons? You know the legend about the Amazons, Caroline? Don't you?'

Rios suddenly and violently pressed the cigarette into the flesh of her right breast.

Caroline screamed again with the searing pain. 'Noooooooo . . . please!'

'It is said that they removed the right breast at puberty so that its full development would not interfere with their ability to draw a bow.' He pressed the cigarette into another spot. 'Tell me about the virus your husband has developed for the Americans.'

'I don't know. Oh God. I don't know. Help me please. *Somebody help.*'

Caroline continued screaming as the blonde Mexican burnt

her more and more. She wanted to die. She couldn't fight the pain any more. Then it suddenly stopped. Rios turned away.

'Shit. I don't think she knows anything,' he said, annoyed.

'The Sheila must know something mate.'

'Unlikely. I've hurt her fairly bad.'

Rios was speaking to somebody else! There was another person in the room. She knew the voice. Caroline turned her head and tried looking up. Her eyes were nearly closed with the bruising caused by her struggle. She cried out in a weak and plaintive voice.

'Rod . . . Is that you, Rod. Oh, thank God. You have come to save me, Rod. Thank God. Help me, Rod. *Roooddd please help me!*'

'What shall I do with her?' Rios was standing over her again.

'Kill her, mate. I don't want the Sheila fingering us. No trace. Understand. A bullet to the brain. Nice and quick.'

'But this is my room! I will be suspected.'

There was a long pause. Caroline could just make out a shadow moving across the room.

'I know, mate.'

'What–'

She watched as Rios turned to look at the approaching figure of Rod Mallory. Suddenly his head jerked back and there was a muffled *sphattt* sound. Tissue and blood sprayed over her from a fist-sized exploding hole in the back of his head and the Mexican policeman was catapulted back, to land across her chest. His collapsing weight forced the breath from her lungs. She had difficulty inhaling and began gasping.

'Oh . . . Oh thank God! Get him off me, Rod. *Get him off.*' Caroline screamed as Diego's body jerked in spasm. One hand finally came to rest on her leg. 'Please hurry. I'm going to puke again. I can't breathe.'

'Sorry, sweetheart but I'm going to have to find a new tennis partner. Shame really. You banged Commander Rios there, like a dunny door. Even I felt like joining in.'

Rod's shadow hovered over her.

'Oh, God no. Not you, Rod. *Nooooooo . . .*' Caroline closed her eyes as the gun discharged.

It was dark, yet flashes of light illuminated the space where I lay. Somebody was shouting, somebody was calling my name.

'Michael, Doctor Mara. Wake up. Wake up.'

My head was pounding and as I tried to sit up the dizziness took over. The flashes of light hurt my eyes.

'Where am I?'

'Near your hotel outside the old cafe.'

It was a girl's voice. American accent. I tried focusing on the face that hovered over me. Hers or somebody's hands were pulling at me.

'How did I get here? What happened?'

'You don't remember anything? You passed out in the apartment and Isabella wanted you to sleep it off. I brought you back here in my car.'

'Is that you Zoë? I can hardly make you out.'

'Yes, Michael. Apparently a mixture of champagne and pot and you're anybody's. Now come on. We'd better get some coffee in you.'

'Where's Isabella?'

'She had to take an early flight from Granada to Madrid. I dropped her at the airport before coming here. She will be back tomorrow. A conference I think.'

'I need to talk to her.'

'She told me to tell you that you and she will meet in a quiet moment again. Whatever that means!'

'What time is it, Zoë?'

'Nearly 6.30.'

'In the morning?'

'Of course. Now come on. Stand on your feet.'

A hazy image of an angry Bob Arnold, his thick-set face glaring at me, suddenly seared into my confusion. I tried to focus on my surroundings. The smell of freshly ground coffee was coming from a small 24-hour café that I recognized as being the one near my hotel. I'd been in there before. I searched my pockets, in an almost flea-bitten frenzy of moving hands, for my wallet and cell phone. Both were still there. The cell phone was still turned on but I could not remember whether I had followed Bob's instructions before I had left the Hotel. It seemed a very long time ago.

'You were there, Zoë, last night. It was you who made . . . eh . . . when Isabella was dancing.'

'It was me who made what, Michael?' she asked as she strong-armed me from the car and across the pavement to stumble through the door of the café.

I sat down at an unoccupied table. The few other patrons present stared in my direction. They, sober, were about to start a day's work whereas I, in abusing their hospitality and morning peace, was another over indulgent layabout tourist.

'Last night when Isabella was dancing. You were there with me. We made love . . . I think.'

'Ha! Ha! In your dreams, my American friend! I think you had better stick to lemonade and coffee in the future. Hold on, I'll just get yours. Sugar?'

'Thanks. Two please.'

While she went to the counter I opened out the cell phone and dialled in the instructions that Bob Arnold had given. I pressed the redial button and left it on the table.

'Here is your coffee.' Zoë looked down at the phone as she brought the steaming cup of coffee to the table. She was suddenly agitated. 'I must go now. I'm sure you will be alright from here.'

'Zoë . . .' She was gone.

I was sitting there for about 20 minutes nursing both coffee and confusion when everybody in the café looked up as three men with short haircuts and large dark glasses walked in. The morning sunlight was not that bright on this side of the street.

'Doctor Mara?' the first of the men to walk up to my table asked.

'Yes.'

'I am colleague of Bob Arnold. He was very anxious about you. You need to come with us?'

'I need this coffee more. Rough night. You know how it is.'

'Yeah right. Where the fuck, have you been? We've been searching for you for two days.' The man barked.

'What?' I was puzzled. My head throbbed. I looked at my watch. 'What day is it?' I asked quietly. I couldn't focus on the date.

'Friday, 7 September.'

'*Friday* . . . but that means I've been gone for two days. Where? I don't remember.'

'Who the fuck knows?' The man looked agitated.

'I *want* to know!' I shouted, banging my hand down on the table. The cell phone fell to the floor.

'I understand Doctor Mara, but we need to go, *now*.'

The man leant down and lifting the cell phone turned off the power, before slipping it into his pocket. While one of the three men remained near the door, the talking haircut and his silent second lifted me to my feet. I did not protest. The other café patrons nodded approvingly.

Gallicinium

COCK CROW

Granada, Spain.
7 September 2001

The hotel lobby was deserted except for the hovering haircuts. They were impatient men and had literally dragged me to the room, forced me into the shower, helped me pack and brought me back down to the lobby. I pressed down on the antique brass reception bell, and when there was no immediate response, did so again before Karl – the chief haircut had reluctantly told me his name – took matters in hand himself. A sleepy Pedro emerged from the reception office and walked unsteadily to the counter.

'*Doctor Mara*. You were missing. Everyone in the hotel was worried. We notified the police.' Pedro looked at the dark-suited men standing in the lobby.

'I want to check out, Pedro. I need my bill please.'

Pedro looked at his watch and then up at the lobby clock to confirm his discomfort.

'But it is only 7.20, *in the morning*!'

'I know Pedro, but I have to go. It's urgent.'

'I am sorry, Doctor Mara, but the receptionist does not start until 8.00. I am not allowed. You will have to wait.'

Big Karl pushed me aside and launched into a tirade in

Spanish, most of which I couldn't understand. In the end I didn't need to, as the impact on the hapless night porter was obvious and by the time Karl had vented his fury, Pedro was quivering. He agreed to get the receptionist to forward the account to my office.

I felt sorry for him, and opening my wallet extracted enough for a more than generous tip. All resistance melted.

'Thank you, Doctor Mara.' Pedro glared at Karl before smiling back at me. 'Are you ok?'

'Yes. These are friends.'

He raised his eyebrows. 'I hope you have a good trip. Please come back and stay with us again.'

'I certainly will, Pedro. Thank you.'

'Doctor Mara. We need to go, *now*!' Karl was pulling at my arm. I shrugged it off but followed him out of the lobby. The other haircuts, adjusted their glasses, and murmured into their suit lapels. It was only then that I noticed the almost invisible earpieces. They fell in behind me, one of them reluctantly carrying my hastily packed luggage. I held onto my rucksack.

'Oh, Doctor Mara. Wait please!' Pedro came rushing from behind the counter and, using his bulk to barge my escorts aside, up to my side. He held out an envelope for me to take. 'This arrived for you late last night. I was going to give it to the police today.'

'Thank you,' I said as I took the envelope from him and inspected it. Only my name, written in fine calligraphic style, appeared on the surface.

'Also, your wife telephoned two nights ago, twice in fact, about 5.00 in the morning. She sounded very upset when you were not in your room. I told her you might be away walking in the mountains. I didn't have a number to call her about you being missing and I think the police were going to try and contact her through your embassy in Madrid.'

'Thank you, Pedro.' I put the envelope in my inside pocket. 'Did she leave a message? My wife.'

'She just said she would be back in Los Angeles in the late afternoon. You are to contact her at home.'

'Thanks again, Pedro. Good bye.'

The government haircuts ushered me into a large black Volvo sedan with darkened glass windows. I was left alone in the back seat with just the driver and one of the agents in the car. I saw him searching beneath the seat and retrieving a machine pistol, which he lay across his lap, one finger hovering near the trigger mechanism. The driver looked back at me, then turned to his compatriot.

'Point that hardware the other way, Dave. I've no fucking desire to be the unlucky victim of friendly fire caused by a Spanish pothole.'

The agent in the passenger seat smiled and made a gesture of aiming the barrel back at me before pointing it at the door side panel. The driver checked his mirrors before pulling out after another blacked-out van, into which all of the other haircuts had disappeared. The streets were quiet and red lights ignored.

I reached into my pocket and retrieved the envelope. I opened it as quietly as I could, extracted and unfolded the letter, and began to read:

"*Dear Michael,*

'By the time you read this I will probably be already . . ."

'Stop the car!' I shouted.

'What's up, Doc?' Dave, the agent in the passenger seat, turned around. 'Jesus, Doctor Mara. You look like death.'

My hand was shaking uncontrollably and the letter was flapping like a trapped butterfly. 'I need to puke. Stop the car!'

There was burst of radio chatter and the Volvo slowed to a halt near a small area of shrubbery. I pushed out the door and even before I could exit the car I was retching viciously. I forced myself out onto the roadway, to the margin of the baking asphalt. What had been in my stomach soon came up to spray a small lizard and drive it from its shade. I rested there, bent-double and sucking in air, for a few minutes until slowly straightening and returning to the car.

As I approached, the front passenger's window wound down and Dave's face peered out.

'Are you ok?'

His concern seemed genuine.

'Yes. We have to make a stop. It's vital,' I said as I wiped my mouth with the back of my sleeve.

'No can do, Doctor Mara. Our orders –'

'Fuck your orders, Dave. We either make the stop or you leave me here. Dead or alive I don't care.'

There was another clatter of radio talk. The van backed up and Karl came storming across to where I stood. I gave him Alonzo's address, adding the same ultimatum.

'Very well. Ten minutes tops! Do you understand?'

'Yes.' I nodded and crawled back into the car. Karl held the door open and leant in. His face, about four inches from mine, had an almost serene sneer creasing it.

'By the way. If there is to be a choice of kidnap or us taking you out, then we are sanctioned to do it. Do you understand that, Doctor Mara?'

'What?' The door slammed shut and the car started up again. Dave turned back to look at me.

'Those are our instructions. You must be very important.' He handed me a clean handkerchief.

'Thanks. I'm sorry about earlier.'

'Part of the job. Let's go, Hal.' Dave pointed to the departing van ahead of us.

The driver nodded his head slightly, eyes firmly fixed on the rear-view mirror as he pulled out. Dave kept his hand on his gun.

We travelled in silence until the Volvo pulled up outside Alonzo's address. I could see that the door of his house was open. I wanted to rush out but couldn't as the central locking was engaged. The van had stopped ahead of us and I watched as agents jumped out and moved to either end of the street. Karl entered the house with his gun drawn. One other agent followed. It was a few minutes before Dave's radio earphone activated.

'We can go in now. The building is secure.'

'What's up? Tell me.'

'According to Karl, it's not very pleasant. I'm sorry.'

'What do –'

'Come on. We have very little time.'

I got out of the car and followed Dave into the house. Karl was waiting by the first courtyard pool. He said nothing but indicated that I should follow him. We walked to the archway that led to the inner garden. I could see Alonzo sitting in a chair beneath the pavilion roof. He was smiling, eyes slightly open, but with no movement, no greeting.

'He's dead, strangled. Couple of hours, maybe.' Karl moved out of the way to let me approach.

'How do you know?'

'Some lividity. Little or no rigor mortis.'

The eyes and smile were fixed and I instinctively put out my hand to close them. The skin of Alonzo's eyelids was still warm to touch.

'He's still warm!' I shouted, pulling away my hand.

'In asphyxiation the body temperature often rises.' Karl spoke in a detached voice as he looked around the garden.

Alonzo's face was a suffused blue-purple colour with the exploded surface capillaries of the hangman's mask. I next saw the cord, interwoven black and red silk, taut still around the neck. There was little sign of a struggle. No soiling. No blood. No fight it seemed.

Across his lap lay a bundle of slender, feathered tamarisk branches tied in the middle by a wrapping of thin bark. I could see that this had been stripped from the nearby potted mulberry bush, which now looked more distressed than ever. Alonzo's hands, the left holding the right wrist in a lock, were resting on the bundle. From his fisted right hand a piece of paper protruded. I tried to release it but it would not budge. I looked at Karl who shrugged his shoulders.

'Cadaveric spasm.'

I prised open the stiffened grip, forcing the fingers back to do so. One snapped with a sickening sound and in my panic I pulled at his hand and caused Alonzo's unresisting body to slide off the chair. His head thumped off the tiles.

'*Jesus, don't do that*,' Karl shouted. 'Spanish forensics will want no disturbance.'

It was too late. As I hurriedly unravelled the paper a small hard stone-like object fell to the ground. I ignored it and looked at the paper. There were ten lines of writing, in Arabic, on the paper. I shook my head. 'Shit.'

'What's up? Doctor Mara. What does it say?'

'I don't know. It's in Arabic.' I handed Karl the paper and knelt down beside the chair to try and retrieve the fallen stone. My stomach was retching again.

'*Neither yours nor ours, he is. . .*'

'What!' I looked up. Dave, my minder, was reading the piece of paper. 'Do you read Arabic?' I tried, vainly, to keep a tone of disbelief out of my voice.

'Yes, but this is not Arabic. It's old Persian.' Dave said this in a matter of fact way as he held up the paper to the light before looking back down at me. He repaid my cynicism with a very superior sneer. 'School of Oriental Studies, Harvard. We are not just "haircuts" you know.'

'I'm sorry, Dave. I did not mean to assume anything. Please go on with . . .'

Dave ignored me as he spotted the stone under Alonzo's shoe and bent down to retrieve it. He turned in his hand a couple of times before handing it to me. 'Anubis charm. Obsidian. Head of the jackal. Guide of the dead into Hades.'

'What does the writing say? Please translate it for me, Dave.'

' "*Neither yours nor ours, he has gone directly to hell. For the Lord of Time the sun rises in the west. The dogs have looked on him and await the scattering*". It is signed by one "*Zilullah*", the shadow of God.' Dave, the agent-orientalist, handed me back the paper.

'Thank you, Dave.'

'Do you know what this all means, Doctor Mara?' Karl was clearly agitated and anxious to leave.

'No I don't,' I truthfully replied. 'How about you, Dave?'

Dave smiled and nodded at my obvious deferral to his greater understanding. 'It's all a little strange and jumbled. The tamarisk bundle and reference to the dogs is strongly associated with the "*ravan barsm*" ceremony of the Persian Zoroastrians celebrating the soul's departure from the recently deceased. The *barsom* plant was originally used, hence the name of the ceremony, but often substituted for by tamarisk.

The Anubis charm is Egyptian but the reference to the Lord of Time, I do not get. As I said, all a bit jumbled.'

'Excuse me,' I blurted, jumping to my feet and rushing back towards the first courtyard. 'I must do something. I will not be long,' I shouted back to Karl not caring whether he heard or not.

Alonzo's office was undisturbed but the door to the library was open. I ran through it and up to the lectern. The plinth was still raised, supporting nothing but a small mound of finely ground sand. The hourglass was gone.

'We *must* go, Mara.' Karl had followed after me and was pulling at my arm. '*Now!*' My thoughts were elsewhere.

'What? Ok. What about Alonzo?'

'Who? Oh the stiff. We will contact the police once we are gone.'

'My friend.'

'Right. I'm sorry for your loss, but it's no longer a concern of mine. Now come on. We're out of here.'

There was no further resistance from me and within a few minutes the van and the Volvo were speeding through the early morning traffic. We were heading north towards the road that would take us up into the Sierra Nevada. Dave said nothing for a while but then turned to look back at me.

'Do you have any idea what all that was about, Doctor Mara? It seems very weird and almost . . .' He hesitated.

'Almost what?'

'Ritual.'

'The way he was killed?'

'Yes.'

'No. Alonzo was a good friend,' I said in a distracted way, trying to think things through.

'Did you find what you were looking for?'

'What?'

'When you rushed off into the house. Did you find what you were looking for?'

'No, the *Voice* was gone.'

'The what!'

'Oh . . . nothing. I said . . . eh . . . my voice was gone. I'm tired, Dave.'

'Sure. Get some shut-eye, Michael. It's a long drive.'

'Dave.'

'Yes.'

'Thanks.'

'De nada.'

Sleep plunged me into a demented dream from which I was woken, abruptly, by being tossed across the car to the accompaniment of screeching tyres.

'Fucking asshole.' Dave was screaming out the window. I looked at my watch. I had slept for about an hour. My head was still groggy.

'What happened?' I asked.

'Bloody farmer. Pulled right out in front of us.'

'Where are we?'

'Near Almaden.'

'The Calatrava mercury mines?'

'Yes. Where the Fuggers and then the Rothschild's made their money.' The previously silent driver, Hal grunted knowingly and then shut up again.

'But that's on the Cordoba side. I thought that we were going to Madrid.'

'We are.' Dave turned round as the driver shoved the car into reverse. 'But we reserved the option of switching to Lisbon, depending on security status.'

The car's tyres were still screeching to no effect.

'Shit. We're jammed against the shoulder.' Hal had his head out the window. He turned back to Dave. 'You'll need to get out and jack her up.'

'I need to take a leak anyway.' I spoke as I opened the door and stepped out. After the air conditioned coolness of the car the arid heat was like a furnace. There was no damage to the car and it did not take long for Dave and me to lever it back onto the road.

'Ok. Let's go.' Dave was continuously talking into his radio mike, updating those in the van ahead.

We sat back in and soon were accelerating towards Madrid. I took Alonzo's letter from my pocket and began to read it again:

"Dear Michael,

By the time you read this I will probably be already dead. I have seen the light of illumination and it is blinding. I am to join the lovers in paradise.

Do not distress yourself on this point unduly, as it is my ordained time. There is however a matter of greater importance that concerns you.

With my death the 'Lordship of Time' passes to another and with it the key to the gathering of all of the Voices. I have no further control on who that might be but I fear the worse. You must try to recover Saclaresh and prevent it falling into the gathering of evil.

Our time together was all too short. In olden days the relationship of a Pir and his or her designated pupil would often last for many years. In addition to guidance towards and through the doors of the Path the pupil would also be instructed in how to identify and surmount the obstacles to that Path. We, you and I, never had the time for this and I fear that the dangers to you as a result are great. Because of this I would understand if you wish to turn away from the Path, away from the responsibility of something that you do not yet fully comprehend or understand. That is my failure not yours.

As my final act of guidance, I want to try and alert you to one of the specific dangers. In the present I gave you the other evening are the original handwritten notes that Sir Thomas Malorye gave to Caxton in 1483 and which eventually comprised the fourth book of his Morte D'Arthur. *Nobody knows of their existence and I would ask that you respect that.*

The book in question, deals with the seduction and eventual destruction of Merlin the Magician (Magian) by the virgin prefect (perfect!) Nymue and the approbation of his powers by her. Caxton spelt it this way but, in the handwritten notes, you will see that Malorye spells the name as Nur'mei, *meaning the Solis or Light of Maat, the Egyptian Goddess of Truth and Justice. Watch out for this light, for it already shines on you. I do not want to offend you in any way but like Merlin with Nur'mei, Isabella was, and is, my downfall. You, on the other hand, are akin to Sir Bab de Magus, a brother coming to Merlin's rescue but being unable to help because of the power of Nur'mei. Isabella carries that power and the potential for both good and evil but because of my love for her its design is obscure to me.*

Take up the mantle of Sir Bab, Michael, for all our sakes. You are now the last of the Magi. Find Saclaresh and prevent its gathering.

I will wait for you by the Tuba tree.

Your friend,

Alonzo"

I read over the letter a number of times before checking my backpack to ensure that Alonzo's package was present. I must have let out an audible sigh of relief as Dave looking concerned, turned around to check on me.

'You all right, Doc?'

'Yeah, fine, still a bit shook. I wished I could have done more.'

'There was no time. Did he have any relatives?'

'I don't know. I'd only met him a couple of times, we never got round to talking about his family.'

'Central has informed us that the police have arrived at the house and begun their work.'

'Will they not want to contact me?'

'Not immediately. One of our crew is a cleanup specialist and stayed behind.' Mike gave a terminal emphasis to the description, a 'do not ask anything further' emphasis. I did not pursue it.

The countryside sped past, unfocused, until gradually changing to urban sprawl and a busy highway on the outskirts of Madrid. Turning off for the city's airport we sped past the departures entrance and headed instead for the military airfield at the far end of the complex. A Lear jet was waiting, engines already fired up. It had a name – *The Nightingale* – painted below the cockpit window but no other markings on the fuselage. Karl and Dave followed me up the steps. Both seemed nervous.

'Where are we headed for Karl?' I asked.

'Corsica.'

'*Corsica?*'

The three dark-suited men stepped out of the large Mercedes, that had drawn up in the quiet street, and hurried up the steps. The door opened, without any need to announce themselves, and they were greeted by another figure who stood in the shadows of the atrium. The car moved away and parked discretely a little further along the road. The driver's window opened a fraction and a thin wisp of smoke could be seen to escape through the crack and rise in the evening air.

One of the visitors, hesitating at the entrance, turned, pushed his dark glasses to the tip of his nose and scanned up and down the street before touching the rim. The hazard lights of the Mercedes and another car almost directly opposite the entrance flickered briefly, in unison. He then looked down at the steps he had just climbed. He was a young man with a pale olive complexion. A scar, running obliquely close to his left eye, was just visible and the same eye opened and closed in an increasingly rapid tic action. Annoyed, he hurriedly relocated the glasses to the bridge of his nose.

The steps seemed to hold an unusual fascination for him and he remained staring at them for a few moments before being called into the house by one of the other men. The door closed with a solid thumping noise behind him. His two older companions were walking ahead, their arms linked by a tall central figure, who as if as an afterthought looked back over his shoulder at the younger man. Rod Mallory's voice had a sarcastic resonance.

'Hello, Domingo. I'm so relieved you could join us. Is everything all right?'

'What? Oh yes . . . All clear.' The younger man was looking around the atrium and the courtyard ahead. He removed his glasses and placed them in an inside pocket. The flickering eye was quiet. 'Mallory!'

'Yes, Domingo.'

'Is this the house where Versace was shot? It looks familiar from the photographs I have seen.'

'No. It's not the Casa Casuarina, but nearly an exact replica. Built by a heartbroken admirer of the great man, he sold it to me when Versace was killed. Much cheaper than the original but in identical taste.'

'I'd forgotten the circles that you move in and find your pleasure.' Domingo sneered.

A flare of anger flashed across Mallory's face and he stopped abruptly. The two older men refused to unlink his arms and pulled him forward again, away from a confrontation. Relaxing a fraction, he shrugged his shoulders and led them across the tiled, open courtyard, its mission bell swaying in the swirling evening wind that was sweeping in from the ocean. They entered into the garden and walking along the pebble-mosaic pathways made for a small circular pavilion that lay in one corner partially hidden by tall palm trees. There was a nearby ornamental pond with its waters rippling in the wind. The pond's lights, sunk into the blue mosaic-tiled depths, shimmered their illumination to the surface to appear like spectral water lilies.

Mallory pulled out the ironwork, Roman-style, senatorial chairs and pointed to a drinks cabinet that was secreted in one wall. The light from the pavilion cupola caught the movement of the frolicking nude figures of the back wall fresco and its ornate gilded border that rose in serpentine coils towards the roof.

'Pour yourselves a drink and take a pew,' Mallory said as he chose a beer and sat in a chair facing the garden.

The two older men joined him but Domingo preferred to sit on the pavilion steps with his back to the Australian. Pursing his lips he was pulsing out perfect rings with the smoke from a lit cigar.

The older man, on Rod Mallory's right, looked first at Domingo's back and then at him. He held his hands up in a silent apology. Mallory nodded and smiled. He waited for the older man to speak.

'What happened in La Paz, Rod?'

'I had to deal with a problem . . .Two problems in fact, and it was the only way. A beaut solution though, it cannot be traced.'

'Are you sure?'

'Listen, Miguel. When I established the money-laundering operation for the cartel in Belize you asked me then, 'are you sure?' When I determined that it was the right time to begin rerouting the cartel's money from traditional avenues into the new high stake business such as gene technology you asked me 'are you sure?' then, as well. Tell me, honestly, that the Columbian cartel families are unhappy with my judgement calls and the profits I have made for you, and I'll walk away.'

Miguel Mendoza smiled knowingly at the Australian. 'You can never walk away Rod, you know that. However, although the cartel families have the greatest respect for your management of our affairs and the direction that it has taken us, we do feel it was an unnecessary risk for you to personally deal with the situation in Mexico.'

Mallory emptied his beer and stood up to retrieve another. 'I had to, Miguel. Diego 'Diablo' Rios trusted very few people enough to expose himself like that without protection. He was on home ground with his cock in the air.'

'Why eliminate him in the first place. I don't understand.' The man on Mallory's left spoke for the first time.

'Listen, Francisco, I took the decision to eliminate Rios

because his greed was driving him to try and achieve overall control of the 'casa de cambio' operation in Mexico. This greed was beginning to attract unwelcome attention, both at government level and from other cartels. The less people who were consulted about the decision, the better. Rios still had very strong Columbian contacts and I did not want him alerted by any loose talk at our end. It was yet another judgement call that I've had to before, and will continue to make on the cartel's behalf.' Mallory took his seat again.

'I understand the point you are making, Rod but please explain how his greed threatened us, a little bit more to me. I only ask, because as you may or may not know, his wife was my own wife's goddaughter.'

'Ex wife!'

'True, but I still need to understand,' the older man demanded, his features impassive and unwavering.

'Certainly, Francisco. When we established the *"casa de cambio"* operation in Mexico, it provided an unregulated paradise into which we were able to channel the "profits" of the cartel. The continued success of the operation, from our point of view, is that no competing Mexican cartel has been able, or allowed, to wrest that overall control from us and thus freeze us out of the market. We have managed to divide and rule.'

'What's that got to do Rios?'

'Diego Rios provided much valuable intelligence over the years but he knew far too much about our cartel's and my own personal operational involvement. Despite my repeated warnings to him about not getting above his station he decided to make a push for total control. This did not bother me unduly from a purely commercial point of view, as the new regime in Mexico and likely regulation of the casas made their future uncertain, but it was important to impose discipline on our associates as well. I had to make an example of him, to send a message to the others.'

Francisco looked at Rod Mallory for a few moments before nodding his head in agreement.

Miguel Mendoza had listened without comment but now took

the opportunity of the silence to question Rod on his reasons for calling them to a meeting at such short notice.

'Why the urgency of this meeting tonight, Rod. Surely it could have waited until the next cartel management meeting in a week's time. I am missing my grandson's confirmation and my daughter will be furious with me.'

'I am sorry about that, Miguel, but it was extremely important that we meet. There is another aspect to the Rios situation that I need to discuss with you.'

'Go on.'

'Not with that crawler present.' Rod Mallory spoke deliberately loudly as he pointed to the slouching Domingo. 'It's too sensitive.'

Domingo turned and glared at the Australian.

'Give us five minutes, Domingo. Check the perimeter security status.' It was Francisco who spoke.

'But –'

'*Now!*'

Domingo moved off reluctantly, swiping angrily at the nearby poolside ornamental urn. To his obvious delight he watched as the urn began to waver on its pedestal and after a few seconds the increasing momentum cause it to topple into the pool.

Mallory rose to chase after him but was once again restrained by the older men. 'The sooner that drongo is put down, the happier I'll be. I'll roast his balls yet.' He fumed as he shook them off.

'Calm down and tell us about this 'other aspect', Rod.'

'I'm sorry, Francisco, I respect you enormously but I cannot stand that son of yours.'

'He is jealous of your power, Rod.'

'You're not wrong there mate.'

Francisco stood up and walked to the balcony. He looked into the pool. The urn had sunk swiftly to the bottom but looked undamaged. Francisco turned to face the table and leant against the wall, his arms folded across his chest.

'Domingo will grow out of it and learn to trust you like we have. Now get to the point, Rod.'

'Sure, Francisco. As you know The Hoxygene Corporation of California, founded and directed by Doctor Michael Mara, was the first major investment vehicle amongst the technology stocks that I identified as being a suitable home for the cartel's money. I was, obviously, very keen to make it work and that is why I took such a personal and direct interest. That personal involvement brings with it some major advantages.'

'What do you mean?'

'Recently a large pharmaceutical company called Alpanna BioPharm has made a hostile bid for Hoxygene which values our stake at about $50,000,000.'

'*Jesu!* That is almost a 150 per cent profit and clean money at that.' Miguel was waving his hands excitedly. '*Magnifico*, Rod.'

'Yes and no, Miguel.' Rod Mallory stared up at the roof. 'There may be a major problem.'

'Go on.' Francisco sat down at the table again.

'When Alpanna and I met to discuss the offer for Hoxygene, the chairman, a man called Charles Alexander, made a veiled enquiry about work that the company might be doing for the American Army. I'd no idea what he was talking about but it set off alarm bells.'

'Surely it would have been mentioned in company strategy meetings.'

'Never. If such work was being done then Michael Mara had kept this to himself. I needed to be sure and in his absence in Spain it was not difficult to take the opportunity to search his 'secure' files.' Mallory paused to gather his thoughts.

'And?' both older men asked in unison.

'What I discovered has profound implications for the cartels.'

'You mean with regard to our investment.'

'No! More than that. *To your very survival!*'

The two older men looked at each other and then at Rod. Miguel spoke for both of them. 'We don't understand.'

'Mara appears to be developing, with the US Army, a virus that attacks the cocaine leaf. I don't understand the science but I have some independent experts analysing the information I managed to obtain. This has all happened in the last week, hence the urgency of this meeting to explain my need to react quickly.'

'Good God. By investing money in Hoxygene, we are funding our own destruction.' Francisco held his head in his hands.

'Yeah. Ironic really.' Mallory smiled.

'Fuck irony, Rod. This is serious. Could you not get any other information as to what stage this work is at?'

'That was the reason I primed Rios to try and seduce the woman, Mara's wife, when they met up in La Paz. It was far too good an opportunity to pass up on.'

'Did she know anything?' Miguel looked concerned as he spoke.

'Diego Rios was quite ruthless in his interrogation and I'm convinced that, like me, she knew nothing of her husband's virus work for the army.'

'Was it necessary to kill her?' Francisco almost whispered. 'I hear she was a federal agent.'

Rod Mallory smiled. 'Yes! She could not be allowed to escape to warn her husband or the authorities. We need time to check this out without risking our position.'

'Why not kidnap. It's a powerful tool.' Francisco spoke wearily.

'I thought of that Francisco, but decided if the US army are involved it would be too dangerous. No, it was better to kill her, making it appear that she was the accidental victim of the assassination of Commander Diego Rios. A real beaut scenario of a tragic case of being in the wrong place at the wrong time.'

'So! No information from her at all?'

'She did give one name, Miguel. A General Arnold. I have my sources checking him out right now.'

'Be careful, Rod.'

'As if I was close to a cut snake!'

'What?' Miguel looked puzzled.

Mallory laughed. 'I'll explain some other time. I'll be careful.'

'What *is* your reading of the situation, Rod?' Miguel persisted in his probing, his mind racing as to what action he needed to initiate.

'I'm certain that Alexander of Alpanna knows more than he has let on. Since our initial meeting I have had our security boys check up on him. I don't . . .' Rod paused again, composing his thoughts.

'You don't what?'

'I don't want to concern you unduly just yet but there are rumours of links between Alexander and the anti-Taliban faction in Afghanistan.'

'So! I don't understand.' Francisco had stood up and was refilling his whiskey glass. A generous pouring was swallowed quickly.

'The anti-Taliban faction controls the illegal drugs trade out of Afghanistan.'

'You mean Alexander is directly involved in the opium trade out of Asia. . .' Miguel looked at Rod, shaking his head from side to side, 'don't you Rod? Our competitors.'

'Perhaps, but I don't think it's commercial.'

'Please explain.'

'My sources indicate that Alexander is heavily involved with many separatist groups, such as the Continuity IRA in Ireland, the Basque *Euzkadi Ta Askatasuna* or ETA in Spain, Shining Path and TUPAC in Peru, and others such as the GIA in Algeria, AUM in Japan, KACH in Israel, as well as the FLNC in Corsica.'

'The FLNC?'

'The *Fronte di Liberazione Nazionale de Corsica*. In fact that is where I am heading now.'

'Where?'

'Corsica. I'm catching Air France to Paris and then an Air Littoral connection to Figari, in Southern Corsica.'

'Why?'

'I contacted Alexander and said I would like to talk to him about the offer for Hoxygene, in more detail. We had planned to meet in New York but he called me back to cancel that arrangement and suggested that I come to his villa near Corte, which is the centre of the island. The arse end of nowhere, it seems.'

'What's his reason for involvement with the terrorists?'

'I'm unsure but all the information points to his involvement with narcotics as being a way of orchestrating and funding international destabilisation. I need to determine if this is his real agenda and what risk it poses to our operations. Cheap opium from Afghanistan could destroy our markets, particularly if Alexander gets control of the ability to destroy our cocaine crops.'

'What about the situation in Columbia, Rod? Does Alexander have any links to the FARC? The recent arrest of the Irish terrorists worries me. Is Alexander responsible for their appearance on the scene?'

'I don't know, Miguel, but certainly FARC is increasingly looking beyond Columbia for its direction.'

'It's becoming increasingly difficult for the cartel families to deal with the FARC leadership. We cannot afford any further disruption to our supplies.'

'Listen, Miguel. If it's any help, I've just received the list, given to the Columbian authorities by Interpol, of foreigners involved with the FARC. I'm trying to identify any possible links with Alexander.'

'Rod. I'm unhappy about all this until we have more concrete information.' Miguel was speaking as Francisco looked up to see Domingo returning to the pavilion. He indicated for him to sit down as Miguel continued to press the Australian. 'Don't you think it's dangerous at this time to go to Corsica? It might attract unwarranted attention.'

'What's up Papa?' Domingo had seen how serious his father was looking.

'Rod has just explained about a possible threat to our interests from the opium dealers in Afghanistan.' Francisco smiled at his son.

'What possible threat could they be to us?' Domingo snorted.

'I will explain later but for the moment, Domingo, I want you to shut up and listen.' Francisco admonished him.

'But Papa –'

'Shut up, Domingo.' It was Miguel who barked at the younger

man. Mallory was smiling as the older man turned back to look at him. 'Go on, Rod.'

'I'll be ok. We need to question Alexander.'

'Agreed. What about security.'

'Two teams. Already flying in there as hiking tourists.'

'Good.'

'And a third will join them when they are finished in Spain.'

'What's in Spain, Mallory?' Domingo butted in

'You never listen Junior, do you?' he spat back.

'Easy, Rod. This animosity will not serve our needs.' Francisco tried to placate him.

'Sorry, Francisco. Michael Mara is in Spain and he is the key. He's the only one who can give us the full information on the virus work with the American army. The team I dispatched are going to extract him.' Mallory looked at his watch. 'About now in fact. I should hear soon.'

'What are your intentions, Rod?' Miguel asked, his face betraying his anticipation of the answer.

'If the information is confirmed I'll take them out?'

'Who?'

'Mara and Alexander, both.'

'Who? Why?' Domingo could not restrain himself.

'Listen, idiot. Do as your Daddy says and shut up.' Rod was enjoying the freedom.

'Rod. I am losing patience. Do not push this any further.' Francisco put his hand on Rod's shoulder and squeezed it hard. Rod nodded.

'Look, Francisco, Mara may or may not have developed a cocaine virus for the Army, but it is my gut feeling that he has. If your cocaine crops are destroyed then the Afghans, perhaps orchestrated by Alexander, will swamp our markets with cheap heroin. We will be out of business and sonny-boy over there will lose his allowance and have to go back to pimping or shining shoes.'

'*Rod!* Enough! You are insulting one of my family.'

'Sorry, Francisco. I would never want to insult you but I just wish that you two were not related.'

'Well we are. Now continue with your assessment.'

'I need to evaluate the double threat to our operations. If convinced by the evidence I'll take both Mara and Alexander out. This will allow us retain control of the market while we delay, if not prevent, the threat to our production.'

The night air had become quite cool. The four men around the table were silent, lost in their own thoughts.

'By the way,' Mallory said quietly.

'Yes, Rod,' Miguel asked.

'I've instructed our broker to sell our stock in Hoxygene. The cartel's money is –'

Suddenly, and with a startling effect on all four, the cell phone in his breast pocket shrilled into action.

'Excuse me for a moment, gentlemen.' Mallory took a deep breath before flipping open the lid. 'Hello,' he said brusquely as he stood up to listen. Every now and then, his face would flicker before he finally terminated the call.

'Was that the team in Spain?' Francisco asked.

'Yes.' Rod Mallory was distracted.

'And?'

'Mara has disappeared. Snatched by what appears to be a goon squad from his hotel this morning.'

'Who were they?'

Mallory left out a deep sigh as he held his hands behind his head. 'Don't know.'

'As our security advisor you appear to know very little, Mallory. Maybe one of your queer friends might help. I hear they are great in tight situations.' Domingo pouted his lips and blew a kiss in Mallory's direction.

Rod sprang from his chair and in one movement had Domingo pinned against the ground with a gun against the younger man's temple and a hand crushing his windpipe.

'Move one muscle and you're dead, you fucker.'

'I doubt it.' Domingo smiled as he looked up to see both the older men with their guns trained on Rod.

'Let him go, Rod. *Now!*' Francisco barked. 'We are leaving.'

Rod also looked up at the two older men and gradually slackened his shoulders. He ran the muzzle of the gun along the length of the younger man's facial scar before uncoiling and standing up. Domingo followed suit, gingerly rubbing his head where it had slammed off the tiled floor, before wiping the dust from his jacket.

'Very well. I'll show you out.'

'That's not necessary.' Miguel had holstered his gun and took Rod's hand in a firm grip. 'Go to Corsica. Keep me informed.'

'Sure.'

'Goodnight, Rod.'

'Goodnight, Miguel. Goodnight, Francisco.'

Francisco was nearly half way across the garden and Miguel hurried to catch up with him. Domingo held back and turned to face Rod.

'Mallory. Next time you do something like that, I will kill you. Understand amigo!'

'In your dreams dingo-shit. In your dreams!'

The younger man touched his scar, sneered and sauntered away. He stopped by the pool edge and peered down into its depths before turning to snap back at Rod.

'Keep your back to the wall you faggot. The next penetration you experience might not be to your liking.'

Isabella felt exhilarated by the freshness of the mountain air. She watched as puffball clouds were first gathered, and then released from the serrated crest of Monte Cinto to the northeast, while below her, down on the floor of the valley, the dammed-up waters of the Calacuccia reservoir shimmered in the afternoon sunlight, awaiting their own release into the eastern gorge. Immediately behind her, on the small plateau that lay above the village of Casamaccioli, the teams of *boule* players were earnest in their concentration and effort. The playing ground was rough and uneven and this made the roll and direction of the steel balls highly unpredictable.

She turned to give her full attention to the sport and soon became enthralled by the highly individual character and expressions of these mountain men. In the game nearest to her, a team of three players were arguing about the next throw. The match was obviously at a critical stage and the team members were as dissimilar as their throwing action. A tall, serious, precise thrower, with a stiff arm and tape measure shouted instructions to another, whose white trousers and pointed cowboy's boots added a flourish to an action that was almost operatic in its movement and excess. His throws arced from the sky to land with a back-spun thud; poseurs in flight but deadly accurate in their finesse and performance.

Then there was the "scowler", who wore the cloth cap and burnt skin of the high summer pastures. He was the assassin, she noted, as he prowled the course to choose the boule of his opponent and blast it from the game with the unerring sang-froid of a mountain guerrilla. After one such shot, one of his boules rolled on to land at Isabella's feet. She waited for the game to be finished before stooping to pick it up. The player-assassin came forward to retrieve it from her with a smile and an invitation with his eyes. She smiled back at him with a slight shake of her head. He shrugged and returned to the game.

Isabella walked around the perimeter of the plateau and down the hill towards the small square of the village. Surrounding the square were the covered stalls of food and drink, as well as the gambling tables and displays of sweets and clothes. Near the entrance of the large tent selling the wares of the merchants and artisans who had bothered to make the trip, was a well-attended demonstration of tree-cutting power saws, whose sawdust sprayed the irritated climbers on a nearby artificial wall.

The square was surrounded by a ring of sentinel chestnut trees whose fruit seemed to cling, in its early autumn abundance, like sea-urchins to the crevices of a wave-swept shoreline. She was painfully reminded as to why so many Mediterranean peoples called sea-urchins, "sea-chestnuts" as the spikes of a prematurely fallen pod drove through the side of her canvas shoes.

Letting out a sharp cry from that pain, she sat on a half-sawn upturned log to dislodge the spikes. All around her, the village children, those with energy still left in them, were searching amongst the market stalls for dropped coins. She could sense the excitement that visitors – most of whom were just arriving for the evening festivities – were already feeling as they greeted old friends.

Isabella got up and walked with a slight limp towards one of the village bars. As she approached, the noise of laughter, the clatter of glasses, the curses of gambling all seemed to fade on cue. Leaning against the door of the bar, his eyes looking up at the mountains behind the village, a young male visitor had interrupted his homecoming to begin a high-pitched chant of coarse-spun primitive rhythm. Just when it seemed like it would unravel, another bass-deep resonant voice joined in, threading the chant to its loom. Their combined sounds echoed from the walls and, it seemed to Isabella, through men's hearts.

As she looked around at the attentive faces, she could see an occasional glistening tear well up in tired emotive eyes and then flow as yet another, third voice, joined in. This time it was a haunting silk-smooth lament that weaved with an almost North-African inflection of passion and pathos between the coloured tapestry of high-pitched chant and bass.

'It's magnificent, is it not?'

Isabella was startled by the intrusion but, recognizing the voice, half-turned to smile up at the tall man with silver-grey hair who stood to one side. She could just make out his eyes behind the tinted glasses before returning her gaze to the source of the singing. She nodded her head slightly in agreement.

'Yes, Charles.'

'Did you have difficulty getting here?'

'I took a taxi from Bastia Airport. The driver was delighted. I think he is here somewhere getting drunk.'

'The "*A Santa Di Niolu*" festival has become a very important part of the expression of Corsican nationhood. Tomorrow is the biggest day.'

'What happens?'

'8 September, is the feast day of the birth of the Virgin and after an open-air mass in the morning, the statue of the Madonna will be paraded from the church to the square where the three swirling and swivelling white-robed *cunfraterna,* following the statue, will then perform the weaving *granitola* procession. Its rhythms are very similar to the music you're listening to.'

'I like the music and the reaction it's provoking.'

'Perhaps tomorrow night we can return to the church to hear the group, A Filetta. They are some of the finest exponents of Corsican music.'

Isabella seemed distracted. She said nothing for a while but continued to listen to the three men singing. It suddenly stopped to loud applause.

'What is the song about?' She asked.

'It is an old shepherd lament, sung in the form of *a paghjella* or three-part combination of voices, about the untimely death of a beloved son to a mountain storm and the regret that his time was so short. The first or *a prima* voice sets the rhythm and the second or *u boldu* voice adds the bass sound. The third or *a terza* voice sings the melody; this particular song tells of the boy's father offering himself to the gods in exchange.'

'It's very evocative.'

'Corsican music is sad, it is fatalistic. An English writer, called Ross, once wrote that Corsicans rehearse death. He was not far from the truth. I find it an attractive quality. '

'Is that not your wish, Charles? A grand rehearsal of death and without any pretence of resurrection!'

'A meaningful resurrection for any of us is only possible when time stands still. I prefer to wish for a renewal as I do not want a return from death to the same life. We have to begin again. A new covenant must be negotiated.'

'The new Jerusalem, Charles?' Isabella turned to look up at Alexander.

'Exactly, but it can only be realised if you join me.' Alexander was looking up at the sky, to the east beyond the village, as he spoke. He suddenly frowned. ' Come Isabella! My car is at the end of the village. We need to get to the villa for the meeting with Zoë and the others. A thunderstorm is approaching and the Santa Regina road can be treacherous when it's wet.'

Charles Alexander linked Isabella's arm and led her down past the hundreds of parked cars to the lowest part of the village where his silver four-wheeled-drive jeep was parked. As they reached the car a peel of thunder rolled up the valley and pounded against the barren upper slopes above the village. The first drops of rain streaked the mud-stained windscreen and guttered to the ground.

He pulled the passenger door open and holding it, waited for her to climb in. She braced slightly as he slammed the door shut and ran around to the driver's side. After engaging the automatic gearshift he gently accelerated to allow the car move off and begin its journey down the hill.

Isabella thought of the shepherd's lament as she watched, through the increasing downpour, a series of lightning charges searing the lower valley walls. Hailstones replaced the rain to dance on the car roof. It was some time before Alexander spoke again.

'I'm glad you have finally come to Corsica, Isabella. This is my spiritual home, the source of my inspiration. I want you to be part of my life here. We can achieve so much together.'

His free right hand hovered near her leg for a moment before, due to the demands of another hairpin-bend in the road, he returned it quickly to the vibrating steering wheel.

'Why Corsica, Charles?'

'Many reasons really, past, present and future.'

'I don't understand.'

He reached into his pocket and removed a small box, which he then handed it to Isabella.

'Open it.'

Isabella lifted off the lid and, after turning on the interior reading light, held up the open box for inspection. She saw that it contained a single antique coin on which the figures of dolphins were easily distinguishable.

'What is it?'

'It is a present for you; a very rare coin from Phocea.'

'Thank you, Charles, but why?'

'My father's family was originally from Aleria on the east coast of this island. It's an old city that Greek colonists established in 564 BCE, when they emigrated from Phocea, an Anatolian town just north of present day Izmir. As a child, the history of the commercial acumen of these people fascinated me and was to be an inspiration for my business interests later in life.'

'It is in beautiful condition,' she remarked as she followed the carvings of dolphins on the face of the coin, with the tip of a fingernail.

He noticed. 'Phocea, which incidentally is the Greek for dolphin, was also one of the first ever places to mint and stamp their own coins. They were usually made of electrum, a natural alloy of silver and gold, and they imposed their standard on other cities. When eventually driven out from Anatolia by the Persians they came to Aleria for a while before leaving again to found the city of Marseille on the mainland. That coin is also made from electrum and was minted in Aleria shortly after the Greeks arrived.'

'Are you expecting an exchange?' Isabella ran her hand over the leather flap of her small handbag as she spoke.

'No. I just wanted to share some of my history with you,' he said earnestly.

'There must be more to it than that?'

'You are right, of course. Of more importance, and far more relevance to your presence here, is that Aleria is the site where armed nationalists of the ARC initiated the first action against the French authorities in 1975 and which subsequently led to the foundation of the FLNC. I was involved then and 25 years later I am still involved.' Alexander watched as Isabella turned the coin to inspect its markings. 'The coin will also be a reminder, to you, of the covenant and commitment I've made. I hope that you'll soon feel the same way.'

There was silence between them for a moment. Isabella coughed as she spoke.

'In promoting worldwide chaos and the unwarranted death of helpless innocents. That is an evil manifesto, Charles.'

A bolt of lightning burst through the rain to earth nearby and the flash lit up the interior of the car. Isabella caught the sneering look on Alexander's face.

'Evil! What do *you* understand by evil, Isabella?'

'The petulance and pestilence of the world, the work of the opponents of the God of Salvation. The strivings of the inhibitor of Nous. The Demiurge!'

'But evil and good are two sides of the same coin. They are not in opposition, they are complementary.'

'I don't agree, Charles. Evil and good are set against each other for eternity but in the end, evil will be defeated. Light will win out and the dark side will be defaced.'

'That's your problem, Isabella.'

She instantly flushed, annoyed by his, almost, sarcastic dismissal. Turning to face him, she switched on the reading light so she could see his face. He was smiling as she snapped at him. 'Explain your perception of me, or should I say your lack of perception, and your concept of evil, Charles. It had better be compromising or our arrangement, present and future, will dissolve.'

'I understand and I will try. Like you Isabella, I also believe in the twin gods of our existence who influence good and evil within the confines of this world. Unlike you however, I believe that mankind is no longer peripheral to that control; God has withdrawn from influencing our lives. And *man*, created from the essence or purity of God's vision, is the Anthropos, the ordained inheritor of that vision. Man is not governed by some cosmic pre-ordained epoch but is free in his will to choose. These are the actions that will then be judged on the Bridge of the Separator. Unlike –'

'*Fuck!* That was close.' Isabella cursed as a speeding car coming from the opposite direction threatened to push them over the edge of a narrow bridge.

Alexander didn't flinch. 'Unlike you, I do not believe that knowledge should be sought to help you escape this prison of worldly matter to achieve paradise, to know God. Even you accept that evil exists, and by experiencing it we can learn from it. We are here and now, Isabella. Failure to fully understand God's intentions and the failure of reason to explain the design of those intentions is not a defeat but a positive consequence of our existence. True knowledge comes from accepting that fact. The . . .'

He paused as he negotiated the jeep around a particularly sharp corner.

'The failure of reason and understanding, the pillars of evil, is a necessary requirement to force us into action. Man has been given the freedom to shape the world into our own vision of Utopia. It is self-determination, Isabella. God for many people is dead, for others he is hidden. It doesn't matter. He has already given man the knowledge and, more importantly, the authority to care for the world, to manipulate it. That is our salvation.'

'You have an appetite for death, Charles, with or without salvation.'

'It's my most attractive feature, particularly to women. I am Dionysus and the women become my *bassarides*.'

'Why the desire to gather the *Voices*? Surely they have little relevance to self-determination.'

'They have every relevance. They cause confusion not clarity. They present a secret vision, impossible to realize, of a relationship with God that is inter-dependant. They are shackles to our destiny, opt-out clauses in our true covenant. Take you for instance. Your path to the Nous is blocked by the responsibility you feel for your guardianship. Let it go, Isabella and you can float free. That is what I am offering.'

'And when they are gathered, what then, Charles?'

'Timeless Utopia. Zurvarism's ultimate design for us achieved. We finally become our own gods, the source of our own salvation. Time and destiny controlled. The final separation.'

'And how will you try and achieve it? Utopia demands that

pre-existing structures are replaced.' Isabella relaxed as the gorge road flattened out.

'Destruction, initially of the current parameters of man's secular existence and later, that of the so called timeless parameters. We need to begin again but a god-head, a leader of curiosity and vision is required.'

'And that's you?' Isabella laughed sarcastically.

Alexander, suddenly annoyed, accelerated up the hill from the junction at Francardu on the main road that would take them to Corte. The hailstones had eased.

'It's already happening.' His tone was chillingly cold.

'What do you mean, Charles?'

The jeep had reached the sharp bend at the Collo di San Quilico when Alexander turned sharply onto the small road that would take them to Tralonca. To the south, Corte could be seen nestled in the amphitheatre of the valley wall, beneath the Punta Finosa. A lightning bolt lit up the forbidding citadel as Alexander looked across at her.

'Did you know, Isabella, that every year at the end of August, Corte hosts the *Ghjurante di U Populu Corse*.'

'What is it?'

'A gathering of another sort, I suppose you might say. The *Ghjurante*, was originally conceived as a festival of Corsican culture but with my financial help, and prompting, it has now become the annual meeting place for the political wings of separatist groups from all over the world. Some of these people we will meet tomorrow to discuss a co-ordinated plan of action for their aspirations for self-determination.'

'*You are using separatist groups to create havoc?*' Isabella's voice betrayed her surprise.

'Yes, a very simple and convenient way of achieving my utopian dream.'

'But how will you control these groups, if they do come into power?'

'Power! *Merde!* They will never achieve power. I'm able to ensure that within all the groups, there are factions continually at odds with each other. Money and drugs will drown their aspirations. Even here in Corsica I have just achieved that.'

'You mean with the killing of the Iguana?'

'Santoni and his friend Rossi were fools. They wanted to keep the *Cuncolta Naziunalista* pure, but lost out to the ambition and interests of the drug and arm dealing factions that I financially supported. I have achieved much the same with the IRA in Ireland and soon, will have the FARC in Columbia and the al-Qaeda organisation in Afghanistan in similar disarray. Even the most indoctrinated terrorist will eventually succumb to the attraction of self-indulgence, and those that don't will be eliminated.'

Isabella kept looking at the castle. 'I see.'

Again there was a long silence between them until Alexander broke it.

'Did you organize for the Israeli to come, Isabella?'

'Yes, but by a different route. Zoë is picking him up in Bastia. He will meet us at your house tonight.'

'Good, I want to deal with him before talking to the others tomorrow. What about Michael Mara? Were you able to trap him as planned? Did you question him?'

'Yes.'

'And?'

'He confirmed our intelligence. Work is underway on a cocaine leaf virus and looks like it might be successful.'

'I see! Were you able to extract any other details?'

'No. He passed out very early on. I gave him too much Pentothal. He was comatose for nearly 24 hours.'

'That's unfortunate. I presume that . . . Shit!'

A lame dog was limping slowly across the middle of the road ahead of them. The half-starved animal stopped as the jeep's light-beams dazzled its pathetic eyes. Isabella watched as Alexander started to swerve away but then, as if suddenly thinking better of it, decided to drive straight over the hapless animal. She could feel its body rebound against the floor of the jeep.

'You presume what, Charles?'

'I presume Zoë disposed of Mara. Where?'

'Zoë didn't kill him. I instructed her not to as it wasn't the right time. Mara's destiny is not yet complete.'

'Isabella! I told you to dispose of him. You were responsible.'

Her voice became icy cold. 'Whatever about Zoë, you do not control me, Charles. I am not yet one of your *bassarides*. Mara was my responsibility and my choice. Don't ever forget that.'

'Sorry. You are right, but I think that decision could damage our path.'

'Your path not mine. Not yet at any rate.'

'Isabella, I hope that you in time, will see that it is the only way.' Alexander's stridency softened. 'What did you mean when you said Mara's destiny is not yet complete?'

Isabella inhaled deeply. She was barely audible when she spoke. 'Mara is, I think, about to become guardian of a *Voice*.'

'*What did you say?*' Alexander shouted as he suddenly applied the brakes. The jeep skidded and screeched to an abrupt halt.

The seat belt tore into Isabella's chest and violently expelled her breath. She glared at Alexander before answering. 'I said that Mara is, or soon will be, a guardian of a *Voice*.'

'Which one?'

'He called it *Saclaresh*.'

'The Voice of the Magi. That is incredible. How is it possible? It's meant to be somewhere in Armenia.'

'Alonzo was involved.'

Alexander slapped his hand against the steering wheel.

'The interfering old fool; him and his Keeper's legacy. No longer though! Alonzo's time is now passed.'

Alexander's cackling laugh instantly chilled the atmosphere.

'What do you mean?'

'Alonzo is dead! The Timekeeper's seal is now . . . or soon will be, mine.'

'Was that necessary?' Isabella was disturbed.

'Yes, and if you really want to know, he was expecting it to happen. Alonzo was prepared for his death and made no effort to conceal the *Voice*. I *am* the ordained inheritor.'

Isabella could only feel a tremendous sense of sadness. Perhaps Alexander was right. Perhaps all of this was ordained. She thought.

'I loved him,' she whispered.

Alexander did not seem to hear. 'Did you bring *Nefradaleth*?'

'Perhaps.'

Alexander went sullenly silent as he waited for Isabella to expand. When she didn't he looked away from her and at the road ahead. The rain had stopped and after a few moments he released the brake and they continued towards the valley descent.

Isabella was thoughtful and it was some time before she spoke again. They were in a dense forest of Holm oak and chestnut and after some time emerged onto a narrow road that still had centre markings. Alexander stopped the car near a large rock. The storm had passed and the sky had brightened. He opened the door and got out to stand and stare at the valley below. Isabella joined him.

'That is the village of Castellare di Mecurio. My mother's family name was Piaggia and they came from that village.' Alexander was pointing at a small village with red tile-roof houses that seemed to perch precariously on a thin outcrop of rock half way up the nearby mountain. 'The land to the west used to be occupied by the Foreign Legion but now it's mine. You can just make out my villa near the edge of the cemetery.'

'Listen, Charles. If I didn't feel that you, or your way, were somewhat attractive to me, then I would not be here. It is just that I need to understand far more about your course of action before giving my complete commitment. Perhaps the meeting tomorrow with the others will help.'

'I hope so, Isabella. I really do need you. You are the only person with whom I can fully share my vision. You and I, together, will be the inheritors of the new Garden of Eden.'

'That is very sweet of you . . . I brought *Nefradaleth* by the way.' Isabella opened her purse and lifted out the seal to show him. Alexander's right hand instinctively reached over to touch it only to find that she quickly replaced it and snapped the bag closed again. His smile was a mixture of annoyance and satisfaction.

'Thank you, Solis, and thank you for saving Michael Mara as well. I will need to give that issue some more thought, but it's better than I could have hoped for.'

'What do you mean, Charles?'

'It leaves only one more *Voice* unaccounted for and that is *Ammonkaph*, the voice of silence, the hidden one. They are all nearly within my grasp. *It's so close, Isabella.*'

Matutinum

DAWN GODDESS

Corsica
7 September 2001

It seemed, as I looked downwards through a cloudless sky to the green-blue Mediterranean far below, that we had hardly reached our cruising altitude when the pilot was already announcing our descent. Dave, Karl and the other Secret Service agents who had travelled with us grumbled at their wakening. Once we had lifted off they had instantly availed of the radio-free cocooned environment to snatch some much-needed sleep.

I could not rest. My thoughts were concentrated on trying to figure out what had happened to me in the time since I arrived at Isabella's apartment. What has she and Zoë done to me? I had no real recollection of any sequence of events, only unchoreographed fleeting pixel images without pattern or reason. They were like many memories, particularly the bad ones, suppressed when at peace, flickering and occasionally rampant when agitated.

My mouth was dry and my stomach, empty save for some concentrated coffee, knotted further as we came into land. There was a very high crosswind, which pushed downwards on the port-side wing, causing the jet to tilt at a lateral angle and away from the plotted tangent to the curve of the earth that rushed up to meet us. The pilot made a late and expert correction to the tilt but the contact with the airport apron still felt like an old Land Rover's traverse of a dry Serengeti river-bed. I breathed out, finally, when the jet shuddered to a crawl and began taxiing to a private part of the complex.

'Jesus, Jake. This is not a fucking helicopter.' Karl had woken with a start and shouted through the open cockpit door at the pilot.

'Sorry about that, gents. We've only got access to a Japanese version of the flying manual.' The captain roared back at him with an exaggerated bowing of his head and a schoolyard parody of a Japanese accent.

Karl shook his own head as he turned to me.

'I would not be surprised. Most of these cute flyboys earn their wings these days on Gameboys or Play-Stations. They never see the friggen sky. Jesus help us!'

'What now, Karl?' I smiled in a conspiratorial fashion.

'Bob Arnold is going to meet us here and we will have a debriefing. He would like to know more of what happened to you over the past few days.'

'So would I . . .' I looked out the window and could see a small group of non-uniformed people waiting beside two large cars for the engines to shut down. 'But I remember very little.'

'That's what concerns us, buddy!'

'What do you mean, Karl?'

'Let me try and put the story together for you. You said you went to a broad's apartment, right?'

'Yes.'

'And the next thing you remember, nearly two days later, is another broad dropping you off at the café.'

'Yes.'

'All of that suggests to me that you might have been slipped a Mickey Finn that first evening in the apartment. After that it would have been easy to drug you up with whatever they wanted to use.'

'Why?'

'Information extraction, usually.'

'Jesus!' I said. There was silence for a few moments.

Karl had a puzzled frown on his face when he, eventually, spoke again. 'There is one untypical feature about it all however.'

'Which is?' I asked. Everything seemed untypical to my way of thinking.

'If someone goes to that much trouble to kidnap and drug, normally they would kill the mark when they have obtained the information. I just wonder why they let you live? It doesn't fit the usual pattern,' he said coldly as if I was a case study.

'I'm not half as disappointed about that fact as you sound, Karl.' I was shaking.

'Don't get upset, Michael. It's just his way. Karl is an avid fan of pattern analysis. In fact we think he'll make a damn good knitter one day. Won't you, Karl?' Dave was laughing as he stood up. He straightened his narrow tie and slipped his still sharply creased jacket on.

'Shut the fuck up, Dave.' Karl was touchy and as the younger agent backed off a little he turned back to look at me. The plane had finally stopped moving. 'We would like to take a blood sample for analysis.'

'To see the combination of drugs used,' Dave added.

I remembered the hashish. 'No . . . it's not necessary. What might have been used, and why?'

'Ketamine and perhaps a benzodiazepine like Rohypnol or Valium for neuroleptanalgesia, perhaps pentothal as well for control of consciousness. There are many combinations that can be used,' Karl explained. Both he and Dave were watching me carefully.

I stood up and retrieved my knapsack. No wonder I felt groggy. 'I don't believe it.'

'Happens all the time. Industrial espionage is a dirty game. Sometimes in the trade, once we figure out what drugs were used, we try to reproduce the episode to determine what information might have been given by the mark.' Karl was warming to the possibility.

'No thanks,' I hastily replied as I moved up the aisle towards the front of the aircraft. The cabin door was open and I could feel the heat rise from the asphalt to greet me.

At the bottom of the steps, Bob Arnold was waiting. 'Hello, Michael. Whassup!'

'Just playing your game, Bob, just playing your game.' I replied with sarcastic humour. I badly needed a stiff drink. 'What about you?'

'Surprisingly good, given the circumstances.' Bob looked agitated. 'I am sorry about all this, but it was necessary.'

An image of Alonzo appeared, sitting in his chair, his still warm blue-blotched face staring at me. 'I understand. What now?'

'We've received reliable information that an important meeting is taking place tomorrow and that one or other of the parties involved in trying to get their hands on the Mara Stealth Virus, will be there. I'll explain a bit more on our way to an observation house set up on the other side of the island.'

Arnold held the door of the car open for me and I sat in behind the driver. I watched as Karl and Dave descended the steps and quickly got into the other vehicle. The two cars then set off at a leisurely pace across the apron and exited onto the normal airport access road through a guarded gate. The route out of the airport took us past the door of the arrivals terminal. It was busy with traffic, meeting an incoming flight. Near the head of the taxi rank the congestion cleared and the car accelerated. I suddenly thought I recognized somebody standing in the rank.

'Pull over, driver.' I shouted.

'What's up, Michael?'

'Pull over and I'll tell you.'

Arnold instructed the driver to comply and we pulled into the kerbside about thirty yards beyond the end of the rank. I looked through the heavily tinted uni-directional glass of the rear window.

'What is it, Michael?'

'I'm not absolutely sure but I think I recognize that man.' I pointed towards the rank.

'Which one?'

'The tall fellow near the front with the small silver-coloured photographer's camera case.'

'Yes. He looks nervous; alert.'

'Exactly. Like a meerkat sentinel.'

'What?' Arnold looked at me in a confused way.

'It doesn't matter. His name is Sancho and he's a waiter in Granada. What's he doing here? It's a very strange coincidence.'

'Why? Where did you see him before?'

'At the restaurant where I first met Isabella. She said that his mother was her landlady.' I felt a strange weariness and a desperate longing to meet Isabella again.

'Who is this Isabella?'

'The girl, whose apartment I went to . . . whose friend brought me to the café. I met her by chance last Saturday and that man in the rank served us at the table. It was Isabella who told me about Alonzo Aldahrze. She's the . . .' I suddenly realized that I could not reveal any more to Arnold. This was my secret.

'Excuse me for a moment, Michael.'

Arnold touched the driver on the shoulder and after the central locking mechanism had been released opened his door, got out, and walked up to where the car carrying Karl and Dave had pulled in ahead of us. The driver of our car kept the engine running and adjusted the rear view mirror to keep me in view. His eyes darted from me to the car ahead. Without looking back, Arnold had pushed his head and shoulders through the passenger window and spoke for a few minutes before standing up straight. I watched as he slapped the roof of the car and waited to see it pull away before returning to ours.

'Everything ok?' I asked as he sat in.

'Sure. No problem.' Arnold touched the driver's shoulder again and as our car accelerated from the kerb he leant forward to retrieve his briefcase from the floor. After keying in the combination he laid it across his lap, opened back the top panel and retrieved a brown cardboard-backed envelope, which he then handed to me.

'What's this?' I asked.

'Photographs. Please look at them, Michael.'

I opened the envelope and extracted a number of good quality paper prints. The plain back was uppermost and it was only when I turned it over that a medium range but well defined picture of Isabella stared back at me. I blushed instantly and looked at Arnold who said nothing. Shuffling this first photograph to the back of the pile the next was a picture of a couple in deep conversation. It was Isabella and . . . Moshe Hertzog, my Israeli collaborator in the cocaine virus work.

'*Christ!*' I said aloud.

'Is that the woman you know as Isabella?'

'Yes,' I nodded.

'Look at the date.'

The digital date print was on the bottom right hand corner. It was from the week before when Isabella said she was in Chicago.

'Where was this taken?' I was hoping against hope.

'Tel Aviv.'

All of the other photographs, apart from the last, were of that same meeting. The last, in contrast, had "today's" date and was a long distance but obvious picture of Isabella standing against a boat's railings. She looked beautiful with the wind in her hair and the sun on her face. I held the photograph up and looked at it for a long time.

'And this?'

'Earlier today at the port in Calvi.'

'*Isabella is in Corsica?*' I almost choked.

'Yes.' Arnold's face was impassive, cold.

I placed the photograph in my inside jacket pocket and returned the others to the envelope and handed it to Arnold.

'What's going on, Bob?'

'Isabella Sanjil has been under observation since that meeting with Hertzog. Up to now, we still have very little information on her but we do know, from a partially intercepted phone-call, that her code name is Solis. It is she who is the conduit to Alexander in Alpanna and that is why she is here in Corsica. Alexander has a summer villa here.'

'Then my meeting her was not accidental. I was set up.' My voice had dropped to a whisper.

'Probably, Michael. I am sorry but industrial espionage is very sophisticated. You weren't to know.'

'Shit. Shit . . .shit . . . *shit*.' I slammed the door with my fist. The driver's eyes locked onto me in the mirror, his right hand moving towards the unoccupied passenger seat where I'd seen a muzzled machine pistol lying waiting, earlier.

'Take it easy, Michael. This is why we had to get you out of Granada in such a hurry. I'm not sure why your friend Aldahrze was killed, but many of the people that Alexander has dealings with are not to be messed with.'

'What do you mean?'

'It appears that in addition to his pharmaceutical company, Alexander has an interesting sideline in sponsoring international terrorism and that drug money from the Afghan opium trade funds it. CIA and Interpol have linked his name to some of the most radical autonomy-seeking groups in the world. No definite proof, mind you, but the whispers are out there. We think that Corsica is the centre of that operation.'

'Why am I here?'

'Two reasons. One was your immediate safety and the second was your relationship with this Isabella Sanjil.'

I looked out the window. The road was beginning to rise through a valley that would take us, according to the signposts, to Corte. Ahead of us, along the mountain-top horizon, dark storm clouds were gathering to blacken the sky. The occasional forked flash of lightning silhouetted peaks and high passes.

'What do you mean by that?'

'If the woman, Sanjil obtained all the information she wanted from you over the last few days, then you would have been expendable. The fact that you are still here suggests that you either managed to conceal the information she was looking for or that she likes you. Either way it is an opportunity for us to get to Alexander through her.'

'Using me as bait, I suppose!' I pretended to be angry. I was thinking of the *Voices*. Maybe Isabella's loyalties were divided.

'In a very protected way . . . yes. If you do not believe that, Michael, or you want out of the Alexander operation, say so now. There'll be no option for changing your mind later. Do you understand?'

'Yes.' I thought about what he had told me for a few moments. There was something I had to do first. 'Bob.'

'Yes, Michael.'

'I need to contact my wife, Caroline. I'll give you an answer after I speak to her.'

'Sure. Work away.'

'I can't. Karl took my cell phone earlier. I need it back.'

'Oh! Sure.' Arnold tapped on the driver's shoulder. 'Stop the car.'

It was about twenty minutes before we got underway again. Arnold returned the phone and left me alone as I tried contacting Caroline both at home and on her mobile. I had no success on either. Rod was also unavailable. I wound down the window and called out to Bob. He rejoined me in the car.

'What's up, Michael?'

'I cannot get hold of Caroline.'

'Did you leave a message?'

'Yes, but I need you to do a favour for me.'

'Sure. What?'

'Caroline was with a State Department mission to La Paz in Mexico. Could you use your lines of communication to track her down?'

'No problem.' Arnold got out of the car again and I could see him speaking to Karl. When he returned he slapped me on the leg. 'That's all underway. We should have word when we get to the villa. *Let's go driver*.'

'Thanks, Bob. It's important.'

'I know, Michael.' Arnold pulled out a packet of cigarettes and offered me one. After lighting up we sat back saying nothing for some time. It was he who finally broke the silence.

'Michael. May I ask you something?'

'Go ahead, Bob.'

'Does Isabella Sanjil turn you on that much?' Arnold had a look of genuine concern on his face.

'No . . . Well, yes she does. Are you worried it might compromise your mission?'

'Frankly. Yes. There is a lot of shit happening that I can't figure. That worries me.'

'I've decided to go all the way with you, Bob, whatever the consequences.'

'Why, Michael?'

'Alexander is after my company, after me personally and is almost certainly responsible for Alonzo Aldahrze's death. I need to be involved to see that he is stopped and also for another reason.'

'What's that, Michael? What does Aldahrze have to do with all this? What was his connection to Alexander?'

'Charles Alexander is the gath . . . I have to stop him.'

'The what, Michael?'

'It doesn't matter. Can this car go any faster?'

The tall Australian wandered out onto the balcony of the converted wine tower that was rented out as a summer villa. In the small pool, set into the rocks on a level below the balcony, one of the team members was taking a leisurely swim and on seeing Mallory, waved up at him.

He ignored the salute to look out beyond the pool and over the gentle slopes to the Bay of Propriano beyond. To the west, the sun was setting and, he realised, it would soon be dark. He turned as he heard footsteps behind him. A small lithe dark-skinned man dressed in a singlet and shorts and with the conditioned physique, Mallory noted in admiration, of the champion boxer he had once been, was coming towards him. The man stopped for a moment and stared up at the sky behind the tower. He carried an opened bottle of wine and two glasses.

'There are some bad storm-clouds to the northeast Rod. It is going to be a rough night. Good for our purposes though.'

Luis Gonzaga grinned as he placed the bottle and glasses on the table and pulled out a chair. Mallory nodded his head, a concurring smile creasing his face.

'Yes.'

Gonzaga took his seat and after pouring a glass of wine for them leaned back in the chair with his legs resting on the table. He looked at the Australian.

'Tell me, Rod, how did your discussions in Miami go. I wonder if the Medellin boys have any idea of –'

'*Shhhhhh*,' Rod Mallory whispered urgently as he held up a finger to his lips and pointed to the balcony rail.

Gonzaga brought his legs down and, after standing up, quietly moved to the fence-like wooden balcony and looked down towards the pool below him. Seeing the floating swimmer he shouted at him in an irritated voice.

'Jorge, get inside. We will be having a full briefing in ten minutes. I want a full radio and weapons check done by then.'

'Sure, Luis.' Mallory could hear the sullen reply as he sat down and watched as Gonzaga waited for the pool area to be cleared. The two men drew their chairs close and sipped at the poured wine.

'Apart from you, Luis, there is nobody else here that I trust. Jorge, for instance, is one of Domingo's men and that bastard is only waiting for an opportunity to cut my throat. We need to be very careful if we are to shed our Columbian friends,' Mallory whispered.

'What do you intend to do, Rod?'

'I've arranged a surprise for the golden boy.'

'I meant about now, here in Corsica.'

'Oh! As we've discussed, Luis. I'll go, as invited, to Alexander's villa tonight and will act as our point man. If the opportunity presents, we'll try and take him out. Alive! All the men must understand this. We need to get as much information as possible before he is disposed of. If there is no opportunity it will still provide good intelligence and we can make our plans accordingly.'

'And the American, Mara?'

'He'll surface again. The authorities will have found his wife's body by now. I've somebody waiting for Mara to arrive in La Paz. I would not like to see his face when the circumstances are explained. The poor bastard.' Mallory looked at his watch.

'You like him then?' Gonzalez looked puzzled.

'Yes, in a way. But that's not the point, is it, Luis? If the rumours are accurate, Mara potentially holds the key to my . . . To our control of the cocaine industry. I believe in luck, Luis and this has fallen into our laps. With the woman gone, it will not be difficult to be rid of Mara once we have the virus. Hoxygene, lock stock and barrel, will be mine and I can launder our profits to my heart's content.'

'What about the FARC rebels.'

'Fuck the FARC . . . And the cartels. We'll soon see the Columbians grovel.'

'Yes. I will enjoy that pleasure.' Gonzalez smiled a gold-cap toothed smile.

'Right, Luis, enough verbals, mate. Let's go inside and get on with the briefing. We need to be very clear on our tactics. Some of the drongos we are stuck with are as thick as shit and we need to tune their wires carefully.'

The night had fully closed in as the convoy of cars turned off the road and drove up a narrow path carved into the side of the hill. To the west, an occasional flash of lightning could still be seen arcing earthwards from the sky, causing the orange-coloured stone outcrops of the mountain ridges to appear and disappear like spectral beacons. After negotiating a final series of rising hairpin turns and putting up with the constant clatter from the showers of small stones sent flying by spinning tyres of the car ahead, the convoy stopped.

Michael saw that they were in the paved courtyard of a stone-built villa, the type of villa usually owned but rarely used by a mainlander. He watched as the occupants of the other cars got out and, after some stretching, entered through the open door of the villa. He also got out but remained in the courtyard looking up at the sky. The night-air was still laden with the threat of further thunderstorms.

Bob Arnold joined him.

'What happens now, Bob?'

'We have Alexander's villa, on the other side of the small valley, under direct observation. We're anxious to know what's going on.'

The two men entered the hallway and crossed its polished marble floor to enter a large lounge. The room was untidy and cluttered, its floor crisscrossed by cables of every colour. The lighting was subdued and the curtains closed. Two agents with large earmuffs were attached to a bank of electronic equipment that reminded Michael of an airport control tower. One of them looked up as Arnold approached.

'Everything is working, General.'

'Good.' Arnold looked around at the cables and monitors. The room was stuffy with the heat they generated. 'What's in place?'

'Two radar mikes set up below the pool, locked onto the balcony and lounge of Alexander's villa. Interpretation difficult at present as they are playing some heavy-duty opera shit. CIA satellite photo updates every fifteen minutes. Infra-red heat detection video unit mounted in bedroom upstairs. Voice analysis and language interpretation links to Langley open and operational. Vibration and movement detectors, in place on the villa driveway. A two agent team is, at this moment, secure within 50 yards of villa.'

'Any hint of counter-detection audio surveillance?'

'No scanning direction mikes obvious, sir, but the house security does have ground-zero vibration and audio sensors in place. High quality, but perimeter yardage varies. Our field team found a 'quiet' corner close to the house.'

'Great.' Arnold patted the man on his shoulder. 'Who's in charge?'

'Hank Sommers. He's upstairs in the bedroom.'

'Thanks.' Arnold turned and climbed the stairs that brought them to the first floor. Michael followed. At the end of a corridor two heavy black curtains had been set up in sequence about 6 feet apart. Pushing through the first Arnold waited for Michael to join him before going through the second set.

'What's this for, Bob?' Michael asked in the pitch darkness.

'We want no light entering that might give away our presence. *Hank Sommers*? Hank are you there?'

'General,' a voice answered quietly from the gloom.

Gradually, Arnold and Michael's vision adjusted to the little light there was to pick out Hank Sommers standing behind a forest of camera tripods. They moved cautiously to join him.

The bedroom had a large balcony window overlooking a valley and by following the direction of the mounted camera lenses, Michael saw that the target of their observation was another villa on the far side of the valley, about 400 yards away. Curtains were drawn but as most of the rooms had lights on he could see shadowy figures passing behind them. Loud music from the villa blared out across the valley

'What's the update, Hank?'

'Alexander and a woman, voice identified by the data banks at Langley as Solis, arrived about fifteen minutes ago. Backs to us, no pictures. The Israeli, Hertzog, has been there since mid afternoon. He came with another woman, young, spiky redhead, no identity as yet. There is a long balcony shot of her downstairs. In the house we estimate three maybe four other persons. Perimeter security is surprisingly lax. Three single rotating patrols, linked by walkie-talkie to the others on the inside. Strangely, they all appear to be women.'

'Jesus! Talking of women, what's with the goddam music. I hate opera. The singer sounds as if she's being strangled,' Bob Arnold mumbled under his breath.

'You're not far off the mark,' Michael whispered back in a distracted way.

'What is it?' Hank Sommers asked as he and Arnold turned to look at him.

'It's Brünnhilde at Siefried's pyre in the last act of Götterdämmerung. A favourite piece of my father,' Michael said quietly. ' "*Summon Loge to Valhalla! For the gods' destruction soon shall be here*".'

'Gotter what?' Arnold asked.

'Götterdämmerung. The Twilight of the Gods. Richard Wagner's opera based on the Teutonic mythology of *ragna rök,* the final destiny, the utter destruction of Valhalla and the old order of Gods, allowing a new cycle to begin. New Gods and new men emerging from the Twilight.'

'Jesus. This guy is doing the full trip. I wonder what other surprises he –'

'Sorry, General. We've got company,' Hank Sommers interrupted.

There was a sudden burst of radio clatter in the room behind them as two other shadows entered. Michael could feel the tension rise as he watched Karl and Dave moving towards the cameras. In the distance the lights of a car were drawing closer to Alexander's villa.

'What's up?' Michael asked.

'Car coming. Two occupants. Two . . .' Hank Sommers pressed his hand hard against his earpiece. 'Repeat! Right. Two men.'

Everybody in the darkened room peered out across the valley towards the villa. The car drew up into a forecourt that was situated in a hollow that was linked by a set of steps to the villa entrance. Automatic sensors lit up the forecourt and steps in bright light.

'Hopefully somebody will come to the door,' Sommers said quietly.

'At least they've turned off that blasted music,' Arnold added.

The car doors opened and the two men got out. Michael could see on a nearby monitor that their backs were to the cameras.

The front door of the villa opened. Two figures stepped out and into the bright light of the forecourt.

'Shit. Zoom in on them first.' Sommers tapped Dave on the shoulder.

The monitor image shifted, focused and then froze.

'Alexander and the woman Sanjil,' Dave said.

'Also known as Solis,' Sommers added.

Michael's heart missed a beat and his mouth went dry. He had hoped they'd been mistaken but knew they had not been. *It was Isabella.* Alexander had placed his arm around her waist as they waited for the two new arrivals to walk up the steps towards them. It was only as the two men neared the top that Alexander released his hold when one of the visitors hesitated,. He looked anxious.

'Focus back on the visitors,' Sommers ordered.

'They've suddenly stopped. One of them is saying something. Do you copy, Base?' Dave whispered into his mike and waited for a reply. 'Arabic. Good. One of them has left something in the car. He's turning back.'

The tall angular figure turned and descended the steps again. The monitor image froze again. Michael almost shouted. 'That's Sancho, the waiter.'

'The man at the airport. He is retrieving something from the car,' Karl confirmed.

'Zoom in on the other. Quick he is looking back down.' Sommers spoke urgently. 'Shit. Did we get it?'

'Just.' Karl spoke and they all waited to see if the image was adequate. Michael didn't recognize the dark-skinned man with piercing eyes.

'Jesus.' It was Dave who spoke first. 'I'm sure that's Hasan al-Sa'igh, the anti-Taliban leader of the *Badhriya* in Afghanistan. Alexander's opium supplier no doubt.' He spoke urgently once again into his lapel mike. 'Base. Patch this through to Langley for confirmation.'

Michael knew it to be true. It had to be. Alonzo had warned him. What had the waiter Sancho got to do with it all? He sighed.

'The gathering.'

'What did you say, Michael?' Bob Arnold spoke without turning to look back at him.

'Emm . . . I said it's some gathering.'

'Yes. They are desperate to get their hands on the Mara Stealth Virus.'

'And me too, it seems!'

Arnold said nothing but watched as all four figures entered into the house. After a minute or so the forecourt lights went out.

'General Arnold.' Hank Sommers was speaking.

'Yes.'

'They need you urgently downstairs.'

'Fine Hank. Thanks. Michael, stay here awhile! I'll be back in a few minutes.'

Alexander greeted the new arrivals to the house warmly once the front door was closed. He kissed the Afghan in the Arab fashion before shaking Sancho's hand. Isabella said nothing and pulled away to one side. Sancho seemed upset at her coolness.

'What's wrong, Isabella?' he asked.

'You did it, Sancho. Didn't you?' Isabella glared at him.

The erstwhile waiter looked down at the small case he was carrying and then at Isabella. His eyes were defiant and scathing of her question.

'Yes, my sister. It was my duty. I do not fail.'

'You bastard. He was no threat to us.' Her words spat out and she moved forward to slap his face.

'*Enough!*' Alexander grabbed her wrist and pulled it down. 'The decision to kill Alonzo was mine. He *was* a threat. It is done, Isabella.' Alexander tried putting his hand around her waist. She pulled away. He ignored her and walked down a short flight of stairs to a closed door. Stopping before opening it he looked back at her. His voice was softer but focused. 'We have much to do. Come on.'

Alexander pushed open the door and they followed him into a large lounge area. The room was spacious with three walls formed by sliding glass panels. A light breeze was wafting through the room but it was not enough to ruffle the heavy drapes that screened out the valley beyond. To one side was a small counter bar with bottles of every hue neatly stacked. Behind the bar a tall shaven-headed girl waited. She smiled as Alexander walked in, shifting the shoulder-strapped Uzi from her side to the small of her back.

There was little furniture apart from a low glass-topped table that displayed a collection of coins within its layers. Surrounding this was a series of white leather-covered sofa chairs with Moroccan pillows. In the furthest chair a flustered, bald and heavyset man was perched on the edge. Behind him, Zoë hovered. She looked to the ceiling, as Alexander approached, shaking her head slightly.

'Alexander. I'm tired of all this. I want to leave. *Now!*' The Israeli tried to be as forceful as he could. Large sweat stains were spreading out from his armpits.

'I will tell you when you can leave, you obnoxious pervert,' Alexander rasped at him before disdainfully pointing to chairs for his other guests to take.

'That's it. I am leaving.' Hertzog made an effort to get off the chair. He was half-erect when Zoë slammed the palm of her hand into the base of his neck causing him to drop back to the seat like a stone. His face was suddenly frightened.

'That's better, you Judas goat. Now, tell me what I need to know about the cocaine virus that Mara has developed. I need the genetic sequence and I do not have much time.'

'I'm a horticulturist. I run the trials not the development. I do not –' His words were cut off by another blow from Zoë. Before he could recover from this she began pressing her two thumbs into his eye-sockets.

'Hertzog. I advise you to tell me everything you know, right now. I do not have any time for games and Zoë there, has even less tolerance. Have you got access to the genetic sequence information?'

'No. I don't. Ahhhhhhhhhhhhhhhh . . .' Hertzog screamed, as Zoë dug deep with her thumb and his left eyeball was half gouged from its socket. Clear fluid squirted across the room. 'I don't. *I don't*! Please stop.'

'Then you should not have pretended that you had, Hertzog. 40 pieces of silver is a real bad bargain. Take him away.'

The tall shaven-headed girl moved from behind the bar and along with Zoë began pulling the still screaming Israeli to his feet. When he resisted, she drove the butt of her gun deep into his groin. He collapsed and it was only with great effort that she and Zoë managed to drag him out of the room.

Alexander watched the scene, silently. Both al-Sa'igh and Sancho were shaking their heads, admiringly.

'I think he might have given us more information if we had given him more time,' Isabella said coolly.

Alexander smiled at her.

'No. I've had him checked him out. Our friend, Hertzog has an ego and a free-spending teenage mistress. He thought he could pull a deal on us. He knows nothing of the virus structure and the samples he brought will have to be analysed. That much was worth it, I suppose.'

'Why torture him? Was that necessary?' Isabella stood up and walked towards the bar. She glared at Sancho who had put a finger to his lips in warning.

'It's irrelevant, Isabella. He is a dead man and death will be a release. The torture will have convinced him of that. Hertzog will die with a sense of escape, a sense of freedom. In comparison to the perils of living he is moving to paradise. What more could one do for another human being?'

Isabella shuddered slightly at the adamant and brutal sincerity of Alexander's logic. The death of any one man or woman did not bother her if it was necessary. She often had to be the instrument of that death but took no pleasure in it. Alexander, on the other hand, seemed to relish it and, as if reading her thoughts, smiled knowingly at her again before turning to walk towards a Hockney painting that dominated one wall of the room.

The frame of the picture swung back on its hinges to reveal a wall safe. Alexander dialled in the combination and after releasing the door bolt leant into the safe. He retrieved a small but thick case made of fireproof titanium. Almost reverentially he carried this with some effort across to the low table. Taking a seat opposite al-Sa'igh and Sancho he let it down carefully and opened its lid.

Both men let out a gasp as they looked at the contents. Carved into a solid gold base were seven wide grooves. At the head of each of the grooves was a small circular well. Two of these wells were filled with hardened wax and the three men could easily make out the impressions made by the small button-shaped seals of bright blue lapis lazuli, which rested in the corresponding grooves. Alexander touched each of them in turn.

'The seals of *Abrape* and *Nergimmel.* Two of the seven *Voices*! They are now to be joined in their place of repose by others. Sancho please!'

Sancho retrieved the small case he had brought. Opening it he removed a bulky silk-wrapped bundle and handed it to Alexander. They all watched as he laid this down on the table and opened out the material carefully. At last the hourglass was uncovered and as it rolled slightly on its axis they could see in its lid, the Timekeeper's seal, *Ayatau.*

'I will get a jeweller to retrieve the stone later.' Alexander sounded disappointed. He wanted the *Voice* to join the others immediately. 'Al-Sa'igh and Isabella. Show me yours please.'

Al-Sa'igh, retrieved from a deep pocket and passed over the dagger with *Syrbeth* imbedded while Isabella lifted *Nefradaleth* from around her neck. They laid these down on the table close to the hourglass. Alexander pulled a stick of golden beeswax from a grove in the lid. Lighting a match he dripped the melting liquid into the wells until they filled.

'I'll wait until they harden somewhat and will then take an impression.'

'Why the impressions, Charles?' Isabella asked.

'It is the combination of the ideograms of each of the seals that controls the power of the *Voices*, not the actual stones. Once I . . . once we have all seven then the formula of mankind's original relationship with God will be revealed and the original design for that relationship explained. I need the message not the messengers. Previous gatherers failed to understand this. Only two more and it is complete. *Saclaresh,* which Isabella informs me is coincidentally to become Mara's responsibility, and the hidden *Voice*, whose name I know not but whose whereabouts is irrelevant.'

'What do you mean, Charles?' Isabella watched as Alexander took an impression of *Nefradaleth* and replaced the seal and the wax well in their grooves. She already regretted the ease in which she had allowed him the opportunity to take the impression and was annoyed at herself for not anticipating his intentions. She had always believed that it was the stone that was the talisman, that it had the philosopher's power, but now realized, with sudden blinding clarity, that Alexander was right. The ideas were the important legacy not the stones.

Alexander must have read her thoughts and he glared over at her.

'With five gathered, and the sixth close by, the last, the hidden one can no longer remain hidden. It is obliged to reveal itself and when that happens I will be waiting. I first just need to get Mara and *Saclaresh*. Where is he, I wonder?'

With Arnold, Karl and Sommers gone the bedroom was suddenly very quiet. Michael could hear Dave's breathing coming in short bursts as he listened intently through the earmuffs of a radio direction mike. Moving closer, he saw that one of the cables coursing across the floor had become detached from the mike's receiver unit. He tapped Dave on the shoulder.

'Dave.'

The agent startled. 'What?'

'One of the cables has come loose.' Michael pointed towards the ground.

'What? Oh thanks.'

Michael watched as the previously cool agent flustered while reattaching the cable. 'Are you picking up anything? May I listen?'

'What? Oh no. It's very garbled. There was a mention of your stealth virus however and Alexander was wondering where you might be.'

'If only he knew!'

'Yeah.'

From where Alexander, Isabella, al-Sa'igh and Sancho were sitting they could watch as the groaning Hertzog was dragged through the front door. His legs trailed behind him, one hand clasped over the weeping eye. Zoë looked back briefly at Alexander before descending the steps. Isabella could see him give a slight but unmistakable nod of his head.

'What is the agenda now, Sahib al-Zuhur?'

The Afghan, al-Sa'igh was speaking as he pulled a tin of tobacco from his pocket and began rolling a cigarette. Expertly he soon finished and offered the tin to Sancho. Soon the smell of hashish wafted through the room. Alexander waited for them to finish. He declined to smoke.

'Mara's business partner, the Australian, Rod Mallory, will be here shortly under the pretence of finalizing my company's plans for Hoxygene. I'll be able to use him to flush Mara out. You, and Sancho are to make yourselves scarce.'

'I did not mean your commercial activities, Overlord, though I wish them well. May Allah watch over you.' Hasan al-Sa'igh spoke in an irritated manner and Isabella could see Alexander bristling. The Nuristani continued. 'I need to know how we are going to tackle the Taliban. You have the *Voice* as requested as well as access to the opium. My people will question my wisdom in these matters unless I can bring back a workable plan as well as funding.'

'I understand your concerns, Sahib al-Sa'igh and that is why I have asked Sancho to be here.'

Isabella threw a quick glance in the tall, thin man's direction. He smiled briefly.

'What do you mean, Overlord?'

'Sancho and his fellow members of the *Khannakiya* have agreed, for a considerable consideration it must be said, to undertake the task of assassinating all of the Taliban leadership. This will –'

'Is that true Sancho? Are you a member of the *Khannakiya*? Tell me!' Isabella looked shocked as she shot out the words.

'It is true, Solis, my sister.'

'I was saying, if you allow me continue.' Alexander had a half-smile on his face and an amused sarcastic tone in his voice. He enjoyed revealing the unexpected. Nobody could relax. 'They will be ready to begin their onerous duty in the New Year. Training camps are at operational status near Khorsud in Tajikistan. Targeting and information gathering is taking place as we speak. At that point, al-Sa'igh, you and your people had better be prepared to move. We will get one opportunity and one only. Do you understand?'

'Of course, Overlord. Forgive my doubts. May Allah bless you. We will hang and gut the dogs on their goalposts in Kabul. It will be a splendid victory. '

'And profitable. You and Sancho will return together to Zurich. Some time will need to be taken to co-ordinate your operations. My chalet in Flims is at your disposal.'

'Thank you again, Overlord.'

In the background they suddenly heard the sounds of muffled shots. Alexander stood up to getter a better view through the open doorway and Isabella joined him. He put an arm around her waist. She did not move away.

'No loose ends, Solis. No loose ends!'

Suddenly the forecourt lights came on. Zoë and the shaven-headed girl who were standing near the rear of the car stopped what they were doing and looked up as if caught by a border post beam. Alexander laughed as he spoke into a small microphone attached to his shirt.

'Security. That must be Mallory. Confirm.'

'One Range Rover. Blacked-out windows. Moving very slowly. Two occupants.'

'Any other activity.'

'No. Vibration sensors and infra-red beams functioning at optimal status.'

'Good.'

Alexander watched as the car drew up. Zoë and the shaven-headed girl rushed up the steps. He moved towards the doorway. Zoë reached him first.

'You and Jena were like rabbits out there. Are you nervous Zoë?'

'I have a strange sensation that we are being watched. I cannot pinpoint it.'

'When Mallory arrives you and Jena check out the car. Go outside and wait on the steps.' Alexander activated his mike again. 'Security! Turn on weapons scan in doorway!'

'Copy that. Are you armed, Overlord.' The woman's tone was polite.

'Yes.'

'Step away a little bit more. You will activate the machine.'

Alexander stepped back into the shadows to where Isabella had waited and they watched as the large vehicle pulled up. The headlights were turned off but there was no movement to open the doors. He waited.

'Security. What the fuck is happening?' Isabella noticed the edge in Alexander's voice.

'Sensors indicate he has opened a telecommunications link from the car. Probably making a telephone call. Cannot be more specific than that.'

'Shit.' Alexander pulled away from Isabella. 'Security. Zoë and Jena are outside and will check the car. Order full perimeter check, section by section. Night vision equipment. *Now!*'

'Permission to shut down vibration and infra-red sensors.'

'Section by section only. Stay ahead of them. Understand!'

'Understood.'

As the car turned the corner Alexander's villa came into view. The two men inhaled deeply.

'It's some set up. Our sensors and cameras confirm vibration mikes and infra-red. What should we do?' Luis Gonzalez was the first to speak.

The car pulled to a halt on the forecourt. Mallory could see two women waiting near the top of the steps that led up to the house. They appeared agitated.

'They look nervous. I suspect that they will check us out and then the car. We'll wait here for a while. Let them stew a bit. Force them to act.' Mallory pressed a console button; there was now an open line to his teams. 'This will get them going.'

They waited and waited. Eventually the two women outside the doorway of the house began to descend the steps. They made no secret of the fact that they carried guns. A small jeep exited from a side entrance and with screeching wheels accelerated down the driveway.

'Bingo, you beauts, a textbook response.' Rod Mallory smiled as he watched. He lifted the console handset and spoke in a low voice. 'Sierra One. Patrol coming, two lizards. Await opportunity to take them out. Once in, use the driveway. Frontal take out. Sierra Two. Probably another patrol dispatched to a different sector. Move to valley side of house. Wait for my signal. Over and out.'

The connection severed, Mallory pushed the door open and exited the car. He bounded, with a big grin on his face past the two women on the steps, towards the doorway.

Bob Arnold sat down in the chair beside the agent who was operating the console of monitors in the downstairs lounge.

'What's going on?'

'Put on this ear piece, General. We've lost the signal from inside the house but I'm getting good reception from the courtyard and doorway area. The villa is going hot.' The agent did not divert his eyes from the screens as he pushed the radio headset towards Arnold.

'What do you mean?' Arnold picked up the headset and put it on.

'Listen and watch, sir. Alexander has started issuing lots of orders and something is happening on the steps.' The agent pointed to one of the screens.

Two shadowy figures could be seen dragging a third person down the steps towards one of the parked cars. Reaching a large Mercedes sedan the bigger of two helpers leant the slumping third over the shinning silver bonnet while the other pulled out a set of keys and deactivated the cars central locking.

'Who's that over the hood?' Arnold moved in close to the screen.

'The Israeli, Hertzog, I think.' The agent answered.

'Drunk?' Arnold offered.

There was a brief silence. 'Perhaps. They are being very rough with him though. Jesus!'

'What?' It was Hank Summers voice. He was standing behind Arnold and the agent at the console.

'Its very dark but the smaller of the two figures is opening the trunk. They are shoving Hertzog into the fucken' trunk.'

'What should we do?' Arnold looked up at Sommers.

'Radio the field team to try and get closer. Hold it . . . Shit!'

They all watched as one of the women drew a gun and pointed it into the trunk. They couldn't see Hertzog's body but two distinct *ppfaaaft* sounds were picked up on the mikes.

'*Jesus*, they've murdered him.' Arnold stood up. 'We're fucken' useless over here.'

Just at that moment the vibration and audio mikes lit up their signals.

'Car coming.' The console agent flicked a switch. 'Bravo team. Car coming. Confirm previous instruction on movement. This is opportunity to move within perimeter. Copy?'

'Copy base. Moving in.' The response was a metallic echo.

The forecourt lights came on again. The scene at the car was lit up like a night hunt.

'They must be activated by the roadway sensors. The two figures look like startled rabbits caught in a torch beam. It's caught them out. Who are they?' Arnold asked.

'Taller shaven-headed woman unidentified but Alexander called her Jena. House security staff probably. Codename assigned Amazon One. Smaller red-headed woman recognized, codename Zoë,' Hank Sommers answered.

'That's Zoë, Isabella Sanjil's cousin, the girl who left me back to the café,' Michael suddenly said quietly from behind them as he and Dave arrived down from the upper floor.

They all watched silently, impotent, as the trunk was closed and the two women ran back up the steps and into the house. After a few minutes they came back out again and took up a position near the top of the steps. The incoming car soon drew up into the forecourt and stopped. They all looked at each other, shrugging their shoulders, as nothing happened for the next five minutes.

'What gives?' Arnold spoke for all of them. Suddenly, the passenger door opened and a tall man unwound himself from the seat and stepped out.

'*Rod Mallory*. What the fuck is he doing *here*?'

Arnold, Sommers and the console agent all turned simultaneously to see Michael Mara staring, his face flushed, at the monitor screens.

'Mallory identity confirmed,' Karl shouted from the far side of the room and a smaller bank of screens.

They watched as he ran up the steps past the descending women. They seemed to hesitate for a moment, glaring at him as they unslung their weapons. Ignoring them, Mallory reached the patio in front of the doorway where he stopped abruptly and turned to walk towards the side of the house that overlooked the valley. There was a small low balcony wall and he leant against it.

'What's he doing?' Arnold spoke again.

'Pretending to take in the view. he's . . . he's planting something on the outside wall, just under the balcony. It's. . . camera three, zoom in. . . there, see!' Karl pointed to the enlarged and rapidly enhancing screen image. 'It looks like a gun. Confirm Bravo One.'

'Confirmed. Automatic pistol. Beretta probably.'

Alexander stepped out of the shadows and was surprised not to find Rod Mallory waiting in the doorway. He barked into his mike.

'Security. What's happening?'

'Visitor on balcony to side of house. Looking over the valley.'

'Shit. Leave doorway scanner on. I'll go out.' Alexander reached inside his jacket and withdrew his small shoulder-holstered gun and handed it to Isabella. 'Solis, go back to the others and put the case for the seals back in the safe. I'll join you in a few minutes. Tell Sancho and al-Sa'igh to withdraw.'

Alexander went out. He could see Zoë talking to the driver of the Land Rover. Jena was inspecting the rear. Turning left he could see Mallory's back as the Australian looked out over the valley.

'Rod how are you? Why did you not come in?'

The Australian turned. He had a warm smile on his face. He held his hand out to take Alexander's and shook it strongly.

'Charles. I'm sorry. I was just taking a look over the valley. It's a fair dinkum place you have here. Really beaut.'

'Thank you, Rod. Come inside.'

Alexander linked arms with Mallory and led him into the house. He relaxed a little when the doorway sensors did not detect a concealed weapon on the Australian. Isabella came to greet them.

'You will have heard me mention my personal assistant, Isabella Sanjil. Isabella this is Rod Mallory, finance director of Hoxygene.'

Isabella held out her hand. She was used to being instantly appraised by the men she met, but this one was different. He did not appear particularly interested. His handshake was cool, professional.

'You are welcome, Mr Mallory. May I get you a drink?'

'Hi. Sure. A tinny please.'

'Sorry!'

'A beer thanks.'

Isabella turned and moved behind the counter bar.

Alexander showed Mallory to a seat. 'What happened in the car Rod? You took a long time to get out. My security staff, were concerned.'

'I noticed. I had to make a telephone call. Sorry.'

'Is there a problem?'

'What . . . Oh . . . Oh no. I was trying to speak to Michael Mara before you and I met.'

'Any luck? I too would like to arrange a meeting with him soon.'

'No. He is in the South of Spain somewhere. I could not track him down. I left a long message on his mobile phone though. That's what delayed me.'

'I see.' Alexander sounded disappointed.

'Don't worry, cobber. Our arrangement is a fait accompli. I have the backing of both the institutional shareholders and his wife's family to proceed with the deal. I just want to use this opportunity to thrash out our personal arrangement. My facilitator's fee, as it were.'

'You do not beat around the bush. Do you, Rod?'

'No, Charles. Kill the snakes where they lie. Check out whether they are poisonous afterwards. That's my approach.'

'I do not understand.' Alexander was genuinely puzzled.

'Sorry, mate. What I mean is that I prefer direct action. Tell it as it is. No misunderstandings. *Comprenez vous*?'

'*Parlez-vous Francais*?'

'*Oui. Bien sûr mon ami. Español, Japanois et Italien aussi.*'

'Surprising.'

'I'm a man of surprises, Charles. Do not underestimate me.'

'Thank you for the warning, Rod. I'll try not to. Ah good, here's your beer. I hope it is cold enough. Thank you, Isabella.'

Rod took the beer from Isabella and quickly downed a large draught. Alexander sat opposite him.

'Perhaps you would –' An urgent voice was speaking into Alexander's earpiece. He stood up suddenly. 'Excuse me a moment, Rod. There is a small matter I need to attend to.'

The radio cackled into life. The voice that spoke did so in a garbled and hurried way.

'Base, this is Bravo Two. Come in. Urgent.'

'Go ahead, Bravo Two.'

'A two man team near the entrance has just taken out the house security patrol.'

'Repeat, Bravo Two.' Karl looked up at Arnold.

'House security patrol down. Both dead. Intruder team on driveway.'

'Copy Bravo Two. Wait.'

Arnold was circling the console station. I felt in the way and moved to one side where I could still see the screens. He eventually stopped and whispered something into Karl's ear.

'Bravo Two. Follow them in. If confronted permission to engage otherwise wait for orders.'

'Copy. Over and out.'

'Bravo One. Come in . . . Bravo One. Please acknowledge.'

There was a silence. Dave came rushing down the stairs.

'Switch to infra-red. Valley in front of house! Bravo One's sector.'

Karl threw a switch and a ghostly green-yellow colour came up on the screen. Occasionally there was a bright flash of white that exploded across the screen's pixels. Arnold leant forward and put the antenna mike on audio. The *pflaaat* sounds of muzzle-silenced shots were mixed with shouts. It suddenly went quiet.

'Bravo One. Do you copy?' Karl almost shouted.

'Base, this is Bravo One. Leader down. Dead.'

'What happened?' Arnold grabbed the mike.

'Intruder team surprised us from behind. No warning.'

'Where are they now.'

'One down, other making for the house.'

'Stay with fallen leader. Bravo Three back-up team dispatched. Bravo Two. *Come in.*'

'Bravo Two,' the voice whispered.

'Take out intruder team in driveway.' Karl looked at Arnold who nodded.

'Repeat.'

'*Take out intruder team!*'

'Copy. Two minutes.'

The audio speakers started wailing. The shrill noise reverberated throughout the room.

'What's that?' I tried shouting over the din.

Hank Sommers leaned forward to turn down the sensitivity.

'House alarm. It's gone active.'

Alexander came rushing back into the room. Sancho and al-Sa'igh with were with him. They were all armed. The house alarm was sounding with a piercing high-pitched screech. It did not stop.

Rod Mallory stood up. 'What's going on, Charles?'

'I don't know. There are intruders in the grounds and one of my security patrols has gone silent. I must go out.'

'I'll go with you.'

'It's too dangerous. Stay here, Mallory.'

'In for a penny, in for a pound. I'm well able to take care of myself and insist on coming with you.' Rod Mallory stood up, shaking his head. He was angry. Had his team been detected? He wondered to himself. He had not given the signal and he needed to be sure. It might however be the opportunity he wanted. Isabella noted the agitation but admired his apparent coolness. He was a man of surprises.

'Very well, but stay close to me. These two gentlemen are Sancho and al-Sa'igh, friends of mine.' Alexander hesitated for a moment, appraising the Australian before agreeing.

'You bet cobber!' Mallory nodded in the direction of the two men.

Alexander led them out the doorway and while al-Sa'igh and Sancho fanned to the right, he and Mallory spun to the left. They saw a single figure darting across the ground beneath the overhanging balcony. He stopped and turned. There was a flash of orange. A bullet ricocheted off the wall beside them, gouging out a piece of masonry that whizzed past Mallory's ear. He smiled. Alexander cursed then started firing. Wildly.

More shots were returned from below. A voice bellowed out. '*Mictlan*!'

Mallory smiled again. It was their team's code word – Aztec for the "Abode of the Dead". He had chosen it. His thoughts were racing. One of his men was below him. His team must have been detected, but it was still an opportunity. He pretended to take cover by dropping to the ground and rolling up against the balcony wall. Happy that Alexander was sufficiently distracted further down the balcony he reached over and retrieved the gun he had secreted earlier. In one movement he released the safety catch and had it pointed at Alexander's back.

'*Charles, look out!*'

It was Isabella who shouted a warning but she was too late. She watched as Alexander half-turned only to be catapulted backwards, as the spray of bullets from Mallory's gun ripped into his chest and shoulder. There was an immediate splattering of the whitewashed walls and windows with a spray of blood. Alexander fell heavily against the balcony rail and seemed to balance there for a moment before the force of the impact caused his body to topple over and crash into the valley below.

Mallory had turned at the sound of Isabella's shout and from his crouched position was now aiming up at her. She pulled back behind the corner of the doorway as bullets tore into the masonry. There was a wild shout from behind her.

Isabella looked around. Zoë was running up the steps and onto the balcony. Her face was wild, agitated, excited. Isabella put out her hand, instinctively, to stop her. She brushed past it and, firing from her hip as she went, rounded the corner where Isabella sheltered. Shots were returned and just as suddenly all went quiet, but only for a brief moment.

Isabella bent down to her knees and cautiously took a quick look around the corner. Zoë was slumped against the house wall, groaning, holding her stomach. Between her and the balcony railing, Mallory lay stretched out. His body was twitching, the eyes staring upwards into space. Blood was pouring from a large rent in his forehead. It pooled like a halo about his neck. Isabella crawled forward.

Zoë was crying. 'I feel so cold, Isabella. Help me.'

'Hold on, Zoë. Hold on!' Isabella reached out her hand.

Zoë took it, her head lolling from side to side. She groaned. 'Where's Charles? Tell Charles I need him. Tell him I loved him. Oh God, Isabella! I'm so cold.' Her mouth was filling with blood. Her body started jerking, then suddenly the grip relaxed, the groans stopped.

There was still the staccato noise of shots being fired. Isabella slipped her hand from Zoë's and cautiously stood up. She moved forward to the railing and peered down into the darkness. Suddenly, from far away, she could hear a familiar voice screaming her name.

'Isabella! Get away. *Run Isabella! Isabellllllla!*'

I had drifted quietly away from the downstairs room where Arnold and the others were huddled around the console. I was in the way and of little or no use to them now and so climbed back up the stairs to the balcony bedroom. The telescopes and audio-mikes were on automatic, whirring and focusing in response to commands from below. I stepped out onto the observation deck, having found a pair of binoculars.

Across the narrow valley Alexander's villa was lit up like a baseball game. Occasionally in the dark shadows bursts of orange flame could be seen. The noise from the alarms and shooting intermingled. It was very real and very immediate. I knelt down, afraid of attracting a stray bullet. There were figures on the balcony. I hardly needed the binoculars to make them out. It was Alexander with Rod Mallory.

The whole scene was being played out for me in cinematic slow motion . . .

I can see Rod reaching over the balcony for his gun and then pointing it at Alexander's back. Alexander half-turns and then falls backwards out of view. Rod turns. He is pointing the gun again at somebody else. It's . . . Isabella. He is pointing it at Isabella. I hear the shots. I try to stand up.

Another figure is running onto the balcony. Isabella disappears. More shots. It's another woman, Isabella's athletic cousin, Zoë, with wild eyes and wild red hair. She's shooting from the hip. She stops suddenly and slumps against the wall. I remember Zoë naked from the bathhouse. Was it her or Isabella who had made love to me in the apartment? She never answered. I cannot see Rod now. He must be on the ground behind the balcony wall.

Isabella . . . I can see Isabella. Thank God! She's standing at the balcony railing, looking down.

'Look over here, Isabella. I'm here,' I whisper. There are more shots. She should get away as fast as possible.

'*Isabella. Get away. Run Isabella. Isabellllla . . .*' I scream out across the valley. She looks up. She must have heard me. She disappears back into the shadows. There's a noise behind me. I turn in fright, lifting the binoculars to swing them in my defence . . .

It was Bob Arnold.

'Steady on Michael! It's me! What's happening up here?' he grunted. 'I heard shouting. I thought something had happened to you.'

'No. Nothing physical anyway,' I replied tersely as I turned back to look at the villa.

'Our teams nearly have control. Both al-Sa'igh and the man Sancho are down.'

'Dead?' I asked, uncaring.

'Unsure.'

'And the others?'

'Withdrawn to . . . Oh fuck! What's that?' Arnold rushed past me to the balcony. Ahead of us a bright blinding flash was bursting through the windows of the villa. Soon a thunderclap rolled across the valley and I thought I felt something pass close to my ear. I was thrown to the ground; Arnold was on top of me.

'What's happened?' I stared up into his face. He looked frightened.

'Alexander's place has blown. Stay down, Michael.'

I could hear the crackling death rattle of glass and masonry.

Occasionally another thunderclap sounded and debris bounced off the observation deck. I pulled out from under Arnold. I lifted my head to the level of the rail. I needed to see.

'*Isabella!* Oh no! Not you too, Isabella,' I cried out loud. Turning slowly away, I began to crawl back towards the bedroom across the glass-strewn deck.

'Where are you going, Michael? Come back!'

'I've got to go over there. Don't stop me, Bob.'

I stood up and began to race towards the door. I could hear Arnold barking orders into his radio-mike. Dave was at the foot of the stairs. I pretended to stop and as he relaxed I ducked under his arm. I was out the main door and, skirting the villa opted for a direct route and a headlong run down the steep valley towards the villa on the other slope.

I soon fell, and tumbled out of control down through the groves of chestnut and oak. I could feel the low-level juniper bushes pulling at my legs. I did not care. I was getting closer to Isabella. Hitting a dry riverbed I got unsteadily to my feet. Somebody was behind me. I began to climb again. A piece of burning wood landed close to my head. Sparks and smoke filled the air cascading from above. My legs were held. I lashed out. I had to keep moving. I lashed out as hard as I could.

'Stop it, Michael, or I will shoot you to prevent you going any further.'

I stopped struggling. His voice told me he meant it.

'Dave! Please let me go. I must . . . I must . . .' I started crying, uncontrollable tears were coursing down my face. 'Isabella's in there. I must try to help her.'

'I know, but it's not possible, Michael. It's too fucken' dangerous this way.'

Sa'id Alkahiri's apartment on the New Jersey shoreline gave him an uninterrupted view across the Hudson River of the Manhattan skyline and the Statue of Liberty. It was a clear day with late summer sunshine glistening off the windows of the skyscrapers.

The cell phone in his pocket began to vibrate and he took note of the caller identification number as he opened its flap.

'*As-salamu aahalaykum*, my brother!'

'And peace, God's mercy and His blessings be upon you too, my brother!'

'How does it go with you?'

'I leave tomorrow to perform my duty. The demon Massoud will take his leave of us soon.'

'You will be remembered as a true martyr of the Bayt Kathir. How will it be achieved?'

'I am posing as a journalist. Musallam al Bahr travels with me.'

'It is good to have friends at this time. God's blessings be upon you both!'

'What of you, my brother.'

'It is very near, Hasan. We are prepared and the fatwa of our glorious leader will soon be achieved. We will punish the unbelievers for their defilement of the Holy Places.'

'Are Radiyyah and the children with you?'

'Yes, but they leave tomorrow for Doha. Tonight we will feast on the *habshah* and chew the *tambul*. Even now there the *hawjiri* frankincense is making the foul air of this putrid place smell of the mountains of the Jabal Samhan.'

'That is good, Sa'id. I will pray for them on their journey.'

'Thank you, Hasan.'

'I must go now, my brother. Goodbye.'

'We will meet each other on the *ezirit* road into paradise, my brother. May God wrap you in a *bisht* cloak of golden thread to help you on that journey. Farewell!'

The echoes from the explosion were still reverberating around the room.

'Michael.' The voice came from behind me. It was Arnold.

'Yes, Bob.'

'Come with me, Michael, I need to talk to you.'

Arnold's tone was tautly serious. Once I managed to adjust my vision to the harsh light beyond the black curtains, I saw that his facial expression was equally trense.

'What is it, Bob?' I asked, my voice quivering with mounting anxiety.

'Let's go in here.' He pushed open the door of one of the other bedrooms and after a quick inspection invited me in. Bob Arnold closed the door behind us. His features were ashen. 'I've some very bad news, Michael.'

'What is it Bob? Have they found Isabella?'

'No. It's not about Isabella Sanjil, It concerns . . .' He began to shake his head. '. . . I don't know how to say this.'

At that exact moment I knew what Arnold was going to tell me. Something had happened to Caroline.

'Caroline?' I whispered.

'Caroline . . .' He looked away. 'Has been found dead.'

'Jesus.'

'I'm so sorry, Michael.'

I hardly heard him. There had often been times in the past where, in lonely moments, I had played out this scenario in my head, particularly when Caroline's fieldwork appeared to become more and more dangerous. Sometimes I wondered whether it was my concern for her or my concern for myself that drove the abstract game of irrational anticipation. In my waking state the concerns were dismissed as responses of reasonable paranoia but sometimes in my sleep the nightmare of my guilt was much more vivid.

I often saw a coffin, draped with a confused top-spread of Union crosses and the Stars and Stripes, being lowered into the snow-blanket-covered ground of an English West Country church's chestnut-pocked graveyard. I could suddenly see her face, smiling up at the sombre and grey-faced mourners as their handfuls of frozen earth hailed down to bounce off the varnished oak of the casket lid.

My legs weakened, and I staggered to the edge of the room's small bed and sat down, staring up at Arnold, wanting to disbelieve him.

'What . . . what happened? When? Where?' I stuttered.

'Mexico. Caroline was found. . .' Arnold stopped. He was unable to look at me.

'Tell me, Bob. *Fuck you!* Don't mess with me. Not with Caroline.' I stood up and pulled at his jacket. He jerked away.

'She was found with somebody else, Michael. A Mexican drugs enforcement officer. It looks like they were the victims of a cartel assassination.'

'Found where, Bob?'

'I . . . I don't have all the details yet, Michael.' He was been evasive.

'The fuck you don't. Tell me, Bob!'

'I'm so sorry, Michael. It's . . . it's just that Caroline was found . . . They were found in his bedroom, in his bed, naked. Both killed with single shots to the head. She didn't suffer, Michael.'

'*I don't believe you*,' I shouted.

'Keep your voice down, Michael. We do not want to draw attention.'

'*Fuck* the attention, Bob. Who was the Mexican?'

'A man called Diego Rios. He is . . . he was a commander in the Federal Preventive Police and apparently part of the combined taskforce she was briefing.'

Somehow, knowing his name made it worse. This man, Rios had an identity, a life, and a past. He breathed, he lived, and he made love. Had he made love to Caroline? What was she doing with him? Why did she do it? She must have been drugged or threatened?

I thought of my own recent behaviour and the tone of our last conversation. Both of us were at risk, both of us had succumbed. Caroline was dead, I was alive. I felt the guilt, she could feel nothing. I slid off the edge of the bed to slump to the floor. I stared at the space between my feet, opening and closing the gap between them like shutters. I thought of Isabella. I needed to contact Caroline's brother. I needed to make arrangements.

I finally looked up at Arnold, who hovered, embarrassed and silent, above me. 'Bob, ask Dave to drive me back to Ajaccio. I need to get back home.'

'Michael, nothing can happen tonight. Our plane will bring you to London in the morning. There is a flight to Mexico at midday. I have you booked.'

'Mexico?'

'Yes. Caroline's body is in the morgue in La Paz. You have to give a formal identification before an autopsy can occur.'

'An autopsy. No way.'

'Michael I'm really sorry but this goes all the way to the top. Both the American and Mexican Presidents have been informed. Caroline was part of a high priority joint federal task force.'

'I know.'

'A forensic autopsy will be automatic.'

'Shit. Not to Caroline it won't!' My medical training had convinced me of the necessity of autopsies but this was personal and difficult to rationalize. I wanted to know everything and nothing about the circumstances of Caroline's death.

'The coroner's court will be *in camera* and all reports secret.'

It was as if he had read my thoughts.

'Will I have access, Bob?'

'Yes. You have top-level security clearance.'

'Shit! Shit! Shit!' I whispered. 'Who would do this to Caroline, to us?'

The room was quiet, I was quiet, but Bob continued to hover like a waiting vulture of sympathy. I was the carrion of his pity and after a few moments he moved closer and hunkered down onto his knees beside me.

'Michael, there is something else I need to tell you about.'

'What else could there be Bob?' I said wearily, not listening and not caring. I was, in any event, beyond caring too much. 'What the fuck else could there be?'

'We think we know who might have been responsible for the kill . . . for shooting, Caroline.'

My head shot up. '*What? Who?*'

'How well did you know –' At that moment the door swung open with a loud bang. Karl, clearly agitated, burst into the room.

'General. Come down to base. *Stat!*'

'What is it, Karl?' Bob Arnold stood up.

'The French Security Minister and our Ambassador in Paris are on the lines downstairs. They are demanding your instant attention and are not happy campers.'

'Shit! Just what I need.'

Karl and Arnold began to hurry out of the room. I shouted after them.

'Bob, what were you going to tell me? *Bob!* Don't leave me alone, *please.*'

Arnold stopped and looked back down at me. 'Michael, I really am very sorry. I wish there was more I could do to make it easier. Throw some water on your face and come downstairs. I'll continue what I was saying there. I must go.'

He was gone, and I couldn't move. Rocking back and forward against the bed, I began to cry. For Caroline, for me; for us.

Diluculum

DAWN TWILIGHT

Corsica
8 September 2001

The lone figure of Michael Mara sat in sullen silence on the observation deck, watching the frantic activity across the valley. The butts of almost continuously smoked and discarded cigarettes lay scattered at his feet. To the east, the first glow of the rising sun was beginning to bubble on the horizon and a warm wind swirled in the charcoal-laden morning twilight.

He constantly used his shirtsleeve to wipe the moist soot particles from his face as he tried to distinguish between the numerous gendarme and fire fighters from the National Parks service, that were swarming over the charred wreckage of Alexander's villa. They had been struggling for nearly two hours to control the violent flames that erupted from the inferno.

From where he was sitting he could still hear the roof tiles as they crackled and split when, every now and then, a tongue of spitting, hissing flame would dance across the pitch. In response, a sudden facial twitch would cause blackened and bloodstained crease lines to distort his otherwise impassive features. He did not look up as Arnold joined him.

'How are you doing, Michael? You didn't come back downstairs.'

'Ok, Bob . . . I think.' Michael kept staring at the smouldering villa. 'What's happening over there? Did you find Isabella?'

'No. No sign of a woman's body with her description yet. There is however, a part of the building where the walls collapsed inwards and it will be a while before they can move the rubble. She might be there.'

'I see. I just need to know, Bob. You understand that don't you? Caroline is dead . . . and Alonzo, Rod, and now Isabella . . . all of them are *fucking* dead. Is all this my fault?'

'No. Of course not!' Arnold pulled up a chair. He said nothing for a while as he watched what Michael watched.

Suddenly there was a crashing noise as something solid hit the decking wood. They both looked down. It was a large rabbit whose life quickly ebbed as they watched.

'What the hell. Where did that come from?' Arnold asked.

'Look up there.' Michael was already pointing upwards. 'I wonder if it's a lammergeyer.' A huge eagle-like bird was patrolling the sky above the valley. There was too little light to make out its colouring. Michael thought he could hear a shrill whistle of annoyance. 'It's very weird. There was a lammergeyer in Alonzo's story of the *Voices*.'

'What voices are you talking about, Michael?'

'Oh. Nothing, Bob.'

Arnold stood up and kicked the lifeless corpse of the rabbit into the ravine below them. A trail of blood smeared across the decking. He looked back at Michael whose attention was still captured by the majesty of the soaring bird.

'Michael there is something else I need to . . .' He stopped, hesitating.

'Go on, Bob. You were going to tell me earlier before being called away. What is it?' Michael didn't divert his eyes from the sky above him.

'It's about Caroline's death . . . and your partner Rod Mallory.'

'Dead partner!'

Arnold didn't answer.

'What about them, Bob?' Michael stopped looking upwards and stared at Arnold. The general's face was a picture of concern and nervousness as he retook his seat.

'We . . . we feel reasonably certain that Mallory might have killed Caroline.'

'*What* . . . Why? I don't fucking believe you. They were friends, tennis partners for God's sake.' Michael stood up and glared down at him.

Arnold shifted uncomfortably in his chair, kicking out at the butts on the decking. 'It appears that Mallory might be . . . might have been, a major figure in the Mexican drug trade and that Caroline was caught in the crossfire of an internal dispute. He couldn't afford to have her knowing about his connections. He killed her.'

'How do you know that?' Michael said coldly, as he stood up.

Arnold said nothing for a considerable time. He didn't look at Michael but instead pretended to be distracted by the activity across the valley. He fingered the collar of his shirt nervously.

'How do you know that, Bob? *Answer me*!'

'One of our agents was tailing him.' The army general was almost inaudible as he spoke.

'What? Why?' Michael shook his head and began pacing across the balcony.

'Once the results of the field trials on the cocaine virus started coming through so positively, everyone who had anything to do with its development, and that included your colleagues in Hoxygene, were placed under surveillance. These orders came from the very top. We had great concerns over security and safety.'

'Well you certainly made a great fucking job of that, didn't you, Bob! In case you've forgotten, you prize prick, Hertzog, Alexander, Mallory and . . . Caroline are all dead. Some fucking protection! Why did you not protect Caroline? Why the fuck could you not save Caroline, if you were watching her. She knew nothing about my work for the army on the virus.' Michael's tone was venomous.

'Listen, Michael. This was all breaking very fast. The order to throw a security blanket over you and the virus work was only issued last Monday, when the first results of the field trials started coming through. We were just getting our surveillance schedules up to speed and could not have suspected that Mallory was such a loose cannon. He was your partner and financial controller in Hoxygene for God's sake!' Arnold paused. 'We knew he had very little access to the scientific work you were doing for us and his initial security screen gave no cause for concern. We considered him low risk and the tail put on him was of minimal intensity. Caroline was already with secret service agents and we were satisfied that we had that ground covered.'

'Were they alerted?' Michael stopped pacing.

Arnold hesitated and appeared to blush. 'No! Not in any specific way. When Mallory flew to Mexico, we thought that they, your wife and Mallory, had arranged to meet there. You know! We wanted to be discreet.'

'You thought that they might be lovers,' Michael said quietly as he remembered that he had levelled the same accusation. 'Is that why?'

'Yes. It's not unusual and from what we had heard they were very close. No one could have expected something like that to happen.'

'Why didn't you pick up the bastard, if you are convinced he might have killed her?'

'Very soon after arriving, Mallory left Mexico again, in a private jet. The agent assigned to tail him was only arriving in La Paz as his aircraft took off. He didn't realize what had gone down in the hotel and was busy trying to determine Mallory's next movements. The jet's pilot had filed a flight plan to Miami so another of our agents was quickly assigned to pick him up on arrival there. It was then, and only then, that we first became aware of the drug people he was dealing with. It was also about that time that the agent in Mexico found Caroline. By the time the news was relayed to Miami and we could react, Mallory had disappeared again.'

'How can you be so sure it was Rod Mallory?'

'The agent assigned to tail him in Miami, luckily, saw him dump a package in an airport garbage can shortly after landing. It was recovered and a gun found. The ballistics match the crime scene in Mexico!'

'*Luckily!* That's a loose fucking description of what's happened. I thought Caroline's post-mortem was not done yet.'

'Michael. Please sit down. This is very hard for me.' Beads of sweat were beginning to appear on Arnold's forehead.

Michael stopped pacing and retook his seat. 'I'm sure it is, Bob, but it's not *your* wife that's fucking dead.'

Arnold was visibly stung by the rebuke. 'My own wife has ovarian cancer. She's likely to die in the next two years. Knowing it will happen makes the pain worse.' He was about to get up when Michael put his hand on his arm to stop him.

'I'm very sorry, Bob. I didn't know. Explain how you know about the ballistics.'

'They come from the body of Diego Rios . . . the man found with Caroline. There is no reason to expect otherwise. It was a clinical kill. Similar modus.'

Michael said nothing. He had all but forgotten about the Mexican, Rios and he suddenly felt his chest tighten. He couldn't breathe and wanted to gag. He needed to scream out. He needed the air. He began to cry with an uncontrollable sobbing that jerked his body into spasms of pain. It was all Arnold could do to stop Michael falling to the ground as he knelt beside his chair holding him as hard as he could. The spasms continued for what seemed an age until just as suddenly they stopped again and Michael's muscles relaxed.

'Let me go, Bob!' Michael's voice was hard and clear. Arnold recoiled at the intensity of it.

'Are you OK, Michael?'

'Yes.' Michael stood up and leant against the balcony railing. Across the valley the burning timbers and roof-tiles of Alexander's villa hissed and jumped as the water cannons sprayed into their flaming embers. He could hear more sirens winding their way up the narrow valley road from Corte. The scorched wind was scented with the aroma of mountain pine.

At that instant, Michael Mara's head suddenly arched back and as he looked up at the sky with wild staring eyes he began to laugh. It was an intense laughter of such visible violence that tears were forced from his eyes and began streaming down his cheeks. Its loudness echoed off the walls and across the valley floor. He turned to Arnold and began wildly shaking the older man's shoulders.

'Ha! Ha! Ha! Ha! This is all just a fucking game, isn't it, Bob?' he shouted.

The general looked puzzled.

Suddenly, Michael's grip on Arnold's jacket eased as quickly as it had begun. The frenzied peels of ghoulish laughter shuddered abruptly to a halt as he glared at the army man with red raw eyes and streaming cheeks. 'Well you can stop it right now, Bob. Enough is enough. Tell Rod Mallory that he's won!'

'What are you talking about, Michael?' Bob Arnold was suddenly very confused.

'The game. *The fucking Silicone Valley game*. Rod Mallory set me up for this. I'll kill him when I see him.'

'What game Michael? Mallory is dead.'

'You're very convincing, Bob but you can stop it now. You can stop messing with my mind. I give in. The game is over.'

'You're making no sense, Michael.' Arnold stood up and moved slowly backwards towards the doorway where the telescopes were set up. He picked up a walkie-talkie from where it hung on the side of one of the tripods and after depressing the transmit button whispered urgently into the microphone. Michael was looking at him and began to laugh again.

'Ha. Ha. You were all really bloody good, Bob. Even down to Alonzo calling me the last Magus. Isn't that the plan? Manipulate the victim. Obscure his tenuous reality with tangible fantasy. I can see it all so clearly now. The happenchance meeting with Isabella and then Alonzo! The story of the *Voices* and the apparent sex in Isabella's apartment to suck me in! Alexander's villa, Caroline's reported death. I never saw the clues.'

'Michael! Get a hold of yourself. What are you talking about?' Arnold started walking slowly towards where Michael was standing.

'The game, Bob! This shit! All this playacting shit is just part of Bellfiore's and Allen's game for bored millionaire nerds. And I'm fucking Michael Douglas. It must have cost a fortune! You tell Mallory to stick the obelisk up his arse.'

'What's going on out here?' Dave shouted as he brushed past the telescopes. He saw Michael laughing hysterically near the balcony with Arnold standing close by.

Suddenly, the general lunged and pinned Michael's arms behind his back. Mara began to struggle. 'He's flipped, Dave.' Arnold looked very frightened as he shouted. 'He's ranting on about some friggen' game. I'm afraid he might hurt himself. Get over here!'

'Fuck off, Dave. You and your Zoroastrian shit. Jesus I should have guessed,' Michael spat out at the agent.

'Com'on, Mike. Calm down.' The agent was walking with his hands extended and palms outstretched towards where the two men were struggling. As he got closer, Michael suddenly lifted up his feet and lashed out at him. The sudden movement caught the agent in the chest and he recoiled backwards.

'Jesus, Mara!'

'Take him out, Dave! I can't hold him much longer.' Bob Arnold was losing with his lock on Michael's arms.

'Are you sure?'

'Certain. *Do it now!*'

'It's over, Dave. The game is over. I give in. *Let me go, you bastards*,' Michael screamed, as he lashed out again.

This time the agent was ready and ducking first to one side then surged forward. His fist came up in a fast uppercut that caught Michael full on the chin. Michael's head flew back to crunch into the bridge of Arnold's nose before rebounding forward again to follow his collapsing legs to the ground. Arnold and Michael fell together in a heap at Dave's feet.

Bob Arnold slowly disentangled himself and gingerly stood up holding his nose. Blood was pouring from behind his hand and down onto his shirt. '*Jesus H Christ!* I think it's fucken' broken.'

'I'm sorry General. Go downstairs, Sir and get it seen to. I'll look after things here.' Dave had stooped down and was turning Michael into a recovery position on the decking. Arnold stared at the prostrate body.

'He really lost it, Dave. Didn't he?'

'Yes, Sir. You never know how someone will react to bad news.'

Francisco Carrillo was sitting in the small pavilion, which was situated at the far end of the swimming pool. From here, high on the southern ridge of mountains which enclosed the valley, he had an uninterrupted view of the twinkling night-lights of the city of Medelin far below. Plumes of soft smoke drifted into the night air from a large cigar that was held with hard hands. Behind him small children were giggling and squealing as they chased each other into and out of the jet spray of the lawn-irrigation nozzles. He didn't turn as a white-suited dark-haired man approached.

'Papa.'

'Yes, Domingo. What is it? I thought you were in the city tonight.'

The younger man pulled out a chair and sat down facing the older man.

'I have some –'

'Have you no kiss for your father. Remember your manners!' Francisco scorned without looking at his son.

'I'm sorry, Papa. Of course.'

The younger man flushed but then meekly leant forward and kissed his father on both cheeks. Francisco smiled, satisfied with the formality of obedience observed.

'What is your news, Domingo? It must be important to drag you away from the casino whores.'

'It is!' Domingo looked up to see that nobody was listening. His children and his wife were on the veranda of the house and he waved over at them.

'Well, get on with it?' Francisco's tone was intolerant, as if fully aware of the charade being played out behind his back.

'Fabio Ochoa is at this moment on his way to Miami to be handed over to the Americans.'

'Shit. It was expected. We are lucky though, that many of his functions have been already assumed by Rod Mallory. The cartels will survive.'

Domingo Carrillo could not prevent the satisfied smile from creasing his face. He gave a loud snort before looking at his father with a mixture of pity and smugness.

'Papa. Your great *amigo,* Rod Mallory was killed in Corsica about ten hours ago.' Domingo did not try to disguise the tone of delight in his voice.

'*What happened?* How do you know?' The cigar fell to the floor as the older man's eyes flared.

'Jorge Quintana, one of my men, was there. There was a gunfight and an explosion. They were surprised when about to attack the villa of the man called Alexander. Jorge managed to escape and contact me.'

'Surprised by whom, Domingo? Alexander's security.'

'No. Americano. Probably CIA or the like.'

'What happened exactly, Domingo?'

The younger man paused for a moment as if trying to control his thoughts. When he spoke again his voice was cold and analytical. 'That moron, Mallory, apparently decided on a frontal assault. There were two teams on the perimeter and one hidden in the car that had brought him, waiting for a signal. Jorge and his partner, in moving into position, unexpectedly encountered an American special-ops team observing the house. There was a gunfight and Jorge managed to escape. Alerted by the gunfire, the house security reacted and set off a sequence of events that resulted in the loss of five of our men as well as Mallory.'

'All dead.'

'Yes.'

'Shit. What is your assessment, Domingo?' The older man

slumped in his chair. He suddenly looked defeated. Too much was going against them.

'The fact that an American special-ops unit was at the villa worries me.'

'Their presence in Corsica might have been a coincidence. They may have been targeting the other man . . . eh . . . Alexander.'

'Sure,' the younger man said dismissively. 'They might have been watching Alexander, but we must also consider that they might have been expecting our teams. That would imply Mallory was being watched and that creates a problem for us. They will have known about the meeting in Miami.'

'There was nothing to suggest that. You were there, Domingo.'

'We cannot take that chance.'

'No . . .' Francisco hesitated. He put out his hand and rested it on his son's. 'You are right, Domingo. We'd better discuss our future plans. Arrange a time with Miguel Mendoza and the others for a meeting.'

'Yes, Papa.'

There was a long silence between them until Francisco Carrillo broke it.

'They are drawing in around us. We must counteract.'

'Who? The Americans?'

'Yes. And their Mexican fox cubs.'

'What do you mean, Papa?'

'There are some specific problems that Rod Mallory and I were discussing, that you now need to be aware of, Domingo.'

'Go on.'

'Since the arrest in June of our contact in the Juarez cartel, the supply of potassium permanganate from that source has dried up. The Mexican president, Vicente Fox is doing all he can to suck as much milk from the big Americano tits as possible, by targeting Mexican cartels with Columbian connections. Our customers are beginning to complain about the lack of high quality oxidised cocaine. The specific targeting of the production and supply of potassium permanganate is hurting us.'

'Operation Purple.'

'Yes, and now the shipment-tracing activities of Operation Topaz are beginning to bite as well.'

'Topaz, Papa? I don't understand.'

'In October of last year, the International Narcotics Control Board announced the targeting of the international trade in the chemical, acetic anhydride which we use to purify our heroin. We need to start fighting back, otherwise we will be out of business.'

'What do you suggest, Papa.'

'Mallory and I had begun discussions about a detailed plan to use his international banking expertise to discredit Fox. Remove Fox and we remove a major obstacle. Now that Mallory's gone we will need to think of another way.'

'Good riddance to the faggot.' Domingo spat out the words. 'I never trusted him and tried to warn you. Now look where it has got us.'

'Don't you ever question my . . .' An angry and shouting Francisco Carrillo shot out of his chair and hovered over his son as if about to strike. 'You had nothing to do with warning the Americans about Mallory, did you Domingo?'

The younger man did not flinch and stared with cold, murderous eyes back up at his father. '*No* . . . of course not . . . but, I'm not unhappy about his death, if that's what you want to know. We should never have given so much control to a gringo. That was a mistake, Papa.'

For a moment it seemed that the older man would actually hit his son but then, suddenly, Francisco hesitated and slowly wilted. The fight was gone from his eyes. He was tired. 'You . . . You are right, Domingo. Mallory was a danger to us and my judgement was faulty. I will inform the cartel families that you will be taking over the operational decisions from now on.'

'Thank you, Papa. I will not betray your trust.'

'Perhaps, perhaps not! In the meantime, there is much to be done. You had best get started.'

'Good night, Papa.'

'Good night, Domingo.'

The two men parted. This time, there was no formality of a parting embrace and the older man sank disconsolately back into his chair.

Very little was said between us, as we negotiated the sharply twisting road that would take us to the villa. It was only when the last of those bends was safely behind us that I turned to him.

'Did you have to hit me so hard, Dave?' My jaw hurt like hell and checking its movement made it worse. A gold crown was working its way loose and I could feel the wobble with my bruised and swollen tongue.

'I'm sorry, Michael but I was afraid that you might hurt yourself. You were really freaking out!' He kept his eyes straight ahead, focused on the gates of Alexander's villa. Two grim-looking and gun-carrying gendarme approached the side of the car. Dave pressed the automatic switch to lower the window.

'*Avetene identification, s'il vous plait!*' The older of the two policemen barked.

As Dave reached into his pocket to pull out his card the younger man circled the jeep tapping against the glass with his gun.

'*Merci, Monsieur. Attendez ici.*' The senior gendarme withdrew and as he inspected Dave's credentials spoke into his walkie-talkie. He was scowling when he returned to the car.

'*Basta!*' he shouted at the younger man as he handed back Dave's card. '*Ouvre la porte!*'

The iron gates swung back and Dave drove the jeep slowly up the gravel road. Parking behind one of the fire tenders he turned to look at me.

'Michael. You don't need to do this. It's not a pleasant sight.'

'Dave. I need to see what happened. I need to be sure.'

'OK! Stay close to me. The gendarmes are being very sensitive about our presence here and our involvement in the gunfight. It has taken a lot of urgent diplomatic manoeuvring to calm their annoyance. The National Park officials and firemen are on the warpath. This is this worst time of the year for forest fires and they have an exploding house spraying its crap over the area. Do not answer any questions, Michael. Is that understood?'

'That's easy. I won't be able to talk . . . Thanks to you.'

'As I said . . . I'm sorry. Now let's go!'

I followed Dave out of the car and up the narrow driveway towards the villa. The ascent was steep and the gravel surface was being seared by the rivers of brown-black water that flowed in torrents down the hill to meet us. Everywhere, like wriggling snakes, fire-hoses jerked and squirmed as a sudden surge of water coursed through their narrow lumens.

I could see the pall of dark smoke as it rose up above the villa into the, now bright, early-morning sky before drifting down again to settle as a choking smog on the valley floor. Most of the fire fighters still wore breathing apparatus and as we approached the one of them handed a pair of masks to Dave.

'Do you get a peculiar smell?' I asked as I strapped on the mask.

'Napalm,' he said bluntly.

I followed him into a tent that had been hastily erected near the burnt-out shell of Mallory's jeep. I could see from where we were that there was still a figure slumped over the wheel of the jeep, half-covered by a plastic yellow sheet. In the tent about ten corpses were laid in a row on the ground. Most were hideously burnt, with features missing or congealed by the force of the explosion.

Rod Mallory, the meerkat Sancho and even the athlete Zoë were all there, all very dead. I could recognise them still. Zoë's body was in two parts and Sancho had lost an arm. Their deaths were now real, and even with the breathing masks the smell of charred flesh haunted the air. Ironically, Hertzog's body was almost pristine it its completeness; it had been protected in the trunk of the car. I looked at the other bodies. Most of the women all had peculiar, and near identical, defects of their left ear lobes, like the type I'd first noticed in Zoë and the blonde Scandinavian, at the bath-house in Granada. The women were otherwise anonymous in death.

I thought of the bathhouse as we left the tent accompanied by a gendarme captain. There had been no sign of either Alexander or Isabella's body. I asked him about them, but with a blunt appraisal he said that the area of collapsed masonry had now been checked and there was no sign of any more bodies.

'Evaporated, I suspect,' he added with a Gallic shrug of the shoulders.

I felt at that moment, as I stared down the valley, that Isabella, like Caroline, was also probably dead and that nothing I could do would bring her back. I hurried back towards the jeep with Dave in close pursuit. I tore off the mask and sucked in great gulps of air. My stomach heaved and I began to puke. One of the gendarmes from the gate laughed as he walked past.

'Are you ok, Michael?'

'Yes. I didn't see Alexander's body. Is it one of the charred ones?'

'I don't know. We all saw him falling over when he was shot, but the area he was in was partially obscured from our cameras behind some trees. Only Mallory's and the girl Zoë's bodies were recovered from the balcony area.'

'You mean he got away!'

'I doubt it. I'd say one of those bodies is his.' Dave pointed back towards the tent where the row of blackened corpses lay. The firemen were removing the dead man from the jeep. A large portion of the leather seating remained stuck to the charred corpse's back as it was peeled out. 'Dental and DNA forensics will confirm.'

'I didn't see Isabella's body either, Dave. Do you think she got away?' I asked hopefully.

'I doubt it, Michael. She had just gone back into the villa when it started exploding.' His answer was hesitant.

'But, there is some hope?' I latched onto his hesitancy.

'Perhaps! If she did, Michael, she was one lucky dame and . . .' Dave put his hand around my shoulders. '. . . we'll have to track her down. You know that, don't you?'

'Yes!'

There was a long silence as thoughts raced through my head.

Suddenly it became clear and pulling away from Dave I began to walk back towards our car.

'What are you doing, Michael?'

'Let's go, Dave. I must contact Caroline's brother in England. Bring me back to the villa. I need to make the phone call in private. I have to make some arrangements.'

'Sure, Michael but we don't have much time.'

'We?'

'Yeah. I'm coming with you to Mexico. For your own protection! Arnold asked and I volunteered.'

'Thanks, Dave.'

As the jeep drove through the gates I could see through the thinning smoke that the lammergeyer was now circling high above Alexander's villa. I remembered again Alonzo's story of the sacred fire and the Hekamaad horse sacrifice in the high valleys of Nuristan long ago. The outstretched wings were still floating, silently, on the updrafts, waiting for an opportunity to strike at the offerings of the fire.

This was someone else's killing zone but the bones would have enough marrow for all.

It was 5.00 am London time. The phone was picked up almost instantly.

'Hello.' The voice sounded tired.

'Hello Max. It's –'

'Is that you, Michael? Christ! Where the hell are you? I've been trying to contact you. Caroline has been –'

'Caroline is dead. I know Max. How did you hear?'

'The Mexican authorities contacted your house and the housekeeper gave them my name. They told me very little other than she was shot. Something to do with her work, they said. What really happened, Michael?'

Michael explained that he was in Corsica and told his brother-in-law as much as he dared about the cocaine virus work and its links to the involvement and death of both Alexander and Rod Mallory.

'Christ, Michael. Mallory is dead too?'

'Yes . . .Will you do something for me, Max?'

'If I can.'

'I need you to go to Mexico.'

'I've already made the arrangements. I leave in two hours.'

'Would you identify Caroline's . . . Caroline for me. I don't think I could face it.'

'What?'

'Please, Max.'

There was a long pause before his brother-in-law answered.

'Right. But don't expect anything more from me, Michael. Caroline's death is your entire fault. You and your bloody virus.'

'Thanks, Max. I will –'

The phone line went dead.

Max had hung up on him and Michael stared at the phone for a few moments. He knew that Max was right. It was his fault and he had to try and make some sense out of all that had happened.

Michael scrolled through the address book of his phone until he found the number he wanted and dialled. While he waited for the connection, he thought about what he was about to do. He knew now that he had one opportunity, and one opportunity only, to follow the trail of *Saclaresh* to Armenia and that it had to be done immediately, before the news of the villa explosion broke.

The business of the living occupied his thoughts. He owed it to Alonzo. He owed it to Caroline and he owed it to himself.

Twenty minutes later Dave called for him. This time they headed for Bastia airport where an unmarked, CIA-operated, Lear jet waited for them. The flight was smooth and they landed at the RAF Northolt Airbase, at about 10.00 hrs GMT, and made the short transfer by car to Heathrow. Once in the terminal it had not been difficult to give the sprawled and snoring Dave the slip. Without sleep for the best part of 48 hours, and his body withdrawing quickly from the caffeine and amphetamine-fuelled operational status, he had quickly fallen into a deep sleep.

Arnold had arranged for Dave and Michael to fly on the

United Airlines 13.55 connection to Los Angeles, with an immediate onward connection on a Mexicana de Aviacion flight to San Jose Cabo in Baja. There was an airport closer to La Paz but the routing chosen offered the quickest connections. A car would be waiting at San Jose Cabo to take them to the morgue in La Paz.

Using Hoxygene's membership of the British Airways Executive Travel Club, Michael had made a booking, before leaving Corsica, on British Airway's scheduled 13.35 flight from Heathrow to Moscow. From there he would connect on Aeroflot's Flight 191 to Yerevan. With hand luggage only Michael had picked up the ticket at the transfer desk and waited until the very last moment before rushing to the designated gate. As he neared it Michael kept looking back. He was suddenly afraid of cutting the boarding time too closely and of Dave being alerted by his name being called over the tannoy system.

The ticket was charged to a coded account, established deliberately by Hoxygene's ex-CIA, but still spookish security consultants, to reduce the risk of industrial espionage. It allowed masking of the commercial movements of Hoxygene's executives and it would be some days before the transaction could be traced. In the meantime, as he settled back into his seat, Michael consoled himself that they, the good and the evil, would never think of Yerevan.

The connection from Moscow was delayed by a couple of hours and as the plane descended from the early-morning sky, Mount Ararat and Little Ararat rose up to meet it. Like Kilimanjaro, a mountain he had once climbed, snow was still present on the higher summit even at the end of the summer heat that had scorched brown the ancient plains below it.

Even at this early-morning hour Michael found the circular spaceship-like terminal to be oppressively hot. After a drawn out passport inspection his 21-day visa was issued – reluctantly – for a consideration of $50. The person ahead of him in the queue, he noticed, an Italian hotelier, had only paid 35. The decision seemed arbitrary.

Once he had finally escaped the terminal Michael took a taxi to the city. The main road was already getting busy and very soon his empty stomach was heaving at the sight of a sheep being slaughtered in a roadside butcher's. There were three of four other sheep awaiting their fate in the small pen next to the dawn killing zone. Michael's memory of the events at the villa and the thought of Caroline's body lying stiff in a morgue in Mexico ebbed and flowed with the waves of nausea.

The centre of Yerevan city itself was small, Michael thought, dominated as it was on the western-bank access route by the French-owned brandy factory. The taxi driver gesticulated with pleasure when pointing the building out, his face cartooning a punch-drunk fighter in the absence of language. Michael nodded as he felt his chin. Thanks to Dave's efforts, he fully understood the characterization, and the helplessness of the pain. The monument to the Armenian genocide was briefly glimpsed as the taxi turned into the wide avenue that would bring them to the hotel. Its stark memorial-granite significance could have been placed anywhere, he felt; even Corsica.

At the Hotel Yerevan the welcome was warm and friendly. Good-looking girls and serious men busied themselves in their attention to his needs. After booking a taxi for the late afternoon to take him to the monastery at Etschmiadzin, he made for his room and a much needed shower and rest.

Sleep came quickly; the telephone call ended it.

'Your taxi is here, Doctor Mara,' the voice announced sweetly.

'Thank you. I'll be down in a minute,' he answered drowsily.

'He will wait. No problem.'

'Excuse me. What is your name?'

'Gaiane.'

'Gaiane, could I have some sandwiches and coffee in the lobby before I leave?'

'Certainly, Doctor Mara. I will arrange that straight away.'

'Thank you.'

Michael showered again and feeling somewhat better, quickly dressed in clean clothes and stepped out onto the balcony corridor that looked down onto the enclosed atrium cafe. There were huddles of people in deep conversation and he was relieved when nobody looked up. The nearby glass-capsule lift had some white-legged children heading for the pool and leisure club on the hotel roof. He took the stairs.

After the much needed coffee and food were hurriedly finished he headed for the reception desk. A tall girl with beautiful eyes and a slightly arched nose was beaming a smile towards him. Her jet-black hair fell in a pageboy cut onto bare shoulders. He looked behind, suspecting she was smiling at someone else. There was no one there.

'Doctor Mara,' she said.

'Yes.'

'I am Gaiane.' She had a polished smile.

'Oh . . . I see.' Michael automatically reached into his pocket to extract some money for a tip. 'Thank you, Gaiane for your trouble.' He peeled off a few dollars from a billfold and proffered them in the power-asserting way of well-off tourists and businessmen.

'That is *not* necessary, Doctor Mara. I was just doing my job.'

Her smile vanished and the tone of her voice became formal and abrasive. She was staring down at the opened billfold in Michael's hand.

He had somehow offended her and didn't know why. The other staff in the lobby seemed to be watching his reactions carefully.

'Nevertheless, Gaiane, I would like you to have the money.' Michael hastily replaced the billfold in his trousers pocket and tried to retrieve the situation. 'I really appreciate your kindness.'

'No thank you. It really is not necessary.' She turned away and retreated behind the reception counter.

Michael waited for a few seconds wondering what to do. He followed her to the counter.

'I'm sorry, Gaiane. Did I offend you in some way? I would like to know because I would hope not to do it again.'

'No . . . I am sorry, Doctor Mara. It is my fault. It is not you. I am just overreacting.'

'To what?' he asked concerned.

'Another guest.' she said in an embarrassed way.

'What happened?'

'A short time ago, just before you arrived, another American guest pulled out a billfold just like you and, making sure everyone could see, started peeling back $100 bills until reaching a single dollar note, which he then handed over. One of those larger bills would be my father's pension for three months, and he knew it. He was trying to buy me and expected that I would comply.'

'Some people are very rude.'

'Sure. It is the price we have to pay to be so dependant on others. Sometimes, it is too high a price.'

'I tell you what, Gaiane. Is there a communal tip box?'

'Yes. On the other counter.'

'Good. I will secret some of Uncle Sam's corrupting influence in that. My conscience will be clear and everyone will benefit.'

Gaiane smiled and her attitude relaxed. 'You are going to Etschmiadzin? To see the monastery?'

'Yes.'

'May I ask of you a favour, Doctor Mara?'

'Sure Gaiane . . . but only if it doesn't involve killing other foreigners. Please call me Michael.'

'No, nothing like that.' She laughed but he couldn't be sure that she meant it from the slightly wistful smile that briefly creased her face. 'May I take a lift with you? I live near the monastery and I'm off duty for a few hours.'

'Of course.'

'Thank you. I'll only be a moment.'

Gaiane explained what she was doing to the duty manager. He appeared, in the very formal way of Armenian men, to disapprove. The other female receptionists smiled and giggled as Michael followed her out the door and into the waiting taxi.

The journey to Etschmiadzin was at funeral pace. Despite the taxi being a gleaming and powerful-looking Mercedes it was underpowered with what appeared, to Michael at least, to be a lawnmower's engine. It eventually chugged into the dusty carpark outside the fortress-like walls and gate of the monastery complex. A new church was being built nearby and the straining hiss of a hydraulic crane echoed at intervals across the space.

Gaiane had given Michael a brief account of her life. She was a trained chemical engineer who refused to take the well-worn road of Armenian emigrants to Russia, France or the USA.

'I did postgraduate work in the Sorbonne but ran away. I liked Paris though. I also went to Imperial College in London. Again I ran away. I am always running away. From situations.'

'Probably not running away,' Michael replied. 'Maybe you were running towards something. Something undefined but better.' Michael found it somehow comforting to hear some of his own thoughts verbalized.

'Perhaps, but I am happy here, for now. The income from the hotel is at least regular.' Gaiane said this with sad eyes and a slightly resigned shrug of her shoulders.

As the car shuddered to a halt she gave him a brief synopsis of the history of the complex. '*Descentdit Unigenitus*: 'The descent of the only Begotten One'. In the Armenian language called Etschmiadzin. Tradition holds that it was here that St Gregory the Illuminator had his vision. You will enjoy its serenity.'

'Thank you very much for your help, Gaiane. I don't want to insult you again but I would like you to accept a tip. Spend it with a will free from any contractual obligation.'

'Thank you, Michael. I never have a problem with spending money. I will accept it.' It was the equivalent of about a week's wages. 'When you go inside the monastery ask for Stephen. He speaks excellent English and is very knowledgeable.'

'Is he a monk?'

'No. He is a lay worker who is a full-time guide to the complex and a friend of my family. Say that I sent you.'

The door opened and Gaiane stepped out. As she leant back in to shake his hand she pushed the hair falling down the left side of her face out of the way for a moment. The handshake finished, she turned and walked away.

Something about her suddenly bothered him and he called after her.

'Gaiane! Wait!' Michael hurriedly got out and pulled out his wallet to pay off the taxi driver. The man looked at the dollars that Michael proffered and protested.

'Too much! Too much!'

'Is this enough?' Michael pulled out a smaller denomination but was annoyed by the driver's slow accounting. 'Gaiane, please wait!' he shouted again.

She appeared not to hear him and continued to walk away, disappearing down a small alleyway. Michael wanted to run after her but the taxi driver was not quite satisfied. Other drivers were gathering round in his pursuit of the proper change. Michael pressed the money on him and with a forced smile walked away from the car and through the monastery gate. He decided to forget about Gaiane. He needed to hurry.

In the small souvenir shop Michael asked for Stephen and a few minutes later a bearded dark-haired man in a long brown cassock appeared. He looked like a monk and his eyes flared at Michael's initial questions until Gaiane's name was mentioned. After that he became very knowledgeable and anxious to help.

'Why is it you are here, Doctor Mara?'

'I am looking for a seal or stone that might have been given to the monastery in the 1850's. It is made of lapis lazuli.'

'What is lapis lazuli?'

'Ultramarine from Afghanistan.'

'Ah. Lazurite. What is the importance of this seal?'

'It might have some very ancient carvings on it. From the dawn of time.'

'I don't know of any such stone but let us go into the museum.'

Michael followed him into the Church dedicated to the Blessed Virgin. The basilica's interior was chairless and spacious and groups of schoolchildren wandered freely about. Stephen the guide, entered into a side room to the right of the nave and here the walls were covered with glass cases containing the relics, jewels and books of the Armenian Church. Browsing slowly through the contents, one book caught Michael's eye. Its cover was embossed with the symbols of freemasonry and he asked Stephen about it.

'Are they not freemasonry symbols?'

'Yes.' No further information was forthcoming. 'Come see the preserved hand of St Gregory.' He pulled insistently at Michael's arm.

The silver encased relic with the thumb approximating the third finger was the centrepiece of the collection. Apparently there was another in Sis, and yet others where schisms of the Armenian Church had dictated. The Illuminator's hand was everywhere but pointing nowhere. There was no sign of the seal however, and Michael was worried that it was lost in the shadow-facets of one of the relics. Stephen appeared to grow bored of his attempted minute examination of every possible artefact.

'Is it possible to have the display cases opened so I can view the relics in more detail?' Michael asked hopefully.

'Perhaps. I will have to ask the curator but it will not be today.' Michael failed to hide his look of disappointment. Stephen suddenly brightened as if wanting to console him. 'Come. There is something else I want to show you. I think you might be interested. Follow me.'

Michael ducked his head as he followed Stephen down through a low-arched heavy door that led off the middle room of the museum. Its direction brought them under the floor of the basilica.

'Did you know that the church was built on the ruins of a pagan temple?' the smiling guide asked.

Michael shook his head as they skirted the white clay crumbling walls along a narrow passageway. The effect was ghostly. Like bones, the clay brick, which in the light of life was red, had lost its hue to the colour-quenching effect of age. Like all catacombs the atmosphere was dust-laden and brittle. The light emitting from a single naked electric bulb was weak but once accustomed to the dimness, he found himself looking at a small, enclosed space, in the centre of which was an urn-like structure. Its rim was irregular, blackened.

'Coloured! Used!' Michael thought. He turned around to look at Stephen who stood there impassively.

'Is this . . . Is this a Zoroastrian fire temple?'

'Yes. You can see where the church foundations were laid directly on the pagan's stone. Look at the wall behind you.'

There was an ancient carving of the Avestan circle of eternity set into the wall. At the centre was a representation of the sun. Stephen touched it but was then anxious to leave.

'It is at this point that we accept donations for the upkeep of the church.'

'May I stay here a while?' Michael asked as he handed him $20. Stephen smiled, nodded and left him alone.

Michael waited there, hearing Alonzo's words in his head: 'It will find you'. He sat on a low wall balancing carefully, afraid of his full weight collapsing its pale frailty. Examining the temple precinct provided no clues or inspiration. Suddenly, the light bulb flickered bright then went out. He was in pitch darkness. He could hear the lock of the far off door engage. Stephen or the other keepers must have assumed he had left. There was only silence. A dense silence.

Michael did not move, nor did he want to cry out. It was if he was expecting something to happen. He needed something to happen. With his cigarette lighter's rapidly diminishing fuel he found a dry corner in a side passage. He hoped there were no rats, or snakes for that matter. A cool breeze flowed in from somewhere. He hunkered down, listening to the silence and soon, still exhausted, fell asleep.

It was some hours later that he was woken by the scraping noise of stone moving on stone. He looked out from the recess of his hiding place. Suddenly the temple's pagan walls were full of flickering shadows thrown up by hand-held candles. Three figures were emerging from a hidden door in the wall where the circle of eternity stood. Maybe this is what Stephen had wanted to indicate. Alonzo's image smiled at him.

Michael retreated back into the recess as far as he could. The figures were all wearing grey-white robes and tightly wrapped turbans on their heads. The first of them carried a bunch of kindling under one arm. Perhaps, Michael thought, this was the sacred barsom of Dave's explanation in Granada. The second figure had a small pitcher of liquid and the third carried no candle but held, with two hands, a platter on which a small object was centred.

The ghostly figures drew closer to where he was hidden but suddenly turned right to enter into the pit. The first man, Michael assumed they were men, placed the kindling in the fire bowel and soon the smell of scented wood-smoke filled the room.

They began chanting:

'*Verethraghnem ahuradhatem yazamaide,*
Verethraghnem ahuradhatem yazamaide,
Verethraghnem ahuradhatem yazamaide.'

Their voices echoed off the walls. The oldest looking of the figures with a white bushy beard lowered the platter he was holding towards the rim of the fire urn. He tilted it slightly. Michael could see a reflection. It was a mirror. The object in the centre caught the light of the candles. It shone a brilliant blue. Specks of gold twinkled from its core. It was a blue button-shaped stone. Michael knew that he had found *Saclaresh*.

He let out a gasp with the realisation and instantly the three hooded heads jerked in unison towards where he was hiding. They began to approach him. They were shouting. At that very moment the lock in the far off door clattered with the sound of keys being inserted. The hooded figures panicked. Michael saw the older man stumbling, the platter mirror tilted some more and the blue stone slid off and toppled into the fire urn. There was a scatter of sparks. The men rushed past him in their anxiousness to escape through the stonewall door. It just closed behind them as the electric light bulb flickered once more into action.

Clattering footsteps were rushing along the narrow passageway at the far end of the temple.

'Doctor Mara! Are you in here still?' It was Stephen's voice.

'Yes.' Michael slid out from his hiding space and hurriedly stepped into the centre of the fire pit, pretending to warm his hands on the fire. Stephen's face soon appeared above the low wall. He appeared breathless and flushed.

'I am so sorry. I should have checked that you had left.'

'It's ok. No problem.' Michael spoke as Stephen lifted his nostrils to scent the air. He was carefully surveying the temple cavern and soon noticed the smoke rising from the urn.

'Were you cold. Where did you get the wood from?'

'There were some twigs and dried leaves in the side passage. I'll just make sure it's out.'

'I will do it.' Stephen offered.

'No, I insist.' Michael was adamant as he picked up a large stick to pat out the embers. The urn was deep and he could feel *Saclaresh* touch against the stick at the base. He patted gently around it.

'Doctor Mara, we must go!' Stephen growled.

'Sure.' Michael hesitated. There was nothing else he could do but pick up the seal in his hand. He would have no other opportunity. He leant down and searching among the embers felt for and found the stone. It was fiercely hot and as he pulled away he could smell the singeing contact of burning flesh. Strangely however, Michael felt very little pain and as he closed his hand tightly about the stone he gave no sign of anything being wrong.

'It's all out now. I wouldn't want to be the cause of a fire in the church.' Michael smiled.

Stephen shaking his head checked the bottom of the urn before leading him out. The night air was cool and fresh.

'Would you like a drink of tea perhaps?'

Michael looked at his watch. It was 2.00 am.

'Please. I would like to use the toilet if I may.'

'Of course. This way.'

Once in the toilet Michael ran the tap and tried opening his clenched fist. He slowly prised his fingers back. In the centre of his palm the stone lay face downwards. The brilliant blue colour had gone. It had turned white in the fire's heat. The stone was stuck to the skin. Michael wrapped a wet handkerchief over the palm and went back out to join Stephen. He noticed the temporary bandage.

'Did you hurt yourself?'

'It's just a small cut.' The pain was now coming and Michael grimaced. 'How did you know I was still in there?'

'Gaiane rang me from the hotel, saying that you had not returned.'

'Why? Was somebody looking for me?' He could not help sounding suspicious.

'No. I don't think so. Are you afraid of something . . . or someone, Doctor Mara?'

'No.' Michael lied and to distract the line of enquiry he quickly asked. 'Stephen. Are there any Zoroastrians still in Armenia?'

'What a strange question? No. Of course not! The Magi are all gone. Long ago. Why?'

'I just wondered. The fire bowl looked like it had been used recently.'

'Probably some children doing it for a challenge. A dare you call it. No?'

Michael said nothing. His hand was now beginning to hurt terribly. Sweat appeared on his forehead as he followed Stephen back into the carpark. It was still dark and checking his watch Michael now saw that it was nearly 3.00 am local time. The same taxi driver was still waiting. Stephen had told him that Michael was a good bet for business, so he had waited. Following the call from Gaiane, the taxi-man had confirmed to Stephen that he had not left the compound and that is when he had begun to look for me. Michael sat in, exhausted.

'Thank you, Stephen.'

'Enjoy the remainder of your stay in Armenia. I will ask the curator about you having the chance to inspect the relics in a little more detail. I can leave a message with Gaiane at the hotel. Is that satisfactory?'

'Very.' The urge to cry out was immense. Michael's hand was throbbing. Stephen looked at it and then at his face.

'I hope the hand is soon better.'

Stephen closed the door and the taxi moved off. Michael looked back to ensure that Stephen had disappeared. He suddenly tapped on the taxi driver's shoulder.

'Stop here!'

The pain was intense. He needed to get out of the car. He opened his hand and unwrapped the handkerchief. The stone was no longer there. It had shattered and in its place was a small mound of white powder. The grains were so fine that they sluiced with ease through the gaps between his fingers. Michael looked at his hand. The pain had eased but burnt deep into his palm were the marks of *Saclaresh*. There were flecks of golden pyrite embedded into the scorched tattoo and they glittered in the light.

Suddenly Michael noticed some movements near the far end of the external monastery wall. There was very little in the way of street lighting and for a moment Michael thought the beams of the idling taxi's headlamps caught the shape of three ghostly figures emerging from the shadows. He strained to make them out but they quickly disappeared again.

The hairs on Michael's neck stood on end. He knew then that he was in danger if they, the guardians, returned to the pit and found the seal missing. With luck it would not be tonight. He jumped back into the taxi and slumped in the seat. He realised that he had failed Alonzo. He had failed in his duty to Caroline. His responsibility for *Saclaresh* had ended in bitter failure; the shattered stone draining away like quicksilver through his fingers.

Michael knew he had to keep moving. But to where? He needed time to think. 'Hotel Yerevan and then the airport, please. Hurry.'

The taxi driver shrugged his shoulders. The lawnmower-engined Mercedes would not be rushed. There was a British Mediterranean flight to Heathrow at 9.35 and he had time to catch it. Just.

The four-wheeled-drive Jeep with blacked-out windows pulled

out onto the dusty street from the entrance of the Kabul Headquarters of the Ministry for Vice and Virtue. Three black-turbaned and bushy-bearded men sat erect in the seats. Pedestrians scattered as the vehicle sped off in the direction of the football stadium.

Behind the turbaned guards, a fourth figure, his long white djellaba streaked with blood, lay curled on the back of the vehicle. He offered no protest, no sound save a croaking gurgle through the distorted anatomy of a broken and sundered jaw. The short journey was quick. He could hear the shouting of the crowds as they entered the stadium built by the Europeans for the entertainment of the deprived Afghani youth. It was now an arena for the depraved. One of the turbaned Taliban guards turned and hit him with the butt of his gun.

'Get up you dog. Your master al-Sa'igh has gone to his just reward and soon you will join him. Look out at the field of your dreams.'

In response to the continual battering, the jawless man uncurled and stared out through the tinted glass. The jeep was making a slow funeral circle of the field. The concrete terraces were full of people. Some were shouting wildly encouraging the spectacle. Others just stood there, impassive, tense, dead in their eyes, looking away and back furtively.

'Stop here,' the guard in the passenger seat ordered. 'Get him out.'

The jeep screeched to a halt. The guards jumped out and opening the rear door pulled the jawless man out.

'Watch this, you son of Satan. You idolater.'

From another jeep that had followed them into the stadium, two women, in their all-obscuring faded blue burkas, were pulled out and dragged across the field. They were forced to kneel on the edge of the lime-marked boundary lines of the penalty area. They shook in fear and with high-pitched, frenzied cries started to plead with their guards. 'Allah have mercy on us. We have done nothing!'

'Myriam. . . Fatima. I am so sorry. Leave . . .' The jawless man began to cry out. He recognised the voices as those of his daughter and wife. He tried to crawl towards the women but was battered to the ground once again.

The guards were laughing as they watched him squirm in pain.

From that sprawled position, through the dust, the pain, and blood-obscured vision, he watched as one of the women's guards slowly raised a gun and after a quick look in his direction, and without any hesitation, pressed it into each of the bases of their skulls in turn. Miriam fell forward first and then Fatima; the single shots had blown the light from their eyes away forever.

Immediately the executioner bent to the ground and then slowly rising walked back to where the jawless man lay shuddering. Bending down the gunman pressed the two spent and still warm bullet casings into the prostrate man's hand before pulling up the weeping man's head to stare into the already dead eyes. The Taliban's voice was harsh and unforgiving.

'Your women were as accountable as you are. How dare they suggest that there was a better way than the path that the Mullah has laid out before them. They have now found the peace that their prostitute friends in Rawa will also find. Look around you, you cringing dog of the devil. This is *our* paradise and the field of Allah's command. Before you die you can make your own peace. Tell us where the camps of the insurgents are. Who are your friends?'

The jawless man didn't care any more. 'You have more to fear from your friends than your enemies. Soon the world's wrath will descend upon your miserable heads.'

'What do you mean by that?'

'Ask what Fazlur Khalil, al-Zawahiri and the others who mock your protection are doing as we speak. Say your prayers friend!'

'Tell us what you know.'

The man shook his head and in a final act of defiance arched back his neck and offered it to the turbaned guards.

Soon that same neck was being stretched and slowly strangled by a coarse rope slung over the goalmouth crossbar at the opposite end of the field. It was the far end of the world. The jawless man's last sight of this earth, through bulging eyes, was of the mountains to the northeast. He thought he could smell the juniper and ideals of the high valleys.

The stadium crowds were drifting away and in the hurry to finish their God's work the guards pulled down on the dangling man's legs until they heard his neck snap.

The Taliban watched without emotion as the lifeless body swayed back and forth. He turned to his companions. ' "*If God wishes, the magic spell of the devils will soon be broken*".'

The journey up the small tributary of the Vaupes River, in the slender, steel flat-bottomed boat had taken the best part of six hours. For most of the time they had had to hug the riverbank closely to hide their presence and Domingo Carrillo was cursing his foolishness in agreeing to make the trip.

"There was no other way", his contacts in FARC had informed him. The leadership were hiding deep in the jungle and if Domingo and the cartel families wanted to negotiate the cocaine supply from the areas that FARC controlled then he would have to go to them.

Suddenly, there was a cackling laugh from the Indian guide who sat at the prow. He was sneering down at Domingo.

'What's he saying?' Domingo looked at the blonde-haired rebel soldier in jungle camouflage uniform who nervously kept scanning the riverbank. A machine gun lay across his lap, one hand resting lightly on the trigger guard.

'He said, 'Tell the city boy to sit up. Only dead men lie down in canoes'.' The soldier smiled as he translated.

'I'm not going to be insulted by any stinking Indian. I'll kill the . . .' Domingo's eyes flared as he reached inside his jacket. 'Fuck!' The shoulder holster was empty. He'd forgotten that his gun had been confiscated as part of the conditions. Domingo's face reddened further with the anger he felt. 'How much more of this fucking river do we have to travel?'

The soldier spoke to the Indian who once again sneered at Domingo before answering. 'About 300 meters.'

'Thank God for that. I'm sick of the insect life.'

The river began to narrow sharply and the banks converged to close in on them. The sky was shut out as the boat slid beneath an archway of spreading ferns and hanging creepers. The Indian on the prow hacked a passage forward for them until suddenly, the tunnel of clinging undergrowth disappeared and the boat shot forward into an open space. Domingo saw that they were in a large horseshoe-shaped pool surrounded on three sides by the amphitheatre walls of a high cliff.

Thousands of yellow butterflies fluttered into the air, with the intrusion, and a large waterfall cascaded to feed the river at the far end of the pool. The boat inched forward over the shallow bottom to dock into a narrow crevice. Domingo nearly slipped on the greasy moss-covered rocks as he stepped out.

Excitedly, the Indian was looking upwards and pointing to the sky. Above the thick canopy of the jungle the whirring muffled drone of a Blackhawk helicopter grew ever louder as it skimmed over the treetops towards the pool. The soldier pulled Domingo into the dense cover of a cave and the three figures waited patiently for the noise of the helicopter to disappear towards the west. In the far distance he could hear the sound of screaming jets and the thudding roar of air-launched rockets.

The light was fading fast when the three men re-emerged slowly from the undergrowth. Domingo was perspiring heavily in the dense humidity. 'Jesus!' He looked bewildered.

'You chose a dangerous time to come here amigo. General Mora's Rapid Reaction Forces are closing in on one of our positions to the east.'

'Have we got far to go?' He turned to look at the soldier. '*What the fuck?*'

The man had his gun levelled at him.

'Take off your shoes!'

'Why?'

'Take off your shoes. Now!' The soldier pressed the gun into Domingo's neck.

Domingo nodded and slipped off his shoes. The Indian bent

down and picked them up. After a careful inspection he began to prise the heel off one of the shoes with a knife. A small transmitter was buried in the hollow.

'Take your hands off me you scum. My friends will follow me and if any harm comes –' Domingo shouted.

'Shut up you prick,' the soldier ordered. He took the shoe away from the Indian and looked at the transmitter for a moment before tossing the shoe into the black froth-covered waters of the pool. He watched it sink before turning to Domingo. 'If, they come, they will be too late.'

'What do you mean?' Domingo Carrillo looked suddenly unsure.

'Move out.' The soldier prodded Domingo in the ribs, forcing him to turn.

They walked along a narrow ledge that led under the waterfall and into a large tunnel cave. He could see light ahead and soon they emerged into a clearing. There was a group of corrugated tin-roofed huts camouflaged from the sky by the canopy of overhanging trees. A single figure was waiting, smoking a cigarette on the doorstep of one of the houses. He remained sitting as Domingo was herded forward.

'Who the fuck, are you? I'm here to see Peres, the leader of FARC.'

'Comrade Peres is busy right now directing a counter assault. He asked that I meet you.'

'I'm not going to discuss my business with a fucking lackey. Bring me to Peres.' Domingo felt more in control. The Blackhawk helicopter was *his* backup. He had bribed the area air-force commandant to provide an escort of Special Forces. The FARC were fools to think he would come alone. They would soon be here. The transmitter would have been tracked to the pool. '*Now!*'

The sitting man smiled as he stood up. He moved close to Domingo and blew a mouthful of smoke into the younger man's face. 'Don't think that your friends can save you, Carrillo.'

'Who are you?' Domingo looked back in the direction of the tunnel leading to the pool. Everything was quiet.

'My name is Jorge Reilly.'

'That's not a very Columbian name!'

'My father was from Belize but I'm more Columbian than you will ever be, you cocaine-snorting pimp. You and your fucking cartels have bled the country dry.'

'What do you want with me?' Domingo's fear was obvious.

'What do you think?'

'I don't . . . I don't know. If it's money I can get that. If this is a kidnapping I can arrange a ransom. Let me contact my friends.'

'That would be far too easy, jerk' The dark-haired Jorge threw his cigarette to the ground and stamped it out with his foot. 'Tie him up . . . over there.' He pointed out a nearby tree to the soldier and the Indian, while he disappeared into the hut.

Domingo tried to break free, to run towards the tunnel. He felt a sharp blow on his neck and the force threw him to the ground. The soldier was immediately on top of him, pinioning his hands behind his back. With the Indian's help, Domingo was lifted up and brought to the tree. His hands were crudely but effectively tied behind the trunk. The thin wire cut into his wrists. The Indian was laughing as he urinated on Domingo's feet.

Jorge Reilly walked slowly from the hut towards him. He had something in his hand.

'What do you want you bastards?' Domingo screamed, hoping someone might hear.

Reilly moved in closer. He placed a strap around Domingo's neck. It was attached to a small canister that rested on his heaving, panicking, chest.

'This my friend is a necklace of paradise. It has a mercury switch and any lateral movement will set it off. I would be careful if I were you.'

'But why?' Domingo's eyes strained to look down towards his chest as he whispered.

'It's a present from Rod Mallory, you fuck. He asked me to say that he wished that he could be here.'

'*Mallory!*'

'Yes! Rod Mallory arranged for this deception. It was easier than we had expected though. Mallory didn't know that you had taken operational control of the cartel's interests. We thought that they might smell a rat if we requested just you, but when we made contact it was you who volunteered for the meeting. Trying to prove that you are the main man. Eh? How fucking convenient for us.'

'Mallory is dead! I'll pay you to let me go.'

Jorge Reilly's features flickered for a moment. 'It doesn't matter. I've repaid my family's debt in Belize to him. Honour is restored. I –'

The sound of a helicopter could suddenly be heard. It was almost dark and a searchlight raked over the canopy roof. Reilly looked at the Indian and with a slight nod he and the soldier followed the small, dark-skinned man into the dense undergrowth. They waited, watching the pale figure of Domingo being picked out by the light. A large moth hovered to sit on the canister, others landed to play on his illuminated face. Soon there were shouts from the sky, and black uniformed figures rappelling down ropes from the hovering Blackhawk.

Domingo was blinking frantically. A soldier had moved in from behind him. He could feel him cutting at the wire that bound his hands. They were soon free. Domingo didn't move. The soldier who had set him free stood facing the jungle and pulled at him. With a free hand Domingo started pointing to his neck.

The other soldiers abruptly stopped advancing, looks of horror etched on their faces. They started to scream at their colleague behind Domingo. He hadn't noticed. He was still pulling at Domingo's arms furiously. They needed to get away from here. Why wouldn't the man move?

With the explosion Domingo's decapitated head landed very close to where Jorge Reilly and the others hid. They smiled before disappearing further into the jungle.

As I looked down, the beaten and battered landscape of the

Iberian Caucasus slipped away to the southwest some 30,000 feet below us. I thought of my own origins and of the western expansion of the Indo-European peoples that had poured through the same gap from the steppes to populate and change forever the Anatolian and Iranian plateaux. Alonzo and I had talked about how historians concern themselves with the intensely immediate nature of mankind and its secular determination to survive chaos, whereas philosophers would rather defend the timeless obligation of that same nature to mankind's survival in the order of things.

What I'd been through those last few days had no place in my own understanding of either history or philosophy. Everything had happened so fast that chaos had replaced the ordered world in which I lived. I'd always imagined that even chaos would have a predictable structure but I felt nothing. My chaos was a vacuum.

Had Alonzo been a figure of that imagination? My memory of our meetings was even by now, already blurred. I remembered him in death more than in life. Were his mystical insights into a hidden underworld of knowledge and freedom merely anticipated responses to my needs and to my confusion?

And what of Caroline? My image of her was in life and living that life. Could it really be possible that she lay dead, distant, alone and cold, in a racked fridge on a different continent? I'd wept but not mourned for her in any meaningful way, as I did not want to accept the brutal reality of her death. For that reason I'd asked Max to go but I would soon pay my dues. In my mind's hope I would arrive and inspect the corpse with solemn attention, and the body shown would be that of somebody else. Another person's loss and pain! Not mine.

A memory from medical school days of the first, almost bloodless, crescent-shaped scalpel-cut to the back of the head and the peeling forward of the skin, like a hairy orange, to uncover the bare bone. My poor Caroline! She would be laid out on the cold steel platform, with constantly running water to shift the detritus of death. Standing somewhat removed from the sacrificial pathologist's table I would wait for the morgue attendant's saw to open the Pandora's box of another person's death. I would insist on watching them perform Caroline's autopsy. I did not understand what had happened to us, but I would stand by her in death. A useless gesture no doubt, my guilt-laden sentinel duty to past dreams and hopes.

And what of Isabella; the most ephemeral of them all? Isabella, who was so in love with the challenge of life and the discipline of death! Had she shown me another way, another possible avenue to find peace? I'd been captivated by her. I had never before sensed someone's soul with such physical presence. I'd not yet found her way, but I had taken the first steps. Could I now retreat? What would Isabella say? What would she think of my moral cowardice? Would she really care? I needed her to care. Had her death, like Caroline's, freed me from moral obligation?

My heart ached at the loss of opportunity to find out. The window steamed up with my short and laboured breaths. Isabella's image flashed before me, it was out of focus, as if I also had trouble remembering her features. I never really knew her after all. She had forewarned me, accused me, of that possibility.

'Excuse me, Michael. May I join you?'

The familiar and unexpected voice tore into my wonderings. I turned away from the window to look up and with wide-eyed suprise to find my minder, Dave, last seen slumped comatose on a chair in Heathrow, hovering over the vacant seat next to mine. I automatically pressed back against my seat with the embarrassed defensive guilt I suddenly felt. 'What?'

'I asked whether I could join you, Michael. We have things to discuss.'

Dave's voice was calm and pleasant. To those around us it must have appeared like a previously arranged and convenient opportunity to talk. I looked around; nobody appeared to be taking any notice.

'Sure . . . sure . . . Sit down, Dave. *Jesus!* How on earth did you . . . did you follow me from London?'

'Hard work really. I eventually tracked your itinerary and just arrived on the incoming flight of this plane this morning. I was in the airport waiting for a car from the Embassy when I spotted you getting out of a taxi. It took some significant bribery to re-board almost immediately. A very brief visit to Armenia I must say, for both of us.'

'Yes. I'm stunned though.'

'What happened to your hand, Michael?' Dave was staring down at the coarse bandage.

'A burn. Stupid accident really.'

'Did you find what you were looking for?'

'What do you mean, Dave?' I was very guarded. My hand was throbbing.

'Don't bite my head off, Michael! To go to the lengths you did to give me the slip in Heathrow, you must have come to Armenia for a purpose. Did you find what you were looking for?'

'No, even though it's none of your business, Dave, it was a wasted journey. I lost . . . I didn't find what I was looking for.'

'That's a shame.' He sounded genuine.

'Why would you, or Bob Arnold, give a shit about something that has no bearing on your responsibilities?'

'Who said anything about Bob Arnold?'

'But –'

'Bob Arnold doesn't know I am here. At the moment he thinks that I lost you in London somewhere. He's having nightmares about losing you to the Dark Side.'

'The Dark Side?'

'Don't let your imagination run wild, Michael. I'm talking about Arnold's enemies, the drug barons.'

'Oh! I see. How will you explain finding me in Armenia so?'

'He'll never know. This is none of his concern.' Dave stared at me with intense eyes.

'What are you up to, Dave? I don't understand.'

'It is my job to ensure that the *gathering* is prevented.'

'The *gathering*. How could *you* possibly know about that?'

I almost shouted at him and a stewardess stopped in her tracks and stared down at me. 'Are you all right, Sir?'

'Yes. Sorry . . . I'm fine. Thank you.' My hand was beginning to throb painfully. I held it with the other as I spoke through gritted teeth.

'You're very edgy, Michael. Calm down.'

'What do you know of the gathering, Dave?'

'Everything!'

'How? I don't understand.'

'I am one of the Keepers of the Truth, as Alonzo was. It was to me that he came on the night of your first visit to his home. He knew that you were to be a guardian but he also realised that you were in danger. He needed my help.'

'Who are the Keepers of the Truth? '

'We are of the people. There are about 30 of us spread throughout the world. We carry the legacy of an ideal world in our hearts. We protect the providence.'

'But Alonzo said that there are only seven seals, seven guardians.'

'We are distinct from the guardians, although at times some individuals like Alonzo may be both.'

'I don't understand.'

'The guardians of the seals have the potential for both good and evil. It is the nature of the covenant. The Keepers are the observers, the recorders of the Truth as it transpires. We can do little to influence the legacy except protect the need for its continuance.'

'Without judgement of the consequences?'

'Without judgement!'

'But when you see evil surely there is a responsibility to intervene.'

'No! Not really! Both good and evil are as necessary as say . . . eh . . . sperm and eggs, to the nature of mankind.'

'What of human cloning? What of the new genetics? My work? No sperm required. That defeats your maxim of necessity?' By now I was irritated with both Dave's passive observance and his smug indifference.

'Cloning, in genetic or human terms, poses no concerns. It is just imitation and throughout history imitation has had an initial but ultimately limited appeal. In adding nothing it changes nothing. The fabric of society is constantly evolving and cloning will not stop that, even in its wildest re-creationist aspirations. It is an utopian indulgence and therefore inherently limiting and self-destructive.'

'But is not the whole objective of the legacy to portray a utopian ideal.'

'No. Not at all! You must understand, Michael that the ordained legacy of the *Voices*, the Truth, is an understanding of the necessity for change. They are a record of the primary covenant which acknowledges mankind's right to determine its own destiny free from constraint, prescription, or guidance from the first authority.'

'Even if that right invokes an evil advocacy, like Alexander's.'

'Alexander is . . . was also one of the Keepers of the Truth.'

'*What?*'

'Most of the attempted *gatherings* throughout history were undertaken by individuals who were Keepers. When you think about it, it's not that illogical. A Keeper would know of the history and legacy of the seals and all of their possible locations.'

'But why would they do it and want to end the legacy?'

'Each of us interprets the world as we see fit. The *gatherers* are seduced by the notion, as Alexander undoubtedly was, that their time was to be the end of time, when the full truth could be revealed.'

'Messianic?'

'Yes. Messiahs are a peculiar and recurrent expression of human nature and its interaction with time. I have no doubt they will soon find a gene to predict its occurrence.'

I turned away from Dave, looked out the window again and said nothing for a considerable while. Far below the sunlight caught the crests of wind-rippled waves of a mountain lake. It was like a dance of frenzied fireflies on a blue-green waterbed.

Our lives, I thought, mine, Caroline's, Alonzo's, Isabella's, Alexander's and even that of the double-crossing bastard Mallory, were like the numbered fluorescent nights of those carefree mating fireflies. Too soon, like exhausted and sated glitterati, we fall spent into the drowning whirlpools of the pitch-dark waters of annihilation. Give or take pollution of the ideals and aspirations of the river-bank or lake, another generation would soon follow, to make the same mistakes, but achieve different victories, before experiencing that one glorious night of light.

'Will it all end, Dave?' I continued to look out the window.

'What, Michael?'

'With the *gathering*.' I turned back to watch his reaction. 'Will it all actually end? – the pain, the suffering, the ecstasy of life?'

'I don't know Michael but . . . it is not yet the time to find out.'

'What do you mean?'

'We are just entering the third, and final, 3,000-year cycle of our development, of the duration of the covenant. The *gathering* cannot take place until that has elapsed. That is the responsibility of the Keepers of the Truth.'

'And the guardians of the *Voices*. What now? What will become of those that Alexander had access to.'

'That is a difficult determination. We don't know where they are. What happened, by the way, to *Saclaresh*?'

'You really did know all along!'

'Yep.' He nodded without any obvious sign of satisfaction. 'What happened?'

I began to tell Dave of what had transpired in the monastery, of the encounter with the three white-robed Zoroastrians and how, when disturbed by the returning Stephen, the chief priest had dropped *Saclaresh* into the ceremonial fire. I was about to tell him about my recovery of the seal when another thought began to bother me.

'How was I chosen, Dave . . . to be a guardian?'

'Even I'm not fully sure of that, Michael. All I can say to you is that your invitation to Granada wasn't an accident.'

'What do you mean?'

'Alvorro Martinez!'

'The Professor of Pharmacology in Granada?'

'Yes! He is Alonzo Aldahrze's son. He took his mother's maiden name.'

'He was also Isabella's supervisor.'

'Yes. It was Martinez who, at Alonzo's request, pointed you out to her.'

'I knew it! I fucking knew it. I said it to Bob.'

'What Michael? What did you say to Arnold?' Dave suddenly looked a little worried.

'I told him it was all a game.'

'Oh! I see! Ha! Ha! Bob Arnold, even on a lucid day, would never understand what you were getting at.'

'What do you mean, Dave?'

'It's not the game that you keep imagining you have been duped into Michael. It is far more important than that. You are involved in time's game. It is older, of greater consequence and far more real than any conceived by bored millionaires. This is the only game; it is the living of the Truth. My responsibility, and that of the other Keepers is to ensure that it continues. Time is the necessary limit to the imagination of man and timelessness will remove those limits. Without limits mankind will self-destruct. That is what Alexander wanted.'

'I'm sorry,' I said.

Dave shrugged his shoulders.

'For what Michael? Losing *Saclaresh*? Your destiny was to witness its destruction. That has determined that a *gathering* of the *Voices* can never now take place. Perhaps we should be grateful. Maybe over the next 3,000 years it's meant to be that each *Voice* will be destroyed in turn, until there is none left. No legacy, no memory, no false hope. Time to start again, a new covenant. A new cycle.'

'And me, Dave. What is left for me?'

'Ladies and Gentlemen. We are beginning our descent into Heathrow. Please return to your seats and fasten your seatbelts. We should be on the ground in fifteen minutes.'

'Michael. Are you sure *Saclaresh* was destroyed?'

'What?' I felt Dave's eyes boring into mine. 'Yes . . .Yes, of course. Eh . . .lapis lazuli turns white and shatters in contact with heat. It's quite a fragile gemstone. I'm assuming that . . . Why do you ask, Dave?'

'I need to be certain. You are telling –'

'Sorry Dave. Could you excuse me for a moment? I have to go to the toilet. I'll be back in a few minutes.'

'Sure, Michael. Sure!'

Dave stood up and stepped into the aisle. The curtains between the executive seating section and steerage had been drawn back for landing. He was looking back anxiously towards the rear of the cabin and didn't appear to notice as I tried to step past him.

'What's up? You seem distracted,' I said as I tried to squeeze past him.

'What? Oh sorry, Michael.' Dave moved aside a little. 'I thought I saw someone I recognised.'

'Who? Where?' I had half-turned to look towards the back of the plane when I found myself suddenly falling forwards. Dave's hand reached out to stop me but he couldn't prevent my shoulder banging off a seat restraint as I stumbled to my knees. My upper arm stung like hell but the embarrassment was worse. Dave helped me up.

'I'm so sorry, buddy. I didn't mean to trip you. My big feet have always been a danger. Are you all right?'

'Yes. No problem.' I smiled as I gingerly rubbed the back of my shoulder and moved towards the toilet door.

'You will have to be quick, Sir. We have started our descent,' an efficient stewardess admonished as she busied herself stowing away the last of the emptied glasses.

'Right.' I smiled at her as I closed the door behind me.

A few minutes later I exited the cubicle with difficulty. My legs felt weak and a sweating wave of nausea swept up from my throat to my forehead.

'Where are you, Dave?' I wondered aloud before realising that he must have returned to his own seat.

I was relieved in a way, as I flopped heavily into the seat that

Dave had occupied beside me. I tried standing up to look back and find him but couldn't find the power. The passenger in front of me glared back, annoyed that his head had been sprung forward after I had released my hold on his headrest. I tried shrugging an apology, as the words wouldn't come. I was having difficulty with the seat belt and with my breathing.

Saeculum

Once upon a time when I had begun to think about the things that are, and my thoughts had soared high aloft, while my bodily senses had been put under restraint by sleep, yet not such sleep as that of men weighed down by fullness of food or by bodily weariness, methought there came to me a being of vast and boundless magnitude, who called to me by name.

The Poimandres

Timegame

All that had happened, all the memories, faded as the nearby voices intruded again. It took a great deal of effort to try and concentrate on what they were saying.

'We've got back most of the emergency work-up including CT and MRI scans. They show no obvious damage to the spinal cord, brainstem or brain cortex. Direct trauma has been excluded and yet he has generalized paralysis. Septic screens, so far, are also negative,' the West Indian woman pronounced.

I'm in a hospital. I suddenly realised, probably ICU from the way the women were talking.

'Where was he flying from?' the girl with the Scottish accent was asking.

'Yerevan, Armenia. His passport shows that he's a well travelled individual.'

'Tropical disease screen. Was that done?'

'Armenia is hardly the tropics but yes, because of his travels, they've all been done. Malaria and Typhus screen is negative. Stool for ova, cysts and parasites have been sent as well. We had to give him an enema to get that. His bowel is completely flaccid.'

'Oh God! I hate giving enemas to coma patients,' the Scottish nurse groaned.

'Tell me about it.'

'He looks very comfortable. Have there been any consults?'

'Yeah. Doctor Cameron, the new neurologist, was called in. He thought it might be an acute poisoning with a plant toxin or curare-like compound. He has tried reversal with no success and thinks that our friend here probably suffered irreversible brain hypoxia when he collapsed and couldn't ventilate. We're waiting for lab results on a toxic drug screen and metabolite spectroscopy.'

Poisoning! Brain hypoxia!

'His current status?'

'Flaccid paralysis. Ventilator settings are pretty constant. Input and output satisfactory. Core temperature is elevated but not spiking. Pupils are dilated and unresponsive, eyelids taped closed. No evidence of papilloedema. He's for a repeat MRI and EEG tomorrow. The contrast is in the fridge.'

The voices drew even closer.

'Are you on your own tonight, Kathy?'

'Two of the regular staff are on holidays in the States and have been caught out by the shutdown in the airports. The night manager said that there's an agency nurse coming in. Delayed in the traffic I think.'

'I still can't believe what happened there.'

'I know. It's unreal. I've been glued to the telly all day. Listen, finish your report Janice, and get off. I can cope until she comes.'

'Michael. *Michael*, can you hear me? Unlikely. The poor sod. *Michael!* This is Nurse Devine and she will be looking after you tonight. I'll see you again in the morning.' Janice, the West Indian fatalist, was leaving me.

Don't go! I tried to scream out.

'Good night Janice, enjoy the party. Give Peter my best,' Nurse Devine teased.

The departing Janice laughed. 'Not on your life. I plan to give him mine. See you.'

The footsteps receded.

'The lucky tart. Did you hear that Michael? You and I will just have to manage. My name is Kathy. Can you move anything for me? Move something if you can hear me.' The accent softened to a plea.

There was an expectant pause. I did try for her. The sweet voice was disappointingly quiet. I could almost hear the pity in the silence.

Then there were footsteps again, this time louder and quicker as if the person was running.

'Oh, Kathy.' The voice was breathless.

'Yes, Janice. What's wrong?'

'There's one other thing I forgot to mention. When he came in, our friend here had a peculiar burn on the palm of his right hand. It's a full thickness injury, almost as if he had tried to hold a hot exhaust pipe or something. We've been dressing it two hourly and the next change is due shortly. The tray is ready.'

'Thanks, Janice. I'll see to it. By the way, has there been any contact from relatives?'

'No, not yet. Admin are on to it but fat lot of good that'll do.'

'Why?'

'I tried contacting them earlier but apparently there was nobody available to deal with it. A management staffing shortage, it seems.'

'That'll be a first in the NHS!'

'Yeah! Perhaps the coffee machine was broken. *Blimey*, look at the time! I'll be late. I must fly Kathy. See you tomorrow.'

'Goodnight, Janice. I'll see . . .'

The footsteps were already disappearing at a running pace. Kathy didn't bother finishing the sentence and from the soft sound of her breathing, remained close by. I was beginning to feel drowsy and it was hard to concentrate.

'Hmmmm. Your oxygen saturations are falling a little Michael. I'm just going to increase the rate a bit. Nothing to worry about.'

She-shup . . . She-shup . . . She-shup . . . She-shup . . .

The mechanical noise increased its rhythm. With the frequency change came a strange sense of euphoria. My mind became clear.

'That's better, sweetheart. Your sats are coming up nicely.' Kathy's voice broke in.

Good for you my angel.

'You'll be more comfortable now, Michael. I'm just slipping out for a minute to check your blood gases. Don't go away – Oh! Hello.'

'Hello,' a different voice answered.

'You must be the agency nurse.'

'Yes.'

'Hi. I'm Kathy. Listen, I was just about to run off this man's blood gases and I need to check on the other isolation patient. Can you hold on here for a few minutes and I'll come back and give you a report?'

'But of course. Is there anything you want done?' The question was formal, another woman, accent European.

She sounded strangely familiar.

'No. . . Oh, yes there is! He has to have a burn dressing changed on his hand. The tray is all set up. Can you handle that?'

'No problem.'

'Thanks. I'll be back in a few minutes.'

Kathy's footsteps faded. I could hear a tap being run and the snap slapping on of latex gloves. The next moment, the voice of the agency nurse was very close.

'Hello, Michael,' she whispered gently.

I convinced myself that I can sense her breath on my face.

She had an angel's voice, like my mother! I suddenly thought, adding to my confusion. I desperately wanted to be able to see. *I'd love to be able to . . .*

The wish faded, unrealised. I felt myself drifting off again, a traveller of the night.

Throughout my life, in those moments suspended between sleeping and being awake, between dreaming and having dreamt, between the spectral and the tangible, I have often felt an acute sense of vertigo as I become aware of the edge of my world. The physical safety net of a gentle awakening in the sleep-warmed embrace of another's arms was not for me. I always needed to get moving, to get away, and by moving, paradoxically, ease the vertigo. Powerlessness would become power if I controlled the direction.

I now needed that direction, that determination. My brain was screaming at me again, to rise and rush towards the light of day and away from the night's horizon, but my body again refused to move.

As I lay there, presuming a horizontal bed, I felt trapped in the sarcophagus of my own flesh.

She-shup . . . She-shup . . . She-shup . . . She-shup . . .

There are some compensations however, I suddenly think, as a dazzling glare of increasing euphoria envelops me. My thoughts are soon racing and are clad in the recalled vibrant colours of a once indulged acid-tripped rainbow.

Suddenly, three men are walking towards me with the sun at their backs. One of them is Gilgamesh, the hero of the Babylonian epics, who had searched long and hard for the secret of immortality, and who when put to the first test by Uta-napishti, the Distant, was unable to even defeat sleep. He is explaining to two other men, one of whom is my father, how the survivor of the flood had taunted him:

'See the fellow who so desired life!
Sleep like a fog already breathes over him.'

I hear Gilgamesh tell the others of how he dived to retrieve the secret coral plant of immortality, the 'Plant of Heartbeat' only to watch helplessly as a serpent snatched the immortal coral before he had a chance to distil its powers, its essence, before he had a chance to help himself . . . or others:

'Now far and wide the tide is rising.
Having opened the channel I abandoned the tools:
What thing would I find that served as my landmark?
Had I only turned back, and left the boat on the shore!'

Gilgamesh, my father and the other man stand there in their radiant light looking pityingly at me. The words are repeated again and again.

"*Had I only turned back!*" Indeed! I think.

The other man then suddenly smiles at me. It is a tormented but kindly smile. He speaks softly:

'The mind is its own place, and in itself
Can make a heaven of hell, a hell of heaven.'

An alarm was ringing. Shrill and sharp. Running footsteps. Coming closer.

'What happened?' A concerned Kathy asked. She was back to me again, breathless and anxious.

'I'm not sure. His core temperature shot up suddenly and he developed a tachycardia. It has just begun to settle again. Were his gases ok?'

'Yeah . . . although the pCO2 is low. We'd better slow the rate again; otherwise he'll get alkalotic. We'd also better make a note in his status chart and let the senior resident know when he makes his rounds,' Kathy said, concerned.

'I can handle that.'

'Are you sure? Thanks. I need about twenty minutes with the other fellow. I'll be with you then.'

'Sure. Take your time. No problem.'

The alarm stopped. Time hitched a ride.

My father is beside me again, wrapping me up in the warm towel of love.

'Remember, Michael, Time, is the castrator of the heavens, it severs the link between man and the Creator. *Saeculum* of the

Romans; *al-dahr* of the Arabs, is our Time, both here and now and from beginning to end, until resurrection. Do what you will with it, Michael, for it's measured by the appearance and disappearance of light, not darkness. Light bathes the ascent of man, the night his descent. The ancients feared that descent, and divided up the night. From *crepesculum*, the evening twilight, until *diluculum*, the morning twilight, the seventh division, they hurried its passage. In the Twilight you will find your destiny. You must take that journey, Michael, but have no fear. I'll be waiting for you.'

My father disappears again.

I'm a feather falling like a stone in the vacuum of space. I'm the geometric point of Foucault's pendulum. I no longer have a physical dimension. I have become opaque, a fugitive. There is no corporeal me!

The footsteps came back again pushing squeaking wheels.

'Michael, it's me,' the familiar voice tenderly intoned. 'Michael. My poor, Michael!'

Her concern entombed me in a casket of silk-lined pity.

I don't want pity! I wanted to be free from the darkness to fly towards the blinding light of day. I wanted the sounds to be that of a nightingale, a harbinger of the dawn.

The voice . . . *I know that voice.*

'Michael. It's me.'

It was Isabella! She was there. Isabella was there with me. She's was alive. How? How did she find me?

I'm getting confused again. The mechanical repeating sound hypnotises me. A university drama group production from a different time and place intrudes. The student actors are portraying a mock debate on the meaning of analogy, between Douglas Hofstadter and Umberto Eco. The departed Borges presides in an analogy of his living self.

She-shup . . . She-shup . . . She-shup . . . She-shup . . .

Perhaps the notion of Isabella being here, was an analogy of my own making. The faithful transport of an abstract notion from one medium, the medium where she exists without me, into mine. My medium, whose only substance is that of an intoxicated notion of my imagination!

Imachination! Another word from the debate. The Hofstadter role-playing student is talking. He poses a problem to the audience. Somebody suggests to him that *machination* would be a good French translation for the title of a book called 'Machines Who Think'.

She-shup . . . She-shup . . . She-shup . . . She-shup . . .

The Hofstadter player smiles and in turn tweaks the word to *Imachination.* This, he says, suggests machinery and mechanicalness and yet because of its similarity in pronunciation to imagination, retains the sense of the living creativity of the human spirit. The only difference is the lack of voicedness of the second consonant, he states.

She-shup . . . She-shup . . . She-shup . . . She-shup . . .

This machine is thinking for me as it completely defines the parameters of my world and my perception.

The machine is the voice of my *imachination,* until startled.

'*Michael!* It's Isabella. I know you can hear me. The heart monitor is displaying your response. It's like when I danced for you, I am able to sense your soul.'

Don't torment me Isabella. I cannot see you dance. I cannot hold you close. There is nothing else. Don't leave me again!

'I am always with you Michael. It was Gaiane and I whom you saw moving in the shadows of the carpark. I saw what happened to the seal and how the sands of its existence crumbled from your hand.'

Gaiane! I don't understand Isabella.

'Gaiane from the hotel in Yerevan! She was one of Alexander's women, one of his *bassarides,* waiting patiently for *Saclaresh* to show itself.'

Her ear. I knew it! I sensed something when she left the taxi! What about Zoë and those other women at the villa? There was a defect in their left ear lobes too. Why?

'Charles Alexander was a Corsican. It is the way that Corsican shepherds used to identify their sheep. He never marked me, Michael.'

What about Saclaresh?

'He always knew that *Saclaresh* was in Armenia somewhere, and that it was just a question of time before it surfaced. When I told him that I suspected that you were to be its next guardian he telephoned Gaiane from the villa and alerted her to your possible arrival. She was waiting, yet was very surprised when you, almost instantly, materialised.'

How did you get to know?

'Gaiane tried to contact Alexander at the villa and when she couldn't, she left a message for me. I only received this about eight hours after escaping from the villa.'

Corsica! How did you get away?

'I always had the authority to use Alexander's jet and after alerting the crew I was able to fly directly from Bastia to Zurich. From there I flew on to Yerevan. I arrived while you were at the monastery.'

What happened to Alexander? They never found his body.

'I don't know what has happened to Charles but his opportunity has now gone. Even if he did survive, he no longer would have any power. 11 September has changed everything, but then of course, Michael, you knew nothing of that, as you rested in your coma.'

What happened to me Isabella?

'I followed you back to the airport and took the same flight as you and Dave Asha.'

I never knew his surname!

'It was Asha, one of the Keepers, who poisoned you on the plane. Remember when you stumbled over his foot in the aisle?'

He thought he saw someone. Was that you Isabella?

'He thought he recognised me and that's what caused him to panic. I saw what happened. The Keepers had decided to protect you, and your guardianship of a *Voice*, by having Dave Asha follow you. When he thought he saw me, thought that I might be alive, he panicked. He assumed that I was working in league with Alexander to recover the seals and decided, there and then, to remove you from your obligation to Alonzo and the guardians, lest I got to you first. He knew how you felt about me.'

You were there and did nothing to help me!

'And you thought Michael, that I might love you or that I could, or would, change my destiny for the devotion of one man. Poor Michael . . . though I must thank you for the warning shout in Corsica. It gave me a chance to retrieve the other seals and get away. I also had time to detonate the explosives that Alexander had the house rigged with as a security measure. He never planned on being there to witness the effect himself.'

And when at last that murder's over
Maybe the bride-bed brings despair,
For each an imagined image brings
And finds a real image there

'I do not have much time, Michael. That kindly nurse Kathy will return soon. She has big sad eyes, you know . . . a little like yours.'

Isabella has stopped talking. I can hear trolley wheels moving and something like a plastic bag being ripped open. Her breathing is coming in short excited breaths.

'I nearly had them all, Michael. But for your interference, all the *Voices* would be mine. *Syrbeth, Abrape, Nergimmel, Ayatau, Nefradaleth* and, of course, *Saclaresh*. I could never allow an evil man like Alexander to have their power.'

You don't have Saclaresh!

'It doesn't matter though, Michael. For all his faults, Charles Alexander showed me that. The only link left to the ancient images of *Saclaresh's* legacy are those that are burnt into your hand. I just need to see them.'

I suddenly remember Alonzo's story of the seals and the old man Ebabu's instructions to the six pathfinders of the Weiministan people to learn the marks of the others. That's what Alonzo had meant in the story! *It is the marks and not the seals themselves that are important.*

'Exactly, Michael. I just need to record the ideas and now I can . . . ah there . . . that's the bandage off. Let me finally look at the legacy.'

Please keep my hand closed!

She-shup . . . She-shup . . . She-shup . . . She-shup . . .

'Good.' Isabella sounds pleased with herself. 'The burnt tattoos are as clear as the day they were carved in stone. I can copy them easily and then I will have them all. I will be the *gatherer*.'

What about Ammonkaph?

'You never really understood, Michael! Did you? Alonzo suspected but he could never be certain. *Nefradaleth* and *Ammonkaph* were always together. Twin destinies: sunrise and sunset. *Ammonkaph* is the judgement *Voice* waiting to welcome you over the Bridge of Separation. I am also *Ammonkaph*. There! That's the copying finished.'

What about me Isabella? Don't I exist? Don't I have a choice?

'You did exist once Michael. But now look at you! Your hearing is the last gift of *Saclaresh*. Without it you do not have a definition and when it is gone so will your being.'

But that is nothingness! I can see the student Eco nodding his head. My father is waiting by the black funnel. *I can be something again. Please Isabella!*

'I'm sorry Michael. This is the *turning point*. Being something is nothing like being.'

She-shup . . . She-shup . . . Sheshh-shup . . . Sheshh-shup . . .

The rhythm was slowing. I'm unable to fight anymore. My

father is smiling at me. He is getting closer. There is a wonderful light on the horizon. I can walk again.

Sheshh-shup . . . . . . Sheshh-shup . . .

I see the bridge. My father and mother are waiting there, waving me forward. I move towards them, feeling safe. Caroline is also there. *I'm ready, Caroline.* I call out:

"*The night has fallen; not a sound*
In the forbidden sacred grove
Unless a petal hit the ground,
Nor any human sight within it
But the crushed grass where we have lain:
And the moon is wilder every minute.
O! Solomon! Let us try again."

Isabella is beside me.

'Goodbye, Michael. You *were* the last of the Magi and we will meet again on the Bridge of Separation. There we will be bathed in the essence of the Creator. Receive your consolamentum and trust in my intuition.'

Sheshh-shup . . . . . . Sheshh –